"America" by Orson Scott Card—When two people share the dream of a new world, everyone may wake to a far different future. . . .

"Trapalanda" by Charles Sheffield—Their search for a legendary El Dorado would take them through a gateway from which few had ever found a way back, and none had ever done so without paying a price. . . .

"Aconcagua" by Tony Daniel—He would forget his grief by challenging the mountain alone—but sometimes help can come when it's least expected. . . .

"The Sky People" by Poul Anderson—After a devastating war, they set out from the safety of their islands to explore the Americas, only to discover that sometimes you have more in common with your "enemies" than with your "friends. . . ."

These are just a few of the expeditions you'll join as you travel to the many possible tomorrows in—

FUTURE EARTHS:
Under South American Skies

FUTURE EARTHS:
Under South American Skies

EDITED BY
Mike Resnick
and
Gardner Dozois

DAW BOOKS, INC.
DONALD A. WOLLHEIM, FOUNDER
375 Hudson Street, New York, NY 10014

ELIZABETH R. WOLLHEIM
SHEILA E. GILBERT
PUBLISHERS

First Printing, August 1993

1 2 3 4 5 6 7 8 9

 DAW TRADEMARK REGISTERED
U.S. PAT. OFF. AND FOREIGN COUNTRIES
—MARCA REGISTRADA
HECHO EN U.S.A.

PRINTED IN THE U.S.A.

ACKNOWLEDGMENTS

Acknowledgment is made for permission to print the following material:

"Introduction," © 1993 by Mike Resnick.

"The Women Men Don't See," by James Tiptree, Jr. Copyright © 1973 by James Tiptree, Jr. First published in *The Magazine of Fantasy and Science Fiction*, December 1973. Reprinted by permission of the author's Estate and the Estate's agent, Virginia Kidd.

"Salvador," by Lucius Shepard. Copyright © 1984 by Mercury Press, Inc. First published in *The Magazine of Fantasy and Science Fiction*, April 1984. Reprinted by permission of the author.

"Doomsday Deferred," by Will F. Jenkins. Copyright © 1949 by Will F. Jenkins. Reprinted by permission of the author's Estate and the Estate's agent, Scott Meredith Literary Agency, Inc.

"On a Hot Summer Night in a Place Far Away," by Pat Murphy. Copyright © 1985 by Davis Publications, Inc. First published in *Isaac Asimov's Science Fiction Magazine*, May 1985. Reprinted by permission of the author.

"Manatee Gal Ain't You Coming Out Tonight," by Avram Davidson. Copyright © 1977 by Mercury Press, Inc. First published in *The Magazine of Fantasy and Science Fiction*, April 1977. Reprinted by permission of the author and the author's agent, Richard D. Grant.

"Trapalanda," by Charles Sheffield. Copyright © 1987 by Davis Publications, Inc. First published in *Isaac Asimov's Science Fiction Magazine*, June 1987. Reprinted by permission of the author.

"America," by Orson Scott Card. Copyright © 1989 by Orson Scott Card. First published in *Isaac Asimov's Science Fiction Magazine*, January 1987. Reprinted by permission of the author.

for
JACK DANN
—who *didn't* go to South America
to have his hair fixed.

The Editors would like to thank the following people for their help and support:

Susan Casper, Carol Resnick, Lawrence Person, Janet Kagan, Pat Cadigan, Jim Cappio, Glen Cox, Dwight Brown, Jack Dann, Sheila Williams, Ian Randall Strock, Scott Towner, Ellen Datlow, Jim Frenkel, Virginia Kidd, Joshua Bilmes, Richard D. Grant, Gordon Van Gelder, Kay McCauley, Pat Murphy, Lucius Shepard, John Kessel, Poul Anderson, Charles Sheffield, Ginjer Buchanan, Tony Daniel, Diane Mapes, G.C. Edmondson, Diane de Avalle-Arce, Orson Scott Card, and special thanks to our own editor, Sheila Gilbert.

CONTENTS

INTRODUCTION

by Mike Resnick

Given that it's our closest continental neighbor, you wouldn't think that we'd know so very little about South America. But the average American, once he tells you that it produces good baseball players, fine music, and tons of revolutions, has just about shot his bolt.

It's amazing, but in this day of instant communication, endless television documentaries, and easy travel, we probably know *less* about South America than about such distant land masses as Australia and Africa.

Which is probably what makes it so exotic, and such a ripe field for science fiction and fantasy writers!

South America has long been associated with the literature of the fantastic, of one sort or another. The Magic Realists, writers such as Jorge Luis Borges, Garcia Marquez, Julio Cortazar, Mario Vargas Llosa, and many others, have built up an impressive body of work set in South American locales—but the bulk of it is, well, *Magic Realism*, after all, and not really appropriate for a science fiction anthology. South America *does* have a flourishing SF market of its own, particularly in Brazil, where several regularly published SF magazines exist, but little of this material has as yet been translated into English, and even less of it translated with any real artistry. So, in looking for realistic science fiction stories set in the future in South America, we turned inevitably to the English-speaking SF genre—where, fortunately for us, there were quite a few excellent ones to be found. (For the purposes of this anthology, to widen the scope as much as possible, we are including stories set in Central America and Mexico, as well as stories set in South America proper. Probably a more accurate title for this book would have been *Under South American, Central American, and Mexican Skies,* but it *also* wouldn't have been a terribly commercial title, and wouldn't fit well on the cover, either.

And yes, we *are* aware that, geographically speaking, Mexico is considered to be part of North America, so don't bother to send us letters informing us of this fact.)

South America has been a fertile ground for science fiction and fantasy literature for more than a century. The classic fantasy novel, *Green Mansions*, was set in South America, and Sir Arthur Conan Doyle gave Sherlock Holmes a rest long enough to send his other hero, Professor Challenger, to *The Lost World* in an unnamed South American country. Some years later L. Sprague de Camp wrote a series of stories (collected in *The Continent Makers)* that presupposed Brazil would be the dominant power of a future Earth (a shocking prediction indeed from the perspective of the early 50s, but one that now looks more likely every day!), and in stories like "Greenslaves," Frank Herbert was writing about mankind's destruction of the tropical rainforest decades before that topic became headline news. James Blish took a Tarzan-like figure to the jungles of South America in 1962's *The Night Shapes*. At about the same time, G.C. Edmonson was writing a series of satrical but hard-edged SF stories set in Mexico and Central America, and a few years later dealt with the phenomenon of First Contact from the unique perspective of a tribe of Yaqui Indians in *Blue Face*. James Tiptree, Jr. was one of the first SF writers to warn of the possibility of the U.S. becoming involved in a Vietnam-style war in South or Central America, in her 1968 story "Beam Us Home," and later, in the 70s, went on to write an entire series of stories set in the eerie but beautiful Quintana Roo country of Yucatan. At about the same time, Avram Davidson was writing a series of stories set in his own richly-imagined version of a Central American country, "British Hidalgo," as well as stories with Latin American backgrounds such as "The Power of Every Root" and "El Vilvoy de las Islas," and the novel *Clash of Star Kings*. At the beginning of the 80s, a young writer of remarkable power, Lucius Shepard, wrote so many first-rate stories set in Central or South America—"The Jaguar Hunter," "R&R," "Surrender," "Black Coral," "Salvador," and the bestselling novel *Life During Wartime*, among many others—that he has become identified with the region, much as Mike Resnick has been identified with Africa. Nor was he the only young writer to become fascinated with that part of the world during the 80s—Pat Murphy won a Nebula Award for her 1986 novel set in Central America, *The Falling Woman*, Lewis Shiner's 1988 Central American novel, *Deserted Cities of the Heart*, was on award ballots a few years later, and writers such as Karen Joy Fowler, S.P. Somtow, Orson Scott Card, John Kessel, Bruce McAllister, Robert Frazier, Diane de Avalle-Arce, Tony Daniel, Robert Silverberg, Bruce Sterling, Richard Mueller, Charles Sheffield, and Richard Paul Russo, among others, all set stories there during the late 80s and early 90s. Still more recently, such bestselling science fiction writers as Jack L. Chalker and Lawrence Watt-Evans have set novels in South America, and the list shows no signs of stopping there.

When you come right down to it, there is very little a writer of imaginative fiction can't do with South America. You want surviving ancient races? Start with the Aztecs and the Incas, and work from there. Ancient cities? Try Machu Picchu and half a dozen others that haven't been unearthed yet. Half-baked scientific theories? Velitkovsky's *The Chariots of the Gods* abounds with them, many centered on our neighboring continent. Exotic adventure? No part of Africa is as unexplored as the Amazon rain forest. Strange religions? There's voodoo and dozens of even weirder rites and rituals. Parables about human rights? Try the jails of Uruguay and Paraguay. Dystopian governments? South America has had everything from Eva Peron to an unending succession of military dictatorships. Isolated communities to tinker with? Try to find three dozen *un*isolated communities on the whole continent.

And so science fiction writers have homed in on South America, and over the years they have produced some truly remarkable stories, from old timers like Murray Leinster to pillars of the field like Poul Anderson to Big New Names like Lucius Shepard and Orson Scott Card and Pat Murphy and John Kessel, and on to rising new stars like Tony Daniel and Diane de Avalle-Arce.

And now that you see why South America appeals to some of the finest writers in science fiction, let's get on with the book so you can enjoy what they *do* with it!

THE WOMEN MEN DON'T SEE

by James Tiptree, Jr.

As most of you probably know by now, multiple Hugo and Nebula Award-winning author James Tiptree, Jr. was actually the pseudonym of the late Dr. Alice Sheldon, a semi-retired experimental psychologist and former member of the American intelligence community who also wrote occasionally under the name of Raccoona Sheldon. Dr. Sheldon's tragic death in 1987 put an end to "both" careers, but not before she had won two Nebula and two Hugo Awards as Tiptree, won another Nebula Award as Raccoona Sheldon, and established herself, under whatever name, as one of the very best science fiction writers of our times. As Tiptree, Dr. Sheldon published two novels, Up the Walls of the World *and* Brightness Falls From the Air, *and nine short-story collections:* Ten Thousand Light Years From Home, Warm Worlds and Otherwise, Starsongs of an Old Primate, Out of the Everywhere, Tales of the Quintana Roo, Byte Beautiful, The Starry Rift, *the posthumously published* Crown of Stars, *and the recent posthumous retrospective collection,* Her Smoke Rose Up Forever.

Dr. Sheldon was no stranger to the part of the world she describes so vividly in the story that follows. She spent much time in the Quintana Roo section of Yucatan over the years, and set a number of her best stories there or in adjacent countries: "Beam Us Home," "Lirios, A Tale of the Quintana Roo," "Yanqui Doodle," "Beyond the Dead Reef," and a number of others. "The Women Men Don't See" is "Tiptree" at her most compelling and powerful, though—which means, almost by definition, that it's among the finest SF stories of the last two decades.

I see her first while the Mexicana 727 is barreling down to Cozumel Island. I come out of the can and lurch into her seat, saying "Sorry," at a double female blur. The near blur nods quietly. The younger one in the window seat goes on looking out. I continue down the aisle, registering nothing. Zero. I never would have looked at them or thought of them again.

Cozumel airport is the usual mix of panicky Yanks dressed for the sand pile and calm Mexicans dressed for lunch at the Presidente. I am a used-up Yank dressed for serious fishing; I extract my rods and duffel from the riot and hike across the field to find my charter pilot. One Captain Estéban has contracted to deliver me to the bonefish flats of Belize three hundred kilometers down the coast.

Captain Estéban turns out to be four feet nine of mahogany Mayan *puro*. He is also in a somber Maya snit. He tells me my Cessna is grounded somewhere and his Bonanza is booked to take a party to Chetumal.

Well, Chetumal is south; can he take me along and go on to Belize after he drops them? Gloomily he concedes the possibility—*if* the other party permits, and *if* there are not too many *equipajes*.

The Chetumal party approaches. It's the woman and her young companion—daughter?—neatly picking their way across the gravel and yucca apron. Their Ventura two-suiters, like themselves, are small, plain and neutral-colored. No problem. When the captain asks if I may ride along, the mother says mildly ''Of course,'' without looking at me.

I think that's when my inner tilt-detector sends up its first faint click. How come this woman has already looked me over carefully enough to accept on her plane? I disregard it. Paranoia hasn't been useful in my business for years, but the habit is hard to break.

As we clamber into the Bonanza, I see the girl has what could be an attractive body if there was any spark at all. There isn't. Captain Estéban folds a serape to sit on so he can see over the cowling and runs a meticulous check-down. And then we're up and trundling over the turquoise Jello of the Caribbean into a stiff south wind.

The coast on our right is the territory of Quintana Roo. If you haven't seen Yucatán, imagine the world's biggest absolutely flat green-gray rug. An empty-looking land. We pass the white ruin of Tulum and the gash of the road to Chichén Itzá, a half-dozen coconut plantations, and then nothing but reef and low scrub jungle all the way to the

horizon, just about the way the conquistadors saw it four
centuries back.

Long strings of cumulus are racing at us, shadowing the
coast. I have gathered that part of our pilot's gloom concerns the weather. A cold front is dying on the henequen
fields of Mérida to the west, and the south wind has piled
up a string of coastal storms: what they call *llovisnos*. Estéban detours methodically around a couple of small thun-
derheads. The Bonanza jinks, and I look back with a vague
notion of reassuring the women. They are calmly intent on
what can be seen of Yucatán. Well, they were offered the
copilot's view, but they turned it down. Too shy?

Another *llovisno* puffs up ahead. Estéban takes the Bonanza upstairs, rising in his seat to sight his course. I relax
for the first time in too long, savoring the latitudes between
me and my desk, the week of fishing ahead. Our captain's
classic Maya profile attracts my gaze: forehead sloping back
from his predatory nose, lips and jaw stepping back below
it. If his slant eyes had been any more crossed, he couldn't
have made his license. That's a handsome combination, believe it or not. On the little Maya chicks in their minishifts
with iridescent gloop on those cockeyes, it's also highly
erotic. Nothing like the oriental doll thing; these people
have stone bones. Captain Estéban's old grandmother could
probably tow the Bonanza . . .

I'm snapped awake by the cabin hitting my ear. Estéban
is barking into his headset over a drumming racket of hail;
the windows are dark gray.

One important noise is missing—the motor. I realize Estéban is fighting a dead plane. Thirty-six hundred; we've
lost two thousand feet!

He slaps tank switches as the storm throws us around; I
catch something about *gasolina* in a snarl that shows his big
teeth. The Bonanza reels down. As he reaches for an overhead toggle, I see the fuel gauges are high. Maybe a clogged
gravity feed line; I've heard of dirty gas down here. He
drops the set; it's a million to one nobody can read us
through the storm at this range anyway. Twenty-five hundred—going down.

His electric feed pump seems to have cut in: the motor
explodes—quits—explodes—and quits again for good. We
are suddenly out of the bottom of the clouds. Below us is a
long white line almost hidden by rain: the reef. But there

isn't any beach behind it, only a big meandering bay with a few mangrove flats—and it's coming up at us fast.

This is going to be bad, I tell myself with great unoriginality. The women behind me haven't made a sound. I look back and see they've braced down with their coats by their heads. With a stalling speed around eighty, all this isn't much use, but I wedge myself in.

Estéban yells some more into his set, flying a falling plane. He is doing one jesus job, too—as the water rushes up at us he dives into a hair-raising turn and hangs us into the wind—with a long pale ridge of sandbar in front of our nose.

Where in hell he found it I'll never know. The Bonanza mushes down, and we belly-hit with a tremendous tearing crash—bounce—hit again—and everything slews wildly as we flat-spin into the mangroves at the end of the bar. Crash! Clang! The plane is wrapping itself into a mound of strangler fig with one wing up. The crashing quits with us all in one piece. And no fire. Fantastic.

Captain Estéban pries open his door, which is now in the roof. Behind me a woman is repeating quietly, "Mother. Mother." I climb up the floor and find the girl trying to free herself from her mother's embrace. The woman's eyes are closed. Then she opens them and suddenly lets go, sane as soap. Estéban starts hauling them out. I grab the Bonanza's aid kit and scramble out after them into brilliant sun and wind. The storm that hit us is already vanishing up the coast.

"Great landing, Captain."

"Oh, *yes!* It was beautiful." The women are shaky, but no hysteria. Estéban is surveying the scenery with the expression his ancestors used on the Spaniards.

If you've been in one of these things, you know the slow-motion inanity that goes on. Euphoria, first. We straggle down the fig tree and out onto the sandbar in the roaring hot wind, noting without alarm that there's nothing but miles of crystalline water on all sides. It's only a foot or so deep, and the bottom is the olive color of silt. The distant shore around us is all flat mangrove swamp, totally uninhabitable.

"Bahía Espiritu Santo." Estéban confirms my guess that we're down in that huge water wilderness. I always wanted to fish it.

"What's all that smoke?" The girl is pointing at the plumes blowing around the horizon.

"Alligator hunters," says Estéban. Mayan poachers have left burn-offs in the swamps. It occurs to me that any signal fires we make aren't going to be too conspicuous. And I now note that our plane is well-buried in the mound of fig. Hard to see it from the air.

Just as the question of how the hell we get out of here surfaces in my mind, the older woman asks composedly, "If they didn't hear you, Captain, when will they start looking for us? Tomorrow?"

"Correct," Estéban agrees dourly. I recall that air-sea rescue is fairly informal here. Like, keep an eye open for Mario, his mother says he hasn't been home all week.

It dawns on me we may be here quite some while.

Furthermore, the diesel-truck noise on our left is the Caribbean piling back into the mouth of the bay. The wind is pushing it at us, and the bare bottoms on the mangroves show that our bar is covered at high tide. I recall seeing a full moon this morning in—believe it, St. Louis—which means maximal tides. Well, we can climb up in the plane. But what about drinking water?

There's a small splat! behind me. The older woman has sampled the bay. She shakes her head, smiling ruefully. It's the first real expression on either of them; I take it as the signal for introductions. When I say I'm Don Fenton from St. Louis, she tells me their name is Parsons, from Bethesda, Maryland. She says it so nicely I don't at first notice we aren't being given first names. We all compliment Captain Estéban again.

His left eye is swelled shut, an inconvenience beneath his attention as a Maya, but Mrs. Parsons spots the way he's bracing his elbow in his ribs.

"You're hurt, Captain."

"*Roto*—I think is broken." He's embarrassed at being in pain. We get him to peel off his Jaime shirt, revealing a nasty bruise in his superb dark-bay torso.

"Is there tape in that kit, Mr. Fenton? I've had a little first-aid training."

She begins to deal competently and very impersonally with the tape. Miss Parsons and I wander to the end of the bar and have a conversation which I am later to recall acutely.

"Roseate spoonbills," I tell her as three pink birds flap away.

"They're beautiful," she says in her tiny voice. They both have tiny voices. "He's a Mayan Indian, isn't he? The pilot, I mean."

"Right. The real thing, straight out of the Bonampak murals. Have you seen Chichén and Uxmal?"

"Yes. We were in Mérida. We're going to Tikal in Guatemala . . . I mean, we were."

"You'll get there." It occurs to me the girl needs cheering up. "Have they told you that Maya mothers used to tie a board on the infant's forehead to get that slant? They also hung a ball of tallow over its nose to make the eyes cross. It was considered aristocratic."

She smiles and takes another peek at Estéban. "People seem different in Yucatán," she says thoughtfully. "Not like the Indians around Mexico City. More, I don't know, independent."

"Comes from never having been conquered. Mayas got massacred and chased a lot, but nobody ever really flattened them. I bet you didn't know that the last Mexican-Maya war ended with a negotiated truce in nineteen thirty-five?"

"No!" Then she says seriously, "I like that."

"So do I."

"The water is really rising very fast," says Mrs. Parsons gently from behind us.

It is, and so is another *llovisno*. We climb back into the Bonanza. I try to rig my parka for a rain catcher, which blows loose as the storm hits fast and furious. We sort a couple of malt bars and my bottle of Jack Daniels out of the jumble in the cabin and make ourselves reasonably comfortable. The Parsons take a sip of whiskey each, Estéban and I considerably more. The Bonanza begins to bump soggily. Estéban makes an ancient one-eyed Mayan face at the water seeping into his cabin and goes to sleep. We all nap.

When the water goes down, the euphoria has gone with it, and we're very, very thirsty. It's also damn near sunset. I get to work with a bait-casting rod and some treble hooks and manage to foul-hook four small mullets. Estéban and the women tie the Bonanza's midget life raft out in the mangroves to catch rain. The wind is parching hot. No planes go by.

Finally another shower comes over and yields us six

ounces of water apiece. When the sunset envelops the world in golden smoke, we squat on the sandbar to eat wet raw mullet and Instant Breakfast crumbs. The women are now in shorts, neat but definitely not sexy.

"I never realized how refreshing raw fish is," Mrs. Parsons says pleasantly. Her daughter chuckles, also pleasantly. She's on Mamma's far side away from Estéban and me. I have Mrs. Parsons figured now; Mother Hen protecting only chick from male predators. That's all right with me. I came here to fish.

But something is irritating me. The damn women haven't complained once, you understand. Not a peep, not a quaver, no personal manifestations whatever. They're like something out of a manual.

"You really seem at home in the wilderness, Mrs. Parsons. You do much camping?"

"Oh goodness no." Diffident laugh. "Not since my girl scout days. Oh, look—are those man-of-war birds?"

Answer a question with a question. I wait while the frigate birds sail nobly into the sunset.

"Bethesda . . . Would I be wrong in guessing you work for Uncle Sam?"

"Why yes. You must be very familiar with Washington, Mr. Fenton. Does your work bring you there often?"

Anywhere but on our sandbar the little ploy would have worked. My hunter's gene twitches.

"Which agency are you with?"

She gives up gracefully. "Oh, just GSA records. I'm a librarian."

Of course. I know her now, all the Mrs. Parsonses in records divisions, accounting sections, research branches, personnel and administration offices. Tell Mrs. Parsons we need a recap on the external service contracts for fiscal '73. So Yucatán is on the tours now? Pity . . . I offer her the tired little joke. "You know where the bodies are buried."

She smiles deprecatingly and stands up. "It does get dark quickly, doesn't it?"

Time to get back into the plane.

A flock of ibis are circling us, evidently accustomed to roosting in our fig tree. Estéban produces a machete and a Mayan string hammock. He proceeds to sling it between tree and plane, refusing help. His machete stroke is noticeably tentative.

The Parsons are taking a pee behind the tail vane. I hear one of them slip and squeal faintly. When they come back over the hull, Mrs. Parsons asks, "Might we sleep in the hammock, Captain?"

Estéban splits an unbelieving grin. I protest about rain and mosquitoes.

"Oh, we have insect repellent and we do enjoy fresh air."

The air is rushing by about force five and colder by the minute.

"We have our raincoats," the girl adds cheerfully.

Well, okay, ladies. We dangerous males retire inside the damp cabin. Through the wind I hear the women laugh softly now and then, apparently coy in their chilly ibis roost. A private insanity, I decide. I know myself for the least threatening of men; my non-charisma has been in fact an asset jobwise, over the years. Are they having fantasies about Estéban? Or maybe they really are fresh-air nuts . . . Sleep comes for me in invisible diesels roaring by on the reef outside.

We emerge dry-mouthed into a vast windy salmon sunrise. A diamond chip of sun breaks out of the sea and promptly submerges in cloud. I go to work with the rod and some mullet bait while two showers detour around us. Breakfast is a strip of wet barracuda apiece.

The Parsons continue stoic and helpful. Under Estéban's direction they set up a section of cowling for a gasoline flare in case we hear a plane, but nothing goes over except one unseen jet droning toward Panama. The wind howls, hot and dry and full of coral dust. So are we.

"They look first in the sea." Estban remarks. His aristocratic frontal slope is beaded with sweat; Mrs. Parsons watches him concernedly. I watch the cloud blanket tearing by above, getting higher and dryer and thicker. While that lasts nobody is going to find us, and the water business is now unfunny.

Finally I borrow Estéban's machete and hack a long light pole. "There's a stream coming in back there, I saw it from the plane. Can't be more than two, three miles."

"I'm afraid the raft's torn." Mrs. Parsons shows me the cracks in the orange plastic; irritatingly, it's a Delaware label.

"All right," I hear myself announce. "The tide's going

down. If we cut the good end of that air tube, I can haul water back in it. I've waded flats before."

Even to me it sounds crazy.

"Stay by plane," Estéban says. He's right, of course. He's also clearly running a fever. I look at the overcast and taste grit and old barracuda. The hell with the manual.

When I start cutting up the raft, Estéban tells me to take the serape. "You stay one night." He's right about that, too; I'll have to wait out the tide.

"I'll come with you," says Mrs. Parsons calmly.

I simply stare at her. What new madness has got into Mother Hen? Does she imagine Estéban is too battered to be functional? While I'm being astounded, my eyes take in the fact that Mrs. Parsons is now quite rosy around the knees, with her hair loose and a sunburn starting on her nose. A trim, in fact a very neat shading-forty.

"Look, that stuff is horrible going. Mud up to your ears and water over your head."

"I'm really quite fit and I swim a great deal. I'll try to keep up. Two would be much safer, Mr. Fenton, and we can bring more water."

She's serious. Well, I'm about as fit as a marshmallow at this time of winter, and I can't pretend I'm depressed by the idea of company. So be it.

"Let me show Miss Parsons how to work this rod."

Miss Parsons is even rosier and more windblown, and she's not clumsy with my tackle. A good girl, Miss Parsons, in her nothing way. We cut another staff and get some gear together. At the last minute Estéban shows how sick he feels: he offers me the machete. I thank him, but, no; I'm used to my Wirkkala knife. We tie some air into the plastic tube for a float and set out along the sandiest looking line.

Estéban raises one dark palm. *"Buen viaje."* Miss Parsons has hugged her mother and gone to cast from the mangrove. She waves. We wave.

An hour later we're barely out of waving distance. The going is surely god-awful. The sand keeps dissolving into silt you can't walk on or swim through, and the bottom is spiked with dead mangrove spears. We flounder from one pothole to the next, scaring up rays and turtles and hoping to god we don't kick a moray eel. Where we're not soaked in slime, we're desiccated, and we smell like the Old Cretaceous.

Mrs. Parsons keeps up doggedly. I only have to pull her out once. When I do so, I notice the sandbar is now out of sight.

Finally we reach the gap in the mangrove line I thought was the creek. It turns out to open into another arm of the bay, with more mangroves ahead. And the tide is coming in.

"I've had the world's lousiest idea."

Mrs. Parsons only says mildly, "It's so different from the view from the plane."

I revise my opinion of the girl scouts, and we plow on past the mangroves toward the smoky haze that has to be shore. The sun is setting in our faces, making it hard to see. Ibises and herons fly up around us, and once a big permit spooks ahead, his fin cutting a rooster tail. We fall into more potholes. The flashlights get soaked. I am having fantasies of the mangrove as universal obstacle; it's hard to recall I ever walked down a street, for instance, without stumbling over or under or through mangrove roots. And the sun is dropping down, down.

Suddenly we hit a ledge and fall over it into a cold flow.

"The stream! It's fresh water!"

We guzzle and garble and douse our heads; it's the best drink I remember. "Oh my, oh my—!" Mrs. Parsons is laughing right out loud.

"That dark place over to the right looks like real land."

We flounder across the flow and follow a hard shelf, which turns into solid bank and rises over our heads. Shortly there's a break beside a clump of spiny bromels, and we scramble up and flop down at the top, dripping and stinking. Out of sheer reflex my arms goes around my companion's shoulder—but Mrs. Parsons isn't there; she's up on her knees peering at the burnt-over plain around is.

"It's so good to see land one can walk on!" The tone is too innocent. *Noli me tangere.*

"Don't try it." I'm exasperated; the muddy little woman, what does she think? "That ground out there is a crush of ashes over muck, and it's full of stubs. You can go in over your knees."

"It seems firm here."

"We're in an alligator nursery. That was the slide we came up. Don't worry, by now the old lady's doubtless on her way to be made into handbags."

"What a shame."

"I better set a line down in the stream while I can still see."

I slide back down and rig a string of hooks that may get us breakfast. When I get back Mrs. Parsons is wringing muck out of the serape.

"I'm glad you warned me, Mr. Fenton. It *is* treacherous."

"Yeah." I'm over my irritation; god knows I don't want to *tangere* Mrs. Parsons, even if I weren't beat down to mush. "In its quiet way, Yucatán is a tough place to get around in. You can see why the Mayas built roads. Speaking of which—look!"

The last of the sunset is silhouetting a small square shape a couple of kilometers inland; a Maya *ruina* with a fig tree growing out of it.

"Lot of those around. People think they were guard towers."

"Let's hope it's deserted by mosquitoes."

We slump down in the 'gator nursery and share the last malt bar, watching the stars slide in and out of the blowing clouds. The bugs aren't too bad; maybe the burn did them in. And it isn't hot any more, either—in fact, it's not even warm, wet as we are. Mrs. Parsons continues tranquilly interested in Yucatán and unmistakably uninterested in togetherness.

Just as I'm beginning to get aggressive notions about how we're going to spend the night if she expects me to give her the serape, she stands up, scuffs at a couple of hummocks and says, "I expect this is as good a place as any, isn't it, Mr. Fenton?"

With which she spreads out the raft bag for a pillow and lies down on her side in the dirt with exactly half the serape over her and the other corner folded neatly open. Her small back is toward me.

The demonstration is so convincing that I'm halfway under my share of serape before the preposterousness of it stops me.

"By the way. My name is Don."

"Oh, of course." Her voice is graciousness itself, "I'm Ruth."

I get in not quite touching her, and we lie there like two fish on a plate, exposed to the stars and smelling the smoke in the wind and feeling things underneath us. It is absolutely the most intimately awkward moment I've had in years.

The woman doesn't mean one thing to me, but the obtrusive recessiveness of her, the defiance of her little rump eight inches from my fly—for two pesos I'd have those shorts down and introduce myself. If I were twenty years younger. If I wasn't so bushed . . . But the twenty years and the exhaustion are there, and it comes to me wryly that Mrs. Ruth Parsons has judged things to a nicety. If I *were* twenty years younger, she wouldn't be here. Like the butterfish that float around a sated barracuda, only to vanish away the instant his intent changes, Mrs. Parsons knows her little shorts are safe. Those firmly filled little shorts, so close . . .

A warm nerve stirs in my groin—and just as it does I become aware of a silent emptiness beside me. Mrs. Parsons is imperceptibly inching away. Did my breathing change? Whatever, I'm perfectly sure that if my hand reached, she'd be elsewhere—probably announcing her intention to take a dip. The twenty years bring a chuckle to my throat, and I relax.

"Good night, Ruth."

"Good night, Don."

And believe it or not, we sleep, while the armadas of the wind roared overhead.

Light wakes me—a cold white glare.

My first thought is 'gator hunters. Best to manifest ourselves as *turistas* as fast as possible. I scramble up, noting that Ruth has dived under the bromel clump.

"Quién estás? A secorro! Help, *señores!"*

No answer except the light goes out, leaving me blind.

I yell some more in a couple of languages. It stays dark. There's a vague scrabbling, whistling sound somewhere in the burn-off. Liking everything less by the minute, I try a speech about our plane having crashed and we need help.

A very narrow pencil of light flicks over us and snaps off.

"Eh-ep," says a blurry voice and something metallic twitters. They for sure aren't locals. I'm getting unpleasant ideas.

"Yes, help!"

Something goes *crackle-crackle whish-whish,* and all sounds fade away.

"What the holy hell!" I stumble toward where they were.

"Look." Ruth whispers behind me. "Over by the ruin."

I look and catch a multiple flicker which winks out fast.
"A camp?"

And I take two more blind strides. My leg goes down through the crust, and a spike spears me just where you stick the knife in to unjoint a drumstick. By the pain that goes through my bladder I recognize that my trick kneecap has caught it.

For instant basket-case you can't beat kneecaps. First you discover your knee doesn't bend any more, so you try putting some weight on it, and a bayonet goes up your spine and unhinges your jaw. Little grains of gristle have got into the sensitive bearing surface. The knee tries to buckle and can't, and mercifully you fall down.

Ruth helps me back to the serape.

"What a fool, what a god-forgotten imbecile—"

"Not at all, Don. It was perfectly natural." We strike matches; her fingers push mine aside, exploring. "I think it's in place, but it's swelling fast. I'll lay a wet handkerchief on it. We'll have to wait for morning to check the cut. Were they poachers, do you think?"

"Probably," I lie. What I think is they were smugglers.

She comes back with a soaked bandanna and drapes it on. "We must have frightened them. That light . . . it seemed so bright."

"Some hunting party. People do crazy things around here."

"Perhaps they'll come back in the morning."

"Could be."

Ruth pulls up the wet serape, and we say goodnight again. Neither of us are mentioning how we're going to get back to the plane without help.

I lie staring south where Alpha Centauri is blinking in and out of the overcast and cursing myself for the sweet mess I've made. My first idea is giving way to an even less pleasing one.

Smuggling, around here, is a couple of guys in an outboard meeting a shrimp boat by the reef. They don't light up the sky or have some kind of swamp buggy that goes whoosh. Plus a big camp . . . paramilitary-type equipment?

I've seen a report of Guevarista infiltrators operating on the British Honduran border, which is about a hundred kilometers—sixty miles—south of here. Right under those clouds. If that's what looked us over, I'll be more than happy if they don't come back . . .

I wake up in pelting rain, alone. My first move confirms that my leg is as expected—a giant misplaced erection bulging out of my shorts. I raise up painfully to see Ruth standing by the bromels, looking over the bay. Solid wet nimbus is pouring out of the south.

"No planes today."

"Oh, good morning, Don. Should we look at that cut now?"

"It's minimal." In fact the skin is hardly broken, and no deep puncture. Totally out of proportion to the havoc inside.

"Well, they have water to drink," Ruth says tranquilly. "Maybe those hunters will come back. I'll go see if we have a fish—that is, can I help you in any way, Don?"

Very tactful. I emit an ungracious negative, and she goes off about her private concerns.

They certainly are private, too; when I recover from my own sanitary efforts, she's still away. Finally I hear splashing.

"It's a big fish!" More splashing. Then she climbs up the bank with a three-pound mangrove snapper—and something else.

It isn't until after the messy work of filleting the fish that I begin to notice.

She's making a smudge of chaff and twigs to singe the fillets, small hands very quick, tension in that female upper lip. The rain has eased off for the moment; we're sluicing wet but warm enough. Ruth brings me my fish on a mangrove skewer and sits back on her heels with an odd breathy sigh.

"Aren't you joining me?"

"Oh, of course." She gets a strip and picks at it, saying quickly, "We either have too much salt or too little, don't we? I should fetch some brine." Her eyes are roving from nothing to noplace.

"Good thought." I hear another sigh and decide the girl scouts need an assist. "Your daughter mentioned you've come from Mérida. Have you seen much of Mexico?"

"Not really. Last year we went to Mazatlán and Cuernavaca . . ." She puts the fish down, frowning.

"And you're going to see Tikal. Going to Bonampak too?"

"No." Suddenly she jumps up brushing rain off her face. "I'll bring you some water, Don."

She ducks down the slide, and after a fair while comes back with a full bromel stalk.

"Thanks." She's standing above me, staring restlessly round the horizon."

"Ruth, I hate to say it, but those guys are not coming back and it's probably just as well. Whatever they were up to, we looked like trouble. The most they'll do is tell some-one we're here. That'll take a day or two to get around, we'll be back at the plane by then."

"I'm sure you're right, Don." She wanders over to the smudge fire.

"And quit fretting about your daughter. She's a big girl."

"Oh, I'm sure Althea's all right . . . They have plenty of water now." Her fingers drum on her thigh. It's raining again.

"Come on, Ruth. Sit down. Tell me about Althea. Is she still in college?"

She gives that sighing little laugh and sits. "Althea got her degree last year. She's in computer programming."

"Good for her. And what about you, what do you do in GSA records?"

"I'm in Foreign Procurement Archives." She smiles me-chanically, but her breathing is shallow. "It's very interest-ing."

"I know a Jack Wittig in Contracts, maybe you know him?"

It sounds pretty absurd, there in the 'gator slide.

"Oh, I've met Mr. Wittig. I'm sure he wouldn't remem-ber me."

"Why not?"

"I'm not very memorable."

Her voice is factual. She's perfectly right, of course. Who was that woman, Mrs. Jannings, Janny, who coped with my per diem for years? Competent, agreeable, impersonal. She had a sick father or something. But dammit, Ruth is a lot younger and better-looking. Comparatively speaking.

"Maybe Mrs. Parsons doesn't want to be memorable."

She makes a vague sound, and I suddenly realize Ruth isn't listening to me at all. Her hands are clenched around her knees, she's staaring inland at the ruin.

"Ruth. I tell you our friends with the light are in the next county by now. Forget it, we don't need them."

Her eyes come back to me as if she'd forgotten I was there, and she nods slowly. It seems to be too much effort to speak. Suddenly she cocks her head and jumps up again.

"I'll go look at the line, Don. I thought I heard something—" She's gone like a rabbit.

While she's away I try getting up onto my good leg and the staff. The pain is sickening; knees seem to have some kind of hot line to the stomach. I take a couple of hops to test whether the Demerol I have in my belt would get me walking. As I do so, Ruth comes up the bank with a fish flapping in her hands.

"Oh, no, Don! *No!*" She actually clasps the snapper to her breast.

"The water will take some of my weight. I'd like to give it a try."

"You mustn't!" Ruth says quite violently and instantly modulates down. "Look at the bay, Don. One can't see a thing."

I teeter there, tasting bile and looking at the mingled curtains of sun and rain driving across the water. She's right, thank god. Even with two good legs we could get into trouble out there.

"I guess one more night won't kill us."

I let her collapse me back onto the gritty plastic, and she positively bustles around, finding me a chunk to lean on, stretching the serape on both staffs to keep rain off me, bringing another drink, grubbing for dry tinder.

"I'll make us a real bonfire as soon as it lets up, Don. They'll see our smoke, they'll know we're all right. We just have to wait." Cheery smile. "Is there any way we can make you more comfortable?"

Holy Saint Sterculius: playing house in a mud puddle. For a fatuous moment I wonder if Mrs. Parsons has designs on me. And then she lets out another sigh and sinks back onto her heels with that listening look. Unconsciously her rump wiggles a little. My ear picks up the operative word: *wait.*

Ruth Parsons is waiting. In fact, she acts as if she's waiting so hard it's killing her. For what? For someone to get us out of here, what else? . . . But why was she so horrified when I got up to try to leave? Why all this tension?

My paranoia stirs. I grab it by the collar and start idly checking back. Up to when whoever it was showed up last night, Mrs. Parson was, I guess, normal. Calm and sensible, anyway. Now she's humming like a high wire. And she seems to want to stay here and wait. Just as an intellectual pastime, why?

Could she have intended to come here? No way. Where she planned to be was Chetumal, which is on the border. Come to think, Chetumal is an odd way round to Tikal. Let's say the scenario was that she's meeting somebody in Chetumal. Somebody who's part of an organization. So now her contact in Chetumal knows she's overdue. And when those types appeared last night, something suggests to her that they're part of the same organization. And she hopes they'll put one and one together and come back for her?

"May I have the knife, Don? I'll clean the fish."

Rather slowly I pass the knife, kicking my subconscious. Such a decent ordinary little woman, a good girl scout. My trouble is that I've bumped into too many professional agilities under the careful stereotypes. *I'm not very memorable* . . .

What's in Foreign Procurement archives? Wittig handles classified contracts. Lots of money stuff; foreign currency negotiations, commodity price schedules, some industrial technology. Or—just as a hypothesis—it could be as simple as a wad of bills back in that modest beige Ventura, to be exchanged for a packet from say, Costa Rica. If she were a courier, they'd want to get at the plane. And then what about me and maybe Estéban? Even hypothetically, not good.

I watch her hacking at the fish, forehead knotted with effort, teeth in her lip. Mrs. Ruth Parsons of Bethesda, this thrumming, private woman. How crazy can I get? *They'll see our smoke* . . .

"Here's your knife, Don. I washed it. Does the leg hurt very badly?"

I blink away the fantasies and see a scared little woman in a mangrove swamp.

"Sit down, rest. You've been going all out."

She sits obediently, like a kid in a dentist chair.

"You're stewing about Althea. And she's probably worried about you. We'll get back tomorrow under our own steam, Ruth."

"Honestly I'm not worried at all, Don." The smile fades; she nibbles her lip, frowning out at the bay.

"You know, Ruth, you surprised me when you offered to come along. Not that I don't appreciate it. But I rather thought you'd be concerned about leaving Althea alone with our good pilot. Or was it only me?"

This gets her attention at last.

"I believe Captain Estéban is a very fine type of man."

The words surprise me a little. Isn't the correct line more like "I trust Althea," or even, indignantly, "Althea is a good girl?"

"He's a man. Althea seemed to think he was interesting."

She goes on staring at the bay. And then I notice her tongue flick out and lick that prehensile upper lip. There's a flush that isn't sunburn around her ears and throat too, and one hand is gently rubbing her thigh. What's she seeing, out there in the flats?

Oho.

Captain Estéban's mahogany arms clasping Miss Althea Parsons' pearly body. Captain Estéban's archaic nostrils snuffling in Miss Parsons' tender neck. Captain Estéban's copper buttocks pumping into Althea's creamy upturned bottom . . . The hammock, very bouncy. Mayas know all about it.

Well, well. So Mother Hen has her little quirks.

I feel fairly silly and more than a little irritated. *Now* I find out . . . But even vicarious lust has much to recommend it, here in the mud and rain. I settle back, recalling that Miss Althea the computer programmer had waved goodbye very composedly. Was she sending her mother to flounder across the bay with me so she can get programmed in Maya? The memory of Honduran mahogany logs drifting in and out of the opalescent sand comes to me. Just as I am about to suggest that Mrs. Parsons might care to share my rain shelter, she remarks serenely, "The Mayas seem to be a very fine type of people. I believe you said so to Althea."

The implications fall on me with the rain. *Type.* As in breeding, bloodline, sire. Am I supposed to have certified Estéban not only as a stud but as a genetic donor?

"Ruth, are you telling me you're prepared to accept a half-Indian grandchild?"

"Why, Don, that's up to Althea, you know."

Looking at the mother, I guess it is. Oh, for mahogany gonads.

Ruth has gone back to listening to the wind, but I'm not about to let her off that easy. Not after all that *noli me tangere* jazz.

"What will Althea's father think?"

Her face snaps around at me, genuinely startled.

"Althea's father?" Complicated semismile. "He won't mind."

"He'll accept it too, eh?" I see her shake her head as if a fly were bothering her, and add with a cripple's malice: "Your husband must be a very fine type of a man."

Ruth looks at me, pushing her wet hair back abruptly. I have the impression that mousy Mrs. Parsons is roaring out of control, but her voice is quiet.

"There isn't any Mr. Parsons, Don. There never was. Althea's father was a Danish medical student . . . I believe he has gained considerable prominence."

"Oh." Something warns me not to say I'm sorry. "You mean he doesn't know about Althea?"

"No." She smiles, her eyes bright and cuckoo.

"Seems like rather a rough deal for her."

"I grew up quite happily under the same circumstances."

Bang, I'm dead. Well, well, well. A mad image blooms in my mind: generations of solitary Parsons women selecting sires, making impregnation trips. Well, I hear the world is moving their way.

"I better look at the fish line."

She leaves. The glow fades. *No.* Just no, no contact. Good-bye, Captain Estéban. My leg is very uncomfortable. The hell with Mrs. Parsons' long-distance orgasm.

We don't talk much after that, which seems to suit Ruth. The odd day drags by. Squall after squall blows over us. Ruth singes up some more fillets, but the rain drowns her smudge; it seems to pour hardest just as the sun's about to show.

Finally she comes to sit under my sagging serape, but there's no warmth there. I doze, aware of her getting up now and then to look around. My subconscious notes that she's still twitchy. I tell my subconscious to knock it off.

Presently I wake up to find her penciling on the water-soaked pages of a little notepad.

"What's that, a shopping list for alligators?"

Automatic polite laugh. "Oh, just an address. In case we—I'm being silly, Don."

"Hey," I sit up, wincing, "Ruth, quit fretting. I mean it. We'll all be out of this soon. You'll have a great story to tell."

She doesn't look up. "Yes . . . I guess we will."

"Come on, we're doing fine. There isn't any real danger here, you know. Unless you're allergic to fish?"

Another good-little-girl laugh, but there's a shiver in it.

"Sometimes I think I'd like to go . . . really far away."

To keep her talking I say the first thing in my head.

"Tell me, Ruth. I'm curious why you would settle for that kind of lonely life, there in Washington? I mean, a woman like you—"

"Should get married?" She gives a shaky sigh, pushing the notebook back in her wet pocket.

"Why not? It's the normal source of companionship. Don't tell me you're trying to be some kind of professional man-hater."

"Lesbian, you mean?" Her laugh sounds better. "With my security rating? No, I'm not."

"Well, then. Whatever trauma you went through, these things don't last forever. You can't hate all men."

The smile is back. "Oh, there wasn't any trauma, Don, and I *don't* hate men. That would be as silly as—as hating the weather." She glances wryly at the blowing rain.

"I think you have a grudge. You're even spooky of me."

Smooth as a mouse bite she says, "I'd love to hear about your family, Don?"

Touché. I give the edited version of how I don't have one any more, and she says she's sorry, how sad. And we chat about what a good life a single person really has, and how she and her friends enjoy plays and concerts and travel, and one of them is head cashier for Ringling Brothers, how about that?

But it's coming out jerkier and jerkier like a bad tape, with her eyes going round the horizon in the pauses and her face listening for something that isn't my voice. What's wrong with her? Well, what's wrong with any furtively un-conventional middle-aged woman with an empty bed. And a security clearance. An old habit of mind remarks unkindly that Mrs. Parsons represents what is known as the classic penetration target.

"—so much more opportunity now." Her voice trails off.

"Hurrah for women's lib, eh?"

"The lib?" Impatiently she leans forward and tugs the serape straight. "Oh, that's doomed."

The apocalyptic word jars my attention.

"What do you mean, doomed?"

She glances at me as if I weren't hanging straight either and says vaguely, "Oh . . ."

"Come on, why doomed? Didn't they get that equal rights bill?"

Long hesitation. When she speaks again her voice is different.

"Women have no rights, Don, except what men allow us. Men are more aggressive and powerful, and they run the world. When the next real crisis upsets them, our so-called rights will vanish like—like that smoke. We'll be back where we always were: property. And whatever has gone wrong will be blamed on our freedom, like the fall of Rome was. You'll see."

Now all this is delivered in a gray tone of total conviction. The last time I heard that tone, the speaker was explaining why he had to keep his file drawers full of dead pigeons.

"Oh, come on. You and your friends are the backbone of the system; if you quit, the country would come to a screeching halt before lunch."

No answering smile.

"That's fantasy." Her voice is still quiet. "Women don't work that way. We're a—a toothless world." She looks around as if she wanted to stop talking. "What women do is survive. We live by ones and twos in the chinks of your world-machine."

"Sounds like a guerrilla operation." I'm not really joking, here in the 'gator den. In fact, I'm wondering if I spent too much thought on mahogany logs.

"Guerrillas have something to hope for." Suddenly she switches on a jolly smile. "Think of us as oppossums, Don. Did you know there are oppossums living all over? Even in New York City."

I smile back with my neck prickling. I thought I was the paranoid one.

"Men and women aren't different species, Ruth. Women do everything men do."

"Do they?" Our eyes meet, but she seems to be seeing ghosts between us in the rain. She mutters something that could be "My Lai" and looks away. "All the endless

wars . . .'' Her voice is a whisper. ''All the huge author-
itarian organizations for doing unreal things. Men live to
struggle against each other; we're just part of the battle-
fields. It'll never change unless you change the whole
world. I dream sometimes of—of going away—'' She
checks and abruptly changes voice. ''Forgive me, Don,
it's so stupid saying all this.''

''Men hate wars too, Ruth,'' I say as gently as I can.

''I know.'' She shrugs and climbs to her feet. ''But that's
your problem, isn't it?''

End of communication. Mrs. Ruth Parsons isn't even living in the same world with me.

I watch her move around restlessly, head turning toward
the ruins. Alienation like that can add up to dead pigeons,
which would be GSA's problem. It could also lead to believing some joker who's promising to change the whole
world. Which could just probably be my problem if one of
them was over in that camp last night, where she keeps
looking. *Guerrillas have something to hope for. . . ?*

Nonsense. I try another position and see that the sky
seems to be clearing as the sun sets. The wind is quieting
down at last too. Insane to think this little woman is acting
out some fantasy in this swamp. But that equipment last
night was no fantasy; if those lads have some connection
with her, I'll be in the way. You couldn't find a handier spot
to dispose of the body . . . Maybe some Guevarista is a fine
type of man?

Absurd. Sure . . . The only thing more absurd would be
to come through the wars and get myself terminated by a
mad librarian's boyfriend on a fishing trip.

A fish flops in the stream below us. Ruth spins around so
fast she hits the serape. ''I better start the fire,'' she says,
her eyes still on the plain and her head cocked, listening.

All right, let's test.

''Expecting company?''

It rocks her. She freezes, and her eyes come swiveling
around at me like a film take captioned Fright. I can see
her decide to smile.

''Oh, one never can tell!'' She laughs weirdly, the eyes
not changed. ''I'll get the—the kindling.'' She fairly scuttles into the brush.

Nobody, paranoid or not, could call *that* a normal reaction.

Ruth Parsons is either psycho or she's expecting something to happen—and it has nothing to do with me; I scared her pissless.

Well, she could be nuts. And I could be wrong, but there are some mistakes you only make once.

Reluctantly I unzip my body belt, telling myself that if I think what I think, my only course is to take something for my leg and get as far as possible from Mrs. Ruth Parsons before whoever she's waiting for arrives.

In my belt also is a .32 caliber asset Ruth doesn't know about—and it's going to stay there. My longevity program leaves the shoot-outs to TV and stresses being somewhere else when the roof falls in. I can spend a perfectly safe and also perfectly horrible night out in one of those mangrove flats . . . Am I insane?

At this moment Ruth stands up and stares blatantly inland with her hand shading her eyes. Then she tucks something into her pocket, buttons up and tightens her belt.

That does it.

I dry-swallow two 100 mg tabs, which should get me ambulatory and still leave me wits to hide. Give it a few minutes. I make sure my compass and some hooks are in my own pocket and sit waiting while Ruth fusses with her smudge fire, sneaking looks away when she thinks I'm not watching.

The flat world around us is turning into an unearthly amber and violet light show as the first numbness sweeps into my leg. Ruth has crawled under the bromels for more dry stuff; I can see her foot. Okay. I reach for my staff.

Suddenly the foot jerks, and Ruth yells—or rather, her throat makes that *Uh-uh-hhh* that means pure horror. The foot disappears in a rattle of bromel stalks.

I lunge upright on the crutch and look over the bank at a frozen scene.

Ruth is crouching sideways on the ledge, clutching her stomach. They are about a yard below, floating on the river in a skiff. While I was making up my stupid mind, her friends have glided right under my ass. There are three of them.

They are tall and white. I try to see them as men in some kind of white jumpsuits. The one nearest the bank is stretching out a long white arm toward Ruth. She jerks and scuttles further away.

The arm stretches after her. It stretches and stretches. It stretches two yards and stays hanging in the air. Small black things are wiggling from its tip.

I look where their faces should be and see black hollow dishes with vertical stripes. The stripes move slowly . . .

There is no more possibility of their being human—or anything else I've ever seen. What has Ruth conjured up?

The scene is totally silent. I blink, blink—this cannot be real. The two in the far end of the skiff are writhing those arms around an apparatus on a tripod. A weapon? Suddenly I hear the same blurry voice I heard in the night.

"Guh-give," it groans. "G-give . . ."

Dear god, it's real, whatever it is. I'm terrified. My mind is trying not to form a word.

And Ruth—Jesus, of course—Ruth is terrified too; she's edging along the bank away from them, gaping at the monsters in the skiff, who are obviously nobody's friends. She's hugging something to her body. Why doesn't she get over the bank and circle back behind me?

"G-g-give." That wheeze is coming from the tripod. "Pee-eeze give." The skiff is moving upstream below Ruth, following her. The arm undulates out at her again, its black digits looping. Ruth scrambles to the top of the bank.

"Ruth!" My voice cracks. "Ruth, get over here behind me!"

She doesn't look at me, only keeps sidling farther away. My terror detonates into anger.

"Come back here!" With my free hand I'm working the .32 out of my belt. The sun has gone down.

She doesn't turn but straightens up warily, still hugging the thing. I see her mouth working. Is she actually trying to *talk* to them?

"Please . . ." She swallows. "Please speak to me. I need your help."

"RUTH!!"

At this moment the nearest white monster whips into a great S-curve and sails right onto the bank at her, eight feet of snowy rippling horror.

And I shoot Ruth.

I don't know that for a minute—I've yanked the gun up so fast that my staff slips and dumps me as I fire. I stagger up, hearing Ruth scream "No! No! No!"

The creature is back down by his boat, and Ruth is still

farther away, clutching herself. Blood is running down her
elbow.

"Stop it, Don! They aren't attacking you!"

"For god's sake! Don't be a fool, I can't help you if you
won't get away from them!"

No reply. Nobody moves. No sound except the drone of
a jet passing far above. In the darkening stream below me
the three white figures shift uneasily; I get the impression
of radar dishes focusing. The word spells itself in my head:
Aliens.

Extraterrestrials.

What do I do, call the President? Capture them single-
handed with my peashooter? . . . I'm alone in the arse end
of nowhere with one leg and my brain cuddled in meperi-
dine hydorchloride.

"Prrr—eese," their machine blurs again. "Wa-wat hep . . ."

"Our plane fell down," Ruth says in a very distinct, eerie
voice. She points up at the jet, out towards the bay. "My—
my child is there. Please take us *there* in your boat."

Dear god. While she's gesturing, I get a look at the thing
she's hugging in her wounded arm. It's metallic, like a big
glimmering distributor head. What—?

Wait a minute. This morning: when she was gone so long,
she could have found that thing. Something they left behind.
Or dropped. And she hid it, not telling me. That's why she
kept going under that bromel clump—she was peeking at it.
Waiting. And the owners came back and caught her. They
want it. She's trying to bargain, by god.

"—Water," Ruth is pointing again. "Take us. Me. And
him."

The black faces turn toward me, blind and horrible. Later
on I may be grateful for that "us." Not now.

"Throw your gun away, Don. They'll take us back." Her
voice is weak.

"Like hell I will. You—who are you? What are you doing
here?"

"Oh god, does it matter? He's frightened," she cries to
them. "Can you understand?"

She's as alien as they, there in the twilight. The beings in
the skiff are twittering among themselves. Their box starts
to moan.

"Ss-stu-dens," I make out. "S-stu-ding . . . not—huh-arm-ing . . . w-we . . . buh . . .'' It fades into garble and then says ''G-give . . . we . . . g-go . . .''

Peace-loving cultural-exchange students—on the interstellar level now. Oh, no.

''Bring that thing here, Ruth—right now!''

But she's starting down the bank toward them saying, ''Take me.''

''Wait! You need a tourniquet on that arm.''

''I know. Please put the gun down, Don.''

She's actually at the skiff, right by them. They aren't moving.

''Jesus Christ.'' Slowly, reluctantly, I drop the .32. When I start down the slide. I find I'm floating; adrenaline and Demerol are a bad mix.

The skiff comes gliding toward me, Ruth in the bow clutching the thing and her arm. The aliens stay in the stern behind their tripod, away from me. I note the skiff is camouflaged tan and green. The world around us is deep shadowy blue.

''Don, bring the water bag!''

As I'm dragging down the plastic bag, it occurs to me that Ruth really is cracking up, the water isn't needed now. But my own brain seems to have gone into overload. All I can focus on is a long white rubbery arm with black worms clutching the far end of the orange tube, helping me fill it. This isn't happening.

''Can you get in, Don?'' As I hoist my numb legs up, two long white pipes reach for me. *No you don't.* I kick and tumble in beside Ruth. She moves away.

A creaky hum starts up, it's coming from a wedge in the center of the skiff. And we're in motion, sliding toward dark mangrove files.

I stare mindlessly at the wedge. Alien technological secrets? I can't see any, the power source is under that triangular cover, about two feet long. The gadgets on the tripod are equally cryptic, except that one has a big lens. Their light?

As we hit the open bay, the hum rises and we start planing faster and faster still. Thirty knots? Hard to judge in the dark. Their hull seems to be a modified trihedral much like ours, with a remarkable absence of slap. Say twenty-two feet. Schemes of capturing it swirl in my mind. I'll need Estéban.

Suddenly a huge flood of white light fans out over us from the tripod, blotting out the aliens in the stern. I see Ruth pulling at a belt around her arm still hugging the gizmo.

"I'll tie that for you."

"It's all right."

The alien device is twinkling or phosphorescing slightly. I lean over to look, whispering, "Give that to me, I'll pass it to Estéban."

"No!" She scoots away, almost over the side. "It's theirs, they need it!"

"What? Are you crazy?" I'm so taken aback by this idiocy I literally stammer. "We have to, we—"

"They haven't hurt us. I'm sure they could." Her eyes are watching me with feral intensity; in the light her face has a lunatic look. Numb as I am, I realize that the wretched woman is poised to throw herself over the side if I move. With the alien thing.

"I think they're gentle," she mutters.

"For Christ's sake, Ruth, they're *aliens!*"

"I'm used to it," she says absently. "There's the island! Stop! Stop here!"

The skiff slows, turning. A mound of foliage is tiny in the light. Metal glints—the plane.

"Althea! Althea! Are you all right?"

Yells, movement on the plane. The water is high, we're floating over the bar. The aliens are keeping us in the lead with the light hiding them. I see one pale figure splashing toward us and a dark one behind, coming more slowly. Estéban must be puzzled by that light.

"Mr. Fenton is hurt, Althea. These people brought us back with the water. Are you all right?"

"A-okay." Althea flounders up, peering excitedly. "You all right? Whew, that light!" Automatically I start handing her the idiotic water bag.

"Leave that for the captain," Ruth says sharply. "Althea, can you climb in the boat? Quickly, it's important."

"Coming."

"No, no!" I protest, but the skiff tilts as Althea swarms in. The aliens twitter, and their voice box starts groaning. 'Gu-give . . . now . . . give . . .''

"*Que llega?*" Estéban's face appears beside me, squinting fiercely into the light.

"Grab it, get it from her—that thing she has—" but Ruth's

voice rides over mine. "Captain, lift Mr. Fenton out of the boat. He's hurt his leg. Hurry, please."

"Goddamn it, wait!" I shout, but an arm has grabbed my middle. When a Maya boosts you, you go. I hear Althea saying, "Mother, your arm!" and fall onto Estéban. We stagger around in water up to my waist; I can't feel my feet at all.

When I get steady, the boat is yards away. The two women are head-to-head, murmuring.

"Get them!" I tug loose from Estéban and flounder forward. Ruth stands up in the boat facing the invisible aliens.

"Take us with you. Please. We want to go with you, away from here."

"Ruth! Estéban, get that boat!" I lunge and lose my feet again. The aliens are chirruping madly behind their light.

"Please take us. We don't mind what your planet is like; we'll learn—we'll do anything! We won't cause any trouble. Please. Oh *please*." The skiff is drifting farther away.

"Ruth! Althea! Are you crazy? Wait—" But I can only shuffle nightmarelike in the ooze, hearing that damn voice box wheeze, "N-not come . . . more . . . not come . . ." Althea's face turns to it, open-mouthed grin.

"Yes, we understand," Ruth cries. "We don't want to come back. Please take us with you!"

I shout and Estéban splashes past me shouting too, something about radio.

"Yes-s-s" groans the voice.

Ruth sits down suddenly, clutching Althea. At that moment Estéban grabs the edge of the skiff beside her.

"Hold them, Estéban! Don't let her go."

He gives me one slit-eyed glance over his shoulder, and I recognize his total uninvolvement. He's had a good look at that camouflage paint and the absence of fishing gear. I make a desperate rush and slip again. When I come up Ruth is saying, "We're going with these people, Captain. Please take your money out of my purse, it's in the plane. And give this to Mr. Fenton."

She passes him something small; the notebook. He takes it slowly.

"Estéban! No!"

He has released the skiff.

"Thank you so much," Ruth says as they float apart. Her voice is shaky; she raises it. "There won't be any trouble,

Don. Please send this cable. It's to a friend of mine, she'll take care of everything.'' Then she adds the craziest touch of the entire night. "She's a grand person; she's director of nursing training at N.I.H."

As the skiff drifts, I hear Althea add something that sounds like "Right on."

Sweet Jesus . . . Next minute the humming has started; the light is receding fast. The last I see of Mrs. Ruth Parsons and Miss Althea Parsons is two small shadows against that light, like two opossums. The light snaps off, the hum deepens—and they're going, going, gone away.

In the dark water beside me Estéban is instructing everybody in general to *chingarse* themselves.

"Friends, or something," I tell him lamely. "She seemed to want to go with them."

He is pointedly silent, hauling me back to the plane. He knows what could be around here better than I do, and Mayas have their own longevity program. His condition seems improved. As we get in I notice the hammock has been repositioned.

In the night—of which I remember little—the wind changes. And at seven thirty next morning a Cessna buzzes the sandbar under cloudless skies.

By noon we're back in Cozumel, Captain Estéban accepts his fees and departs laconically for his insurance wars. I leave the Parsons' bags with the Caribe agent, who couldn't care less. The cable goes to a Mrs. Priscilla Hayes Smith, also of Bethesda. I take myself to a medico and by three P.M. I'm sitting on the Cabañas terrace with a fat leg and a double margharita, trying to believe the whole thing.

The cable said, *Althea and I taking extraordinary opportunity for travel. Gone several years. Please take charge our affairs. Love, Ruth.*

She'd written it that afternoon, you understand.

I order another double, wishing to hell I'd gotten a good look at that gizmo. Did it have a label. Made by Betelgeusians? No matter how weird it was, *how* could a person be crazy enough to imagine—?

Not only that but to hope, to plan? *If I could only go away* . . . That's what she was doing, all day. Waiting, hoping, figuring how to get Althea. To go sight unseen to an alien world . . .

With the third margharita I try a joke about alienated

women, but my heart's not in it. And I'm certain there won't be any bother, any trouble at all. Two human women, one of them possibly pregnant, have departed for, I guess, the stars; and the fabric of society will never show a ripple. I brood: do all Mrs. Parsons' friends hold themselves in readiness for any eventuality, including leaving Earth? And will Mrs. Parsons somehow one day contrive to send for Mrs. Priscilla Hayes Smith, that grand person?

I can only send for another cold one, musing on Althea. What suns will Captain Estéban's sloe-eyed offspring, if any, look upon? "Get in, Althea, we're taking off for Orion." "A-okay, Mother." Is that some system of upbringing? *We survive by ones and twos in the chinks of your world-machine . . . I'm used to aliens . . .* She'd meant every word. Insane. How could a woman choose to live among unknown monsters, to say good-bye to her home, her world?

As the margaritas take hold, the whole mad scenario melts down to the image of those two small shapes sitting side by side in the receding alien glare.

Two of our opossums are missing.

SALVADOR

by Lucius Shepard

Lucius Shepard was one of the most popular and influential new writers of the 80s, and his popularity has persisted right into the 90s as well. Stories set in authentically described Third World milieus are a specialty of Shepard's, and as a writer he has become as strongly identified with Central and South America as Mike Resnick is with Africa. In fact, so many Shepard stories were qualified for this anthology—stories such as "R&R," "The Jaguar Hunter," "Black Coral," "Fire Zone Emerald," "Surrender," "On The Border," "The End of Life As We Know It," "A Traveller's Tale," and others—that it was difficult to decide which one of them to use.

In the end, we decided on the harrowing story that follows, in which he shows us that we do learn from the experience of war—the only question is, learn what?

Lucius Shepard won the John W. Campbell Award in 1985 as the year's Best New Writer, and no year since has gone by without him adorning the final ballot for one major award or another, and often for several. In 1987, he won the Nebula Award for his landmark novella "R & R," and in 1988 he picked up a World Fantasy Award for his monumental short-story collection The Jaguar Hunter, *following it in 1992 with a second World Fantasy Award for his second collection,* The Ends of the Earth. *His novels include* Green Eyes, *the bestselling* Life During Wartime, *and* Kalimantan. *His most recent books are the novels* The Golden *and* The Off-Season. *He's currently at work on a mainstream novel,* Family Values. *Born in Lynchburg, Virginia, he now lives in Seattle, Washington.*

Three weeks before they wasted Tecolutla, Dantzler had his baptism of fire. The platoon was crossing a meadow at the foot of an emerald-green volcano, and being a dreamy sort, he was idling along, swatting tall grasses with his rifle barrel and thinking how it might have been a first-grader with crayons who had devised this elementary landscape of a perfect cone rising into a cloudless sky, when cap-pistol noises sounded on the slope. Someone screamed for the medic, and Dantzler dove into the grass, fumbling for his ampules. He slipped one from the dispenser and popped it under his nose, inhaling frantically; then, to be on the safe side, he popped another—"A double helpin' of martial arts," as DT would say—and lay with his head down until the drugs had worked their magic. There was dirt in his mouth, and he was very afraid.

Gradually his arms and legs lost their heaviness, and his heart rate slowed. His vision sharpened to the point that he could see not only the pinpricks of fire blooming on the slope, but also the figures behind them, half-obscured by brush. A bubble of grim anger welled up in his brain, hardened to a fierce resolve, and he started moving toward the volcano. By the time he reached the base of the cone, he was all rage and reflexes. He spent the next forty minutes spinning acrobatically through the thickets, spraying shadows with bursts of his M-18; yet part of his mind remained distant from the action, marveling at his efficiency, at the comic-strip enthusiasm he felt for the task of killing. He shouted at the men he shot, and he shot them many more times than was necessary, like a child playing soldier.

"Playin' my ass!" DT would say. "You just actin' natural."

DT was a firm believer in the ampules; though the official line was that they contained tailored RNA compounds and pseudoendorphins modified to an inhalant form, he held the opinion that they opened a man up to his inner nature. He was big, black, with heavily muscled arms and crudely stamped features, and he had come to the Special Forces direct from prison, where he had done a stretch for attempted murder; the palms of his hands were covered by jail tattoos—a pentagram and a horned monster. The words DIE HIGH were painted on his helmet. This was his second tour in Salvador, and Moody—who was Dantzler's buddy—said the drugs had addled DT's brains, that he was crazy and gone to hell.

"He collects trophies," Moody had said. "And not just ears like they done in 'Nam."

When Dantzler had finally gotten a glimpse of the trophies, he had been appalled. They were kept in a tin box in DT's pack and were nearly unrecognizable; they looked like withered brown orchids. But despite his revulsion, despite the fact that he was afraid of DT, he admired the man's capacity for survival and had taken to heart his advice to rely on the drugs.

On the way back down the slope they discovered a live casualty, an Indian kid about Dantzler's age, nineteen or twenty. Black hair, adobe skin, and heavy-lidded brown eyes. Dantzler, whose father was an anthropologist and had done fieldwork in Salvador, figured him for a Santa Ana tribesman; before leaving the States, Dantzler had pored over his father's notes, hoping this would give him an edge, and had learned to identify the various regional types. The kid had a minor leg wound and was wearing fatigue pants and a faded COKE ADDS LIFE T-shirt. This T-shirt irritated DT no end.

"What the hell you know 'bout Coke?" he asked the kid as they headed for the chopper that was to carry them deeper into Morazán Province. "You think it's funny or somethin'?" He whacked the kid in the back with his rifle butt, and when they reached the chopper, he slung him inside and had him sit by the door. He sat beside him, tapped out a joint from a pack of Kools, and asked, "Where's Infante?"

"Dead," said the medic.

"Shit!" DT licked the joint so it would burn evenly. "Goddamn beaner ain't no use 'cept somebody else know Spanish."

"I know a little," Dantzler volunteered.

Staring at Dantzler, DT's eyes went empty and unfocused. "Naw," he said. "You don't know no Spanish."

Dantzler ducked his head to avoid DT's stare and said nothing; he thought he understood what DT meant, but he ducked away from the understanding as well. The chopper bore them aloft, and DT lit the joint. He let the smoke out his nostrils and passed the joint to the kid, who accepted gratefully.

"Qué sabor!" he said, exhaling a billow; he smiled and nodded, wanting to be friends.

Dantzler turned his gaze to the open door. They were flying low between the hills, and looking at the deep bays of shadow in their folds acted to drain away the residue of the drugs, leaving him weary and frazzled. Sunlight poured in, dazzling the oil-smeared floor.

"Hey, Dantzler!" DT had to shout over the noise of the rotors. "Ask him whass his name!"

The kid's eyelids were drooping from the joint, but on hearing Spanish he perked up; he shook his head, though, refusing to answer. Dantzler smiled and told him not to be afraid.

"Ricardo Quu," said the kid.

"Kool!" said DT with false heartiness. "Thass my brand!" He offered his pack to the kid.

"Gracias, no." The kid waved the joint and grinned.

"Dude's named for a goddamn cigarette," said DT disparagingly, as if this were the height of insanity.

of a coven than a platoon. The other two guys were singing
their lungs out, and even the kid was getting into the spirit
of things. "*Música!*" he said at one point, smiling at everybody, trying to fan the flame of good feeling. He swayed
to the rhythm and essayed a "la-la" now and again. But no
one else was responding.

The singing stopped, and Dantzler saw that the whole
platoon was staring at the kid, their expressions slack and
dispirited.

"Space!" shouted DT, giving the kid a little shove. "The
final frontier!"

The smile had not yet left the kid's face when he toppled
out the door. DT peered after him; a few seconds later he
smacked his hand against the floor and sat back, grinning.
Dantzler felt like screaming, the stupid horror of the joke
was so at odds with the languor of his homesickness. He
looked to the others for reaction. They were sitting with
their heads down, fiddling with trigger guards and pack
straps, studying their bootlaces, and seeing this, he quickly
imitated them.

Morazán Province was spook country. Santa Ana spooks.
Flights of birds had been reported to attack patrols; animals
appeared at the perimeters of campsites and vanished when
you shot at them; dreams afflicted everyone who ventured
there. Dantzler could not testify to the birds and animals,
but he did have a recurring dream. In it the kid DT had
killed was pinwheeling down through a golden fog, his
T-shirt visible against the roiling backdrop, and sometimes
a voice would boom out of the fog, saying, "You are killing
my son." No, no, Dantzler would reply, it wasn't me, and
besides, he's already dead. Then he would wake covered
with sweat, groping for his rifle, his heart racing.

But the dream was not an important terror, and he assigned it no significance. The land was far more terrifying.
Pine-forested ridges that stood out against the sky like
fringes of electrified hair; little trails winding off into thickets and petering out, as if what they led to had been mag-
icked away; gray rock faces along which they were forced
to walk, hopelessly exposed to ambush. There were innumerable booby traps set by the guerrillas, and they lost several men to rockfalls. It was the emptiest place of Dantzler's
experience. No people, no animals, just a few hawks cir-

cling the solitudes between the ridges. Once in a while they
found tunnels, and these they blew with the new gas grenades; the gas ignited the rich concentrations of hydrocar-
bons and sent flame sweeping through the entire system.
DT would praise whoever had discovered the tunnel and
would estimate in a loud voice how many beaners they had
"refried." But Dantzler knew they were traversing pure
emptiness and burning empty holes. Days, under debilitat-
ing heat, they humped the mountains, traveling seven, eight,
even ten klicks up trails so steep that frequently the feet of
the guy ahead of you would be on a level with your face;
nights, it was cold, the darkness absolute, the silence so
profound that Dantzler imagined he could hear the great
humming vibration of the earth. They might have been anywhere or nowhere. Their fear was nourished by the isolation, and the only remedy was "martial arts."

Dantzler took to popping the pills without the excuse of
combat. Moody cautioned him against abusing the drugs,
citing rumors of bad side effects and DT's madness; but
even he was using them more and more often. During basic
training, Dantzler's D.I. had told the boots that the drugs
were available only to the Special Forces, that their use was
optional; but there had been too many instances of lacklus-
ter battlefield performance in the last war, and this was to
prevent a reoccurrence.

"The chickenshit infantry should take 'em," the D.I. had
said. "You bastards are brave already. You're born killers,
right?"

"Right, sir!" they had shouted.

"What are you?"

"Born killers, sir!"

But Dantzler was not a born killer; he was not even clear
as to how he had been drafted, less clear as to how he had
been manipulated into the Special Forces, and he had
learned that nothing was optional in Salvador, with the possible exception of life itself.

The platoon's mission was reconnaissance and mop-up.
Along with other Special Forces platoons, they were to secure Morazán prior to the invasion of Nicaragua; specifically, they were to proceed to the village of Tecolutla, where
a Sandinista patrol had recently been spotted, and following
that they were to join up with the First Infantry and take
part in the offensive against León, a provincial capital just

across the Nicaraguan border. As Dantzler and Moody walked together, they frequently talked about the offensive, how it would be good to get down into flat country; occasionally they talked about the possibility of reporting DT, and once, after he had led them on a forced night march, they toyed with the idea of killing him. But most often they discussed the ways of the Indians and the land, since this was what had caused them to become buddies.

Moody was slightly built, freckled, and red-haired; his eyes had the "thousand-yard stare" that came from too much war. Dantzler had seen winos with such vacant, lusterless stares. Moody's father had been in 'Nam, and Moody said it had been worse than Salvador because there had been no real commitment to win; but he thought Nicaragua and Guatemala might be the worst of all, especially if the Cubans sent in troops as they had threatened. He was adept at locating tunnels and detecting booby traps, and it was for this reason Dantzler had cultivated his friendship. Essentially a loner, Moody had resisted all advances until learning of Dantzler's father; thereafter he had buddied up, eager to hear about the field notes, believing they might give him an edge.

"They think the land has animal traits," said Dantzler one day as they climbed along a ridgetop. "Just like some kinds of fish look like plants or sea bottom, parts of the land look like plain ground, jungle . . . whatever. But when you enter them, you find you've entered the spirit world, the world of *Sukias*."

"What's *Sukias*?" asked Moody.

"Magicians." A twig snapped behind Dantzler, and he spun around, twitching off the safety of his rifle. It was only Hodge—a lanky kid with the beginnings of a beer gut. He stared hollow-eyed at Dantzler and popped an ampule.

Moody made a noise of disbelief. "If they got magicians, why ain't they winnin'? Why ain't they zappin' us off the cliffs?"

"It's not their business," said Dantzler. "They don't believe in messing with worldly affairs unless it concerns them directly. Anyway, these places—the ones that look like normal land but aren't—they're called. . . ." He drew a blank on the name. "*Aya*-something. I can't remember. But they have different laws. They're where your spirit goes to die after your body dies."

"Don't they got no Heaven?"

"Nope. It just takes longer for your spirit to die, and so it goes to one of these places that's between everything and nothing."

"Nothin'," said Moody disconsolately, as if all his hopes for an afterlife had been dashed. "Don't make no sense to have spirits and not have no Heaven."

"Hey," said Dantzler, tensing as wind rustled the pine boughs. "They're just a bunch of damn primitives. You know what their sacred drink is? Hot chocolate! My old man was a guest at one of their funerals, and he said they carried cups of hot chocolate balanced on these little red towers and acted like drinking it was going to wake them to the secrets of the universe." He laughed, and the laughter sounded tinny and psychotic to his own ears. "So you're going to worry about fools who think hot chocolate's holy water?"

"Maybe they just like it," said Moody. "Maybe somebody dyin' just give 'em an excuse to drink it."

But Dantzler was no longer listening. A moment before, as they emerged from pine cover onto the highest point of the ridge, a stony scarp open to the winds and providing a view of rumpled mountains and valleys extending to the horizon, he had popped an ampule. He felt so strong, so full of righteous purpose and controlled fury, it seemed only the sky was around him, that he was still ascending, preparing to do battle with the gods themselves.

Tecolutla was a village of whitewashed stone tucked into a notch between two hills. From above, the houses—with their shadow-blackened windows and doorways—looked like an unlucky throw of dice. The streets ran uphill and down, diverging around boulders. Bougainvilleas and hibiscuses speckled the hillsides, and there were tilled fields on the gentler slopes. It was a sweet, peaceful place when they arrived, and after they had gone it was once again peaceful; but its sweetness had been permanently banished. The reports of Sandinistas had proved accurate, and though they were casualties left behind to recuperate, DT had decided their presence called for extreme measures. Fu gas, frag grenades, and such. He had fired an M-60 until the barrel melted down, and then had manned the flamethrower. Afterward, as they rested atop the next ridge, exhausted and begrimed, having radioed in a chopper for resupply, he could not get over how one of the houses he had torched had come to resemble a toasted marshmallow.

"Ain't that how it was, man?" he asked, striding up and down the line. He did not care if they agreed about the house; it was a deeper question he was asking, one concerning the ethics of their actions.

"Yeah," said Dantzler, forcing a smile. "Sure did."

DT grunted with laughter. "You *know* I'm right, don'tcha man?"

The sun hung directly behind his head, a golden corona rimming a black oval, and Dantzler could not turn his eyes away. He felt weak and weakening, as if threads of himself were being spun loose and sucked into the blackness. He had popped three ampules prior to the firefight, and his experience of Tecolutla had been a kind of mad whirling dance through the streets, spraying erratic bursts that appeared to be writing weird names on the walls. The leader of the Sandinistas had worn a mask—a gray face with a surprised hole of a mouth and pink circles around the eyes. A ghost face. Dantzler had been afraid of the mask and had poured round after round into it. Then, leaving the village, he had seen a small girl standing beside the shell of the last house, watching them, her colorless rag of a dress tattering in the breeze. She had been a victim of that malnutrition disease, the one that paled your skin and whitened your hair and left you retarded. He could not recall the name of the disease—things like names were slipping away from him—nor could he believe anyone had survived, and for a moment he had thought the spirit of the village had come out to mark their trail.

That was all he could remember of Tecolutla, all he wanted to remember. But he knew he had been brave.

Four days later, they headed up into a cloud forest. It was the dry season, but dry season or not, blackish gray clouds always shrouded these peaks. They were shot through by ugly glimmers of lightning, making it seem that malfunctioning neon signs were hidden beneath them, advertisements for evil. Everyone was jittery, and Jerry LeDoux—a slim dark-haired Cajun kid—flat-out refused to go.

"It ain't reasonable," he said. "Be easier to go through the passes."

"We're on recon, man! You think the beaners be waitin'

in the passes, wavin' their white flags?'' DT whipped his
rifle into firing position and pointed it at LeDoux. ''C'mon,
Louisiana man. Pop a few, and you feel different.''

As LeDoux popped the ampules, DT talked to him.

''Look at it this way, man. This is your big adventure.
Up there it be like all them animal shows on the tube. The
savage kingdom, the unknown. Could be like Mars or somethin'. Monsters and shit, with big red eyes and tentacles.
You wanna miss that, man? You wanna miss bein' the first
grunt on Mars?''

Soon LeDoux was raring to go, giggling at DT's rap.

Moody kept his mouth shut, but he fingered the safety of
his rifle and glared at DT's back. When DT turned to him,
however, he relaxed. Since Tecolutla he had grown taciturn,
and there seemed to be a shifting of lights and darks in his
eyes, as if something were scurrying back and forth behind
them. He had taken to wearing banana leaves on his head,
arranging them under his helmet so the frayed ends stuck
out the sides like strange green hair. He said this was camouflage, but Dantzler was certain it bespoke some secretive
irrational purpose. Of course DT had noticed Moody's spiritual erosion, and as they prepared to move out, he called
Dantzler aside.

''He done found someplace inside his head that feel good
to him,'' said DT. ''He's tryin' to curl up into it, and once
he do that he ain't gon' be responsible. Keep an eye on
him.''

Dantzler mumbled his assent, but was not enthused.

''I know he your fren', man, but that don't mean shit.
Not the way things are. Now me, I don't give a damn 'bout
you personally. But I'm your brother-in-arms, and thass
somethin' you can count on . . . y'understand.''

To Dantzler's shame, he did understand.

They had planned on negotiating the cloud forest by
nightfall, but they had underestimated the difficulty. The
vegetation beneath the clouds was lush—thick, juicy leaves
that mashed underfoot, tangles of vines, trees with slick,
pale bark and waxy leaves—and the visibility was only about
fifteen feet. They were gray wraiths passing through gray-
ness. The vague shapes of the foliage reminded Dantzler of
fancifully engraved letters, and for a while he entertained
himself with the notion that they were walking among the
half-formed phrases of a constitution not yet manifest in the

land. They barged off the trail, losing it completely, becoming veiled in spiderwebs and drenched by spills of water; their voices were oddly muffled, the tag ends of words swallowed up. After seven hours of this, DT reluctantly gave the order to pitch camp. They set electric lamps around the perimeter so they could see to string the jungle hammocks; the beam of light illuminated the moisture in the air, piercing the murk with jeweled blades. They talked in hushed tones, alarmed by the eerie atmosphere. When they had done with the hammocks, DT posted four sentries—Moody, LeDoux, Dantzler, and himself. Then they switched off the lamps.

It grew pitch-dark, and the darkness was picked out by plips and plops, the entire spectrum of dripping sounds. To Dantzler's ears they blended into a gabbling speech. He imagined tiny Santa Ana demons talking about him, and to stave off paranoia he popped two ampules. He continued to pop them, trying to limit himself to one every half hour; but he was uneasy, unsure where to train his rifle in the dark, and he exceeded his limit. Soon it began to grow light again, and he assumed that more time had passed than he had thought. That often happened with the ampules—it was easy to lose yourself in being alert, in the wealth of perceptual detail available to your sharpened senses. Yet on checking his watch, he saw it was only a few minutes after two o'clock. His system was too inundated with the drugs to allow panic, but he twitched his head from side to side in tight little arcs to determine the source of the brightness. There did not appear to be a single source; it was simply that filaments of the cloud were gleaming, casting a diffuse golden glow, as if they were elements of a nervous system coming to life. He started to call out, then held back. The others must have seen the light, and they had given no cry; they probably had a good reason for their silence. He scrunched down flat, pointing his rifle out from the campsite.

Bathed in the golden mist, the forest had acquired an alchemic beauty. Beads of water glittered with gemmy brilliance; the leaves and vines and bark were gilded. Every surface shimmered with light . . . everything except a fleck of blackness hovering between two of the trunks, its size gradually increasing. As it swelled in his vision, he saw it had the shape of a bird, its wings beating, flying toward him

from an inconceivable distance—inconceivable, because the
dense vegetation did not permit you to see very far in a
straight line, and yet the bird was growing larger with such
slowness that it must have been coming from a long way
off. It was not really flying, he realized; rather, it was as if
the forest were painted on a piece of paper, as if someone
were holding a lit match behind it and burning a hole, a
hole that maintained the shape of a bird as it spread. He
was transfixed, unable to react. Even when it had blotted
out half the light, when he lay before it no bigger than a
mote in relation to its huge span, he could not move or
squeeze the trigger. And then the blackness swept over him.
He had the sensation of being borne along at incredible
speed, and he could no longer hear the dripping of the forest.

"Moody!" he shouted. "DT!"

But the voice that answered belonged to neither of them.
It was hoarse, issuing from every part of the surrounding
blackness, and he recognized it as the voice of his recurring
dream.

"You are killing my son," it said. "I have led you here,
to this *ayahuamaco*, so he may judge you."

Dantzler knew to his bones the voice was that of the *Sukia*
of the village of Santander Jiménez. He wanted to offer a
denial, to explain his innocence, but all he could manage
was, "No." He said it tearfully, hopelessly, his forehead
resting on his rifle barrel. Then his mind gave a savage
twist, and his soldiery self regained control. He ejected an
ampule from his dispenser and popped it.

The voice laughed—malefic, damning laughter whose vi-
brations shuddered Dantzler. He opened up with the rifle,
spraying fire in all directions. Filigrees of golden holes appeared in the blackness, tendrils of mist coiled through
them. He kept on firing until the blackness shattered and
fell in jagged sections toward him. Slowly. Like shards of
black glass dropping through water. He emptied the rifle
and flung himself flat, shielding his head with his arms,
expecting to be sliced into bits; but nothing touched him.
At last he peeked between his arms; then—amazed, because
the forest was now a uniform lustrous yellow—he rose to
his knees. He scraped his hand on one of the crushed leaves
beneath him, and blood welled from the cut. The broken
fibers of the leaf were as stiff as wires. He stood, a giddy

trickle of hysteria leaking up from the bottom of his soul. It was no forest, but a building of solid gold worked to resemble a forest—the sort of conceit that might have been fabricated for the child of an emperor. Canopied by golden leaves, columned by slender golden trunks, carpeted by golden grasses. The water beads were diamonds. All the gleam and glitter soothed his apprehension; here was something out of a myth, a habitat for princesses and wizards and dragons. Almost gleeful, he turned to the campsite to see how the others were reacting.

Once, when he was nine years old, he had sneaked into the attic to rummage through the boxes and trunks, and he had run across an old morocco-bound copy of *Gulliver's Travels*. He had been taught to treasure old books, and so he had opened it eagerly to look at the illustrations, only to find that the centers of the pages had been eaten away, and there, right in the heart of the fiction, was a nest of larvae. Pulpy, horrid things. It had been an awful sight, but one unique in his experience, and he might have studied those crawling scraps of life for a very long time if his father had not interrupted. Such a sight was now before him, and he was numb with it.

They were all dead. He should have guessed they would be; he had given no thought to them while firing his rifle. They had been struggling out of their hammocks when the bullets hit, and as a result they were hanging half-in, half-out, their limbs dangling, blood pooled beneath them. The veils of golden mist made them look dark and mysterious and malformed, like monsters killed as they emerged from their cocoons. Dantzler could not stop staring, but he was shrinking inside himself. It was not his fault. That thought kept swooping in and out of a flock of less acceptable thoughts; he wanted it to stay put, to be true, to alleviate the sick horror he was beginning to feel.

"What's your name?" asked a girl's voice behind him.

She was sitting on a stone about twenty feet away. Her hair was a tawny shade of gold, her skin a half-tone lighter, and her dress was cunningly formed out of the mist. Only her eyes were real. Brown heavy-lidded eyes—they were at variance with the rest of her face, which had the fresh, unaffected beauty of an American teenager.

"Don't be afraid," she said, and patted the ground, inviting him to sit beside her.

He recognized the eyes, but it was no matter. He badly needed the consolation she could offer; he walked over and sat down. She let him lean his head against her thigh.

"What's your name?" she repeated.

"Dantzler," he said. "John Dantzler." And then he added, "I'm from Boston. My father's . . ." It would be too difficult to explain about anthropology. "He's a teacher."

"Are there many soldiers in Boston?" She stroked his cheek with a golden finger.

The caress made Dantzler happy. "Oh, no,"he said. "They hardly know there's a war going on."

"This is true?" she said, incredulous.

"Well, they *do* know about it, but it's just news on the TV to them. They've got more pressing problems. Their jobs, families."

"Will you let them know about the war when you return home?" she asked. "Will you do that for me?"

Dantzler had given up hope of returning home, of surviving, and her assumption that he would do both acted to awaken his gratitude. "Yes," he said fervently. "I will."

"You must hurry," she said. "If you stay in the *ayahuamaco* too long, you will never leave. You must find the way out. It is a way not of directions or trails, but of events."

"Where is this place?" he asked, suddenly aware of how much he had taken it for granted.

She shifted her leg away, and if he had not caught himself on the stone, he would have fallen. When he looked up, she had vanished. He was surprised that her disappearance did not alarm him; in reflex he slipped out a couple of ampules, but after a moment's reflection he decided not to use them. It was impossible to slip them back into the dispenser, so he tucked them into the interior webbing of his helmet for later. He doubted he would need them, though. He felt strong, competent, and unafraid.

Dantzler stepped carefully between the hammocks, not wanting to brush against them; it might have been his imagination, but they seemed to be bulged down lower than before, as if death had weighed out heavier than life. That heaviness was in the air, pressuring him. Mist rose like golden steam from the corpses, but the sight no longer affected him—perhaps because the mist gave the illusion of being their souls. He picked up a rifle with a full magazine and headed off into the forest.

The tips of the golden leaves were sharp, and he had to ease past them to avoid being cut; but he was at the top of his form, moving gracefully, and the obstacles barely slowed his pace. He was not even anxious about the girl's warning to hurry; he was certain the way out would soon present itself. After a minute or so he heard voices, and after another few seconds he came to a clearing divided by a stream, one so perfectly reflecting that its banks appeared to enclose a wedge of golden mist. Moody was squatting to the left of the stream, staring at the blade of his survival knife and singing under his breath—a wordless melody that had the erratic rhythm of a trapped fly. Beside him lay Jerry LeDoux, his throat slashed from ear to ear. DT was sitting on the other side of the stream; he had been shot just above the knee, and though he had ripped up his shirt for bandages and tied off the leg with a tourniquet, he was not in good shape. He was sweating, and a gray chalky pallor infused his skin. The entire scene had the weird vitality of something that had materialized in a magic mirror, a bubble of reality enclosed within a gilt frame.

DT heard Dantzler's footfalls and glanced up. "Waste him!" he shouted, pointing to Moody.

Moody did not turn from contemplation of the knife. "No," he said, as if speaking to someone whose image was held in the blade.

"Waste him, man!" screamed DT. "He killed LeDoux!"

"Please," said Moody to the knife. "I don't want to."

There was blood clotted on his face, more blood on the banana leaves sticking out of his helmet.

"Did you kill Jerry?" asked Dantzler; while he addressed the question to Moody, he did not relate to him as an individual, only as part of a design whose message he had to unravel.

"Jesus Christ! Waste him!" DT smashed his fist against the ground in frustration.

"Okay," said Moody. With an apologetic look, he sprang to his feet and charged Dantzler, swinging the knife.

Emotionless, Dantzler stitched a line of fire across Moody's chest; he went sideways into the bushes and down.

"What the hell was you waitin' for!" DT tried to rise,

but winced and fell back. "Damn! Don't know if I can walk."

"Pop a few," Dantzler suggested mildly.

"Yeah. Good thinkin', man." DT fumbled for his dispenser.

Dantzler peered into the bushes to see where Moody had fallen. He felt nothing, and this pleased him. He was weary of feeling.

DT popped an ampule with a flourish, as if making a toast, and inhaled. "Ain't you gon' to do some, man?"

"I don't need them," said Dantzler. "I'm fine."

The stream interested him; it did not reflect the mist, as he had supposed, but was itself a seam of the mist.

"How many you think they was?" asked DT.

"How many what?"

"Beaners, man! I wasted three or four after they hit us, but I couldn't tell how many they was."

Dantzler considered this in light of his own interpretation of events and Moody's conversation with the knife. It made sense. A Santa Ana kind of sense.

"Beats me," he said. "But I guess there's less than there used to be."

DT snorted. "You got *that* right!" He heaved to his feet and limped to the edge of the stream. "Gimme a hand across."

Dantzler reached out to him, but instead of taking his hand, he grabbed his wrist and pulled him off-balance. DT teetered on his good leg, then toppled and vanished beneath the mist. Dantzler had expected him to fall, but he surfaced instantly, mist clinging to his skin. Of course, thought Dantzler; his body would have to die before his spirit would fall.

"What you doin', man?" DT was more disbelieving than enraged.

Dantzler planted a foot in the middle of his back and pushed him down until his head was submerged. DT bucked and clawed at the foot and managed to come to his hands and knees. Mist slithered from his eyes, his nose, and he choked out the words ". . . kill you . . ." Dantzler pushed him down again; he got into pushing him down and letting him up, over and over. Not so as to torture him. Not really. It was because he had suddenly understood the nature of the *ayahuamaco*'s laws, that they were approximations of

normal laws, and he further understood that his actions had
to approximate those of someone jiggling a key in a lock.
DT was the key to the way out, and Dantzler was jiggling
him, making sure all the tumblers were engaged.

Some of the vessels in DT's eyes had burst, and the whites
were occluded by films of blood. When he tried to speak,
mist curled from his mouth. Gradually his struggles subsided; he clawed runnels in the gleaming yellow dirt of the
bank and shuddered. His shoulders were knobs of black
land foundering in a mystic sea.

For a long time after DT sank from view, Dantzler stood
beside the stream, uncertain of what was left to do and unable to remember a lesson he had been taught. Finally he
shouldered his rifle and walked away from the clearing.
Morning had broken, the mist had thinned, and the forest
had regained its usual coloration. But he scarcely noticed
these changes, still troubled by his faulty memory. Eventually, he let it slide—it would all come clear sooner or
later. He was just happy to be alive. After a while he began
to kick the stones as he went, and to swing his rifle in a
carefree fashion against the weeds.

When the First Infantry poured across the Nicaraguan
border and wasted León, Dantzler was having a quiet time
at the VA hospital in Ann Arbor, Michigan; and at the pre-
cise moment the bulletin was flashed nationwide, he was
sitting in the lounge, watching the American League play-
offs between Detroit and Texas. Some of the patients ranted
at the interruption, while others shouted them down, wanting to hear the details. Dantzler expressed no reaction whatsoever. He was solely concerned with being a model patient;
however, noticing that one of the staff was giving him a
clinical stare, he added his weight on the side of the baseball
fans. He did not want to appear too controlled. The doctors
were as suspicious of that sort of behavior as they were of
its contrary. But the funny thing was—at least it was funny
to Dantzler—that his feigned annoyance at the bulletin was
an exemplary proof of his control, his expertise at moving
through life the way he had moved through the golden leaves
of the cloud forest. Cautiously, gracefully, efficiently.
Touching nothing, and being touched by nothing. That was
the lesson he had learned—to be as perfect a counterfeit of
a man as the *ayahuamaco* had been of the land; to adopt

the various stances of a man, and yet, by virtue of his distance from things human, to be all the more prepared for the onset of crisis or a call to action. He saw nothing aberrant in this; even the doctors would admit that men were little more than organized pretense. If he was different from other men, it was only that he had a deeper awareness of the principles on which his personality was founded.

When the battle of Managua was joined, Dantzler was living at home. His parents had urged him to go easy in readjusting to civilian life, but he had immediately gotten a job as a management trainee in a bank. Each morning he would drive to work and spend a controlled, quiet eight hours; each night he would watch TV with his mother, and before going to bed, he would climb to the attic and inspect the trunk containing his souvenirs of war—helmet, fatigues, knife, boots. The doctors had insisted he face his experiences, and this ritual was his way of following their instructions. All in all, he was quite pleased with his progress, but he still had problems. He had not been able to force himself to venture out at night, remembering too well the darkness in the cloud forest, and he had rejected his friends, refusing to see them or answer their calls—he was not secure with the idea of friendship. Further, despite his methodical approach to life, he was prone to a nagging restlessness, the feeling of a chore left undone.

One night his mother came into his room and told him that an old friend, Phil Curry, was on the phone. "Please talk to him, Johnny," she said. "He's been drafted, and I think he's a little scared."

The word *drafted* struck a responsive chord in Dantzler's soul, and after brief deliberation he went downstairs and picked up the receiver.

"Hey," said Phil. "What's the story, man? Three months, and you don't even give me a call."

"I'm sorry," said Dantzler. "I haven't been feeling so hot."

"Yeah, I understand." Phil was silent a moment. "Listen, man. I'm leavin', y'know, and we're havin' a big send-off at Sparky's. It's goin' on right now. Why don't you come down?"

"I don't know."

"Jeanine's here, man. Y'know, she's still crazy 'bout you, talks 'bout you alla time. She don't go out with nobody."

Dantzler was unable to think of anything to say.

"Look," said Phil, "I'm pretty weirded out by this soldier shit. I hear it's pretty bad down there. If you got anything you can tell me 'bout what it's like, man I'd 'preciate it."

Dantzler could relate to Phil's concern, his desire for an edge, and besides, it felt right to go. Very right. He would take some precautions against the darkness.

"I'll be there," he said.

It was a foul night, spitting snow, but Sparky's parking lot was jammed. Dantzler's mind was flurried like the snow, crowded like the lot—thoughts whirling in, jockeying for position, melting away. He hoped his mother would not wait up, he wondered if Jeanine still wore her hair long, he was worried because the palms of his hands were unnaturally warm. Even with the car windows rolled up, he could hear loud music coming from inside the club. Above the door the words SPARKY'S ROCK CITY were being spelled out a letter at a time in red neon, and when the spelling was complete, the letters flashed off and on and a golden neon explosion bloomed around them. After the explosion, the entire sign went dark for a split second, and the big ramshackle building seemed to grow large and merge with the black sky. He had an idea it was watching him, and he shuddered—one of those sudden lurches downward of the kind that take you just before you fall asleep. He knew the people inside did not intend him any harm, but he also knew that places have a way of changing people's intent, and he did not want to be caught off guard. Sparky's might be such a place, might be a huge black presence camouflaged by neon, its true substance one with the abyss of the sky, the phosphorescent snowflakes jittering in his headlights, the wind keening through the side vent. He would have liked very much to drive home and forget about his promise to Phil; however, he felt a responsibility to explain about the war. More than a responsibility, an evangelistic urge. He would tell them about the kid falling out of the chopper, the white-haired girl in Tecolutla, the emptiness. God, yes! How you went down chock-full of ordinary American thoughts and dreams, memories of smoking weed and chasing tail and hanging out and freeway flying with a case of something cold, and how you smuggled back a human-shaped container of pure Salvadorian emptiness. Primo grade. Smuggled it back to the land of silk and money, of mindfuck video games and topless tennis matches and fast-food solutions to the nutritional problem. Just a taste of Salvador would banish all those trivial obsessions. Just a taste. It would be easy to explain.

Of course, some things beggared explanation.

He bent down and adjusted the survival knife in his boots so the hilt would not rub against his calf. From his coat pocket he withdrew the two ampules he had secreted in his helmet that long-ago night in the cloud forest. As the neon explosion flashed once more, glimmers of gold coursed along their shiny surfaces. He did not think he would need them; his hand was steady, and his purpose was clear. But to be on the safe side, he popped them both.

DOOMSDAY DEFERRED

by Will F. Jenkins

"Will F. Jenkins" was one of the writing names used by the late William Fitzgerald Jenkins, who will be more familiar to the genre audience under his best-known pseudonym, Murray Leinster. Although he wrote copiously in many other fields (and was a successful inventor as well, known, for instance, for the invention of a front projection method for filming backgrounds still used in the film industry today), as "Murray Leinster" Jenkins had a profound effect on the development of modern science fiction. Jenkins sold his first SF story to Argosy *in 1919, had work published in Hugo Gernsback's* Amazing *during the 20s, and went on to be one of the mainstays of John W. Campbell's "Golden Age"* Astounding *in the 40s. Among other accomplishments, he is credited with writing one of the first Alternate History stories, in "Sideways in Time," and one of the earliest First Contact stories, the famous "First Contact," and stories like his Hugo Award-winning "Exploration Team" are still models of how to write an intricate and intelligent adventure set on an alien world. His books include* The Wailing Asteroid, The Planet Explorer, The Time Tunnel, The Mutant Weapon, *and the collections* Monsters and Such *and* The Best of Murray Leinster.*

Although much of Jenkins' work is heavily dated now, the best of his short stories remain as fresh and powerful today as they were on the day they were written. As demonstrated by the hair-raising story that follows, the oldest story in this book by a decade, and almost forty-five years older than the most recently-published story here, and still a story that will make your blood run cold, and will have you sitting on the edge of your seat.

If I were sensible, I'd say that somebody else told me this story, and then cast doubts on his veracity. But I saw it all.

I was part of it. I have an invoice of a shipment I made from Brazil, with a notation on it, "José Ribiera's stuff." The shipment went through. The invoice, I noticed only today, has a mashed *soldado* ant sticking to the page. There is nothing unusual about it as a specimen. On the face of things, every element is irritatingly commonplace. But if I were sensible, I wouldn't tell it this way.

It began in Milhao, where José Ribiera came to me. Milhao is in Brazil, but from it the Andes can be seen against the sky at sunset. It is a town the jungle unfortunately did not finish burying when the rubber boom collapsed. It is so far up the Amazon basin that its principal contacts with the outer world are smugglers and fugitives from Peruvian justice who come across the mountains, and nobody at all goes there except for his sins. I don't know what took José Ribiera there. I went because one of the three known specimens of *Morpho andiensis* was captured nearby by Böhler in 1911, and a lunatic millionaire in Chicago was willing to pay for a try at a fourth for his collection.

I got there after a river steamer refused to go any further, and after four days more in a canoe with paddlers who had lived on or near river water all their lives without once taking a bath in it. When I got to Milhao, I wished myself back in the canoe. It's that sort of place.

But that's where José Ribiera was, and in back-country Brazil there is a remarkable superstition that *os Senhores Norteamericanos* are honest men. I do not explain it. I simply record it. And just as I was getting settled in a particularly noisome inn, José knocked on my door and came in. He was a small brown man, and he was scared all the way down deep inside. He tried to hide that. The thing I noticed first was that he was clean. He was barefoot, but his tattered duck garments were immaculate, and the rest of him had been washed, and recently. In a town like Milhao, that was startling.

"*Senhor,*" said José in a sort of apologetic desperation, "you are a *Senhor Norteamericano*. I—I beg your aid."

I grunted. Being an American is embarrassing, sometimes and in some places. José closed the door behind him and fumbled inside his garments. His eyes anxious, he pulled out a small cloth bundle. He opened it with shaking fingers. And I blinked. The lamplight glittered and glinted on the most amazing mass of tiny gold nuggets I'd ever seen. I hadn't a doubt it was gold, but even at first glance I wondered how on earth it had been gathered. There was no flour gold at all—that fine powder which is the largest part of any placer yield. Most of it was gravelly particles of pinhead size. There was no nugget larger than a half pea. There must have been five pounds of it altogether, though, and it was a rather remarkable spectacle.

"*Senhor,*" said José tensely, "I beg that you will help me turn this into cattle! It is a matter of life or death."

I hardened my expression. Of course, in thick jungle like that around Milhao, a cow or a bull would be as much out of place as an Eskimo, but that wasn't the point. I had business of my own at Milhao. If I started gold buying or cattle dealing out of amiability, my own affairs would suffer. So I said in polite regret, "I am not a businessman, *senhor*. I don't deal in gold or cattle either. To buy cattle, you should go down to São Pedro"—that was four days' paddle downstream, or considering the current perhaps three—"and take this gold to a banker. He will give you money for it if you can prove that it is yours. You can then buy cattle if you wish."

José looked at me desperately. Certainly half the population of Milhao—and positively the Peruvian-refugee half—would have cut his throat for a fraction of his hoard. He almost panted: "But, *senhor!* This would be enough to buy cattle in São Pedro and send them here, would it not?"

I agreed that at a guess it should buy all the cattle in São Pedro, twice over, and hire the town's wheezy steam launch to tow them upriver besides. José looked sick with relief. But, I said, one should buy his livestock himself, so he ought to go to São Pedro in person. And I could not see what good cattle would be in the jungle anyhow.

"Yet—it would buy cattle!" said José, gulping. "That is what I told—my friends. But I cannot go farther than Milhao, *senhor*. I cannot go to São Pedro. Yet I must—I need to buy cattle for—my friends! It is life and death! How can I do this, *senhor?*"

Naturally, I considered that he exaggerated the emergency.

"I am not a businessman," I repeated. "I would not be able to help you." Then at the terrified look in his eyes I explained, "I am here after butterflies."

He couldn't understand that. He began to stammer, pleading. So I explained.

"There is a rich man," I said wryly, "who wishes to possess a certain butterfly. I have pictures of it. I am sent to find it. I can pay one thousand milreis for one butterfly of a certain sort. But I have no authority to do other business, such as the purchase of gold or cattle."

José looked extraordinarily despairing. He looked numbed by the loss of hope. So, merely to say or do something, I showed him a color photograph of the specimen of *Morpho andiensis* which is in the Goriot collection in Paris. Bug collectors were in despair about it during the war. They were sure the Nazis would manage to seize it. Then José's eyes lighted hopefully.

"*Senhor!*" he said urgently. "Perhaps my—friends can find you such a butterfly! Will you pay for such a butterfly in cattle sent here from São Pedro, *senhor?*"

I said rather blankly that I would, but—Then I was talking to myself. José had bolted out of my room, leaving maybe five pounds of gravelly gold nuggets in my hands. That was not usual.

I went after him, but he'd disappeared. So I hid his small fortune in the bottom of my collection kit. A few drops of formaldehyde, spilled before closing up a kit of collection bottles and insects, is very effective in chasing away pilferers. I make use of it regularly.

Next morning I asked about José. My queries were greeted with shrugs. He was a very low person. He did not live in Milhao, but had a clearing, a homestead, some miles upstream, where he lived with his wife. They had one child. He was suspected of much evil. He had bought pigs, and taken them to his clearing and behold he had no pigs there! His wife was very pretty, and a Peruvian had gone swaggering to pay court to her, and he had never come back. It is notable, as I think of it, that up to this time no ant of any sort has come into my story. Butterflies, but no ants. Especially not *soldados*—army ants. It is queer.

I learned nothing useful about José, but I had come to Milhao on business, so I stated it publicly. I wished a certain butterfly, I said. I would pay one thousand milreis for a perfect specimen. I would show a picture of what I wanted to any interested person, and I would show how to make a butterfly net and how to use it, and how to handle butterflies without injuring them. But I wanted only one kind, and it must not be squashed.

The inhabitants of Milhao became happily convinced that I was insane, and that it might be profitable insanity for them. Each person leaped to the nearest butterfly and blandly brought it to me. I spent a whole day explaining to bright-eyed people that matching the picture of *Morpho andiensis* required more than that the number of legs and wings should be the same. But, I repeated, I would pay one thousand milreis for a butterfly exactly like the picture. I had plenty of margin for profit and loss, at that. The last time a *Morpho andiensis* was sold, it brought $25,000 at auction. I'd a lot rather have the money, myself.

José Ribiera came back. His expression was tense beyond belief. He plucked at my arm and said, *"Senhor,"* and I grabbed him and dragged him to my inn.

I hauled out his treasure. "Here!" I said angrily. "This is not mine! Take it!"

He paid no attention. He trembled. *"Senhor,"* he said, and swallowed. "My friends—my friends do not think they can catch the butterfly you seek. But if you will tell them—" He wrinkled his brows. *"Senhor,* before a butterfly is born, is it a little soft nut with a worm in it?"

That could pass for a description of a cocoon. José's friends—he was said not to have any—were close observers. I said so. José seemed to grasp at hope as at a straw.

"My—friends will find you the nut which produces the butterfly," he said urgently, "if you tell them which kind it is and what it looks like."

I blinked. Just three specimens of *Morpho andiensis* had ever been captured, so far as was known. All were adult insects. Of course nobody knew what the cocoon was like. For that matter, any naturalist can name a hundred species—and in the Amazon valley alone—of which only the adult forms have been named. But who would hunt for cocoons in jungle like that outside of Milhao?

"My friend," I said skeptically, "there are thousands of different such things. I will buy five of each different kind you can discover, and I will pay one milreis apiece. But only five of each kind, remember!"

I didn't think he'd even try, of course. I meant to insist that he take back his gold nuggets. But again he was gone before I could stop him. I had an uncomfortable impression that when I made my offer, his face lighted as if he'd been given a reprieve from a death sentence. In the light of later events, I think he had.

I angrily made up my mind to take his gold back to him next day. It was a responsibility. Besides, one gets interested in a man—especially of the half-breed class—who can unfeignedly ignore five pounds of gold. I arranged to be paddled up to his clearing next morning.

It was on the river, of course. There are no footpaths in Amazon-basin jungle. The river flowing past Milhao is a broad deep stream perhaps two hundred yards wide. Its width seems less because of the jungle walls on either side. And the jungle is daunting. It is trees and vines and lianas as seen from the stream, but it is more than that. Smells come out, and you can't identify them. Sounds come out, and you can't interpret them. You cut your way into its mass, and you can see nothing. You come out, and you have learned nothing. You cannot affect it. It ignores you. It made me feel insignificant.

My paddlers would have taken me right on past José's clearing without seeing it, if he hadn't been on the river bank. He shouted. He'd been fishing, and now that I think, there were no fish near him, but there were some picked-clean fish skeletons. And I think the ground was very dark about him when we first saw him, and quite normal when we approached. I know he was sweating, but he looked terribly hopeful at the sight of me.

I left my two paddlers to smoke and slumber in the canoe. I followed José into the jungle. It was like walking in a tunnel of lucent green light. Everywhere there were tree trunks and vines and leaves, but green light overlay everything. I saw a purple butterfly with crimson wing tips, floating abstractedly in the jungle as if in an undersea grotto.

Then the path widened, and there was José's dwelling. It was a perfect proof that man does not need civilization to live in comfort. Save for cotton garments, an iron pot and a machete, there was literally nothing in the clearing or the house which was not of and from the jungle, to be replaced merely by stretching out one's hand. To a man who lives like this, gold has no value. While he keeps his wants at this level, he can have no temptations. My thoughts at the moment were almost sentimental.

I beamed politely at José's wife. She was a pretty young girl

with beautifully regular features. But, disturbingly, her eyes were
as panic-filled as José's. She spoke, but she seemed tremblingly
absorbed in the contemplation of some crawling horror. The
two of them seemed to live with terror. It was too odd to be
quite believable. But their child—a brown-skinned three-year-
old quite innocent of clothing—was unaffected. He stared at me,
wide-eyed.

"*Senhor,*" said José in a trembling voice, "here are the
things you desire, the small nuts with worms in them."

His wife had woven a basket of flat green strands. He put
it before me. And I looked into it tolerantly, expecting nothing. But I saw the sort of thing that simply does not happen.
I saw a half bushel of cocoons!

José had acquired them somehow in less than twenty-four
hours. Some were miniature capsules of silk which would
yield little butterflies of wing spread no greater than a mosquito's. Some were sturdy fat cocoons of stout brown silk.
There were cocoons which cunningly mimicked the look of
bird droppings, and cocoons cleverly concealed in twisted
leaves. Some were green—I swear it—and would pass for
buds upon some unnamed vine. And—

It was simply, starkly impossible. I was stupefied. The
Amazon basin has been collected, after a fashion, but the
pupa and cocoon of any reasonably rare species is at least
twenty times more rare than the adult insect. And these
cocoons were fresh! They were alive! I could not believe it,
but I could not doubt it. My hands shook as I turned them
over.

I said, "This is excellent, José! I will pay for all of them
at the rate agreed on—one milreis each. I will send them to
São Pedro today, and their price will be spent for cattle and
the bringing of the cattle here. I promise it!"

José did not relax. I saw him wipe sweat off his face.

"I—beg you to command haste, *Senhor,*" he said thinly.

I almost did not hear. I carried that basket of cocoons
back to the riverbank. I practically crooned over it all the way
back to Milhao. I forgot altogether about returning the gold
pellets. And I began to work frenziedly at the inn.

I made sure, of course, that the men who would cart the
parcel would know that it contained only valueless objects
like cocoons. Then I slipped in the parcel of José's gold. I
wrote a letter to the one man in São Pedro who, if God was

good, might have sense enough to attend to the affair for me. And I was almost idiotically elated.

While I was making out the invoice that would carry my shipment by refrigerated air express from the nearest airport it could be got to, a large ant walked across my paper. One takes insects very casually in back-country Brazil. I mashed him, without noticing what he was. I went blissfully to start the parcel off. I had a shipment that would make history among bug collectors. It was something that simply could not be done!

The fact of the impossibility hit me after the canoe with the parcel started downstream. How the devil those cocoons had been gathered—

The problem loomed larger as I thought. In less than one day, José had collected a half bushel of cocoons, of at least one hundred different species of moths and butterflies. It could not be done! The information to make it possible did not exist! Yet it had happened. How?

The question would not down. I had to find out. I bought a pig for a present and had myself ferried up to the clearing again. My paddlers pulled me upstream with languid strokes. The pig made irritated noises in the bottom of the canoe. Now I am sorry about that pig. I would apologize to its ghost if opportunity offered. But I didn't know.

I landed on the narrow beach and shouted. Presently José came through the tunnel of foliage that led to his house. He thanked me, dry-throated, for the pig. I told him I had ordered cattle sent up from São Pedro. I told him humorously that every ounce of meat on the hoof the town contained would soon be on the way behind a wheezing steam launch. José swallowed and nodded numbly. He still looked like someone who contemplated pure horror.

We got the pig to the house. José's wife sat and rocked her child, her eyes sick with fear. I probably should have felt embarrassed in the presence of such tragedy, even if I could not guess at its cause. But instead, I thought about the questions I wanted to ask. José sat down dully beside me.

I was oblivious of the atmosphere of doom. I said blandly, "Your friends are capable naturalists, José. I am much pleased. Many of the 'little nuts' they gathered are quite new to me. I would like to meet such students of the ways of nature."

José's teeth clicked. His wife caught her breath. She looked at me with an oddly despairing irony. It puzzled me. I looked at José, sharply. And then the hair stood up on my head. My heart tried to stop. Because a large ant walked on José's shoulder, and I saw what kind of ant it was.

"My God!" I said shrilly. "*Soldados!* Army ants!"

I acted through pure instinct. I snatched up the baby from its mother's arms and raced for the river. One does not think at such times. The *soldado* ant, the army ant, the driver ant, is the absolute and undisputed monarch of all jungles everywhere. He travels by millions of millions, and nothing can stand against him. He is ravening ferocity and inexhaustible number. Even man abandons his settlements when the army ant marches in, and returns only after he has left—to find every bit of flesh devoured to the last morsel, from the earwigs in the thatch to a horse that may have been tethered too firmly to break away. The army ant on the march can and does kill anything alive, by tearing the flesh from it in tiny bites, regardless of defense. So—I grabbed the child and ran.

José Ribiera screamed at me, *"No! Senhor! No!"*

He sat still and he screamed. I'd never heard such undiluted horror in any man's voice.

I stopped. I don't know why. I was stunned to see José and his wife sitting frozen where I'd left them. I was more stunned, I think, to see the tiny clearing and the house unchanged. The army ant moves usually on a solid front. The ground is covered with a glistening, shifting horde. The air is filled with tiny clickings of limbs and mandibles. Ants swarm up every tree and shrub. Caterpillars, worms, bird nestlings, snakes, monkeys unable to flee—anything living becomes buried under a mass of ferociously rending small forms which tear off the living flesh in shreds until only white bones are left.

But José sat still, his throat working convulsively. I had seen *soldados* on him. But there were no *soldados*. After a moment José got to his feet and came stumbling toward me. He looked like a dead man. He could not speak.

"But look!" I cried. My voice was high-pitched. "I saw *soldado* ants! I saw them!"

José gulped by pure effort of will. I put down the child. He ran back to his mother.

"*S-sí.* Yes," said José, as if his lips were very stiff and his throat without moisture. "But they are—special *solda-dos*. They are—pets. Yes. They are tame. They are my—friends. They—do tricks, *senhor*. I will show you!"

He held out his hand and made sucking noises with his mouth. What followed is not to be believed. An ant—a large ant, an inch or more long—walked calmly out of his sleeve and onto his outstretched hand. It perched there passively while the hand quivered like an aspen leaf.

"But yes!" said José hysterically. "He does tricks, *senhor*! Observe! He will stand on his head!"

Now, this I saw, but I do not believe it. The ant did something so that it seemed to stand on its head. Then it turned and crawled tranquilly over his hand and wrist and up his sleeve again.

There was silence, or as much silence as the jungle ever holds. My own throat went dry. And what I have said is insanity, but this is much worse. I felt Something waiting to see what I would do. It was, unquestionably, the most horrible sensation I had ever felt. I do not know how to describe it. What I felt was—not a personality, but a mind. I had a ghastly feeling that Something was looking at me from thousands of pairs of eyes, that it was all around me.

I shared, for an instant, what that Something saw and thought. I was surrounded by a mind which waited to see what I would do. It would act upon my action. But it was not a sophisticated mind. It was murderous, but innocent. It was merciless, but naïve.

That is what I felt. The feeling doubtless has a natural explanation which reduces it to nonsense, but at the moment I believed it. I acted on my belief. I am glad I did.

"Ah, I see!" I said in apparent amazement. "That is clever, José! It is remarkable to train an ant! I was absurd to be alarmed. But—your cattle will be on the way, José! They should get here very soon! There will be many of them!"

Then I felt that the mind would let me go. And I went.

My canoe was a quarter mile downstream when one of the paddlers lifted his blade from the water and held it there, listening. The other stopped and listened too. There was a noise in the jungle. It was mercifully far away, but it sounded like a pig. I have heard the squealing of pigs at slaughtering time, when instinct tells them of the deadly intent of men and they try punily to fight. This was not that sort of noise. It was worse; much worse.

I made a hopeless spectacle of myself in the canoe. Now, of course, I can see that, from this time on, my actions were not those of a reasoning human being. I did not think with proper scientific skepticism. It suddenly seemed to me that Norton's theory of mass consciousness among social insects was very plausible. Bees, says Norton, are not only units in an organization. They are units of an organism. The hive or the swarm is a creature—one creature—says Norton. Each insect is a body cell only, just as the corpuscles in our blood stream are individuals and yet only parts of us. We can destroy a part of our body if the welfare of the whole organism requires it, though we destroy many cells. The swarm or the hive can sacrifice its members for the hive's defense. Each bee is a mobile body cell. Its consciousness is a part of the whole intelligence, which is that of the group. The group is the actual creature. And ants, says Norton, show the fact more clearly still; the ability of the creature which is an ant colony to sacrifice a part of itself for the whole. . . . He gives illustrations of what he means. His book is not accepted by naturalists generally, but there in the canoe, going down-river from José's clearing, I believed it utterly.

I believed that an army-ant army was as much a single creature as a sponge. I believed that the Something in José's jungle clearing—its body cells were *soldado* ants—had discovered that other creatures perceived and thought as it did. Nothing more was needed to explain everything. An army-ant creature, without physical linkages, could know what its own members saw and knew and felt. It should need only to open its mind to perceive what other creatures saw and knew and felt.

The frightening thing was that when it could interpret such unantish sensations, it could find its prey with a terrible infallibility. It could flow through the jungle in a streaming, crawling tide of billions of tiny stridulating bodies. It could know the whereabouts and thoughts of every living thing around it. Nothing could avoid it, as nothing could withstand it. And if it came upon a man, it could know his thoughts too. It could perceive in his mind vast horizons beyond its former ken. It could know of food—

animal food—in quantities never before imagined. It could, intelligently, try to arrange to secure that food.

It had.

But if so much was true, there was something else it could do. The thought made the blood seem to cake in my veins. I began frantically to thrust away the idea. The Something in José's clearing hadn't discovered it yet. But pure terror of the discovery had me drenched in sweat when I got back to Milhao.

All this, of course, was plainly delusion. It was at least a most unscientific attitude. But I'd stopped being scientific. I even stopped using good sense. Believing what I did, I should have got away from there as if all hell were after me. But the Something in José's clearing may already have been practicing its next logical step without knowing it. Maybe that's why I stayed.

Because I did stay in Milhao. I didn't leave the town again, even for José's clearing. I stayed about the inn, half-heartedly dealing with gentry who tried every known device, except seeking the *Morpho andiensis,* to extract a thousand milreis from me. Mostly they offered mangled corpses which would have been useless for my purpose even if they'd been the butterfly I was after. No argument would change their idea that I was insane, nor dash their happy hope of making money out of my hallucination that butterflies were worth money. But I was only halfhearted in these dealings, at best. I waited feverishly for the cattle from São Pedro. I was obsessed.

I couldn't sleep. By day I fought the thought that tried to come into my head. At night I lay in the abominable inn—in a hammock, because there are no beds in back-country Brazilian inns, and a man would be a fool to sleep in them if there were—and listened to the small, muted, unidentifiable noises from the jungle. *And* fought away the thought that kept trying to come into my mind. It was very bad.

I don't remember much about the time I spent waiting. It was purest nightmare. But several centuries after the shipment of the cocoons, the launch from São Pedro came puffing asthmatically up the reaches of the river. I was twitching all over, by that time, from the strain of not thinking about what the Something might discover next.

I didn't let the launch tie up to shore. I went out to meet it in a canoe, and I carried my collection kit with me, and an automatic pistol and an extra box of cartridges. I had a machete too. It was not normal commercial equipment for consummating a business deal, but I feverishly kept my mind on what I was going to do. The Something in José's clearing wouldn't be made suspicious by that. It was blessedly naïve.

The launch puffed loudly and wheezed horribly, going past Milhao between tall banks of jungle. It towed a flatboat on which were twenty head of cattle—poor, dispirited, tick-infested creatures. I had them tethered fast. My teeth chattered as I stepped on the flatboat. If the Something realized what it could do—But my hands obeyed me. I shot a dull-eyed cow through the head. I assassinated an emaciated steer. I systematically murdered every one. I was probably wild-eyed and certainly fever-thin and positively lunatic in the eyes of the Brazilian launch crew. But to them *os Senhores Norteamericanos* are notoriously mad.

I was especially close to justifying their belief because of the thought that kept trying to invade my mind. It was, baldly, that if without physical linkage the Something knew what its separate body cells saw, then without physical linkage it also controlled what they did. And if it could know what deer and monkeys saw and knew, then by the same process it could control what *they* did. It held within itself, in its terrifying innocence, the power to cause animals to march docilely and blindly to it and into the tiny maws of its millions of millions of parts. As soon as it realized the perfectly inescapable fact, it could increase in number almost without limit by this fact alone. More, in the increase its intelligence should increase too. It should grow stronger, and be able to draw its prey from greater distances. The time should come when it could incorporate men into its organism by a mere act of will. They would report to it and be controlled by it. And of course they would march to it and drive their livestock to it so it could increase still more and grow wiser and more powerful still.

I grew hysterical, on the flatboat. The thought I'd fought so long wouldn't stay out of my mind any longer. I slashed the slain animals with the machete until the flatboat was more gruesome than any knacker's yard. I sprinkled everywhere a fine white powder from my collection kit—which did not stay white where it fell, but turned red—and pictured the Amazon basin taken over and filled with endlessly marching armies of *soldado* ants. I saw the cities emptied of humanity, and the jungle of all other life. And then, making whimpering noises to myself, I pictured all the people of all the world loading their ships with their cattle and then themselves—because that was what the Something would desire—and all the ships coming to bring food to the organism for which all earth would labor and die.

José Ribiera screamed from the edge of the jungle. The launch and the flatboat were about to pass his clearing. The reek of spilled blood had surrounded the flatboat with a haze of metallic-bodied insects. And José, so weakened by long terror and despair that he barely tottered, screamed at me from the shore line, and his wife added her voice pipingly to echo his cry.

Then I knew that the Something was impatient and eager and utterly satisfied, and I shouted commands to the launch, and I got into the canoe and paddled ashore. I let the bow of the canoe touch the sand. I think that, actually, everything was lost at that moment, and that the Something knew what I could no longer keep from thinking. It knew its power as I did. But there were thousands of flying things about the flatboat load of murdered cattle, and they smelled spilt blood, and the Something in the jungle picked their brains of pure ecstasy. Therefore, I think, it paid little heed to José or his wife or me. It was too eager. And it was naïve.

"José," I said with deep cunning, "get into the canoe with your wife and baby. We will watch our friends at their banquet."

There were bellowings from the launch. I had commanded that the flatboat be beached. The Brazilians obeyed, but they were upset. I looked like a thing of horror from the butchering I had done. I put José and his family on the launch, and I tried to thrust out my mind to the Something in the jungle. I imagined a jungle tree undermined—a little tree, I specified—to fall in the river.

The men of the launch had the flatboat grounded when a slender tree trunk quivered. It toppled slowly outward, delayed in its fall by lianas that had to break. But it fell on the flatboat and the carcasses of slaughtered cattle. The rest was automatic. Army ants swarmed out the thin tree trunk. The gory deck of the flatboat turned black with them. Cries of *"Soldados!"* arose in the launch. The towline was abandoned instantly.

I think José caused me to be hauled up into the launch,

but I was responsible for all the rest. We paused at Milhao, going downstream, exactly long enough to tell that there were *soldados* in the jungle three miles upstream. I got my stuff from the inn. I paid. I hysterically brushed aside the final effort of a whiskery half-breed to sell me an unrecognizable paste of legs and wings as a *Morpho andiensis*. Then I fled.

After the first day or so I slept most of the time, twitching. At São Pedro I feverishly got fast passage on a steamer going downstream. I wanted to get out of Brazil, and nothing else; but I did take José and his family on board.

I didn't talk to him, though. I didn't want to. I don't even know where he elected to go ashore from the steamer, or where he is now. I didn't draw a single deep breath until I had boarded a plane at Belem and it was airborne and I was on the way home.

Which was unreasonable. I had ended all the danger from the Something in José's clearing. When I slaughtered the cattle and made that shambles on the flatboat's deck, I spread the contents of a three-pound, formerly airtight can of sodium arsenate over everything. It is wonderful stuff. No mite, fungus, mold or beetle will attack specimens preserved by it. I'd hoped to use a fraction of a milligram to preserve a *Morpho andiensis*. I didn't. I poisoned the carcasses of twenty cattle with it. The army ants which were the Something would consume those cattle to bare white bones. Not all would die of the sodium arsenate, though. Not at first.

But the Something was naïve. And always, among the army ants as among all other members of the ant family, dead and wounded members of the organism are consumed by the sound and living. It is like the way white corpuscles remove damaged red cells from our human blood stream. So the corpses of army ants—*soldados*—that died of sodium arsenate would be consumed by those that survived, and they would die, and their corpses in turn would be consumed by others that would die. . . .

Three pounds of sodium arsenate will kill a lot of ants anyhow, but in practice not one grain of it would go to waste. Because no *soldado* corpse would be left for birds or beetles to feed on, so long as a single body cell of the naïve Something remained alive.

And that is that. There are times when I think the whole thing was a fever dream, because it is plainly unbelievable. If it is true—why, I saved a good part of South American civilization. Maybe I saved the human race, for that matter. Somehow, though, that doesn't seem likely. But I certainly did ship a half bushel of cocoons from Milhao, and I certainly did make some money out of the deal.

I didn't get a *Morpho andiensis* in Milhao, of course. But I made out. When those cocoons began to hatch, in Chicago, there were actually four beautiful *andiensis* in the crop. I anesthetized them with loving care. They were mounted under absolutely perfect conditions. But there's an ironic side light on that. When there were only three known specimens in the collections of the whole world, the last *andiensis* sold for $25,000. But with four new ones perfect and available, the price broke, and I got only $6800 apiece! I'd have got as much for one!

Which is the whole business. But if I were sensible I wouldn't tell about it this way. I'd say that somebody else told me this story, and then I'd cast doubts on his veracity.

ON A HOT SUMMER NIGHT IN A PLACE FAR AWAY

by Pat Murphy

Here's a compelling story that demonstrates that most people are not what they seem—and that some *of them are even more* not *so than others. . . .*

Pat Murphy lives in San Francisco, where she works for a science museum, the Exploratorium. Her elegant and incisive stories appeared throughout the decade of the 1980s in Isaac Asimov's Science Fiction Magazine, Elsewhere, Amazing, Universe, Shadows, Chrysalis, Interzone, *and other places. One of them, the classic "Rachel in Love," one of the most popular stories of the decade, won a Nebula Award in 1988. Murphy's first novel,* The Shadow Hunter, *appeared in 1982, to no particular notice, but her second novel,* The Falling Woman, *won her a second Nebula Award in 1988, and was one of the most critically-acclaimed novels of the late 80s. Murphy also won a World Fantasy Award in 1992 for her story "Bones." Her third novel was the well-received* The City, Not Long After. *Her most recent book is a collection of her short fiction,* Points of Departure, *and she is at work on another novel.*

Gregorio is a hammock vendor in the ancient Mayan city of T'hoo, known to the Mexicans as Merida. He is a good salesman—*El mejor,* the best salesman of hammocks. He works in Parque Hidalgo and the Zocalo, T'hoo's main square, hailing tourists as they pass, calling in English, "Hey, you want to buy a hammock?"

Gregorio is short—only about five feet tall—but he is strong. His hands are strong and the nails are rimmed with purple from the plant dyes that he uses to tint the hammocks. Two of his front teeth are rimmed with gold. He is, most of the time, a good man. He was married once, and he has two little daughters who live far away in the village of Pixoy, near the city of Valladolid, on the other side of the Yucatan peninsula. Gregorio's wife threw him out because he drank too much and slept with other women. When she married another man, Gregorio left his village and traveled to Merida. He sold hammocks and lived in the nearby village of Tixkokob. Once, he went back to his village to visit his daughters, but they looked at him as if he were a stranger and they called the other man Papa. He did not go back to visit again.

Gregorio was sad when his wife threw him out, and he misses his village and his daughters, but he knows that drinking and sleeping with women does not make him a bad man. He has stopped drinking so much, but he has not stopped sleeping with women. He believes in moderation in virtue as well as vice.

Gregorio met the very thin woman in the sidewalk café beside the Parque Hidalgo. She was watching him bargain with an American couple: The bearded man in the Hawaiian shirt had been determined to get a good deal, and the bargaining took about an hour. Gregorio won, though the tourist never knew it; the final price was slightly higher than Gregorio's lowest, though lower than he would usually drop for a tourist. The gringo was pleased and Gregorio was pleased.

Gregorio noticed the woman when he was tying up his bundle of hammocks. She was a thin woman with pale blond hair cropped close to her head and small breasts and long thin legs that she had stretched underneath the table. She held a notebook on her lap and a pen in one hand. She wore white pants and a white shirt and dark glasses that hid her eyes.

"Hey, you want to buy a hammock?"

She shook her head slightly. "No, *gracias.*"

"*¿Porqué no?* Why not? You ever try sleeping in a hammock?"

"No." She was watching him, but he did not know what was going on behind the dark glasses. There was something strange about her face. The eyebrows, the cheekbones, the mouth—all looked fine. But there was something strange about the way that they were put together.

Gregorio set down his bundle of hammocks and looked around. It was late in the morning on a sunny Sunday. Chances were that most tourists were out visiting Uxmal or some other ancient site. He pulled out a chair. "Okay if I rest here a while?"

She shrugged again, setting her notebook on the table. Her fingers, like her legs, were long and thin. Gregorio noticed that she wore no rings. And even though there was something strange about her face, she was a good-looking woman.

He whistled for the waiter and ordered *café con leche*, coffee with milk. When it came, he poured six teaspoons of sugar into the cup and sat back in the chair. "Where are you from?"

"Here and there," she said. And then, when he kept looking at her, "California, most recently. Los Angeles."

She did not act like a Californian—Californians talked too much and were very friendly—but he let that pass. "You on vacation?" he asked.

"More or less," she said. "Always a tourist."

They talked about the weather for a time, about Merida, about the surrounding ruins. Gregorio could not put this woman in a category. She did not seem like a tourist. She was not relaxed. Her long fingers were always busy—twisting the paper napkin into meaningless shapes, tapping on the table, tracing the lines of the checks on the tablecloth.

He asked her if she had been to visit Uxmal and Chichen Itza.

"Not this trip," she said. "I visited them before. A long time ago."

The church bell at the nearby church rang to call the people to noon mass; the pajaritos screamed in the trees. The woman sipped her café and stared moodily into the distance. She made him think of the tall storks that stand in the marshes near Progresso, waiting. He liked her; he liked her long legs and the small breasts that he knew must be hidden by her baggy shirt. He liked her silences and moodiness. Quiet women could be very passionate.

"You would sleep well in one of my hammocks," he said.

She smiled, an expression as fleeting as a hummingbird. "I doubt that."

"You will never know until you try it," he said. "Why don't you buy a hammock?"

"How much are your hammocks?"

Gregorio grinned. He quoted her his asking price, double

the price he would accept. She bargained well. She seemed to know exactly when he was serious in his claim that he could accept no lower price, and she seemed, in a quiet way, to enjoy working him down to the lowest price he would accept. The hammock she bought was dyed a deep purple that shimmered in the sun.

Gregorio finished his coffee, hoisted his bundle of hammocks, and returned to work, hailing two blond gringos in university T-shirts. He lured them into a bargaining session before they realized what was what.

Tourists stroll through the Zocalo, stare up at the cathedral built from the ancient stones of Mayan temples, admire the colonial architecture of the buildings in the city. Many regard the hammock vendors as pests, like the pigeons that coo and make messes on the lintel above the cathedral door. Many tourists are fools.

The hammock vendors know what happens in T'hoo. They are a select company: only thirty men sell hammocks on T'hoo's streets, though often it seems like much more. Each man carries a bundle of hammocks, neatly bound with a cord. Each man carries one hammock loose, using it as a cushion for the cord looped over his shoulder. When he hails a tourist, he stretches the loose hammock open wide so that the tropical sun catches in the bright threads and dazzles the eyes.

Hammock vendors live at a different tempo than the tourists. They sit in the shade and talk, knowing that the luck will come when the luck comes. They can't rush the luck. Sometimes, tourists buy. Sometimes, they do not. A hammock vendor can only wander in the Zocalo and wait for the luck to come.

While they are waiting, the hammock vendors watch people and talk. The French tourists who are staying at the Hotel Caribe will never buy a hammock; they bargain but never buy. There are pretty women among the Texans who have come to study Spanish at the University of the Yucatan, but all of them have boyfriends. The tall thin woman with pale hair is always awake very early and goes to her hotel very late.

"There she is," said Ricardo, looking up from the hammocks he was tying into a bundle. "She was in Restaurant Express last night until it closed. Drinking *aguardiente*."

Gregorio glanced up to see the thin woman sitting at the same table as the day before. She had a lost look about her, as if she waited for a friend who had not come.

"She was here at seven this morning," observed Pich, a gray-haired, slow-moving hammock vendor. "She needs a man."

Ricardo looked sour and Gregorio guessed that he had suggested that to the thin woman the night before without success. The hammock vendors discussed the woman's probable needs for a time, then continued an earlier discussion of the boxing match to be held that evening. The woman was of passing interest only.

Still, when Gregorio wandered on to search for customers, he passed her table and said hello. Her notebook was on the table before her, but he could not read the writing. Not Spanish, but it did not look much like English either. Though the morning sun was not very bright, she wore the dark glasses, hiding her eyes behind them. *"Buenos días,"* she said to him. *"¿Qué tal?"*

"Good," he said. He sat down at her table. "What are you writing?" He peered at the notebook on the table.

"Poetry," she said. "Bad poetry."

"What about?"

She glanced at the notebook. "Do you know the fairy tale about the princess who slept for a thousand years? I've written one about a woman who did not sleep for a thousand years."

"Why do you look so sad today? You are on vacation and the sun is shining."

She shrugged, the slightest movement of her shoulders. "I am tired of being on vacation," she said. "But I can't go home. I am waiting for my friends. They're going to meet me here."

"I understand." He knew what it was like to be homesick. She looked at him long and hard and he wondered about the color of her eyes behind her dark glasses. "Did you sleep in my hammock?" he asked her at last.

"I strung it in my hotel room."

"But you did not sleep in it?"

She shook her head. "No."

"Why not?"

She shrugged lightly. "I don't sleep."

"Not at all?"

"Not at all."

"Why not?"

"I slept at home," she said. "I can't sleep here."

"Bad dreams? I know a *curandera* who can help you with that. She'll mix you a powder that will keep bad dreams away."

She shook her head, a tiny denial that seemed almost a habit.

"Why not then? Why can't you sleep?"

She shrugged and repeated the head shake. "I don't know."

He stared at her face, wishing that she would remove her glasses. "What color are your eyes?" he asked.

She moved her sunglasses down on her nose and peered at him over the frames with eyes as violet as the sky at dusk. Her eyes were underlined with darkness. A little lost, a little scary. She replaced her sunglasses after only a moment.

"You don't sleep really?" Gregorio asked.

"Really."

"You need a man."

"I doubt that." Her tone was cool, distant, curious. It did not match the lost look in the violet eyes he had seen a moment before. She gestured at two American women taking a table at the other end of the café. "Those two look like they need a hammock," she said.

Gregorio went to sell them a hammock.

Gregorio did not mention to the other hammock vendors that the thin woman did not sleep. Odd that he should forget to mention it—it was an interesting fact about a strange woman. Nevertheless, he forgot until he met her again, very late at night. He was wandering through the Zocalo, cursing his bad luck. He had missed the last bus to his village, Tixkokob, because he had taken a pretty young woman to the movies. But the young woman had declined to share her bed with him and he had no way home. He was in the Zocalo looking for a friend who might have a spot to hang a hammock.

He noticed the thin woman sitting alone on a bench, watching the stars. "What are you doing out here so late?" he asked.

She shrugged. "The cafés are closed. What are you doing here? All your customers have gone home."

He explained and she nodded thoughtfully and offered

him a drink from the bottle of *aguardiente* that sat beside her on the bench. *Aguardiente* was a potent brandy and the bottle was half-empty. He sat beside her on the bench and drank deeply. With his foot, he nudged the paper bag that rested on the ground by her feet and it clinked: more bottles.

"I like this drink," she said slowly, her head tilted back to look at the stars. "It makes me feel warm. I am always cold here. I think, sometimes, if I found a place that was warm enough, then I would sleep."

The guitarists who serenaded tourists were putting away their instruments, grumbling a little at the evening's take. The Zocalo was almost deserted. Gregorio shifted uneasily on the bench. "I should go to Parque Hidalgo and see if Pich is still there. He would let me stay at his house."

"Keep me company a while," she said. "You can stay in my room." She glanced at him. "And don't bother looking at me like that. I plan to sit up by the hotel pool tonight. It's a good night to watch the stars." She leaned back to look at the night sky. "Tell me—have you always lived in Tixkokob?"

"I come from Pixoy. But it is better that I am not there now."

"Better for you?" Her eyes were on the sky, but he felt vaguely uncomfortable, as if she were watching him closely.

"Better for everyone," he said.

"I understand," she said. She drank from the bottle and gave it back to him. They watched the moon rise.

Her room was on the bottom floor of the Hotel Reforma. It was a small dark room, very stuffy and hot. His hammock was strung from rings set in the walls. A stack of notebooks rested on the small table beside the bed. On the dresser, there was a strange small machine that looked a little like a cassette player, a little like a radio. "What's this?" he asked, picking it up.

She took it from his hand and set it gently back on the table. The *aguardiente* made her sway just a little, like a tall tree in the wind. "My lifeline. My anchor. And maybe an albatross around my neck."

Gregorio shook his head, puzzled by her answer, but unwilling to pursue it. The brandy was warm in his blood, and he was very close to deciding that the thin woman had invited him here because she wanted a man. He came close to her and wrapped his arms around her, leaning his head against her chest. He could feel her small breasts and that excited him.

She pushed him away with surprising strength and he fell back against the bed. She picked up her notebook and the strange small machine, tucked the bottle of *aquardiente* under her arm, and stepped toward the door. "Sleep," she said.

He slept badly. The tendrils of someone else's thoughts invaded his dreams. He wandered through a warm humid place where the light was the deep purple color of his hammock. The place was crowded with men and women as tall and thin as the thin woman. He asked them where he was, and they looked at him curiously with dark violet eyes. He wanted to go home, but when he asked if they could tell him the way, they said nothing. He was tired, very tired, but he could not rest in that place. The air was too thick and hot.

He woke, sweating, in the thin woman's room, and went to the patio to find her. The first light of dawn was touching the eastern sky, but stars were still visible overhead. She sat in a lounge chair beside the pool, speaking softly into the machine. He could not understand the words. Two empty *aquardiente* bottles were at her feet and another was on the table at her side. He sat in a chair beside her.

Fireflies were dancing over the pool. She gestured at the bottle that rested on the table and Gregorio saw that a firefly had blundered inside the bottle and seemed unable to find its way out. It crawled on the inside of the glass, its feeble light flickering. "I can't get her out," the woman said in a harsh voice blurred with brandy and filled with uncertainty. "And she can't find her way. She just keeps flashing her light, but no one answers. No one at all."

Without speaking, Gregorio took the bottle to the ornamental flower bed by the side of the pool. He took a brick from the border, lay the bottle on the cement, and tapped it lightly with the brick—once, twice, three times. A starburst of fine cracks spread from each place he struck the bottle, and when he pulled on the neck, the cracks separated and the bottle broke. The insect rose, sluggishly at first, then faster, dancing toward the other lights.

She smiled, and he could tell that the brandy had affected her. The smile was slow and full, like a flower unfolding.

"She returns to her place," the woman said, blinking at the dancing lights. "Sometimes I think that I have returned home and maybe I am asleep and dreaming of this place. Sometimes I try to think that. I go for days believing that I am asleep. Then I come to my senses and I know this is real." She reached for the last bottle, but it was empty.

"Where do you come from?" Gregorio asked.

She lifted one thin arm and pointed up at a bright spot of light high in the sky. "That one."

Gregorio looked at her and frowned. "Why are you here?"

She shrugged. "Merida is as good a place to wait as any. It's warm here, warmer than most places. My friends are supposed to come get me. They're late."

"How late?"

She looked down at her thin hands, now locked together in her lap. "Very late. Just over one hundred years now." Her hands twisted, one around the other. "Or maybe they never intended to come back. That's what bothers me. I send out reports regularly, and maybe that was all they wanted. Maybe they will leave me here forever."

"Forever?"

"Or for as long as I live." She glanced at him. In the light of the rising sun, he could see her strange violet eyes— wide and mournful. "I don't belong here. I don't . . ." She stopped and put her head in her hands. "Why are they so late? I want to go home." He did not understand what she said next—the language was not English and not Spanish. She was crying and he did not know what to say or do. She looked up at him with a face like an open wound. Her violet eyes were wet and the circles beneath them stood out like bruises. "I want to go home," she said again. "I don't belong here."

"Who are you?"

She closed her eyes for a moment and seemed to gather strength to her. "The explorers brought us here," she said. "The ones in the spacecraft. They left us to gather information about your people." She looked down for a moment and he thought she would stop talking, but she looked up again. "We travel with the explorers but we are a different people. When we meet with new ways, we adapt. We learn. We take on a little bit of the other, retaining a little bit of ourselves. We blend the two." She spread her hands on her knees. "We are diplomats, translators, go-betweens for merchants. We live on the border, neither fish nor fowl, not one thing and not the other." Her hands closed into fists. "There were three of us, but Mayra died two years ago. Seena, last year. We grew tired, so tired. They left us here too long. I have lost myself. I don't know who I am.

"I should not speak, but it has been so long." She shook her head and rubbed her eyes with her slender fingers. "You will forget this. I will make you forget." She leaned back in her chair and stared at the sky. The stars were gone now, washed out by the light of the rising sun. "I send them poetry instead of reports, but still they do not come for me. Maybe they don't care. Maybe none of this matters." Her voice had a high, ragged note of hysteria. "It did not bother me at first," she said. "Not while the others were alive. Only recently. It bothers me now. I would like to curl up and sleep for days. For weeks."

Gregorio took her long thin hand in his, squeezing it gently for comfort. This woman, she needed help. And he wanted her. She was aloof and foreign and he wanted to hold her. He wanted her because of her long thin legs, like a heron's legs, her long thin hands, like the cool hands of the Madonna.

He said nothing, but he was thinking of the place that the dream had brought to his mind, the dark, warm, limestone cavern just outside the nearby village of Homun. He had been thinking about seeing the thin woman naked, swimming in the waters of the cavern, alone with him.

She looked at his face and suddenly laughed, a small chuckle that seemed drawn from her against her will. "Sometimes, I can find my way out of my own self-pity, and I see you, son of the strange men who built those cities, goggling at me for . . . what? What do you want?" She stared at him, her violet eyes filled with amusement, then suddenly widening as if she were trying to see something in dim light. "Wait . . . where is this . . . this place . . . where?"

Her thin fingers were playing over his face as if searching for something. She reached out and ran a cool finger along the back of one hand. She had moved closer to him, her eyes wide and eager.

The quiet ones, he thought to himself. They are always the most passionate. And he imagined her clearly again, a long pale naked woman stepping into the warm water and smiling at him in invitation.

But she pulled back then, leaning back in her chair and slipping the dark glasses over her violet eyes, hiding behind the tinted lenses.

Later that day, Gregorio could not remember all that had happened out by the pool. He remembered the woman's hand in his; he remembered telling the woman that he would take her to the caves of Homun, to a very private cave he knew. But there was a curiously incomplete blurred feel to his memory.

Gregorio liked the woman, but he did not like the vague feeling that he was being tricked and he acted to prevent such a thing from happening again. In his right pocket, for clarity of mind, he carried a clear polished stone that had been thrice blessed with holy water. In his left, for good luck, he carried a jade bead that had been carved on one side with the face of Kin Ahau, the sun god who watches by day, and on the other side with the face of Akbal, the jaguar-headed god who watches by night. With these talismans he was confident. His mind would not be clouded.

The bus to Homun was hot and crowded. It dropped them on the edge of the village and Gregorio led the woman through the monte, the scrubby brush that covers much of the Yucatan, to the entrance to the cavern.

The Yucatan peninsula is riddled with limestone caverns that lead to deep dark places beneath the earth. Here and there, the caves dip beneath the water table, forming subterranean pools. Gregorio knew of such a cave, a secluded subterranean pool that was a fine place to bring cute American tourists for seduction.

A tunnel led deep into the underworld to a pool of clear water in a limestone cave. Shells—all that remained of ancient clams and oysters—were embedded in the rock. Another tunnel, extending back from the first pool, led to an even more secluded pool.

Gregorio took the woman to the most remote pool. Stalactites hung low over the pool. The air was close and humid, very hot and moist. He carried a small flashlight and shone it on the limestone to show her the way. She was smiling now, following close behind him.

Gregorio strung his hammock on the two hooks that he

had set in the limestone walls long ago. As soon as he had it strung, the woman sat on the edge of the hammock and then lay back with a soft sigh.

"We can swim," Gregorio said. He was quietly stripping off his clothing.

No reply from the woman in the hammock.

He went, naked, to the hammock. She was curled on her side, one hand tucked under her cheek, the other resting on her breast like a bird who has found her nest. Her eyes were closed and she breathed softly, gently, rhythmically. He touched her cheek, warm at last, brushing a stray tendril of hair back into place, and kissed her lightly. When he touched her, he felt a bright warm sensation, like the spreading warmth of brandy but quicker, cleaner, more pure. He saw in the darkness the tall thin people, holding out their long arms in welcome. He felt content and loved and very much at home.

He did not wake her. He swam alone in the warm water, dressed, and left her there, sleeping peacefully.

In a limestone cavern at Homun, a woman sleeps like a princess in a fairy tale. Gregorio knows she is there, but few others know the way to the hidden cave and if anyone does chance to find her, Gregorio knows that the person's mind will be clouded and he will forget. Gregorio visits her sometimes, touches her lightly on the cheek and feels the warm glow of homecoming. And he watches for the day when a tall thin man who does not sleep comes to town and sits in the cafés, sitting up late as if waiting for a friend. This one, Gregorio will take to the cavern to wake the woman who sleeps so soundly, wake her with a kiss and take her home.

MANATEE GAL AIN'T YOU COMING OUT TONIGHT?

by Avram Davidson

One of the most eloquent and individual voices in modern SF and fantasy, Avram Davidson is also one of the finest short story writers of our times. He won the Hugo Award for his famous story "Or All the Seas with Oysters," and his short work has been assembled in landmark collections such as Strange Seas and Shores, The Best of Avram Davidson, Or All The Seas With Oysters, The Redward Edward Papers, *and* Collected Fantasies. *His novels include* The Phoenix and the Mirror, Masters of the Maze, Rork!, Rogue Dragon, *and* Vergil in Averno. *He has also won the Edgar and the World Fantasy Award. His most recent book is one of the best collections of the decade, the marvelous* The Adventures of Doctor Eszterhazy.

In recent years, Davidson has been producing a series of stories (as yet uncollected, alas) detailing the strange adventures of Jack Limekiller. The Limekiller stories are set against the lushly evocative background of "British Hidalgo," Davidson's vividly realized, richly imagined version of one of those tiny, eccentric Central American nations that exist in near-total isolation on the edge of the busy twentieth-century world . . . a place somehow at once flamboyant and languorous, where strange things can—and do—happen. . . .

As the brilliant story that follows will amply demonstrate!

The Cupid Club was the only waterhole on the Port Cockatoo waterfront. To be sure, there were two or three liquor booths back in the part where the tiny town ebbed away into the bush. But they were closed for siesta, certainly. And they sold nothing but watered rum and warm soft-drinks and loose cigarettes. Also, they were away from the breezes off

the Bay which kept away the flies. In British Hidalgo gnats
were flies, mosquitoes were flies, sand-flies—worst of all—
were flies—*flies* were also flies: and if anyone were inclined
to question this nomenclature, there was the unquestionable
fact that mosquito itself was merely Spanish for little fly.

It was not really cool in the Cupid Club (Alfonso Key,
prop., LICENSED TO SELL WINE, SPIRITS, BEER,
ALE, CYDER AND PERRY). But it was certainly less hot
than outside. Outside the sun burned the Bay, turning it into
molten sparkles. Limekiller's boat stood at mooring, by very
slightly raising his head he could see her, and every so often
he did raise it. There wasn't much aboard to tempt thieves,
and there weren't many thieves in Port Cockatoo, anyway.
On the other hand, what was aboard the *Sacarissa* he could
not very well spare; and it only took one thief, after all. So
every now and then he did raise his head and make sure
that no small boat was put by his own. No skiff or dory.

Probably the only thief in town was taking his own siesta.

"Nutmeg P'int," said Alfonso Key. "You been to Nutmeg P'int?"

"Been there."

Every place needs another place to make light fun of. In
King Town, the old colonial capital, it was Port Cockatoo.
Limekiller wondered what it was they made fun of, down
at Nutmeg Point.

"What brings it into your mind, Alfonso?" he asked,
taking his eyes from the boat. All clear. Briefly he met his
own face in the mirror. Wasn't much of a face, in his own
opinion. Someone had once called him "Young Count Tol-
stoy." Wasn't much point in shaving, anyway.

Key shrugged. "Sometimes somebody goes down there, goes
up the river, along the old bush trails, buys carn. About now,
you know, mon, carn bring good price, up in King Town."

Limekiller knew that. He often did think about that. He could
quote the prices Brad Welcome paid for corn: white corn, yellow
corn, cracked and ground. "I know," he said. "In King Town
they have a lot of money and only a little corn. Along Nutmeg
River they have a lot of corn and only a little money. Someone
who brings down money from the Town can buy corn along the
Nutmeg. Too bad I didn't think of that before I left."

Key allowed himself a small sigh. He knew that it wasn't
any lack of thought, and that Limekiller had had no money
before he left, or, likely, he wouldn't have left. "May-be

they trust you down along the Nutmeg. They trust old Bob
Blaine. Year after year he go up the Nutmeg, he go up and
down the bush trail, he buy carn on credit, bring it bock up
to King *Town*.''

Off in the shadow at the other end of the barroom someone began to sing, softly.

> *W'ol' Bob Blaine, he done gone.*
> *W'ol' Bob Blaine, he done gone.*
> *Ahl, ahl me money gone—*
> *Gone to Spahnish Hidalgo . . .*

In King Town, Old Bob Blaine had sold corn, season after
season. Old Bob Blaine had bought salt, he had bought shotgun shells, canned milk, white flour, cotton cloth from the
Turkish merchants. Fish hooks, sweet candy, rubber boots,
kerosene, lamp *chim*ney. Old Bob Blaine had returned and
paid for corn in kind—not, to be sure, immediately after
selling the corn. Things did not move that swiftly even today, in British Hidalgo, and certainly had not Back When.
Old Bob Blaine returned with the merchandise on his next
buying trip. It was more convenient, he did not have to
make so many trips up and down the mangrove coast. By
and by it must almost have seemed that he was paying in
advance, when he came, buying corn down along the Nutmeg River, the boundary between the Colony of British Hidalgo and the country which the Colony still called Spanish
Hidalgo, though it had not been Spain's for a century and a
half.

"Yes, mon," Alfonso Key agreed. "Only, that one last
time, he *not* come bock. They say he buy one marine engine
yard, down in Republican waters."

"I heard," Limekiller said, "that he bought a garage
down there."

The soft voice from the back of the bar said, "No, mon.
Twas a coconut walk he bought. Yes, mon."

Jack wondered why people, foreign people, usually,
sometimes complained that it was difficult to get information in British Hidalgo. In his experience, information was
the easiest thing in the world, there—all the information you
wanted. In fact, sometimes you could get more than you
wanted. Sometimes, of course, it was contradictory. Some-

times it was outright wrong. But that, of course, was another matter.

"Anybody else ever take up the trade down there?" Even
if the information, the answer, if there was an answer, even
if it were negative, what difference would it make?

"No," said Key. "No-body. May-be you try, eh, Jock?
May-be they trust you."

There was no reason why the small cultivators, slashing
their small cornfields by main force out of the almighty bush
and then burning the slash and then planting corn in the
ashes, so to speak—maybe they would trust him, even though
there was no reason *why* they should trust him. Still . . . Who
knows . . . They might. They just might. Well . . . some of
them just might. For a moment a brief hope rose in his mind.

"Naaa . . . I haven't even got any crocus sacks." There
wasn't much point in any of it after all. Not if he'd have to
tote the corn wrapped up in his shirt. The jute sacks were
fifty cents apiece in local currency; they were as good as
money, sometimes even better than money.

Key, who had been watching rather unsleepingly as these
thoughts were passing through Jack's mind, slowly sank
back in his chair. "Ah," he said, very softly. "You haven't
got any crocus sack."

"Een de 'ol' days," the voice from the back said, "every
good 'oman, she di know which bush yerb good fah wyes,
fah kid-ney, which bush yerb good fah heart, which bush
yerb good fah fever. But ahl of dem good w'ol' 'omen, new,
dey dead, you see. Yes mon. Ahl poss ahway. No-body know
bush medicine nowadays. Only *bush-doc-tor*. And dey very
few, sah, very few."

"What you say, Captain Cudgel, you not bush *doc*-tor
you w'own self? Nah true, Coptain?"

Slowly, almost reluctantly, the old man answered. "Well
sah. Me know few teeng. Fah true. Me know few teeng.
Not like in w'ol' days. In w'ol' days, me dive fah conch.
Yes, mon. Fetch up plan-ty conch. De sahlt wah-tah hort
me eyes, take bush-yerb fah cure dem. But nomah. No,
mon. Me no dive no mah. Ahl de time, me wyes hort, stay
out of strahng sun now . . . Yes, mon . . ."

Limekiller yawned, politely, behind his hand. To make
conversation, he repeated something he had heard. "They

say some of the old-time people used to get herbs down at
Cape Manatee.''

Alfonso Key flashed him a look. The old man said, a
different note suddenly in his voice, different from the mel-
ancholy one of a moment before, ''Mon-ah-*tee*. Mon-ah-*tee*
is hahf-*mon,* you know, sah. Fah true. Yes sah, mon-ah-*tee* is
hahf-*mon*. Which reason de lah w'only allow you to tehk one
mon-ah-*tee* a year.''

Covertly, Jack felt his beer. Sure enough, it was warm.
Key said, ''Yes, but who even bother nowadays? The leather
is so tough you can't even sole a boot with it. And you
dasn't bring the meat up to the Central Market in King *Town*,
you *know*.''

The last thing on Limekiller's mind was to apply for a
license to shoot manatee, even if the limit were one a week.
''How come?'' he asked. ''How come you're not?'' King
Town. King Town was the reason that he was down in Port
Cockatoo. There was no money to be made here, now. But
there was none to be lost here, either. His creditors were
all in King Town, though if they wanted to, they could reach
him even down here. But it would hardly be worth anyone's
while to fee a lawyer to come down and feed him during
the court session. Mainly, though, it was a matter of, Out
of sight, somewhat out of mind. And, anyway—who knows?
The Micawber Principle was weaker down here than up in
the capital. But still and all: something might turn up.

''Because, they say it is because Manatee have teats like
a woman.''

''One time, you know, one time dere is a mahn who mehk
mellow wit ah mon-ah-tee, yes, sah. And hahv pickney by
mon-ah-tee.'' It did seem that the old man had begun to say
something more, but someone else said, *''Ha-ha-ha!''* And
the same someone else next said, in a sharp, all-but-
demanding voice, ''Shoe *shine?* Shoe *shine?*''

''I don't have those kind of shoes,'' Limekiller told the
boy.

''Suede *brush?* Suede *brush?*''

Still no business being forthcoming, the bootblack withdrew, muttering.

Softly, the owner of the Cupid Club murmured, ''That is
one bod bobboon.''

Limekiller waited, then he said, ''I'd like to hear more
about that, Captain Cudgel . . .''

But the story of the man who "made mellow" with a manatee and fathered a child up on her would have to wait, it seemed, upon another occasion. Old Captain Cudgel had departed, via the back door. Jack decided to do the same, via the front.

The sun, having vexed the Atlantic coast most of the morning and afternoon, was now on its equal way towards the Pacific. The Bay of Hidalgo stretched away on all sides, out to the faint white line which marked the barrier reef, the great coral wall which had for so long safeguarded this small, almost forgotten nation for the British Crown and the Protestant Religion. To the south, faint and high and blue against the lighter blue of the sky, however faint, darker: Pico Guapo, in the Republic of Hidalgo. Faint, also, though recurrent, was Limekiller's thought that he might, just might, try his luck down there. His papers were in order. Port Cockatoo was a Port of Entry and of Exit. The wind was free.

But from day to day, from one hot day to another hot day, he kept putting the decision off.

He nodded politely to the District Commissioner and the District Medical Officer and was nodded to, politely, in return. A way down the front street strolled white-haired Mr. Stuart, who had come out here in The Year Thirty-Nine, to help the war effort, and had been here ever since: too far for nodding. Coming from the market shed where she had been buying the latest eggs and ground-victuals was good Miss Gwen; if she saw him she would insist on giving him his supper at her boarding-house on credit: her suppers (her breakfasts and lunches as well) were just fine. But he had debts enough already. So, with a sigh, and a fond recollection of her fried fish, her country-style chicken, and her candied breadfruit, he sidled down the little lane, and he avoided Miss Gwen.

One side of the lane was the one-story white-painted wooden building with the sign DENDRY WASHBURN, LICENCED TO SELL DRUGS AND POISONS, the other side of the lane was the one-story white-painted wooden building where Captain Cumberbatch kept shop. The lane itself was paved with the crushed decomposed coral called pipeshank—and, indeed, the stuff did look like so much busted-up clay pipe stems. At the end of the lane was a

small wharf and a flight of steps, at the bottom of the steps
was his skiff.

He poled out to his boat, where he was greeted by his
first mate, Skippy, an off-white cat with no tail. Skippy was
very neat, and always used the ashes of the caboose: and if
Jack didn't remember to sweep them *out* of the caboose as
soon as they had cooled, and off to one side, why, that was
his own carelessness, and no fault of Skippy's.

"All clear?" he asked the small tiger, as it rubbed against
his leg. The small tiger growled something which might
have been "Portuguese man o'war off the starboard bow at
three bells," or "Musket-men to the futtock-shrouds," or
perhaps only, "where in the Hell have *you* been, all day,
you creep?"

"Tell you what, Skip," as he tied the skiff, untied the
Sacarissa, and, taking up the boat's pole, leaned against her
in a yo-heave-ho manner; "let's us bugger off from this
teeming tropical metropolis and go timely down the coast
. . . say, to off Crocodile Creek, lovely name, proof there
really is no Chamber of Commerce in these parts . . . then
take the dawn tide and drop a line or two for some grunts
or jacks or who knows what . . . sawfish, maybe . . . maybe
. . . *some*thing to go with the rice-and-beans tomorrow . . .
Corn what we catch but can't eat," he grunted, leaned,
hastily released his weight and grabbed the pole up from
the sucking bottom, dropped it on deck, and made swift
shift to raise sail; *slap/slap/* . . . and then he took the tiller.

"And *thennn* . . . Oh, shite and onions, *I* don't know.
Out to the Welshman's Cayes, maybe."

"Harebrained idea if ever I heard one," the first mate
growled, trying to take Jack by the left great toe. "Why
don't you cut your hair and shave that beard and get a job
and get drunk, like any decent, civilized son of a bitch would
do?"

The white buildings and red roofs and tall palms wavering
along the front street, the small boats riding and reflecting,
the green mass of the bush behind: all contributed to give
Port Cockatoo and environs the look and feel of a South
Sea Island. Or, looked at from the viewpoint of another
culture, the District Medical Officer (who was due for a
retirement which he would not spend in his natal country),
said that Port Cockatoo was "*gemütlich*." It was certainly
a quiet and a gentle and undemanding sort of place.

But, somehow, it did not seem the totally ideal place for a man not yet thirty, with debts, with energy, with uncertainties, and with a thirty-foot boat.

A bright star slowly detached itself from the darkening land and swam up and up and then stopped and swayed a bit. This was the immense kerosene lamp which was nightly swung to the top of the great flagpole in the Police yard: it could be seen, the local Baymen assured J. Limekiller, as far out as Serpent Caye . . . Serpent Caye, the impression was, lay hard upon the very verge of the known and habitable earth, beyond which the River Ocean probably poured its stream into The Abyss.

Taking the hint, Limekiller took his own kerosene lamp, by no means immense, lit it, and set it firmly between two chocks of wood. Technically, there should have been two lamps and of different colors. But the local vessels seldom showed any lights at all. "He see me forst, he blow he conch-*shell;* me see *he* forst, me blow *my* conch-shell." And if neither saw the other. "Well, we suppose to meet each othah . . ." And if they didn't? Well, there was Divine Providence—hardly any lives were lost from such misadventures: unless, of course, someone was drunk.

The dimlight lingered and lingered to the west, and then the stars started to come out. It was time, Limekiller thought, to stop for the night.

He was eating his rice and beans and looking at the chart when he heard a voice nearby saying, "Sheep a-high!"

Startled, but by no means alarmed, he called out, "Come aboard!"

What came aboard first was a basket, then a man. A man of no great singularity of appearance, save that he was lacking one eye. "Me name," said the man, "is John Samuel, barn in dis very Colony, me friend, and hence ah subject of de Queen, God bless hah." Mr. Samuel was evidently a White Creole, a member of a class never very large, and steadily dwindling away: sometimes by way of absorption into the non-White majority, sometimes by way of emigration, and sometimes just by way of Death the Leveler. "I tehks de libahty of bringing you some of de forst fruits of de sile," said John S.

"Say, mighty thoughtful of you, Mr. Samuel, care for some rice and beans?—My name's Jack Limekiller."

"—to weet, sour*sop,* bread*fruit,* Oh-*ronge,* coco*nut*—

what I care for, Mr. Limekiller, is some *rum. Rum* is what I has come to beg of you. De hond of mon, sah, has yet to perfect any medicine de superior of *rum.*''

Jack groped in the cubbyhold. "What about all those bush medicines down at Cape Manatee?'' he asked, grunting. There was supposed to be a small bottle, a *chaparita,* as they called it. Where—Oh. It must be . . . No. Then it must be . . .

Mr. Samuel rubbed the grey bristles on his strong jaw. "I does gront you, sah, de vertue of de country yerba. But you must steep de *yerba* een de *rum,* sah. Yes mon.''

Jack's fingers finally found the bottle and his one glass and his one cup and poured. Mr. Samuel said nothing until he had downed his, and then gave a sigh of satisfaction. Jack, who had found a mawmee-apple in the basket of fruit, nodded as he peeled it. The flesh was tawny, and reminded him of wintergreen.

After a moment, he decided that he didn't want to finish his rum, and, with a questioning look, passed it over to his guest. It was pleasant there on the open deck, the breeze faint but sufficient, and comparatively few flies of any sort had cared to make the voyage from shore. The boat swayed gently, there was no surf to speak of, the waves of the Atlantic having spent themselves, miles out, upon the reef; and only a few loose items of gear knocked softly as the vessel rose and fell upon the soft bosom of the inner bay.

"Well sah,'' said Mr. Samuel, with a slight smack of his lips, "I weesh to acknowledge your generosity. I ahsked you to wahk weet me wan mile, and you wahk weet me twain.'' Something splashed in the water, and he looked out, sharply.

"Shark?''

"No, mon. Too far een-shore.'' His eyes gazed out where there was nothing to be seen.

"Porpoise, maybe. Turtle. Or a sting-ray . . .''

After a moment, Samuel said, "Suppose to be ah tortle.'' He turned back and gave Limekiller a long, steady look.

Moved by some sudden devil, Limekiller said, "I hope, Mr. Samuel, that you are not about to tell me about some Indian caves or ruins, full of gold, back in the bush, which you are willing to go shares on with me and all I have to do is put up the money—because, you see, Mr. Samuel, I haven't got any money." And added, "Besides, they tell me it's illegal and that all those things belong to the Queen."

Solemnly, Samuel said, "God save de Queen." Then his eyes somehow seemed to become wider, and his mouth as well, and a sound like hissing steam escaped him, and he sat on the coaming and shook with almost-silent laughter. Then he said, "I sees dot you hahs been ahproached ahlready. No sah. No such teeng. My proposition eenclude only two quality: Expedition. Discretion." And he proceded to explain that what he meant was that Jack should, at regular intervals, bring him supplies in small quantities and that he would advance the money for this and pay a small amount for the service. Delivery was to be made at night. And nothing was to be said about it, back at Port Cockatoo, or anywhere else.

Evidently Jack Limekiller wasn't the only one who had creditors.

"Anything else, Mr. Samuel?"

Samuel gave a deep sigh. "Ah, mon, I would like to sogjest dat you breeng me out ah woman . . . but best no. Best not . . . not yet . . . Oh, Mon, I om so lustful, ahlone out here, eef you tie ah rottlesnake down fah me I weel freeg eet!"

"Well, Mr. Samuel, the fact is, I will not tie a rattlesnake down for you, or up for you, for any purpose at all. However, I will keep my eyes open for a board with a knot-hole in it."

Samuel guffawed. Then he got up, his machete slap-flapping against his side, and with a few more words, clambered down into his dory—no plank-boat, in these waters, but a dug-out—and began to paddle. Bayman, bushman, the machete was almost an article of clothing, though there was nothing to chop out here on the gentle waters of the bay. There was a splash, out there in the darkness, and a cry—Samuel's voice—

"Are you all right out there?" Limekiller called.

"Yes mon . . ." faintly. "Fine . . . bloddy Oxville tortle . . ."

Limekiller fell easily asleep. Presently he dreamed of seeing a large Hawksbill turtle languidly pursuing John Samuel, who languidly evaded the pursuit. Later, he awoke, knowing that he knew what had awakened him, but for the moment unable to name it. The awakeners soon enough

identified themselves. Manatees. Sea-cows. The most harm-
less creatures God ever made. He drowsed off again, but
again and again he lightly awoke and always he could hear
them sighing and sounding.

Early up, he dropped his line, made a small fire in the
sheet-iron caboose set in its box of sand, and put on the pot
of rice and beans to cook in coconut oil. The head and tail
of the first fish went into a second pot, the top of the double
boiler, to make fish-tea, as the chowder was called; when
they were done, he gave them to Skippy. He fried the fillets
with sliced breadfruit, which had as near no taste of its own
as made no matter, but was a great extender of tastes. The
second fish he cut and corned—that is, he spread coarse salt
on it: there was nothing else to do to preserve it in this hot
climate, without ice, and where the art of smoking fish was
not known. And more than those two he did not bother to
take, he had no license for commercial fishing, could not
sell a catch in the market, and the "sport" of taking fish he
could neither eat nor sell, and would have to throw back,
was a pleasure which eluded his understanding.

It promised to be a hot day and it kept its promise, and
he told himself, as he often did on hot, hot days, that it beat
shoveling snow in Toronto.

He observed a vacant mooring towards the south of town,
recollected that it always had been vacant, and so, for no
better reason than that, he tied up to it. Half of the remainder of his catch came ashore with him. This was too far
south for any plank houses or tin roofs. Port Cockatoo at
both ends straggled out into 'trash houses,' as they were
called—sides of wild cane allowing the cooling breezes to
pass, and largely keeping out the brute sun; roofs of thatch,
usually of the bay or cohune palm. The people were poorer
here than elsewhere in this town where no one at all by
North American standards was rich, but 'trash' had no ref-
erence to that: *Loppings, twigs, and leaves of trees, bruised
sugar cane, corn husks, etc.*, his dictionary explained.

An old, old woman in the ankle-length skirts and the kerchief of her generation stood in the doorway of her little
house and looked, first at him, then at his catch. And kept
on looking at it. All the coastal people of Hidalgo were
fascinated by fish: rice and beans was the staple dish, but
fish was the roast beef, the steak, the chicken, of this small,

small country which had never been rich and was now—with the growing depletion of its mahogany and rosewood—even poorer than ever. Moved, not so much by conscious consideration of this as by a sudden impulse, he held up his hand and what it was holding. "Care for some corned fish, Grandy?"

Automatically, she reached out her tiny, dark hand, all twisted and withered, and took it. Her lips moved. She looked from the fish to him and from him to the fish; asked, doubtfully, "How much I have for you?"—meaning, how much did she owe him.

"Your prayers," he said, equally on impulse.

Her head flew up and she looked at him full in the face, then. "T'ank you, Buckra," she said. "And I weel do so. I weel pray for you." And she went back into her trash house.

Up the dusty, palm-lined path a ways, just before it branched into the cemetery road and the front street, he encountered Mr. Stuart—white-haired, learned, benevolent, deaf, and vague—and wearing what was surely the very last sola topee in everyday use in the Western Hemisphere (and perhaps, what with one thing and another, in the Eastern, as well).

"Did you hear the baboons last night?" asked Mr. Stuart.

Jack knew that "baboons," hereabouts, were howler-monkeys. Even their daytime noises, a hollow and repetitive *Rrr-Rrr-Rrrr,* sounded uncanny enough; as for their night-time wailings—

"I was anchored offshore, down the coast, last night," he explained. "All I heard were the manatees."

Mr. Stuart looked at him with faint, grey eyes, smoothed his long moustache. "Ah, *those* poor chaps," he said. "They've slipped back down the scale . . . much *too* far down, I expect, for any quick return. Tried to help them, you know. Tried the Herodotus method. Carthaginians. Mute trade, you know. Set out some bright red cloth, put trade-goods on, went away. Returned. Things were knocked about, as though animals had been at them. *Some* of the items were gone, though. But nothing left in return. Too bad, oh yes, too bad . . ." His voice died away into a low moan, and he shook his ancient head. In another moment, before Jack could say anything, or even think of anything to say, Mr. Stuart had flashed him a smile of pure friendliness, and was gone. A bunch of flowers was in one hand, and the path he took was the cemetery road. He had gone to visit one of "the great company of the dead, which increase around us as we grow older."

From this mute offering, laid also upon the earth, nothing would be expected in return. There are those whom we do not see and whom we do not desire that they should ever show themselves at all.

The shop of Captain Cumberbatch was open. The rules as to what stores or offices were open and closed at which times were exactly the opposite of the laws of the Medes and the Persians. The time to go shopping was when one saw the shop open. Any shop. They opened, closed, opened, closed . . . And as to why stores with a staff of only one closed so often, why, they closed not only to allow the proprietor to siesta, they also closed to allow him to eat. It was no part of the national culture for Ma to send Pa's "tea" for Pa to eat behind the counter: Pa came home. Period. And as for establishments with a staff of more than one, why could the staff not have taken turns? Answer: De baas, of whatsoever race, creed, or color, might trust an employee with his life, but he would never trust his employee with his cash or stock, never, never, never.

Captain Cumberbatch had for many years puffed up and down the coast in his tiny packet-and-passenger boat, bringing cargo merchandise for the shopkeepers of Port Caroline, Port Cockatoo, and—very, very semi-occasionally—anywhere else as chartered. But some years ago he had swallowed the anchor and set up business as shopkeeper in Port Cockatoo. And one day an epiphany of sorts had occurred: Captain Cumberbatch had asked himself why he should bring cargo for others to sell and/or why he should pay others to bring cargo for he himself to sell. Why should he not bring his own cargo and sell it himself?

The scheme was brilliant as it was unprecedented. And indeed it had but one discernable flaw: Whilst Captain Cumberbatch was at sea, he could not tend shop to sell what he had shipped. And while he was tending his shop he could not put to sea to replenish stock. And, tossing ceaselessly from the one horn of this dilemma to the other, he often thought resentfully of the difficulties of competing with such peoples as the Chinas, Turks, and 'Paniards, who—most unfairly—were able to trust the members of their own families to mind the store.

Be all this as it may, the shop of Captain Cumberbatch was at this very moment open, and the captain himself was leaning upon his counter and smoking a pipe.

"Marneen, Jock. Hoew de day?"

"Bless God."

"Forever and ever, ehhh-men."

A certain amount of tinned corned-beef and corned-beef hash, of white sugar (it was nearer grey), of bread (it was dead white, as unsuitable an item of diet as could be designed for the country and the country would have rioted at the thought of being asked to eat dark), salt, lamp-oil, tea, tinned milk, cheese, were packed and passed across the worn counter; a certain amount of national currency made the same trip in reverse.

As for the prime purchaser of the items, Limekiller said nothing. That was part of the Discretion.

Outside again, he scanned the somnolent street for any signs that anyone might have—somehow—arrived in town who might want to charter a boat for . . . well, for anything. Short of smuggling, there was scarcely a purpose for which he would have not chartered the *Sacarissa*. It was not that he had an invincible repugnance to the midnight trade, there might well be places and times where he would have considered it. But Government, in British Hidalgo (here, as elsewhere in what was left of the Empire, the definite article was conspicuously absent: "Government will do this," they said—or, often as not, "Government will not do this") had not vexed him in any way and he saw no reason to vex it. And, furthermore, he had heard many reports of the accommodations at the Queen's Hotel, as the King Town "gaol" was called: and they were uniformly unfavorable.

But the front street was looking the same as ever, and, exemplifying, as ever, the observation of The Preacher, that there was no new thing under the sun. So, with only the smallest of sighs, he had started for the Cupid Club, when the clop . . . clop of hooves made him look up. Coming along the street was the horse-drawn equivalent of a pickup truck. The back was open, and contained a few well-filled crocus sacks and some sawn timber; the front was roofed, but open at the sides; and for passengers it had a white-haired woman and a middle-aged man. It drew to a stop.

"Well, young man. And who are *you?*" the woman asked. Some elements of the soft local accent overlaid her speech, but underneath was something else, something equally soft, but different. Her "Man" was not *mon,* it was *mayun,* and her "you" was more like *yieww.*

He took off his hat. "Jack Limekiller is my name, ma'am."

"Put it right back on, Mr. Limekiller. I do appreciate the gesture, but it has already been gestured, now. Draft-dodger, are you?"

That was a common guess. Any North American who didn't fit into an old and familiar category—tourist, sport fisherman, sport huntsman, missionary, businessman—was assumed to be either a draft-dodger or a trafficker in "weed" . . . or maybe both. "No, ma'am. I've served my time and, anyway, I'm a Canadian, and we don't have a draft."

"Well," she said, "doesn't matter even if you are, I don't *cay*-uh. Now, sir, I am Amelia Lebedee. And this is my nephew, Tom McFee." Tom smiled a faint and abstract smile, shook hands. He was sun-dark and had a slim moustache and he wore a felt hat which had perhaps been crisper than it was now. Jack had not seen many men like Tom McFee in Canada, but he had seen many men like Tom McFee in the United States. Tom McFee sold crab in Baltimore. Tom McFee managed the smaller cotton gin in a two-gin town in Alabama. Tom McFee was foreman at the shrimp-packing plant in one of the Florida Parishes in Louisiana. And Tom McFee was railroad freight agent in whatever dusty town in Texas it was that advertised itself as "Blue Vetch Seed Capital of the World."

"We are carrying you off to Shiloh for lunch," said Amelia, and a handsome old woman she was, and sat up straight at the reins. "So you just climb up in. Tom will carry you back later, when he goes for some more of this wood. Land! You'd think it was *teak,* they cut it so slow. Instead of pine."

Limekiller had no notion who or what or where Shiloh was, although it clearly could not be very far, and he could think of no reason why he should not go there. So in he climbed.

"Yes," said Amelia Lebedee, "the war wiped us out

completely. So we came down here and we planted sugar, yes, we planted sugar and we made sugar for, oh, most eighty years. But we didn't move with the times, and so that's all over with now. We plant most anything *but* sugar nowadays. And when we see a new and a civilized face, we plant them down at the table.'' By this time the wagon was out of town. The bush to either side of the road looked like just bushtype bush to Jack. But to Mrs. Lebedee each acre had an identity of its own. ''That was the Cullen's place,'' she'd say. And, ''The Robinsons lived there. Beautiful horses, they had. Nobody has horses anymore, just us. Yonder used to be the Simmonses. Part of the house is still standing, but, land!—you cain't see it from the road anymore. They've gone back. Most everybody has gone back, who hasn't died off. . . .'' For a while she said nothing. The road gradually grew narrower, and all three of them began thoughtfully to slap at ''flies.''

A bridge now appeared and they rattled across it, a dark-green stream rushing below. There was a glimpse of an old grey house in the archaic, universal-tropical style, and then the bush closed in again. ''And *they*-uh,'' Miss Amelia gestured, backwards, ''is Texas. Oh, what a fine place that was, in its day! Nobody lives there, now. Old Captain Rutherford, the original settler, he was with Hood. *Gen*eral Hood, I mean.''

It all flashed on Jack at once, and it all came clear, and he wondered that it had not been clear from the beginning. They were now passing through the site of the old Confederate colony. There had been such in Venezuela, in Colombia, even in Brazil; for all he knew, there might still be. But this one here in Hidalgo, it had not been wiped out in a year or two, like the Mormon colonies in Mexico—there had been no Revolution here, no gringo-hating Villistas—it had just ebbed away. Tiny little old B.H., ''a country,'' as someone (who?) had said, ''which you can put your arms around,'' had put its arms around the Rebel refugees . . . its thin, green arms . . . and it had let them clear the bush and build their houses . . . and it had waited . . . and waited . . . and, as, one by one, the Southern American families had ''died out'' or ''gone back,'' why, as easy as easy, the bush had slipped back. And, for the present, it seemed like it was going to stay back. It had, after all, closed in after the Old Empire Mayans had so mysteriously left, and that was a thousand years ago. What was a hundred years, to the bush?

The house at Shiloh was small and neat and trim and freshly painted, and one end of the veranda was undergoing repairs. There had been no nonsense, down here, of reproducing any of the ten thousand imitations of Mount Vernon. A neatly-mowed lawn surrounded the house; in a moment, as the wagon made its last circuit, Jack saw that the lawnmowers were a small herd of cattle. A line of cedars accompanied the road, and Miss Amelia pointed to a gap in the line. "That tree that was there," she said, calmly, "was the one that fell on my husband and on John Samuel. It had been obviously weakened in the hurricane, you know, and they went over to see how badly—that was a mistake. John Samuel lost his left eye and my husband lost his life."

Discretion . . . Would it be indiscreet to ask—? He asked. "How long ago was this, Miss Amelia?" All respectable women down here were "Miss," followed by the first name, regardless of marital state.

"It was ten years ago, come September," she said. "Let's go in out of the sun, now, and Tom will take care of the horse."

In out of the sun was cool and neat and, though shady, the living room-dining room was as bright as fresh paint and flowered wall-paper—the only wall-paper he had seen in the colony—could make it. There were flowers in vases, too, fresh flowers, not the widely-popular plastic ones. Somehow the Bayfolk did not make much of flowers.

For lunch there was heart-of-palm, something not often had, for a palm had to die to provide it, and palms were not idly cut down: there was the vegetable pear, or chayote, here called cho-cho; venison chops, tomato with okra; there was cashew wine, made from the fruit of which the Northern Lands know only the seed, which they ignorantly call "nut." And, even, there was coffee, not powdered ick, not grown-in-Brazil-shipped-to-the-United-States-roasted-ground-canned-shipped-to-Hidalgo-coffee, but actual local coffee. Here, where coffee grew with no more care than weeds, hardly anyone except the Indians bothered to grow it, and what *they* grew, *they* used.

"Yes," Miss Amelia said, "it can be a very good life here. It is necessary to work, of course, but the work is well-rewarded, oh, not in terms of large sums of money, but in so many other ways. But it's coming to an end. There is just no way that working this good land can bring you all the riches you see in the moving pictures. And that is what they all want, and dream of, all the young people. And there is just no way they are going to get it."

Tom McFee made one of his rare comments. "*I* don't dream of any white Christmas," he said. "I am saying here, where it is always green. I told Malcolm Stuart that."

Limekiller said, "I was just talking to him this morning, myself. But I couldn't understand what he was talking about . . . something about trying to trade with the manatees. . . ."

The Shiloh people, clearly, had no trouble understanding what Stuart had been talking about; they did not even think it was particularly bizarre. "Ah, those poor folks down at Mantee," said Amelia Lebedee; "—now, mind you, I mean *Mantee*, Cape Mantee, I am *not* referring to the people up on Manatee River and the Lagoons, who are just as civilized as you and I: I mean *Cape* Mantee, which is its correct name, you know—"

"Where the medicine herbs grew?"

"Why, yes, Mr. Limekiller. Where they grew. As I suppose they still do. No one really knows, of course, *what* still grows down at Cape Mantee, though Nature, I suppose, would not change her ways. It was the hurricanes, you see. The War Year hurricanes. Until then, you know, Government had kept a road open, and once a month a police constable would ride down and, well, at least, take a look around. Not that any of the people there would ever bring any of their troubles to the police. They were . . . well, how should I put it? Tom, how would *you* put it?"

Tom thought a long moment. "Simple. They were always simple."

What he meant by "simple," it developed, was simple-minded. His aunt did not entirely agree with that. They gave that impression, the Mantee people, she said, but that was only because their ways were so different. "There is a story," she said, slowly, and, it seemed to Jack Limekiller, rather reluctantly, "that a British man-of-war took a Spanish slave-ship. I don't know when this would have been, it was well before we came down and settled here. Well before The War. Our own War, I mean. It was a small Spanish slaver and there weren't many captives in her. As I under-

stand it, between the time that Britain abolished slavery and
the dreadful Atlantic slave-trade finally disappeared, if slav-
ers were taken anywhere near Africa, the British would bring
the captives either to Saint Helena or Sierra Leone, and
liberate them there. But this one was taken fairly near the
American coast. I suppose she was heading for Cuba. So
the British ship brought them *here*. To British Hidalgo.
And the people were released down at Cape Mantee, and
told they could settle there and no one would 'vex' them,
as they say here.''

Where the slaves had come from, originally, she did not
know, but she thought the tradition was that they had come
from somewhere well back in the African interior. Over the
course of the many subsequent years, some had trickled into
the more settled parts of the old colony. "But some of them
just stayed down there," she said. "Keeping up their own
ways."

"Too much intermarrying," Tom offered.

"So the Bayfolk say. The Bayfolk were always, *I* think,
rather afraid of them. None of them would ever go there
alone. And, after the hurricanes, when the road went out,
and the police just couldn't get there, none of the Bayfolk
would *go* there at *all*. By sea, I mean. You must remember,
Mr. Limekiller, that in the 1940s this little colony was very
much as it was in the 1840s. There were no airplanes. There
wasn't one single highway. When I say there used to be a
road to Mantee, you mustn't think it was a road such as
we've got between Port Cockatoo and Shiloh.''

Limekiller, thinking of the dirt road between Port Cockatoo and Shiloh, tried to think what the one between Port
Cockatoo and the region behind Cape Mantee must have
been like. Evidently a trail, nothing more, down which an
occasional man on a mule might make his way, boiling the
potato-like fruit of the breadnut tree for his food and feed-
ing his mule the leaves: a trail that had to be "chopped,"
had to be "cleaned" by machete-work, at least twice a year,
to keep the all-consuming bush from closing over it the way
the flesh closes over a cut. An occasional trader, an occasional buyer or gatherer of chicle or herbs or hides, an occasional missioner or medical officer, at infrequent intervals
would pass along this corridor in the eternal jungle.

And then came a hurricane, smashing flat everything in
its path. And the trail vanished. And the trail was never re-

cut. British Hidalgo had probably never been high on any list of colonial priorities at the best of times. During the War of 1939-1945, they may have forgotten all about it in London. Many of Hidalgo's able-bodied men were off on distant fronts. An equal number had gone off to cut the remaining forests of the Isle of Britain, to supply anyway a fraction of the wood which was then impossible to import. Nothing could be spared for Mantee and its people; in King Town, Mantee was deemed as distant as King Town was in London. The p.c. never went there again. No missioner ever returned. Neither had a medical officer or nurse. Nor any trader. No one. Except for Malcolm Stuart . . .

"He did try. Of course, he had his own concerns. During the War he had his war work. Afterwards, he took up a block of land a few miles back from here, and he had his hands full with that. And then, after, oh, I don't remember how many years of stories, stories—there is no television here, you know, and few people have time for books—stories about the Mantee people, well, he decided he had to go have a look, see for himself, you know."

Were the Mantee people really eating raw meat and raw fish? He would bring them matches. Had they actually reverted to the use of stone for tools? He would bring them machetes, axes, knives. And . . . as for the rest of it . . . the rest of the rather awful and certainly very odd stories . . . he would see for himself.

But he had seen nothing. There had been nothing to see. That is, nothing which he could be sure he had seen. Perhaps he had thought that he had seen some few things which he had not cared to mention to Jack, but had spoken of to the Shiloh people.

They, however, were not about to speak of it to Jack.

"Adventure," said Amelia Lebedee, dismissing the matter of Mantee with sigh. "Nobody wants the adventure of cutting bush to plant yams. They want the adventure of night clubs and large automobiles. They see it in the moving pictures. And you, Mr. Limekiller, what is it that *you* want? —coming, having come, from the land of night clubs and large automobiles. . . ."

The truth was simple. "I wanted the adventure of sailing a boat with white sails through tropic seas," he said. "I saw it in the moving pictures. I never had a night club but

I had a large automobile, and I sold it and came down here
and bought the boat. And, well, here I am.''

They had talked right through the siesta time. Tom McFee
was ready, now, to return for the few more planks which
the sawmill might—or might not—have managed to produce
since the morning. It was time to stand up now and to make
thanks and say good-bye. "Yes," said Amelia Lebedee,
pensively "Here we are. Here we all are. We are all here.
And some of us are more content being here than others."

Half-past three at the Cupid Club. On Limekiller's table,
the usual single bottle of beer. Also, the three chaparitas of
rum which he had bought—but they were in a paper bag,
lest the sight of them, plus the fact that he could invite no
one to drink of them, give rise to talk that he was ''mean.''
Behind the bar, Alfonso Key. In the dark, dark back, slowly
sipping a lemonade (all soft drinks were ''lemonade''—coke
was lemonade, strawberry pop was lemonade, ginger stout
was lemonade . . . sometimes, though not often, for reasons inexplicable, there was also lemon-flavored lemonade)—in the dark rear part of the room, resting his
perpetually sore eyes, was old Captain Cudgel.

"Well, how you spend the night, Jock?" Alfonso ready
for a tale of amour, ready with a quip, a joke.

"Oh, just quietly. Except for the manatees." Limekiller,
saying this, had a sudden feeling that he had said all this
before, been all this before, was caught on the moebius strip
which life in picturesque Port Cockatoo had already become, caught, caught, never would be released. *Adventure!*
Hah!

At this point, however, a slightly different note, a slightly
different comment from the old, old man.

"Een Eedalgo," he said, dolefully, "de monatee hahv no
leg, mon. Becahs Eedalgo ees a smahl coun-*tree,* ahn every-
teeng smahl. Every-teeng *weak.* Now, een Ahfrica, mon,
de monatee *does* hahv leg.''

Key said, incredulous, but still respectful, "What you tell
we, Coptain Cudgel? *What?*" His last word, pronounced in
the local manner of using it as a particular indication of
skepticism, of criticism, of denial, seemed to have at least
three *T*s at the end of it; he repeated "Wh*attt?*"

"Yes, mon. Yes sah. Een Ahfrica, de monatee hahv *leg,*
mon. Eet be ah poerful beast, een Ahfrica, come up on de
lond, mon.''

"I tell you. *Me* di hear eet befoah. Een Ahfrica," he repeated, doggedly, "de monatee hahv leg, de monatee be ah poerful beast, come up on de *lond,* mon, no lahf, mon—"

"Me no di lahf, sah—"

"—de w'ol' people, dey tell me so, fah true."

Alfonso Key gave his head a single shake, gave a single click of his tongue, gave Jack a single look.

Far down the street, the bell of the Church of Saint Benedict the Moor sounded. Whatever time it was marking had nothing to do with Greenwich Meridian Time or any variation thereof.

The weak, feeble old voice resumed the thread of conversation. "Me grahndy di tell me dot she grahndy di tell *she*. Motta hav foct, eet me grahndy di give me me name, b'y. Cudgel. Ahfrica name. Fah true. Fah True."

A slight sound of surprise broke Limekiller's silence. He said, "Excuse me, Captain. Could it have been 'Cudjoe' . . . maybe?"

For a while he thought that the question had either not been heard or had, perhaps, been resented. Then the old man said, "Eet could be so. Sah, eet might be so. Lahng, lahng time ah-go. . . . Me Christian name, Pe-tah. Me w'ol'grahndy she say. "Pickney: you hahv ah Christian name, Pe-tah. But me give you Ahfrica name, too. Cahdjo. No fah-get, pickney? Time poss, time poss, de people dey ahl cahl me 'Cudgel,' you see, sah. So me fah-get . . . Sah, hoew you know dees teeng, sah?"

Limekiller said that he thought he had read it in a book. The old captain repeated the word, lengthening it in his local speech. "Ah boook, sah. To t'eenk ahv dot. Een ah boook. Me w'own name een ah boook." By and by he departed as silently as always.

In the dusk a white cloth waved behind the thin line of white beach. He took off his shirt and waved back. Then he transferred the groceries into the skiff and, as soon as it was dark and he had lit and securely fixed his lamp, set about rowing ashore. By and by a voice called out, "Mon, where de Hell you gwyen? You keep on to de right, you gweyn wine up een *Sponeesh* Hidalgo: Mah to de lef, mon: mah to de *lef!*" And with such assistances, soon enough the skiff softly scraped the beach.

Mr. John Samuel's greeting was, "You bring de rum?" The rum put in his hand, he took up one of the sacks, gestured Limekiller towards the other. "Les go timely, noew," he said. For a moment, in what was left of the dimmest dimlight, Jack thought the man was going to walk straight into an enormous tree: instead, he walked across the enormous roots and behind the tree. Limekiller followed the faint white patch of shirt bobbing in front of him. Sometimes the ground was firm, sometimes it went squilchy, sometimes it was simply running water—shallow, fortunately—sometimes it felt like gravel. The bush noises were still fairly soft. A rustle. He hoped it was only a wish-willy lizard, or a bamboo-chicken—an iguana—and not a yellowjaw, that snake of which it was said . . . but this was no time to remember scare stories about snakes.

Without warning—although what sort of warning there could have been was a stupid question, anyway—there they were. Gertrude Stein, returning to her old home town after an absence of almost forty years, and finding the old home itself demolished, had observed (with a lot more objectivity than she was usually credited with) that there was no *there,* there. The *there,* here, was simply a clearing, with a very small fire, and a *ramada:* four poles holding up a low thatched roof. John Samuel let his sack drop. "Ahnd noew," he said, portentously, "let us broach de rum."

After the chaparita had been not only broached but drained, for the second time that day Limekiller dined ashore. The cooking was done on a raised fire-hearth of clay-and-sticks, and what was cooked was a breadfruit, simply strewn, when done, with sugar; and a gibnut. To say that the gibnut, or paca, is a rodent, is perhaps—though accurate—unfair: it is larger than a rabbit, and it eats well. After that Samuel made black tea and laced it with more rum. After that he gave a vast belch and a vast sigh. "Can you play de bon*joe?*" he next asked.

"Well . . . I have been known to try . . ."

The lamp flared and smoked. Samuel adjusted it . . . somewhat. . . . He got up and took a bulky object down from a peg on one of the roof-poles. It was a sheet of thick plastic, laced with raw-hide thongs, which he laboriously unknotted. Inside that was a deerskin. And inside *that,* an ordinary banjo-case, which contained an ordinary, if rather old and worn, banjo.

"Mehk I hear ah sahng . . . ah sahng ahv *you* country."

What song should he make him hear? No particularly Canadian song brought itself to mind. Ah well, he would dip down below the border just a bit . . . His fingers strummed idly on the strings, The words grew, the tune grew, he lifted up what some (if not very many) had considered a not-bad-baritone, and began to sing and play.

> *Manatee gal, ain't you coming out tonight,*
> *Coming out tonight, coming out tonight?*
> *Oh, Manatee gal, ain't you coming out tonight,*
> *To dance by the light of the—*

An enormous hand suddenly covered his own and pressed it down. The tune subsided into a jumble of chords, and an echo, and a silence.

"Mon, mon, you not do me right. I no di say, "Mehk I hear a sahng ahv *you* country?" Samuel, on his knees, breathed heavily. His breath was heavy with rum and his voice was heavy with reproof . . . and with a something else for which Limekiller had no immediate name. But, friendly it was not.

Puzzled more than apologetic, Jack said, "Well, it *is* a North American song, anyway. It was an old Erie Canal song. It— Oh. I'll be damned. Only it's supposed to go, '*Buffalo gal, ain't you coming out tonight,*' And I dunno what made me change it, what difference does it make?"

"What different? What different it mehk? Ah, Christ me King! You lee' buckra b'y, you not know w'ehnnah-teeng?"

It was all too much for Limekiller. The last thing he wanted was anything resembling an argument, here in the deep, dark bush, with an all-but-stranger. Samuel having lifted his heavy hand from the instrument, Limekiller, moved by a sudden spirit, began,

> *Amazing grace, how sweet the sound,*
> *To save a wretch like me.*

With a rough catch of his breath, Samuel muttered, "Yes. Yes. Dot ees good. Go on, b'y. No stop."

> *I once was halt, but now can walk:*
> *Was blind, but now I see . . .*

He sang the beautiful old hymn to the end: and, by that time, if not overpowered by Grace, John Samuel—having evidently broached the second and the third chaparita—was certainly overpowered: and it did not look as though the dinner-guest was going to get any kind of guided tour back to the shore and the skiff. He sighed and he looked around him. A bed rack had roughly been fixed up, and its lashings were covered with a few deer hides and an old Indian blanket. Samuel not responding to any shakings or urgings, Limekiller, with a shrug and a "Well what the hell," covered him with the blanket as he lay upon the ground. Then, having rolled up the sacks the supplies had come in and propped them under his head, Limekiller disposed himself for slumber on the hides. Some lines were running through his head and he paused a moment to consider what they were. What they were, they were, *From ghoulies and ghosties, long leggedy beasties, and bugges that go* boomp *in the night, Good Lord, deliver us.* With an almost absolute certainty that this was not the Authorized Version or Text, he heard himself give a grottle and a snore and knew he was fallen asleep.

He awoke to slap heartily at some flies, and the sound perhaps awoke the host, who was heard to mutter and mumble. Limekiller leaned over. "What did you say?"

The lines said, Limekiller learned that he had heard them before.

"Eef you tie ah rottlesnake doewn fah me, I weel freeg eet."

"I yield," said Limekiller, "to any man so much hornier than myself. Produce the snake, sir, and I will consider the rest of the matter."

The red eye of the expiring fire winked at him. It was still winking at him when he awoke from a horrid nightmare of screams and thrashings-about, in the course of which he had evidently fallen or had thrown himself from the bed rack to the far side. Furthermore, he must have knocked against one of the roof-poles in doing so, because a good deal of the thatch had landed on top of him. He threw it off, and, getting up, began to apologize.

"Sorry if I woke you, Mr. Samuel. I don't know what—" There was no answer, and looking around in the faint light of the fire, he saw no one.

"Mr. Samuel? Mr. *Samuel?* John? oh, hey, *Johhn!? . . .*"

No answer. If the man had merely gone out to "ease himself," as the Bayfolk delicately put it, he would have surely been near enough to answer. No one in the colony engaged in strolling in the bush at night for fun. "Son of a bitch," he muttered. He felt for and found his matches, struck one, found the lamp, lit it, looked around.

There was still no sign of John Samuel, but what there were signs of was some sort of horrid violence. Hastily he ran his hands over himself, but, despite his fall, despite part of the roof having fallen on him, he found no trace of blood.

All the blood which lay around, then, must have been—could only have been—John Samuel's blood.

All the screaming and the sounds of something—or some things—heavily thrashing around, they had not been in any dream. They had been the sounds of truth.

And as for what else he saw, as he walked, delicate as Agag, around the perimeter of the clearing, he preferred not to speculate.

There was a shotgun and there were shells. He put the shells into the chambers and he stood up, weapon in his hand, all the rest of the night.

"Now, if it took you perhaps less than an hour to reach the shore, and if you left immediately, how is it that you were so long in arriving at Port?" The District Commissioner asked. He asked politely, but he did ask. He asked a great many questions, for, in addition to his other duties, he was the Examining Magistrate.

"Didn't you observe the wind, D.C.? Ask anyone who was out on the water yesterday. I spent most of the day tacking—"

Corporal Huggin said, softly, from the wheel, "That would be correct, Mr. Blossom."

They were in the police boat, the *George* . . . once, Jack had said to P.C. Ed Huggin, "For George VI, I suppose?" and Ed, toiling over the balky and antique engine, his clear tan skin smudged with grease, had scowled, and said, "More for bloody George III, you ask *me.* . . ." At earliest daylight, yesterday, Limekiller, red-eyed and twitching, had briefly cast around in the bush near the camp, decided that, ignorant of bush-lore as he was, having not even a compass, let alone a pair of boots or a snake-bite kit, it would have been insane to attempt any explorations. He found his way along the path, found his skiff tied up, and had rowed to his boat. Unfavorable winds had destroyed his hope of getting back to Port Cockatoo in minimum time: it had been night when he arrived.

The police had listened to his story, had summoned Mr. Florian Blossom, the District Commissioner; all had agreed that "No purpose would be served by attempting anything until next morning." They had taken his story down, word by word, and by hand—if there was an official stenographer anywhere in the country, Limekiller had yet to hear of it—and by longhand, too; and in their own accustomed style and method, too, so that he was officially recorded as having said things such as *Awakened by loud sounds of distress, I arose and hailed the man known to me as John Samuel. Upon receiving no response,* etcetera.

After Jack had signed the statement, and stood up, thinking to return to his boat, the District Commissioner said, "I believe that they can accommodate you with a bed in the Unmarried Police Constables' Quarters, Mr. Limekiller. Just for the night."

He looked at the official. A slight shiver ran up and down him. "Do you mean that I am a prisoner?"

"Certainly not, Mr. Limekiller. No such thing."

"You know, if I had wanted to, I could have been in Republican waters by now."

Mr. Blossom's politeness never flagged. "We realize it and we take it into consideration, Mr. Limekiller. But if we are all of us here together it will make an early start in the morning more efficacious."

Anyway, Jack was able to shower, and Ed Huggins loaned him clean clothes. Of course they had not gotten an early start in the morning. Only fishermen and sandboatmen got early starts. Her Majesty's Government moved at its accustomed pace. In the police launch, besides Limekiller, was P.C. Huggin, D.C. Blossom, a very small and very black and very wiry man called Harlow the Hunter, Police-Sergeant Ruiz, and whitehaired Dr. Rafael, the District Medical Officer.

"I wouldn't have been able to come at all, you know," he said to Limekiller, "except my assistant has returned from his holidays a day earlier. Oh, there is so much to see in this colony! Fascinating, fascinating!"

D.C. Blossom smiled. "Doctor Rafael is a famous antiquarian, you know, Mr. Limekiller. It was he who discovered the grave-*stone* of my three or four times great-grand-sir and -grandy.''

Sounds of surprise and interest—polite on Limekiller's part, gravestones perhaps not being what he would have most wished to think of—genuine on the part of everyone else, ancestral stones not being numerous in British Hidalgo.

''Yes, Yes,'' Dr. Rafael agreed. ''Two years ago I was on *my* holidays, and I went out to St. Saviour's Caye . . . well, to what is left of St. Saviour's Caye after the last few hurricanes. You can imagine what is left of the old settlement. Oh, the Caye is dead, it is like a skeleton, bleached and bare!'' Limekiller felt he could slightly gladly have tipped the medico over the side and watched the bubbles; but, unaware, on the man went. ''—so, difficult though it was making my old map agree with the present outlines, still, I did find the site of the old burial-ground, and I cast about and I prodded with my iron rod, and I felt stone underneath the sand, and I dug!''

More sounds of excited interest. Digging in the sand on the bit of ravished sand and coral where the ancient settlement had been—but was no more—was certainly of more interest than digging for yams on the fertile soil of the mainland. And, even though they already knew that it was not a chest of gold, still, they listened and they murmured *oh* and *ah*. ''The letters were still very clear, I had no difficulty reading them. *Sacred to the memory of Ferdinando Rousseau, a native of Guernsey, and of Marianna his Wife, a native of Mandingo, in Africa.* Plus a poem in three stanzas, of which I have deposited a copy in the National Archives, and of course I have a copy myself and a third copy I offered to old Mr. Ferdinand Rousseau in King Town—''

Smiling, Mr. Blossom asked, ''And what he tell you, then, Doctor?''

Dr. Rafael's smile was a trifle rueful. ''He said, 'Let the dead bury their dead'—'' The others all laughed. Mr. Ferdinand Rousseau was evidently known to all of them. ''—and he declined to take it. Well, I was aware that Mr. Blossom's mother was a cousin of Mr. Rousseau's mother—'' (''Double-cousin,'' said Mr. Blossom.)

Said Mr. Blossom, ''And the doctor has even been there,

too, to that country. I don't mean Guernsey; in Africa, I mean; not true, Doctor?''

Up ahead, where the coast thrust itself out into the blue, blue Bay, Jack thought he saw the three isolated palms which were his landmark. But there was no hurry. He found himself unwilling to hurry anything at all.

Doctor Rafael, in whose voice only the slightest trace of alien accent still lingered, said that after leaving Vienna, he had gone to London, in London he had been offered and had accepted work in a British West African colonial medical service. ''I was just a bit surprised that the old gravestone referred to Mandingo as a country, there is no such country on the maps today, but there are such a people.''

''What they like, Doc-tah? What they like, these people who dey mehk some ahv Mr. Blossom ahn-*ces*-tah?''

There was another chuckle. This one had slight overtones.

The DMO's round, pink face furrowed in concentration among memories a quarter of a century old. ''Why,'' he said, ''they are like elephants. They never forget.''

There was a burst of laughter. Mr. Blossom laughed loudest of them all. Twenty-five years earlier he would have asked about Guernsey; today. . . .

Harlow the Hunter, his question answered, gestured towards the shore. A slight swell had come up, the blue was flecked, with bits of white. ''W'over dere, suppose to be wan ahv w'ol' Bob Blaine cahmp, in de w'ol' days.''

''Filthy fellow,'' Dr. Rafael said, suddenly, concisely.

''Yes sah.'' Harlow agreed. ''He was ah lewd fellow, fah true, fah true. What he use to say, he use to say, 'Eef you tie ah rottle-snehk doewn fah me, I weel freeg eet. . . .' ''

Mr. Blossom leaned forward. ''Something the matter, Mr. Limekiller?''

Mr. Limekiller did not at that moment feel like talking. Instead, he lifted his hand and pointed towards the headland with the three isolated palms.

''Cape Man'tee, Mr. Limekiller? What about it?''

Jack cleared his throat. ''I thought that was farther down the coast . . . according to my chart. . . .''

Ed Huggin snorted. ''Chart! Washington chart copies London chart and London chart I think must copy the original *chart* made by old Captain Cook. *Chart!*'' He snorted again.

Mr. Florian Blossom asked, softly, "Do you recognize your landfall, Mr. Limekiller? I suppose it would not be at the cape itself, which is pure mangrove bog and does not fit the description which you gave us. . . ."

Mr. Limekiller's eyes hugged the coast. Suppose he couldn't *find* the goddamned place? Police and Government wouldn't like that at all. Every ounce of fuel had to be accounted for. Chasing the wild goose was not approved. He might find an extension of his stay refused when next he went applying for it. He might even find himself officially listed as a Proscribed Person, trans.: haul-ass, Jack, and don't try coming back. And he realized that he did not want that at all, at all. The whole coast looked the same to him, all of a sudden. And then, all of a sudden, it didn't . . . somehow. There was something about that solid-seeming mass of bush—

"I think there may be a creek. Right there."

Harlow nodded. "Yes, mon. Is a creek. Right dere."

And right there, at the mouth of the creek—in this instance, meaning, not a stream, but an inlet—Limekiller recognized the huge tree. And Harlow the Hunter recognized something else. "Dot mark suppose to be where Mr. Limekiller drah up the skiff."

"Best we ahl put boots *on*," said Sergeant Ruiz, who had said not a word until now. They all put boots on. Harlow shouldered an axe. Ruiz and Huggin took up machetes. Dr. Rafael had, besides his medical bag, a bundle of what appeared to be plastic sheets and crocus sacks. "You doesn't mind to cahry ah shovel, Mr. Jock?" Jack decided that he could think of a number of things he had rather carry: but he took the thing. And Mr. Blossom carefully picked up an enormous camera, with tripod. The Governments of His and/or Her Majesties had never been known for throwing money around in these parts; the camera could hardly have dated back to George III but was certainly earlier than the latter part of the reign of George V.

"You must lead us, Mr. Limekiller." The District Commissioner was not grim. He was not smiling. He was grave.

Limekiller nodded. Climbed over the sprawling trunk of the tree. Suddenly remembered that it had been night when he had first come this way, that it had been from the other direction that he had made his way the next morning, hesitated. And then Harlow the Hunter spoke up.

"Eef you please, Mistah Blossom. I believes I knows dees pahth bet-tah.''

And, at any rate, he knew it well enough to lead them there in less time, surely, than Jack Limekiller could have.

Blood was no longer fresh and red, but a hundred swarms of flies suddenly rose to show where the blood had been. Doctor Rafael snipped leaves, scooped up soil, deposited his take in containers.

And in regard to other evidence, whatever it was evidence of, for one thing, Mr. Blossom handed the camera over to Police-Corporal Huggin, who set up his measuring tape, first along one deep depression and photographed it; then along another . . . another . . . another. . . .

"Mountain-cow," said the District Commissioner. He did not sound utterly persuaded.

Harlow shook his head. "No, Mistah Florian. No sah. No, no."

"Well, if not a tapir: what?"

Harlow shrugged.

Something heavy had been dragged through the bush. And it had been dragged by something heavier . . . something much, much heavier. . . . It was horridly hot in the bush, and every kind of "fly" seemed to be ready and waiting for them: sand-fly, bottle fly, doctor-fly. They made unavoidable noise, but whenever they stopped, the silence closed in on them. No wild parrot shrieked. No "baboons" rottled or growled. No warree grunted or squealed. Just the waiting silence of the bush. Not friendly. Not hostile. Just indifferent.

And when they came to the little river (afterwards, Jack could not even find it on the maps) and scanned the opposite bank and saw nothing, the District Commissioner said, "Well, Harlow. What you think?"

The wiry little man looked up and around. After a moment he nodded, plunged into the bush. A faint sound, as of someone—or of something?—Then Ed Huggin pointed. Limekiller would never even have noticed that particular tree was there; indeed, he was able to pick it out now only because a small figure was slowly but surely climbing it. The tree was tall, and it leaned at an angle—old enough to have experienced the brute force of a hurricane, strong enough to have survived, though bent.

Harlow called something Jack did not understand, but he

followed the others, splashing down the shallows of the
river. The river slowly became a swamp. Harlow was suddenly next to them. "Eet not fah," he muttered.

Nor was it.

What there was of it.

An eye in a monstrously swollen head winked at them.
Then an insect leisurely crawled out, flapped its horridly-
damp wings in the hot and humid air, and sluggishly flew
off. There was no wink. There was no eye.

"Mr. Limekiller," said District Commissioner Blossom,
"I will now ask you if you identify this body as that of the
man known to you as John Samuel."

"It's him. Yes sir."

It was as though the commissioner had been holding his
breath and had now released it. "Well, well," he said.
"And he was supposed to have gone to Jamaica and died
there. I never heard he'd come back. Well, he is dead now,
for true."

But little Doctor Rafael shook his snowy head. "He is
certainly dead. And he is certainly not John Samuel."

"Why—" Limekiller swallowed bile, pointed. "Look.
The eye is missing, John Samuel lost that eye when the tree
fell—"

"Ah, yes, young man. John Samuel did. *But not that
eye.*"

The bush was not so silent now. Every time the masses
and masses of flies were waved away, they rose, buzzing,
into the heavy, squalid air. Buzzing, hovered. Buzzing, returned.

"Then who in the Hell—?"

Harlow wiped his face on his sleeve. "Well, sah. I cahn
tell you. Lord hahv mercy on heem. Eet ees Bob Blaine."

There was a long outdrawn *ahhh* from the others. Then
Ed Huggin said, "But Bob Blaine had both his eyes."

Harlow stopped, picked a stone from the river bed, with
dripping hand threw it into the bush . . . one would have
said, at random. With an ugly croak, a buzzard burst up and
away. Then Harlow said something, as true—and as dreadful—as it was unarguable. "He not hahv either of them,
noew."

By what misadventure and in what place Bob Blaine had
lost one eye whilst alive and after decamping from his native

land, no one knew: and perhaps it did not matter. He had trusted on "discretion" not to reveal his hideout, there at the site of his old bush-camp. But he had not trusted to it one hundred percent. Suppose that Limekiller were deceitfully or accidently, to let drop the fact that a man was camping out there. A man with only one eye. What was the man's name? John Samuel. What? John *Samuel.* . . . Ah. Then John Samuel had not, after all, died in Jamaica, according to report. Report had been known to be wrong before. John Samuel alive, then. No big thing. Nobody then would have been moved to go down there to check up. Nobody, now, knew why Bob Blaine had returned. Perhaps he had made things too hot for himself, down in "republican waters"— where hot water could be so very much hotter than back here. Perhaps some day a report would drift back up, and it might be a true report or it might be false or it might be a mixture of both.

As for the report, the official, Government one, on the circumstances surrounding the death of Roberto Blaine, a.k.a. Bob Blaine . . . as for Limekiller's statement and the statements of the District Commissioner and the District Medical Officer and the autopsy and the photographs: why, that had all been neatly transcribed and neatly (and literally) laced with red tape, and forwarded up the coast to King Town. And as to what happened to it there—

"What do you think they will do about it, Doctor?"

Rafael's rooms were larger, perhaps, than a bachelor needed. But they were the official quarters for the DMO, and so the DMO lived in them. The wide floors gleamed with polish. The spotless walls showed, here a shield, there a paddle, a harpoon with barbed head, the carapace of a huge turtle, a few paintings. The symmetry and conventionality of it was slightly marred by the bookcases which were everywhere, against every wall, adjacent to desk and chairs. And all were full, crammed, overflowing.

Doctor Rafael shrugged. "Perhaps the woodlice will eat the papers," he said. "Or the roaches, or the *wee-wee* ants. The mildew. The damp. Hurricane. . . . This is not a climate which helps preserve the history of men. I work hard to keep my own books and papers from going that way. But I am not Government, and Government lacks time and money and personnel, and . . . perhaps, also . . . Government has so many, many things pressing upon it. . . . Perhaps, too, Government lacks interest.''

"What were those tracks, Doctor Rafael?''

Doctor Rafael shrugged.

"You do know, don't you?''

Doctor Rafael grimaced.

"Have you seen them, or anything like them, before?''

Doctor Rafael, very slowly, very slowly nodded.

"Well . . . for God's sake . . . can you even give me a, well a *hint?* I mean: that was a rather rotten experience for me, you know. And—''

The sunlight, kept at bay outside, broke in through a crack in the jalousies, sun making the scant white hair for an instant ablaze: like the brow of Moses. Doctor Rafael got up and busied himself with a fresh lime and the sweetened lime juice and the gin and ice. He was rapt in this task, like an ancient apothecary mingling strange unguents and syrups. Then he gave one of the gimlets to his guest and from one he took a long, long pull.

"You see. I have two years to go before my retirement. The pension, well, it is not spectacular, but I have no complaint. I will be able to rest. Not for an hour, or an evening . . . an evening! only on my holidays, once a year, do I even have an evening all my own! Well. You may imagine how I look forward. And I am not going to risk premature and enforced retirement by presenting Government with an impossible situation. One which wouldn't be its fault, anyway. By insisting on impossible things. By demonstrating—''

He finished his drink. He gave Jack a long, shrewd look.

"So I have nothing more to say . . . about *that*. If they want to believe, up in King Town, that the abominable Bob Blaine was mauled by a crocodile, let them. If they prefer to make it a jaguar or even a tapir, why, that is fine with Robert Rafael, M.D., DMO. It might be, probably, the first time in history that anybody anywhere was killed by a tapir, but that is not my affair. The matter is, so far as I am concerned, so far—in fact—as *you* and I are concerned—over.

"Do you understand?''

Limekiller nodded. At once the older man's manner changed. "I have many, many books, as you can see. Maybe some of them would be of interest to you. Pick any one you like. Pick one at random.'' So saying, he took a book from his desk and put it in Jack's hands. It was just a book-looking book. It was, in fact, volume II of the Everyman edition of Plutarch's Lives. There was a wide card, of the kind on which medical notes or records are sometimes made, and so Jack Limekiller opened the book at that place.

seasons, as the gods sent them, seemed natural to him. The Greeks that inhabited Asia were very much pleased to see the great lords and governors of Persia, with all the pride, cruelty, and

"Well, now, what the Hell," he muttered. The card slipped, he clutched. He glanced at it. He put down vol. II of the Lives and he sat back and read the notes on the card.

It is in the nature of things [they began] for men, in a new country and faced with new things, to name them after old, familiar things. Even when resemblance unlikely. Example: *Mountain-cow* for tapir. ('Tapir' from Tupi Indian *tapira*, big beast.) Example: Mawmee-*apple* not apple at all. Ex.: *Sea-cow* for manatee. Early British settlers not entomologists. Quest.: Whence word *manatee?* From Carib? Perhaps. After the British, what other people came to this corner of the world? Ans.: Black people. Calabars, Ashantee, Mantee, Mandingo. Re last two names. Related peoples. Named after totemic animal. *Also,* not likely? *likely*—named unfamiliar animals after familiar (i.e., familiar in Africa) animals. Mantee, Mandee-hippo. Refer legend

Limekiller's mouth fell open. "Oh, my God!" he groaned. In his ear now, he heard the old, old, quavering voice of Captain Cudgel (once Cudjoe): *"Mon, een Ahfrica, de mon-ah-tee hahv leg, I tell you. Een Ahfrica eet be ah powerful beast, come up on de lond, I tell you . . . de w'ol' people, dey tell me so, fah true . . ."*

He heard the old voice, repeating the old words, no longer even half-understood: but, in some measure, at least half-true.

Refer legend of were-animals, universal. Were-wolf, were-tiger, were-shark, were-dolphin. Quest.: Were-manatee?

"Mon-ah-tee ees hahlf ah mon . . . hahv teats like a womahn . . . Dere ees wahn mon, mehk mellow weet mon-ah-tee, hahv pickney by mon-ah-tee . . ."

And he heard another voice saying, not only once, saying, *"Mon, eef you tie ah rottlesnake doewn fah me. I weel freeg eet . . ."*

He thought of the wretched captives in the Spanish slave-ship, set free to fend for themselves in a bush by far wilder than the one left behind. Few, to begin with, fewer as time went on; marrying and intermarrying, no new blood, no new thoughts. And, finally, the one road in to them, destroyed. Left alone. Left quite alone. Or . . . almost . . .

He shuddered.

How desperate for refuge must Blaine have been, to have sought to hide himself anywhere near Cape Mantee—

And what miserable happenstance had brought he himself, Jack Limekiller, to improvise on that old song that dreadful night? —And what had he called up out of the darkness . . . out of the bush . . . out of the mindless present which was the past and future and the timeless tropical forever? . . .

There was something pressing gently against his finger, something on the other side of the card. He turned it over. A clipping from a magazine had been roughly pasted there.

Valentry has pointed out that, despite a seeming resemblance to such aquatic mammals as seals and walrus, the manatee is actually more closely related anatomically to the elephant.

. . . out of the bush . . . out of the darkness . . . out of the mindless present which was also the past and the timeless tropical forever . . .

"They are like elephants. They never forget."

"Ukh," he said, though clenched teeth. "My God, Uff. Jesus . . .

The card was suddenly, swiftly, snatched from his hands. He looked up still in a state of shock, to see Doctor Rafael tearing it into pieces.

"Doña 'Sana!"

A moment. Then the house-keeper, old, all in white. "Doctór?"

"Burn this."

A moment passed. Just the two of them again. Then Rafael, in a tone which was nothing but kindly, said, "Jack, you are still young and you are still healthy. My advice to you: Go away. Go to a cooler climate. One with cooler ways

and cooler memories.'' The old woman called something
from the back of the house. The old man sighed. "It is the
summons to supper," he said. "Not only must I eat in haste
because I have my clinic in less than half-an-hour, but
suddenly-invited guests make Dona 'Saña very nervous.
Good night, then, Jack.''

Jack had had two gin drinks. He felt that he needed two
more. At least two more. Or, if not gin, rum. Beer would
not do. He wanted to pull the blanket of booze over him,
awfully, awfully quickly. He had this in his mind as though
it were a vow as he walked up the front street towards the
Cupid Club.

Someone hailed him, someone out of the gathering dusk.

"Jock! Hey, mon, Jock! Hey, b'y! Where you gweyn so
fahst? Bide, b'y, bide a bit!''

The voice was familiar. It was that of Harry Hazeed, his
principal creditor in King Town. Ah, well. He had had his
chance, Limekiller had. He could have gone on down the
coast, down into the republican waters, where the Queen's
writ runneth not. Now it was too late.

"Oh, hello, Harry," he said, dully.

Hazeed took him by the hand. Took him by both hands.
"Mon, show me where is your boat? She serviceable? She
is? Good: Mon, you don't hear de news: Welcome's ware-
house take fire and born up! Yes, mon. Ahl de carn in King
Town born up! No carn ah-tahl: No tortilla, no empinada,
no tamale, no carn-*cake!* Oh, mon, how de people going to
punish! Soon as I hear de news, I drah me money from de
bonk, I buy ahl de crocus sock I can find, I jump on de
pocket-*boat*—and here I am, oh, mon, I pray fah you . . .
I pray I fine you!''

Limekiller shook his head. It had been one daze, one
shock after another. The only thing clear was that Harry
Hazeed didn't seem angry. "You no understond?" Hazeed
cried. "Mon! We going take your boat, we going doewn to
Nutmeg P'int, we going to buy carn, mon! We going to buy
ahl de carn dere is to buy! Nevah mine dat lee' bit money
you di owe me, b'y! We going to make plenty money, mon!
And we going make de cultivators plenty money, too! What
you theenk of eet, Jock, me b'y? Eh? Hey? What you
theenk?''

Jack put his forefinger in his mouth, held it up. The wind
was in the right quarter. The wind would, if it held up, and,

somehow, it felt like a wind which would hold up, the wind would carry them straight and clear to Nutmeg Point: the clear, clean wind in the clear and starry night.

Softly, he said—and, old Hazeed leaning closer to make the words out, Limekiller said them again, louder, ''I think it's great. Just great. I think it's great.''

TRAPALANDA

by Charles Sheffield

One of the best contemporary "hard science" writers, British-born Charles Sheffield is a theoretical physicist who has worked on the American space program, and is currently chief scientist of the Earth Satellite Corporation. Sheffield is also the only person who has ever served as president of both the American Astronautical Society and the Science Fiction Writers of America. His books include the bestselling nonfiction title Earthwatch, *the novels* Sight of Proteus, The Web Between the Worlds, Hidden Variables, My Brother's Keeper, Between the Strokes of Night, The Nimrod Hunt, Trader's World, Proteus Unbound, Summertide, *and* Divergence, *and the collections* Erasmus Magister *and* The McAndrew Chronicles. *His most recent books are the novels* Transcendence, Cold as Ice, *and* Brother To Dragons. *Upcoming are a new novel,* The Mind Pool, *and a collection,* Dancing With Myself. *He lives in Bethesda, Maryland.*

Here he takes us to the wild border country between Chile and Argentina, to the wind-swept barrens of Patagonia, for an encounter with a very strange and frightening Object— one that will forever change the lives of those who come in contact with it.

John Kenyon Martindale seldom did things the usual way. Until a first-class return air ticket and a check for $10,000 arrived at my home in Lausanne I did not know he existed. The enclosed note said only: "For consulting services of Klaus Jacobi in New York, June 6–7." It was typed on his letterhead and initialed, JKM. The check was drawn on the Riggs Bank of Washington, D.C. The tickets were for Geneva–New York on June 5, with an open return.

I did not need work. I did not need money. I had no particular interest in New York, and a trans-Atlantic telephone call to John Kenyon Martindale revealed only that he was out of town until June 5. Why would I bother with him? It is easy to forget what killed the cat.

The limousine that met me at Kennedy Airport drove to a stone mansion on the East River, with a garden that went right down to the water's edge. An old woman with the nose, chin, and hairy moles of a storybook witch opened the door. She took me upstairs to the fourth floor, while my baggage disappeared under the house with the limousine. The mansion was amazingly quiet. The elevator made no noise at all, and when we stepped out of it the deeply carpeted floors of the corridor were matched by walls thick with oriental tapestries. I was not used to so much silence. When I was ushered into a long, shadowed conservatory filled with flowering plants and found myself in the presence of a man and woman, I wanted to shout. Instead I stared.

Shirley Martindale was a brunette, with black hair, thick eyebrows, and a flawless, creamy skin. She was no more than five feet three, but full-figured and strongly built. In normal company she would have been a center of attention; with John Kenyon Martindale present, she was ignored.

He was of medium height and slender build, with a wide, smiling mouth. His hair was thin and wheat-colored, combed straight back from his face. Any other expression he might have had was invisible. From an inch below his eyes to two inches above them, a flat, black shield extended across his whole face. Within that curved strip of darkness colored shadows moved, little darting points and glints of light that flared red and green and electric blue. They were hypnotic, moving in patterns that could be followed but never quite predicted, and they drew and held the attention. They were so striking that it took me a few moments to realize that John Kenyon Martindale must be blind.

He did not act like a person without sight. When I came into the room he at once came forward and confidently shook my hand. His grip was firm, and surprisingly strong for so slight a man.

"A long trip," he said, when the introductions were complete. "May I offer a little refreshment?"

Although the witch was still standing in the room, waiting, he mixed the drinks himself, cracking ice, selecting bottles, and pouring the correct measures slowly but without error. When he handed a glass to me and smilingly said

"There! How's that?" I glanced at Shirley Martindale and replied, "It's fine; but before we start the toasts I'd like to learn what we are toasting. Why am I here?"

"No messing about, eh? You are very direct. Very Swiss—even though you are not one." He turned his head to his wife, and the little lights twinkled behind the black mask. "What did I tell you, Shirley? This is the man." And then to me. "You are here to make a million dollars. Is that enough reason?"

"No. Mr. Martindale, it is not. It was not money that brought me here. I have enough money."

"Then perhaps you are here to become a Swiss citizen. Is that a better offer?"

"Yes. If you can pay in advance." Already I had an idea what John Martindale wanted of me. I am not psychic, but I can read and see. The inner wall of the conservatory was papered with maps of South America.

"Let us say, I will pay half in advance. You will receive five hundred thousand dollars in your account before we leave. The remainder, and the Swiss citizenship papers, will be waiting when we return from Patagonia."

"We? Who are 'we'?"

"You and I. Other guides if you need them. We will be going through difficult country, though I understand that you know it better than anyone."

I looked at Shirley Martindale, and she shook her head decisively. "Not me, Klaus. Not for one million dollars, not for ten million dollars. This is all John's baby."

"Then my answer must be no." I sipped the best pisco sour I had tasted since I was last in Peru, and wondered where he had learned the technique. "Mr. Martindale, I retired four years ago to Switzerland. Since then I have not set foot in Argentina, even though I still carry those citizenship papers. If you want someone to lead you through the *echter Rand* of Patagonia, there must now be a dozen others more qualified than I. But that is beside the point. Even when I was in my best condition, even when I was so young and cocky that I thought nothing could kill me or touch me—even then I would have refused to lead a blind man to the high places that you display on your walls. With your wife's presence and her assistance to you for personal matters, it might barely be possible. Without her—have you any idea at all what conditions are like there?"

"Better than most people." He leaned forward. "Mr. Jacobi, let us perform a little test. Take something from your pocket, and hold it up in front of you. Something that should be completely unfamiliar to me."

I hate games, and this smacked of one; but there was something infinitely persuasive about that thin, smiling man. What did I have in my pocket? I reached in, felt my wallet, and slipped out a photograph. I did not look at it, and I was not sure myself what I had selected. I held it between thumb and forefinger, a few feet away from Martindale's intent face.

"Hold it very steady," he said. Then, while the points of light twinkled and shivered, "It is a picture, a photograph of a woman. It is your assistant, Helga Korein. Correct?"

I turned it to me. It was a portrait of Helga, smiling into the camera. "You apparently know far more about me than I know of you. However, you are not quite correct. It is a picture of my wife, Helga Jacobi. I married her four years ago, when I retired. You are not blind?"

"Legally, I am completely blind and have been since my twenty-second year, when I was foolish enough to drive a racing car into a retaining wall." Martindale tapped the black shield. "Without this, I can see nothing. With it, I am neither blind nor seeing. I receive charge-coupled diode inputs directly to my optic nerves, and I interpret them. I see neither at the wavelengths nor with the resolution provided by the human eye, nor is what I reconstruct anything like the images that I remember from the time before I became blind; but I see. On another occasion I will be happy to tell you all that I know about the technology. What you need to know tonight is that I will be able to pull my own weight on any journey. I can give you that assurance. And now I ask again: will you do it?"

It was, of course, curiosity that killed the cat. Martindale had given me almost no information as to where he wanted to go, or when, or why. But something was driving John Martindale, and I wanted to hear what it was.

I nodded my head, convinced now that he would see my movement. "We certainly need to talk in detail; but for the moment let us use that fine old legal phrase, and say there is agreement in principle."

There is agreement in principle. With that sentence, I destroyed my life.

Shirley Martindale came to my room last night. I was not surprised. John Martindale's surrogate vision was a miracle of technology, but it had certain limitations. The device could not resolve the fleeting look in a woman's eye, or the millimeter jut to a lower lip. I had caught the signal in the first minute.

We did not speak until it was done and we were lying side by side in my bed. I knew it was not finished. She had not relaxed against me. I waited. "There is more than he told you," she said at last.

I nodded. "There is always more. But he was quite right about that place. I have felt it myself, many times."

As South America narrows from the great equatorial swell of the Amazon Basin, the land becomes colder and more broken. The great spine of the Andean cordillera loses height as one travels south. Ranges that tower to twenty-three thousand feet in the tropics dwindle to a modest twelve thousand. The land is shared between Argentina and Chile, and along their border, beginning with the chill depths of Lago Buenos Aires (sixty miles long, ten miles wide; bigger than anything in Switzerland), a great chain of mountain lakes straddles the frontier, all the way south to Tierra del Fuego and the flowering Chilean city of Puntas Arenas.

For fourteen years, the Argentina-Chile borderland between latitude 46 and 50 South had been my home, roughly from Lago Buenos Aires to Lago Argentina. It had become closer to me than any human, closer even than Helga. The east side of the Andes in this region is a bitter, parched desert, where gale-force winds blow incessantly three hundred and sixty days of the year. They come from the snow-bound slopes of the mountains, freezing whatever they touch. I knew the country and I loved it, but Helga had persuaded me that it was not a land to which a man could retire. The buffeting wind was an endless drain, too much for old blood. Better, she said, to leave in early middle age, when a life elsewhere could still be shaped.

When the time came for us to board the aircraft that would take me away to Buenos Aires and then to Europe, I wanted to throw away my ticket. I am not a sentimental man, but only Helga's presence allowed me to leave the Kingdom of the Winds.

Now John Martindale was tempting me to return there, with more than money. At one end of his conservatory-study stood a massive globe, about six feet across. Presumably it dated from the time before he had acquired his artificial eyes, because it differed from all other globes I had ever seen in one important respect; namely, it was a relief globe. Oceans were all smooth surface, while mountain ranges of the world stood out from the surface of the flattened sphere. The degree of relief had been exaggerated, but everything was in proportion. Himalayan and Karakoram ranges projected a few tenths of an inch more than the Rockies and the Andes, and they in turn were a little higher than the Alps or the volcanic ranges of Indonesia.

When my drink was finished Martindale had walked me across to that globe. He ran his finger down the backbone of the Americas, following the continuous mountain chains from their beginning in Alaska, through the American Rockies, through Central America, and on to the rising Andes and northern Chile. When he finally came to Patagonia his fingers slowed and stopped.

"Here," he said. "It begins here."

His fingertip was resting on an area very familiar to me. It was right on the Argentina–Chile border, with another of the cold mountain lakes at the center of it. I knew the lake as Lago Pueyrredon, but as usual with bodies of water that straddle the border there was a different name–Lago Cochrane–in use on the Chilean side. The little town of Paso Roballo, where I had spent a dozen nights in a dozen years, lay just to the northeast.

If I closed my eyes I could see the whole landscape that lay beneath his finger. To the east it was dry and dusty, sustaining only thornbush and tough grasses on the dark surface of old volcanic flows; westward were the tall flowering grasses and the thicketed forests of redwood, cypress, and Antarctic beech. Even in the springtime of late November there would be snow on the higher ground, with snow-fed lake waters lying black as jet under a Prussian-blue sky.

I could see all this, but it seemed impossible that John Martindale could do so. His blind skull must hold a different vision.

"*What* begins here?" I asked, and wondered again how

much he could receive through those arrays of inorganic crystal.

"The anomalies. This region has weather patterns that defy all logic and all models."

"I agree with that, from personal experience. That area has the most curious pattern of winds of any place in the world." It had been a long flight and a long day, and by this time I was feeling a little weary. I was ready to defer discussion of the weather until tomorrow, and I wanted time to reflect on our "agreement in principle." I continued, "However, I do not see why those winds should interest you."

"I am a meteorologist. Now wait a moment." His sensor array must have caught something of my expression. "Do not jump to a wrong conclusion. Mine was a perfect profession for a blind man. Who can see the weather? I was ten times as sensitive as a sighted person to winds, to warmth, to changes in humidity and barometric pressure. What I could not see was cloud formations, and those are consequences rather than causes. I could deduce their appearance from other variables. Eight years ago I began to develop my own computer models of weather patterns, analyzing the interaction of snow, winds, and topography. Five years ago I believed that my method was completely general, and completely accurate. Then I studied the Andean system; and in one area—only one—it failed." He tapped the globe. "Here. Here there are winds with no sustaining source of energy. I can define a circulation pattern and locate a vortex, but I cannot account for its existence."

"The area you show is known locally as the Kingdom of the Winds."

"I know. I want to go there."

And so did I.

When he spoke I felt a great longing to return, to see again the *altiplano* of the eastern Andean slopes and hear the banshee music of the western wind. It was all behind me. I had sworn to myself that Argentina existed only in my past, that the Patagonian spell was broken forever. John Martindale was giving me a million dollars and Swiss citizenship, but more than that he was giving me an *excuse*. For four years I had been unconsciously searching for one.

I held out my glass. "I think, Mr. Martindale, that I would like another drink."

Or two. Or three.

Shirley Martindale was moving by my side now, running her hand restlessly along my arm. "There is more. He wants to understand the winds, but there is more. He hopes to find Trapalanda."

She did not ask me if I had heard of it. No one who spends more than a week in central Patagonia can be ignorant of Trapalanda. For three hundred years, explorers have searched for the "City of the Caesars," *Trapalanda*, the Patagonian version of El Dorado. Rumor and speculation said that Trapalanda would be found at about 47 degrees South, at the same latitude as Paso Roballo. Its fabled treasure-houses of gold and gemstones had drawn hundreds of men to their death in the high Andes. People did not come back, and say, "I sought Trapalanda, and I failed to find it." They did not come back at all. I was an exception.

"I am disappointed," I said. "I had thought your husband to be a wiser man."

"What do you mean?"

"Everyone wants to find Trapalanda. Four years of my life went into the search for it, and I had the best equipment and the best knowledge. I told your husband that there were a dozen better guides, but I was lying. I know that country better than any man alive. He is certain to fail."

"He believes that he has special knowledge. And you are going to do it. You are going to take him there. For Trapalanda."

She knew better than I. Until she spoke, I did not know what I would do. But she was right. Forget the "agreement in principle." I would go.

"You want me to do it, don't you?" I said. "But I do not understand *your* reasons. You are married to a very wealthy man. He seems to have as much money as he can ever spend."

"John is curious, always curious. He is like a little boy. He is not doing this for money. He does not care about money."

She had not answered my implied question. I had never asked for John Kenyon Martindale's motives, I had been looking for *her* reasons why he should go. Then it occurred to me that her presence, here in my bed, told me all I needed to know. He would go to the Kingdom of the Winds. If he found what he was looking for, it would bring enormous wealth. Should he fail to return, Shirley Martindale would be a free and very wealthy widow.

"Sex with your husband is not good?" I asked.

"What do you think? I am here, am I not?" Then she relented. "It is worse than not good, it is terrible. It is as bad with him as it is exciting with you. John is a gentle, thoughtful man, but I need someone who takes me and does not ask or explain. You are a strong man, and I suspect that you are a cold, selfish man. Since we have been together, you have not once spoken my name, or said a single word of affection. You do not feel it is necessary to pretend to commitments. And you are sexist. I noticed John's reaction when you said, 'I married Helga.' He would always say it differently, perhaps 'Shirley and I got married.' " Her hands moved from my arm, and were touching me more intimately. She sighed. "I do not mind your attitude. What John finds hard to stand, I *need*. You saw what you did to me here, without one word. You make me shiver."

I turned to bring our bodies into full contact. "And John?" I said. "Why did he marry you?" There was no need to ask why she had married him.

"What do you think," she said. "Was it my wit, my looks, my charm? Give me your hand." She gently moved my fingers along her face and breasts. "It was five years ago. John was still blind. We met, and when we said good-night he felt my cheek." Her voice was bitter. "He married me for my pelt."

The texture was astonishing. I could feel no roughness, no blemish, not even the most delicate of hairs. Shirley Martindale had the warm, flawless skin of a six-month-old baby. It was growing warm under my touch.

Before we began she raised herself high above me, propping herself on straight arms. "Helga. What is she like? I cannot imagine her."

"You will see," I said. "Tomorrow I will telephone Lausanne and tell her to come to New York. She will go with us to Trapalanda."

Trapalanda. Had I said that? I was very tired, I had meant to say Patagonia.

I reached up to touch her breasts. "No talk now," I said. "No more talk." Her eyes were as black as jet, as dark as mountain lakes. I dived into their depths.

* * *

Shirley Martindale did not meet Helga; not in New York, not anywhere, not ever. John Kenyon Martindale made his position clear to me the next morning as we walked together around the seventh floor library. "I won't allow her to stay in this house," he said. "It's not for my sake or yours, and certainly not for Shirley's. It is for her sake. I know how Shirley would treat her."

He did not seem at all annoyed, but I stared at the blind black mask and revised my ideas about how much he could see with his CCD's and fiber optic bundles.

"Did she tell you last night why I am going to Patagonia?" he asked, as he picked out a book and placed it in the hopper of an iron pot-bellied stove with electronic aspirations.

I hesitated, and told the truth. "She said you were seeking Trapalanda."

He laughed. "I wanted to go to Patagonia. The easiest way to do it without an argument from Shirley was to hold out a fifty billion dollar bait. The odd thing, though, is that she is quite right. I am seeking Trapalanda." And he laughed again, more heartily than anything he had said would justify.

The black machine in front of us made a little purr of contentment, and a pleasant woman's voice began to read aloud. It was a mathematics text on the foundations of geometry. I had noticed that although Martindale described himself as a meteorologist, four-fifths of the books in the library were mathematics and theoretical physics. There were too many things about John Martindale that were not what they seemed.

"Shirley's voice," he said, while we stood by the machine and listened to a mystifying definition of the intrinsic curvature of a surface. "And a very pleasant voice, don't you think, to have whispering sweet epsilons in your ear? I borrowed it for use with this optical character recognition equipment, before I got my eyes."

"I didn't think there was a machine in the world that could do that."

"Oh, yes." He switched it off, and Shirley halted in midword. "This isn't even state-of-the-art any more. It was, when it was made, and it cost the earth. Next year it will be an antique, and they'll give this much capability out in cereal packets. Come on, let's go and join Shirley for a pre-lunch aperitif.''

If John Martindale were angry with me or with his wife, he concealed it well. I realized that the mask extended well beyond the black casing.

Five days later we flew to Argentina. When Martindale mentioned his idea of being in the Kingdom of the Winds in time for the winter solstice, season of the anomaly's strongest showing, I dropped any thoughts of a trip back to Lausanne. I arranged for Helga to pack what I needed and meet us in Buenos Aires. She would wait at Ezeiza Airport without going into the city proper, and we would fly farther south at once. Even if our travels went well, we would need luck as well as efficiency to have a week near Paso Roballo before solstice.

It amused me to see Martindale searching for Helga in the airport arrival lounge as we walked off the plane. He had seen her photograph, and I assured him that she would be there. He could not find her. Within seconds, long before it was possible to see her features, I had picked her out. She was staring down at a book on her lap. Every fifteen seconds her head lifted for a rapid radar-like scan of the passenger lounge, and returned to the page. Martindale did not notice her until we were at her side.

I introduced them. Helga nodded but did not speak. She stood up and led the way. She had rented a four-seater plane on open charter, and in her usual efficient way she had arranged for our luggage to be transferred to it.

Customs clearance, you ask? Let us be realistic. The Customs Office in Argentina is no more corrupt than that of, say, Bolivia or Ecuador; that is quite sufficient. Should John Martindale be successful in divining the legendary treasures of Trapalanda, plenty of hands would help to remove them illegally from the country.

Helga led the way through the airport. She was apparently not what he had expected of my wife, and I could see him studying her closely. Helga stood no more than five feet two, to my six-two, and her thin body was not quite straight. Her left shoulder dipped a bit, and she favored her left leg a trifle as she walked.

Since I was the only one with a pilot's license I sat forward in the copilot's chair, next to Owen Davies. I had used Owen before as a by-the-day hired pilot. He knew the King-

dom of the Winds, and he respected it. He would not take
risks. In spite of his name he was Argentina born—one of
the many Welshmen who found almost any job preferable
to their parents' Argentinian sheep-farming. Martindale and
Helga sat behind us, side-by-side in the back, as we flew to
Comodora Rivadavia on the Atlantic coast. It was the last
real airfield we would see for a while unless we dipped
across the Chilean border to Cochrane. I preferred not to
try that. In the old days, you risked a few machine-gun
bullets from frontier posts. Today it is likely to be a surface-
to-air missile.

We would complete our supplies in Comodoro Rivadavia,
then use dry dirt airstrips the rest of the way. The provisions
were supposed to be waiting for us. While Helga and Owen
were checking to make sure that the delivery included everything we had ordered, Martindale came up to my side.

"Does she never talk?" he said. "Or is it just my lack
of charm?" He did not sound annoyed, merely puzzled.

"Give her time." I looked to see what Owen and Helga
were doing. They were pointing at three open chests of supplies, and Owen was becoming rather loud.

"You noticed how Helga walks, and how she holds her
left arm?"

The black shield dipped down and up, making me suddenly curious as to what lay behind it. "I even tried to hint
at a question in that direction," he said. "Quite properly
she ignored it."

"She was not born that way. When Helga walked into my
office nine years ago, I assumed that I was looking at some
congenital condition. She said nothing, nor did I. I was
looking for an assistant, someone who was as interested in
the high border country as I was, and Helga fitted. She was
only twenty-one years old and still green, but I could tell
she was intelligent and trainable."

"Biddable," said Martindale. "Sorry, go on."

"You have to be fit to wander around in freezing temperatures at ten thousand feet," I said. "As part of Helga's
condition of employment, she had to take a full physical.
She didn't want to. She agreed only when she saw that the
job depended on it. She was in excellent shape and passed
easily; but the doctor—quite improperly—allowed me to
look at her X-rays."

Were the eyebrows raised, behind that obsidian visor?

Martindale cocked his head to the right, a small gesture of inquiry. Helga and Owen Davies were walking our way.

"She was put together like a jigsaw puzzle. Almost every bone in her arms and legs showed marks of fracture and healing. Her ribs, too. When she was small she had been what these enlightened times call 'abused.' Tortured. As a very small child, Helga learned to keep quiet. The best thing she could hope for was to be ignored. You saw already how invisible she can be."

"I have never heard you angry before," he said. "You sound like her father, not her husband." His tone was calm, but something new hid behind that mask. "And is that," he continued, "why in New York—"

He was interrupted. "Tomorrow," said Owen from behind him. "He says he'll have the rest then. I believe him. I told him he's a fat idle bastard, and if we weren't on our way by noon I'd personally kick the shit out of him."

Martindale nodded at me. Conversation closed. We headed into town for Alberto McShane's bar and the uncertain pleasures of nightlife in Comodoro Rivadavia. Martindale didn't give up. All the way there he talked quietly to Helga. He may have received ten words in return.

It had been five years. Alberto McShane didn't blink when we walked in. He took my order without comment, but when Helga walked past him he reached out his good arm and gave her a big hug. She smiled like the sun. She was home. She had hung around the *Guanaco* bar since she was twelve years old, an oil brat brought here in the boom years. When her parents left, she stayed. She hid among the beer barrels in McShane's cellar until the plane took off. Then she could relax for the first time in her life. Poverty and hard work were luxury after what she had been through.

The decor of the bar hadn't changed since last time. The bottle of dirty black oil (the first one pumped at Comodoro Rivadavia, if you believe McShane) hung over the bar, and the same stuffed guanaco and rhea stood beside it. McShane's pet armadillo, or its grandson, ambled among the tables looking for beer heel-taps.

I knew our search plans, but Helga and Owen Davies needed briefing. Martindale took Owen's 1:1,000,000 scale ONC's, with their emendations and local detail in Owen's careful hand, added to them the 1:250,000 color photomaps that had been made for him in the United States, and spread the collection out to cover the whole table.

"From here, to here," he said. His fingers tapped the map near Laguna del Sello, then moved south and west until they reached Lago Belgrano.

Owen studied them for a few moments. "All on this side of the border," he said. "That's good. What do you want to do there?"

"I want to land. Here, and here, and here." Martindale indicated seven points, on a roughly north-south line.

Owen Davies squinted down, assessing each location. "Lago Gio, Paso Roballo, Lago Posadas. Know 'em all. Tough landing at two, and that last point is in the middle of the Perito Moreno National Park; but we can find a place." He looked up, not at Martindale but at me. "You're not in the true high country, though. You're twenty miles too far east. What do you want to do when you get there?"

"I want to get out, and look west," said Martindale. "After that, I'll tell you where we have to go."

Owen Davies said nothing more, but when we were at the bar picking up more drinks he gave me a shrug. *Too far east*, it said. *You're not in the high country. You won't find Trapalanda there, where he's proposing to land. What's the story?*

Owen was an honest man and a great pilot, who had made his own failed attempt at Trapalanda (sometimes I thought that was true of everyone who lived below 46 degrees South). He found it hard to believe that anyone could succeed where he had not, but he couldn't resist the lure.

"He knows something he's not telling us," I said. "He's keeping information to himself. Wouldn't you?"

Owen nodded. Barrels of star rubies and tons of platinum and gold bars shone in his dark Welsh eyes.

When he returned to the table John Martindale had made his breakthrough. Helga was talking and bubbling with laughter. "How did you *do* that," she was saying. "He's untouchable. What did you *do* to him?" McShane's armadillo was sitting on top of the table, chewing happily at a piece of apple. Martindale was rubbing the ruffle of horny plates behind its neck, and the armadillo was pushing itself against his hand.

"He thinks I'm one of them." Martindale touched the black screen across his eyes. "See? We've both got plates.

I'm just one of the family.'' His face turned up to me. I read satisfaction behind the mask. *And should I do to your wife, Klaus, what you did to mine?* it said. *It would be no more than justice.*

Those were not Martindale's thoughts. I realized that. They were mine. And that was the moment when my liking for John Kenyon Martindale began to tilt toward resentment.

At ground level, the western winds skim off the Andean slopes at seventy knots or more. At nine thousand feet, they blow at less than thirty. Owen was an economy-minded pilot. He flew west at ten thousand until we were at the preferred landing point, then dropped us to the ground in three sickening sideslips.

He had his landing already planned. Most of Patagonia is built of great level slabs, rising like terraces from the high coastal cliffs on the Atlantic Ocean to the Andean heights in the west. The exception was in the area we were exploring. Volcanic eruptions there have pushed great layers of basalt out onto the surface. The ground is cracked and irregular, and scarred by the scouring of endless winds. It takes special skill to land a plane when the wind speed exceeds the landing air-speed, and Owen Davies had it. We showed an airspeed of over a hundred knots when we touched down, light as a dust mote, and rolled to a perfect landing. ''Good enough,'' said Owen.

He had brought us down on a flat strip of dark lava, at three o'clock in the afternoon. The sun hung low on the northwest horizon, and we stepped out into the teeth of a cold and dust-filled gale. The wind beat and tugged and pushed our bodies, trying to blow us back to the Atlantic. Owen, Helga, and I wore goggles and helmets against the driving clouds of grit and sand.

Martindale was bare-headed. He planted a GPS transponder on the ground to confirm our exact position, and faced west. With his head tilted upward and his straw-colored hair blowing wild, he made an adjustment to the side of his visor, then nodded. ''It is there,'' he said. ''I knew it must be.''

We looked, and saw nothing. ''What is there?'' said Helga.

''I'll tell you in a moment. Note these down. I'm going

to read off heights and headings.'' Martindale looked at the
sun and the compass. He began to turn slowly from north
to south. Every fifteen degrees he stopped, stared at the
featureless sky, and read off a list of numbers. When he was
finished he nodded to Owen. ''All right. We can do the next
one now.''

''You mean that's *it? The whole thing?* All you're going
to do is stand there?'' Owen is many good things, but he is
not diplomatic.

''That's it—for the moment.'' Martindale led the way
back to the aircraft.

I could not follow. Not at once. I had lifted my goggles
and was peering with wind-teared eyes to the west. The land
there fell upward to the dark-blue twilight sky. It was the
surge of the Andes, less than twenty miles away, rolling up
in long, snow-capped breakers. I walked across the tufts of
bunch grass and reached out a hand to steady myself on an
isolated ten-foot beech tree. Wind-shaped and stunted it
stood, trunk and branches curved to the east, hiding its head
from the deadly western wind. It was the only one within
sight.

This was my Patagonia, the true, the terrible.

I felt a gentle touch on my arm. Helga stood there, waiting. I patted her hand in reply, and she instinctively re-
coiled. Together we followed Martindale and Davies back
to the aircraft.

''I found what I was looking for,'' Martindale said, when
we were all safely inside. The gale buffeted and rocked the
craft, resenting our presence. ''It's no secret now. When
the winds approach the Andes from the Chilean side, they
shed all the moisture they have picked up over the Pacific;
and they accelerate. The energy balance equation is the same
everywhere in the world. It depends on terrain, moisture,
heating, and atmospheric layers. The same equation everywhere—except that *here,* in the Kingdom of the Winds,
something goes wrong. The winds pick up so much speed
that they are thermodynamically impossible. There is a
mechanism at work, pumping energy into the moving air. I
knew it before I left New York City; and I knew what it
must be. There had to be a long, horizontal line-vortex,
running north to south and transmitting energy to the western wind. But that too was impossible. First, then, I had to
confirm that the vortex existed.'' He nodded vigorously. ''It

does. With my vision sensors I can see the patterns of compression and rarefaction. In other words, I can see direct evidence of the vortex. With half a dozen more readings, I will pinpoint the exact origin of its energy source.''

''But what's all that got to do with finding . . .'' Owen trailed off and looked at me guiltily. I had told him what Martindale was after, but I had also cautioned him never to mention it.

''With finding Trapalanda?'' finished Martindale. ''Why, it has everything to do with it. There must be one site, a specific place where the generator exists to power the vortex line. Find that, and we will have found Trapalanda.''

Like God, Duty, or Paradise, Trapalanda means different things to different people. I could see from the expression on Owen's face that a line vortex power generator was not *his* Trapalanda, no matter what it meant to Martindale.

I had allowed six days; it took three. On the evening of June 17, we sat around the tiny table in the aircraft's rear cabin. There would be no flying tomorrow, and Owen had produced a bottle of *usquebaugh australis;* ''southern whiskey,'' the worst drink in the world.

''On foot,'' John Martindale was saying. ''Now it has to be on foot—and just in case, one of us will stay at the camp in radio contact.''

''Helga,'' I said. She and Martindale shook heads in unison. ''Suppose you have to carry somebody out?'' she said. ''I can't do that. It must be you or Owen.''

At least she was taking this seriously, which Owen Davies was not. He had watched with increasing disgust while Martindale made atmospheric observations at seven sites. Afterward he came to me secretly. ''We're working for a madman,'' he said. ''We'll find no treasure. I'd almost rather work for Diego.''

Diego Luria—''Mad Diego''—believed that the location of Trapalanda could be found by a correct interpretation of the Gospel according to Saint John. He had made five expeditions to the altiplano, four of them with Owen as pilot. It was harder on Owen than you might think, since Diego sometimes said that human sacrifice would be needed before Trapalanda could be discovered. They had found nothing; but they had come back, and that in itself was no mean feat.

Martindale had done his own exact triangulation, and pinpointed a place on the map. He had calculated UTM coordinates accurate to within twenty meters. They were not promising. When we flew as close as possible to his chosen location we found that we were looking at a point halfway up a steep rock face, where a set of broken waterfalls cascaded down a near-vertical cliff.

"I am sure," he said, in reply to my implied question. "The data-fit residuals are too small to leave any doubt." He tapped the map, and looked out of the aircraft window at the distant rock face. "Tomorrow. You, and Helga, and I will go. You, Owen, you stay here and monitor our transmission frequency. If we are off the air for more than twelve hours, come and get us."

He was taking this *too* seriously. Before the light faded I went outside again and trained my binoculars on the rock face. According to Martindale, at that location was a power generator that could modify the flow of winds along two hundred and fifty miles of mountain range. I saw nothing but the blown white spray of falls and cataracts, and a grey highland fox picking its way easily up the vertical rock face.

"Trust me." Martindale had appeared suddenly at my side. "I can *see* those wind patterns when I set my sensors to function at the right wavelengths. What's your problem?"

"Size." I turned to him. "Can you make your sensors provide telescopic images?"

"Up to three-inch effective aperture."

"Then take a look up there. You're predicting that we'll find a machine which produces tremendous power—"

"Many gigawatts."

"—more power than a whole power station. And there is nothing there, nothing to see. That's impossible."

"Not at all." The sun was crawling along the northern horizon. The thin daylight lasted for only eight hours, and already it was fading. John Kenyon Martindale peered off westward and shook his head. He tapped his black visor. "You've had a good look at this," he said. "Suppose I had wanted to buy something that could do what this does, say, five years ago. Do you know what it would have weighed?"

"*Weighed?*" I shook my head.

"At least a ton. And ten years ago, it would have been impossible to build, no matter how big you allowed it to be. In another ten years, this assembly will fit easily inside a prosthetic eye. The way is toward miniaturization, higher energy densities, more compact design. I expect the generator to be small.'' He suddenly turned again to look right into my face. ''I have a question for you, and it is an unforgivably personal one. Have you ever consummated your marriage with Helga?''

He had anticipated my lunge at him, and he backed away rapidly. ''Do not misunderstand me,'' he said. ''Helga's extreme aversion to physical contact is obvious. If it is total, there are New York specialists who can probably help her. I have influence there.''

I looked down at my hands as they held the binoculars. They were trembling. ''It is—total,'' I said.

''You knew that—and yet you married her. Why?''

''Why did you marry *your* wife, knowing you would be cuckolded?'' I was lashing out, not expecting an answer.

''Did she tell you it was for her skin?'' His voice was weary, and he was turning away as he spoke. ''I'm sure she did. Well, I will tell you. I married Shirley—because she wanted me to.''

Then I was standing alone in the deepening darkness. Shirley Martindale had warned me, back in New York. He was like a child, curious about everything. Including me, including Helga, including me and Helga.

Damn you, John Martindale. I looked at the bare hillside, and prayed that Trapalanda would somehow swallow him whole. Then I would never again have to endure that insidious, probing voice, asking the unanswerable.

The plane had landed on the only level piece of ground in miles. Our destination was a mile and a half away, but it was across some formidable territory. We would have to descend a steep scree, cross a quarter mile of boulders until we came to a fast-moving stream, and follow that watercourse upward, until we were in the middle of the waterfalls themselves.

The plain of boulders showed the translucent sheen of a thin ice coating. The journey could not be done in poor light. We would wait until morning, and leave promptly at ten.

Helga and I went to bed early, leaving Martindale with his calculations and Owen Davies with his *usquebaugh australis*. At a pinch the aircraft would sleep four, but Helga and I slept outside in a small reinforced tent brought along for the purpose. The floor area was five feet by seven. We had pitched the tent in the lee of the aircraft, where the howl of the wind was muted. I listened to Helga's breathing, and knew after half an hour that she was still awake.

"Think we'll find anything?" I said softly.

"I don't know." And then, after maybe one minute. "It's not that. It's you, Klaus."

"I've never been better."

"That's the problem. I've seen you, these last few days. You love it here. I should never have taken you away."

"I'm not complaining."

"That's part of the problem, too. You never complain. I wish you would." I heard her turn to face me in the dark, and for one second I imagined a hand was reaching out towards me. It was an illusion. She went on, "When I said I wanted to leave Patagonia and live in Europe, you agreed without an argument. But your heart has always been here."

"Oh, well, I don't know . . ." The lie stuck in my throat.

"And there's something else. I wasn't going to tell you, because I was afraid that you would misunderstand. But I will tell you. John Martindale tried to touch me."

I stirred, began to sit up, and felt the rough canvas against my forehead. Outside, the wind gave a sudden scream around the tent. "You mean he tried to—to—"

"No. He reached out, and tried to touch the back of my hand. That was all. I don't know why he did it, but I think it was just curiosity. He watches everything, and he has been watching us. I pulled my hand away before he got near. But it made me think of you. I have not been a wife to you, Klaus. You've done your best, and I've tried my hardest but it hasn't improved at all. Be honest with yourself, you know it hasn't. So if you want to stay here when his work is finished . . ."

I hated to hear her sound so confused and lost. "Let's not discuss it now," I said.

In other words, I can't bear to talk about it.

We had tried so hard at first, with Helga gritting her teeth at every gentle touch. When I finally realized that the sweat on her forehead and the quiver in her thin limbs was a hundred percent fear and zero percent arousal, I stopped trying. After that we had been happy—or at least, I had. I had not been faithful physically, but I could explain that well enough. And then, with this trip and the arrival on the scene of John Kenyon Martindale, the whole relationship between Helga and me felt threatened. And I did not know why.

"We ought to get as much sleep as we can tonight," I said, after another twenty seconds or so. "Tomorrow will be a tough day."

She said nothing, but she remained awake for a long, long time.

And so, of course, did I.

The first quarter mile was easy, a walk down a gently sloping incline of weathered basalt. Owen Davies had watched us leave with an odd mixture of disdain and greed on his face. We were not going to find anything, he was quite sure of that—but on the other hand, if by some miracle we *did* and he was not there to see it . . .

We carried minimal packs. I thought it would be no more than a two-hour trek to our target point, and we had no intention of being away overnight.

When we came to the field of boulders I revised my estimate. Every square millimeter of surface was coated with the thinnest and most treacherous layer of clear ice. In principle its presence was impossible. With an atmosphere of this temperature and dryness, that ice should have sublimed away.

We picked our way carefully across, concentrating on balance far more than progress. The wind buffeted us, always at the worst moments. It took another hour and a half before we were at the bottom of the waterfalls and could see how to tackle the rock face. It didn't look too bad. There were enough cracks and ledges to make the climb fairly easy.

"That's the spot," said Martindale. "Right in there."

We followed his pointing finger. About seventy feet above our heads one of the bigger waterfalls came cascading its way out from the cliff for a thirty-foot vertical drop.

"The waterfall?" said Helga. Her tone of voice said more than her words. *That's supposed to be a generator of two hundred and fifty miles of gale-force winds?* she was saying. *Tell me another one.*

"Behind it." Martindale was walking along the base of the cliff, looking for a likely point where he could begin the climb. "The coordinates are actually *inside* the cliff. Which means we have to look *behind* the waterfall. And that means we have to come at it from the side.''

We had brought rock-climbing gear with us. We did not need it. Martindale found a diagonal groove that ran at an angle of thirty degrees up the side of the cliff, and after following it to a vertical chimney, we found another slanting ledge running the other way. Two more changes of route, neither difficult, and we were on a ledge about two feet wide that ran up to the right behind our waterfall.

Two feet is a lot less when you are seventy feet up and walking a rock ledge slippery with water. Even here, the winds plucked restlessly at our clothes. We roped ourselves together, Martindale leading, and inched our way forward. When we were a few feet from the waterfall Martindale lengthened the rope between him and me, and went on alone behind the cascading water.

''It's all right.'' He had to shout to be heard above the crash of water. ''It gets easier. The ledge gets wider. It runs into a cave in the face of the cliff. Come on.''

We were carrying powerful electric flashlights, and we needed them. Once we were in behind the screen of water, the light paled and dwindled. We shone the lights toward the back of the cave. We were standing on a flat area, maybe ten feet wide and twelve feet deep. So much for Owen's dream of endless caverns of treasure; so much for my dreams, too, though they had been a lot less grandiose than his.

Standing about nine feet in from the edge of the ledge stood a dark blue cylinder, maybe four feet long and as thick as a man's thigh. It was smooth-surfaced and uniform, with no sign of controls or markings on its surface. I heard Martindale grunt in satisfaction.

''Bingo,'' he said. ''that's it.''

''The whole thing?''

''Certainly. Remember what I said last night, about advanced technology making this smaller? There's the source of the line-vortex—the power unit for the whole Kingdom of the Winds.'' He took two steps towards it, and as he did so Helga cried out, ''Look out!''

The blank wall at the back of the cave had suddenly changed. Instead of damp grey stone, a rectangle of striated darkness had formed, maybe seven feet high and five feet wide.

Martindale laughed in triumph, and turned back to us. "Don't move for the moment. But don't worry, this is exactly what I hoped we might find. I suspected something like this when I first saw that anomaly. The winds are just an accidental by-product—like an eddy. The equipment here must be a little bit off in its tuning. But it's still working, no doubt about that. Feel the inertial dragging?"

I could feel something, a weak but persistent force drawing me toward the dark rectangle. I leaned backward to counteract it and looked more closely at the opening. As my eyes adjusted I realized that it was not true darkness there. Faint blue lines of luminescence started in from the edges of the aperture and flew rapidly toward a vanishing point at the center. There they disappeared, while new blue threads came into being at the outside.

"Where did the opening come from?" said Helga. "It wasn't there when we came in."

"No. It's a portal. I'm sure it only switches on when it senses the right object within range." Martindale took another couple of steps forward. Now he was standing at the very edge of the aperture, staring through at something invisible to me.

"What is it?" I said. In spite of Martindale's words I too had taken a couple of steps closer, and so had Helga.

"A portal—a gate to some other part of the Universe, built around a gravitational line singularity." He laughed, and his voice sounded half an octave lower in pitch. "Somebody left it here for us humans, and it leads to the stars. You wanted Trapalanda? This is it—the most priceless discovery in the history of the human race."

He took one more step forward. His moving leg stretched out forever in front of him, lengthening and lengthening. When his foot came down, the leg looked fifty yards long and it dwindled away to the tiny, distant speck of his foot. He lifted his back foot from the ground, and as he leaned forward his whole body rippled and distorted, stretching away from me. Now he looked his usual self—but he was a hundred yards away, carried with one stride along a tunnel that ran as far as the eye could follow.

Martindale turned, and reached out his hand. A long arm zoomed back towards us, still attached to that distant body, and a normal-sized right hand appeared out of the aperture. "Come on." The voice was lower again in tone, and strangely slowed. "Both of you. Don't you want to see the rest of the Universe? Here's the best chance that you will ever have."

Helga and I took another step forward, staring in to the very edge of the opening. Martindale reached out his left hand too, and it hurtled toward us, growing rapidly, until it was there to be taken and held. I took another step, and I was within the portal itself. I felt normal, but I was aware of that force again, tugging us harder toward the tunnel. Suddenly I was gripped by an irrational and irresistible fear. I had to get away. I turned to move back from the aperture, and found myself looking at Helga. She was thirty yards away, drastically diminished, standing in front of a tiny wall of falling water.

One more step would have taken me outside again to safety, clear of the aperture and its persistent, tugging field. But as I was poised to take that step, Helga acted. She closed her eyes and took a long, trembling step forward. I could see her mouth moving, almost as though in prayer. And then the action I could not believe: she leaned forward to grasp convulsively at John Martindale's outstretched hand.

I heard her gasp, and saw her shiver. Then she was taking another step forward. And another.

"Helga!" I changed my direction and blundered after her along that endless tunnel. "This way. I'll get us out."

"No." She had taken another shivering step, and she was still clutching Martindale's hand. "No, Klaus." Her voice was breathless. "He's right. This is the biggest adventure ever. It's worth everything."

"Don't be afraid," said a hollow, booming voice. It was Martindale, and now all I could see of him was a shimmering silhouette. The man had been replaced by a sparkling outline. "Come on, Klaus. It's almost here."

The tugging force was stronger, pulling on every cell of my body. I looked at Helga, a shining outline now like John Martindale. They were dwindling, vanishing. They were gone. I wearily turned around and tried to walk back the way we had come. Tons of weight hung on me, wreathed themselves around every limb. I was trying to drag the whole world up an endless hill. I forced my legs to take one small step, then another. It was impossible to see if I was making progress. I was surrounded by that roaring silent pattern of rushing blue lines, all going in the opposite direction from me, every one doing its best to drag me back.

I inched along. Finally I could see the white of the waterfall ahead. It was growing in size, but at the same time it was losing definition. My eyes ached. By the time I took the final step and fell on my face on the stone floor of the cave, the waterfall was no more than a milky haze and a sound of rushing water.

Owen Davies saved my life, what there is of it. I did my part to help him. I wanted to live when I woke up, and weak as I was, and half-blind, I managed to crawl down that steep rock face. I was dragging myself over the icy boulders when he found me. My clothes were shredding, falling off my body, and I was shivering and weeping from cold and fear. He wrapped me in his own jacket and helped me back to the aircraft.

Then he went off to look for John Martindale and Helga. He never came back. I do not know to this day if he found and entered the portal, or if he came to grief somewhere on the way.

I spent two days in the aircraft, knowing that I was too sick and my eyes were too bad to dream of flying anywhere. My front teeth had all gone, and I ate porridge or biscuits soaked in tea. Three more days, and I began to realize that if I did not fly myself, I was not going anywhere. On the seventh day I managed a faltering, incompetent takeoff and flew northeast, peering at the instruments with my newly purblind eyes. I made a crash landing at Comodoro Rivadavia, was dragged from the wreckage, and flown to a hospital in Bahia Blanca. They did what they could for me, which was not too much. By that time I was beginning to have some faint idea what had happened to my body, and as soon as the hospital was willing to release me I took a flight to Buenos Aires, and on at once to Geneva's Lakeside Hospital. They removed the cataracts from my eyes. Three weeks later I could see again without that filmy mist over everything.

Before I left the hospital I insisted on a complete physical. Thanks to John Martindale's half-million deposit, money was not going to be a problem. The doctor who went over the results with me was about thirty years old, a Viennese Jew who had been practicing for only a couple of years. He looked oddly similar to one of my cousins at that age. "Well, Mr. Jacobi," he said (after a quick look at his dossier to make sure of my name), "there are no organic abnormalities, no cardiovascular problems, only slight circulation problems. You have some osteo-arthritis in your hips and your knees. I'm delighted to be able to tell you that you are in excellent overall health for your age."

"If you didn't know," I said, "how old would you think I am?"

He looked again at his crib sheet, but found no help there. I had deliberately left out my age at the place where the hospital entry form required it. "Well," he said. He was going to humor me. "Seventy-six?"

"Spot on," I said.

I had the feeling that he had knocked a couple of years off his estimate, just to make me feel good. So let's say my biological age was seventy-eight or seventy-nine. When I flew with John Martindale to Buenos Aires, I had been one month short of my forty-fourth birthday.

At that point I flew to New York, and went to John Kenyon Martindale's house. I met with Shirley—briefly. She did not recognize me, and I did not try to identify myself. I gave my name as Owen Davies. In John's absence, I said, I was interested in contacting some of the mathematician friends that he had told me I would like to meet. Could she remember the names of any of them, so I could call them even before John came back? She looked bored, but she came back with a telephone book and produced three names. One was in San Francisco, one was in Boston, and the third was here in New York, at the Courant Institute.

He was in his middle twenties, a fit-looking curly haired man with bright blue eyes and a big smile. The thing that astonished him about my visit, I think, was not the subject matter. It was the fact that I made the visit. He found it astonishing that a spavined antique like me would come to his office to ask about this sort of topic in theoretical physics.

"What you are suggesting is not just *permitted* in today's view of space and time, Mr. Davies," he said. "It's absolutely *required*. You can't do something to *space*—such as making an instantaneous link between two places, as you have been suggesting—without at the same time having profound effects on *time*. Space and time are really a single entity. Distances and elapsed times are intimately related, like two sides of the same coin.''

''And the line-vortex generator?'' I said. I had told him far less about this, mainly because all I knew of it had been told to us by John Martindale.

''Well, if the generator in some sense approximated an infinitely long, rapidly rotating cylinder, then yes. General relativity insists that very peculiar things would happen there. There could be global causality violations—'before' and 'after' getting confused, cause and effect becoming mixed up, that sort of thing. God knows what time and space look like near the line singularity itself. But don't misunderstand me. Before any of these things could happen, you would have to be dealing with a huge system, something many times as massive as the Sun.''

I resisted the urge to tell him he was wrong. Apparently he did not accept John Martindale's unshakable confidence in the idea that with better technology came increase in capability *and* decrease in size. I stood up and leaned on my cane. My left hip was a little dodgy and became tired if I walked too far. ''You've been very helpful.''

''Not at all.'' He stood up, too, and said, ''Actually, I'm going to be giving a lecture at the Institute on these subjects in a couple of weeks. If you'd like to come . . .''

I noted down the time and place, but I knew I would not be there. It was three months to the day since John Martindale, Helga, and I had climbed the rock face and walked behind the waterfall. Time—my time—was short. I had to head south again.

The flight to Argentina was uneventful. Comodoro Rivadavia was the same as always. Now I am sitting in Alberto McShane's bar, drinking one last beer (all that my digestion today will permit) and waiting for the pilot. McShane did not recognize me, but the armadillo did. It trundled to my table, and sat looking up at me. *Where's my friend John Martindale?* it was saying.

Where indeed? I will tell you soon. The plane is ready. We are going to Trapalanda.

It will take all my strength, but I think I can do it. I have added equipment that will help me to cross that icy field of boulders and ascend the rock face. It is September. The weather will be warmer, and the going easier. If I close my eyes I can see the portal now, behind the waterfall, its black depths and shimmering blue streaks rushing away toward the vanishing point.

Thirty-five years. That is what the portal owes me. It sucked them out of my body as I struggled back against the gravity gradient. Maybe it is impossible to get them back. I don't know. My young mathematician friend insisted that time is infinitely fluid, with no more constraints on movement through it than there are on travel through space. I don't know, but I want my thirty-five years. If I die in the attempt, I will be losing little.

I am terrified of that open gate, with its alien twisting of the world's geometry. I am more afraid of it than I have ever been of anything. Last time I failed, and I could not go through it. But I will go through it now.

This time I have something more than Martindale's scientific curiosity to drive me on. It is not thoughts of danger or death that fill my mind as I sit here. I have that final image of Helga, reaching out and taking John Martindale's hand in hers. Reaching out, to grasp his hand, voluntarily. I love Helga, I am sure of that, but I cannot make sense of my other emotions; fear, jealousy, resentment, hope, excitement. She was *touching* him. Did she do it because she wanted to go through the portal, wanted it so much that every fear was insignificant? Or had she, after thirty years, finally found someone whom she could touch without cringing and loathing?

The pilot has arrived. My glass is empty. Tomorrow I will know.

AMERICA

by Orson Scott Card

Orson Scott Card began publishing in 1977, and by 1978 had won the John W. Campbell Award as best new writer of the year. His short fiction has appeared in Omni, Isaac Asimov's Science Fiction Magazine, Analog, The Magazine of Fantasy and Science Fiction, *and elsewhere. His novels include* Hot Sleep, A Planet Called Treason, Songmaster, Hart's Hope, Wyrms, Seventh Son, Red Prophet, *and* Prentice Alvin. *In 1986 his novel* Ender's Game *won both the Hugo and the Nebula Award; next year his novel* Speaker For the Dead *also won both awards. Card has also won the World Fantasy Award, for his story "Hatrack River." His most recent books are the novels* Xenocide *and* Lost Boys, *and two collections,* The Folk of the Fringe, *and the immense* Maps in A Mirror: the Short Fiction of Orson Scott Card. *Card lives with his family in Greensboro, North Carolina.*

In the story that follows, he takes us deep into the steaming jungles of Brazil for an engrossing tale of a young boy's obsession with a mysterious Indian woman, and the stunning consequences for the whole world that unfold from it.

Sam Monson and Anamari Boagente had two encounters in their lives, forty years apart. The first encounter lasted for several weeks in the high Amazon jungle, the village of Agualinda. The second was for only an hour near the ruins of the Glen Canyon Dam, on the border between Navaho country and the State of Deseret.

When they met the first time, Sam was a scrawny teenager from Utah and Anamari was a middle-aged spinster Indian from Brazil. When they met the second time, he was governor of Deseret, the last European state in America, and she was, to some people's way of thinking, the mother of God. It never occurred to anyone that they had ever met before, except me. I saw it plain as day, and pestered Sam until he told me the whole story. Now Sam is dead, and she's long gone, and I'm the only one who knows the truth. I thought for a long time that I'd take this story untold to my grave, but I see now that I can't do that. The way I see it, I won't be allowed to die until I write this down. All my real work was done long since, so why else am I alive? I figure the land has kept me breathing so I can tell the story of its victory, and it has kept *you* alive so you can hear it. Gods are like that. It isn't enough for them to run everything. They want to be famous, too.

Agualinda, Amazonas

Passengers were nothing to her. Anamari only cared about helicopters when they brought medical supplies. This chopper carried a precious packet of benaxidene; Anamari barely noticed the skinny, awkward boy who sat by the crates, looking hostile. Another Yanqui who doesn't want to be stuck out in the jungle. Nothing new about that. Northeamericanos were almost invisible to Anamari by now. They came and went.

It was the Brazilian government people she had to worry about, the petty bureaucrats suffering through years of virtual exile in Manaus, working out their frustrations by being petty tyrants over the helpless Indians. No I'm sorry we don't have any more penicillin, no more syringes, what did you do with the AIDS vaccine we gave you three years ago? Do you think we're made of money here? Let them come to town if they want to get well. There's a hospital in São Paulo de Olivença, send them there, we're not going to turn you into a second hospital out there in the middle of nowhere, not for a village of a hundred filthy Baniwas, it's not as if you're a doctor, you're just an old withered-up Indian woman yourself, you never graduated from the medical schools, we can't spare medicines for you. It made them feel so important, to decide whether or not an Indian child would live or die. As often as not they passed sentence of death by refusing to send supplies. It made them feel powerful as God.

Anamari knew better than to protest or argue—it would only make that bureaucrat likelier to kill again in the future. But sometimes, when the need was great and the medicine was common, Anamari would go to the Yanqui geologists and ask if they had this or that. Sometimes they did. What she knew about Yanquis was that if they had some extra, they would share, but if they didn't, they wouldn't lift a finger to get any. They were not tyrants like Brazilian bureaucrats. They just didn't give a damn. They were there to make money.

That was what Anamari saw when she looked at the sullen light-haired boy in the helicopter—another Norteamericano, just like all the other Norteamericanos, only younger.

She had the benaxidene, and so she immediately began spreading word that all the Baniwas should come for injections. It was a disease introduced during the war between Guyana and Venezuela two years ago; as usual, most of the victims were not citizens of either country, just the Indios of the jungle, waking up one morning with their joints stiffening, hardening until no movement was possible. Benaxidene was the antidote, but you had to have it every few months or your joints would stiffen up again. As usual, the bureaucrats had diverted a shipment and there were a dozen Baniwas bedridden in the village. As usual, one or two of the Indians would be too far gone for the cure; one or two of their joints would be stiff for the rest of their lives. As usual, Anamari said little as she gave the injections, and the Baniwas said less to her.

It was not until the next day that Anamari had time to notice the young Yanqui boy wandering around the village. He was wearing rumpled white clothing, already somewhat soiled with the greens and browns of life along the rivers of the Amazon jungle. He showed no sign of being interested in anything, but an hour into her rounds, checking on the results of yesterday's benaxidene treatments, she became aware that he was following her.

She turned around in the doorway of the government-built hovel and faced him. "O que?" she demanded. What do you want?

To her surprise, he answered in halting Portuguese. Most of these Yanquis never bothered to learn the language at all, expecting her and everybody else to speak English. "Posso ajudar?" he asked. Can I help?

"Não," she said. "Mas pode olhar." You can watch.

He looked at her in bafflement.

She repeated her sentence slowly, enunciating clearly.
"Pode olhar."

"Eu?" Me?

"Você, sim. And I can speak English."

"I don't want to speak English."

"Tanto faz," she said. Makes no difference.

He followed her into the hut. It was a little girl, lying naked in her own feces. She had palsy from a bout with meningitis years ago, when she was an infant, and Anamari figured that the girl would probably be one of the ones for whom the benaxidene came too late. That's how things usually worked—the weak suffer most. But no, her joints were flexing again, and the girl smiled at them, that heartbreaking happy smile that made palsy victims so beautiful at times.

So. Some luck after all, the benaxidene had been in time for her. Anamari took the lid off the clay waterjar that stood on the one table in the room, and dipped one of her clean rags in it. She used it to wipe the girl, then lifted her frail, atrophied body and pulled the soiled sheet out from under her. On impulse, she handed the sheet to the boy.

"Leva fora," she said. And, when he didn't understand, "Take it outside."

He did not hesitate to take it, which surprised her. "Do you want me to wash it?"

"You could shake off the worst of it," she said. "Out over the garden in back. I'll wash it later."

He came back in, carrying the wadded-up sheet, just as she was leaving. "All done here," she said. "We'll stop by my house to start that soaking. I'll carry it now."

He didn't hand it to her. "I've got it," he said. "Aren't you going to give her a clean sheet?"

"There are only four sheets in the village," she said. "Two of them are on my bed. She won't mind lying on the mat. I'm the only one in the village who cares about linens. I'm also the only one who cares about this girl."

"She likes you," he said.

"She smiles like that at everybody."

"So maybe she likes everybody."

Anamari grunted and led the way to her house. It was two government hovels pushed together. The one served as her clinic, the other as her home. Out back she had two metal washtubs. She handed one of them to the Yanqui boy, pointed at the rainwater tank, and told him to fill it. He did. It made her furious.

"What do you want!" she demanded.

"Nothing," he said.

"Why do you keep hanging around!"

"I thought I was helping." His voice was full of injured pride.

"I don't need your help." She forgot that she had meant to leave the sheet to soak. She began rubbing it on the washboard.

"Then why did you ask me to . . ."

She did not answer him, and he did not complete the question.

After a long time he said, "You were trying to get rid of me, weren't you?"

"What do you want here?" she said. "Don't I have enough to do, without a Norteamericano *boy* to look after?"

Anger flashed in his eyes, but he did not answer until the anger was gone. "If you're tired of scrubbing, I can take over."

She reached out and took his hand, examined it for a moment. "Soft hands," she said. "Lady hands. You'd scrape your knuckles on the washboard and bleed all over the sheet."

Ashamed, he put his hands in his pockets. A parrot flew past him, dazzling green and red; he turned in surprise to look at it. It landed on the rainwater tank. "Those sell for a thousand dollars in the States," he said.

Of course the Yanqui boy evaluates everything by price. "Here they're free," she said. "The Baniwa eat them. And wear the feathers."

He looked around at the other huts, the scraggly gardens. "The people are very poor here," he said. "The jungle life must be hard."

"Do you think so?" she snapped. "The jungle is very kind to these people. It has plenty for them to eat, all year. The Indians of the Amazon did not know they were poor until Europeans came and made them buy pants, which they couldn't afford, and build houses, which they couldn't keep up, and plant gardens. Plant gardens! In the midst of this magnificent Eden. The jungle life was good. The Europeans made them poor."

"Europeans?" asked the boy.

"Brazilians. They're all Europeans. Even the black ones have turned European. Brazil is just another European country, speaking a European language. Just like you Norteamericanos. You're Europeans too."

"I was born in America," he said. "So were my parents and grandparents and great-grandparents."

"But your bis-bis-avós, they came on a boat."

"That was a long time ago," he said.

"A long time!" She laughed. "I am a pure Indian. For ten thousand generations I belong to this land. You are a stranger here. A fourth-generation stranger."

"But I'm a stranger who isn't afraid to touch a dirty sheet," he said. He was grinning defiantly.

That was when she started to like him. "How old are you?" she asked.

"Fifteen," he said.

"Your father's a geologist?"

"No. He heads up the drilling team. They're going to sink a test well here. He doesn't think they'll find anything, though."

"They will find plenty of oil," she said.

"How do you know?"

"Because I dreamed it," she said. "Bulldozers cutting down the trees, making the airstrip, and planes coming and going. They'd never do that, unless they found oil. Lots of oil."

She waited for him to make fun of the idea of dreaming true dreams. But he didn't. He just looked at her.

So she was the one who broke the silence. "You came to this village to kill time while your father is away from you, on the job, right?"

"No," he said. "I came here because he hasn't started to work yet. The choppers start bringing in equipment tomorrow."

"You would rather be away from your father?"

He looked away. "I'd rather see him in hell."

"This *is* hell," she said, and the boy laughed. "Why did you come here with him?"

"Because I'm only fifteen years old, and he has custody of me this summer."

"Custody," she said. "Like a criminal."

"He's a criminal," he said bitterly.

"And his crime?"

He waited a moment, as if deciding whether to answer. When he spoke, he spoke quietly and looked away. Ashamed. Of his father's crime. "Adultery," he said. The word hung in the air. The boy turned back and looked her in the face again. His face was tinged with red.

Europeans have such transparent skin, she thought. All their emotions show through. She guessed a whole story from his word—a beloved mother betrayed, and now he had to spend the summer with her betrayer. "Is that a *crime?*"

He shrugged. "Maybe not to Catholics."

"You're Protestant?"

He shook his head. "Mormon. But I'm a heretic."

She laughed. "You're a heretic, and your father is an adulterer."

He didn't like her laughter. "And you're a virgin," he said. His words seemed calculated to hurt her.

She stopped scrubbing, stood there looking at her hands. "Also a crime?" she murmured.

"I had a dream last night," he said. "In my dream your name was Anna Marie, but when I tried to call you that, I couldn't. I could only call you by another name."

"What name?" she asked.

"What does it matter? It was only a dream." He was taunting her. He knew she trusted in dreams.

"You dreamed of me, and in the dream my name was Anamari?"

"It's true, isn't it? That *is* your name, isn't it?" He didn't have to add the other half of the question: You *are* a virgin, aren't you?

She lifted the sheet from the water, wrung it out and tossed it to him. He caught it, vile water spattering his face. He grimaced. She poured the washwater onto the dirt. It spattered mud all over his trousers. He did not step back. Then she carried the tub to the water tank and began to fill it with clean water. "Time to rinse," she said.

"You dreamed about an airstrip," he said. "And I dreamed about you."

"In your dreams you better start to mind your own business," she said.

"I didn't ask for it, you know," he said. "But I followed

the dream out to this village, and you turned out to be a dreamer, too.''

''That doesn't mean you're going to end up with your pinto between my legs, so you can forget it,'' she said.

He looked genuinely horrified. ''Geez, what are you talking about! That would be fornication! Plus you've got to be old enough to be my mother!''

''I'm forty-two,'' she said. ''If it's any of your business.''

''You're *older* than my mother,'' he said. ''I couldn't possibly think of you sexually. I'm sorry if I gave that impression.''

She giggled. ''You are a very funny boy, Yanqui. First you say I'm a virgin—''

''That was in the dream,'' he said.

''And then you tell me I'm older than your mother and too ugly to think of me sexually.''

He looked ashen with shame. ''I'm sorry, I was just trying to make sure you knew that I would never—''

''You're trying to tell me that you're a good boy.''

''Yes,'' he said.

She giggled again. ''You probably don't even play with yourself,'' she said.

His face went red. He struggled to find something to say. Then he threw the wet sheet back at her and walked furiously away. She laughed and laughed. She liked this boy very much.

The next morning he came back and helped her in the clinic all day. His name was Sam Monson, and he was the first European she ever knew who dreamed true dreams. She had thought only Indios could do that. Whatever god it was that gave her dreams to her, perhaps it was the same god giving dreams to Sam. Perhaps it was that god brought them together here in the jungle. Perhaps it was that god who would lead the drill to oil, so that Sam's father would have to keep him here long enough to accomplish whatever the god had in mind.

It annoyed her that the god had mentioned she was a virgin. That was nobody's business but her own.

* * *

Life in the jungle was better than Sam ever expected. Back in Utah, when Mother first told him that he had to go to the Amazon with the old bastard, he had feared the worst. Hacking through thick viney jungles with a machete, crossing rivers of piranha in tick-infested dugouts, and always sweat and mosquitos and thick, heavy air. Instead the American oilmen lived in a pretty decent camp, with a generator for electric light. Even though it rained all the time and when it didn't it was so hot you wished it would, it wasn't constant danger as he had feared, and he never had to hack through jungle at all. There were paths, sometimes almost roads, and the thick, vivid green of the jungle was more beautiful than he had ever imagined. He had not realized that the American West was such a desert. Even California, where the old bastard lived when he wasn't traveling to drill wells, even those wooded hills and mountains were grey compared to the jungle green.

The Indians were quiet little people, not headhunters. Instead of avoiding them, like the adult Americans did, Sam found that he could be with them, come to know them, even help them by working with Anamari. The old bastard could sit around and drink his beer with the guys—adultery *and* beer, as if one contemptible sin of the flesh weren't enough—but Sam was actually doing some good here. If there was anything Sam could do to prove he was the opposite of his father, he would do it; and because his father was a weak, carnal, earthy man with no self-control, then Sam had to be a strong, spiritual, intellectual man who did not let any passions of the body rule him. Watching his father succumb to alcohol, remembering how his father could not even last a month away from Mother without having to get some whore into his bed, Sam was proud of his self-discipline. He ruled his body; his body did not rule him.

He was also proud to have passed Anamari's test on the first day. What did he care if human excrement touched his body? He was not afraid to breathe the hot stink of suffering, he was not afraid of the innocent dirt of a crippled child. Didn't Jesus touch lepers? Dirt of the body did not disgust him. Only dirt of the soul.

Which was why his dreams of Anamari troubled him. During the day they were friends. They talked about important ideas, and she told him stories of the Indians of the

Amazon, and about her education as a teacher in São Paulo. She listened when he talked about history and religion and evolution and all the theories and ideas that danced in his head. Even Mother never had time for that, always taking care of the younger kids or doing her endless jobs for the Church. Anamari treated him like his ideas mattered.

But at night, when he dreamed, it was something else entirely. In those dreams he kept seeing her naked, and the voice kept calling her "Virgem America." What her virginity had to do with America he had no idea—even true dreams didn't always make sense—but he knew this much: when he dreamed of Anamari naked, she was always reaching out to him, and he was filled with such strong passions that more than once he awoke from the dream to find himself throbbing with imaginary pleasure, like Onan in the Bible, Judah's son, who spilled his seed upon the ground and was struck dead for it.

Sam lay awake for a long time each time this happened, trembling, fearful. Not because he thought God would strike him down—he knew that if God hadn't struck his father dead for adultery, Sam was certainly in no danger because of an erotic dream. He was afraid because he knew that in these dreams he revealed himself to be exactly as lustful and evil as his father. He did not want to feel any sexual desire for Anamari. She was old and lean and tough, and he was afraid of her, but most of all Sam didn't want to desire her because he was not like his father, he would never have sexual intercourse with a woman who was not his wife.

Yet when he walked into the village of Agualinda, he felt eager to see her again, and when he found her—the village was small, it never took long—he could not erase from his mind the vivid memory of how she looked in the dreams, reaching out to him, her breasts loose and jostling, her slim hips rolling toward him—and he would bite his cheek for the pain of it, to distract him from desire.

It was because he was living with Father; the old bastard's goatishness was rubbing off on him, that's all. So he spent as little time with his father as possible, going home only to sleep at night.

The harder he worked at the jobs Anamari gave him to do, the easier it was to keep himself from remembering his dream of her kneeling over him, touching him, sliding along

his body. Hoe the weeds out of the corn until your back is
on fire with pain! Wash the Baniwa hunter's wound and replace the bandage! Sterilize the instruments in the alcohol!
Above all, do not, even accidentally, let any part of your
body brush against hers; pull away when she is near you,
turn away so you don't feel her warm breath as she leans
over your shoulder, start a bright conversation whenever
there is a silence filled only with the sound of insects and
the sight of a bead of sweat slowly etching its way from her
neck down her chest to disappear between her breasts where
she only tied her shirt instead of buttoning it.

How could she possibly be a virgin, after the way she
acted in his dreams?

"Where do you think the dreams come from?" she asked.

He blushed, even though she could not have guessed what
he was thinking. Could she?

"The dreams," she said. "Why do you think we have
dreams that come true?"

It was nearly dark. "I have to get home," he said. She
was holding his hand. When had she taken his hand like
that, and why?

"I have the strangest dream," she said. "I dream of a
huge snake, covered with bright green and red feathers."

"Not all the dreams come true," he said.

"I hope not," she answered. "Because this snake comes
out of—I give birth to this snake."

"Quetzal," he said.

"What does that mean?"

"The feathered serpent god of the Aztecs. Or maybe the
Mayas. Mexican, anyway. I have to go home."

"But what does it mean?"

"It's almost dark," he said.

"Stay and talk to me!" she demanded. "I have room,
you can stay the night."

But Sam had to get back. Much as he hated staying with
his father, he dared not spend a night in this place. Even
her invitation aroused him. He would never last a night in
the same house with her. The dream would be too strong
for him. So he left her and headed back along the path
through the jungle. All during the walk he couldn't get Anamari out of his mind. It was as if the plants were sending
him the vision of her, so his desire was even stronger than
when he was with her.

The leaves gradually turned from green to black in the seeping dark. The hot darkness did not frighten him; it seemed to invite him to step away from the path into the shadows, where he would find the moist relief, the cool relief of all his tension. He stayed on the path, and hurried faster.

He came with relief to the oilmen's town. The generator was loud, but the insects were louder, swarming around the huge area light, casting shadows of their demonic dance. He and his father shared a large one-room house on the far edge of the compound. The oil company provided much nicer hovels than the Brazilian government.

A few men called out to greet him. He waved, even answered once or twice, but hurried on. His groin felt so hot and tight with desire that he was sure that only the shadows and his quick stride kept everyone from seeing. It was maddening: the more he thought of trying to calm himself, the more visions of Anamari slipped in and out of his waking mind, almost to the point of hallucination. His body would not relax. He was almost running when he burst into the house.

Inside, Father was washing his dinner plate. He glanced up, but Sam was already past him. "I'll heat up your dinner."

Sam flopped down on his bed. "Not hungry."

"Why are you so late?" asked his father.

"We got to talking."

"It's dangerous in the jungle at night. You think it's safe because nothing bad ever happens to you in the daytime, but it's dangerous."

"Sure Dad. I know." Sam got up, turned his back to take off his pants. Maddeningly, he was still aroused; he didn't want his father to see.

But with the unerring instinct of prying parents, the old bastard must have sensed that Sam was hiding something. When Sam was buck naked, Father walked around and *looked*, just as if he never heard of privacy. Sam blushed in spite of himself. His father's eyes went small and hard. I hope I don't ever look like that, thought Sam. I hope my face doesn't get that ugly suspicious expression on it. I'd rather die than look like that.

"Well, put on your pajamas," Father said. "I don't want to look at that forever."

Sam pulled on his sleeping shorts.

"What's going on over there?" asked Father.

"Nothing," said Sam.

"You must do *something* all day."

"I told you, I help her. She runs a clinic, and she also tends a garden. She's got no electricity, so it takes a lot of work."

"I've done a lot of work in my time, Sam, but I don't come home like *that*."

"No, you always stopped and got it off with some whore along the way."

The old bastard whipped out his hand and slapped Sam across the face. It stung, and the surprise of it wrung tears from Sam before he had time to decide not to cry.

"I never slept with a whore in my life," said the old bastard.

"You only slept with one woman who wasn't," said Sam.

Father slapped him again, only this time Sam was ready, and he bore the slap stoically, almost without flinching.

"I had one affair," said Father.

"You got caught once," said Sam. "There were dozens of women."

Father laughed derisively. "What did you do, hire a detective? There was only the one."

But Sam knew better. He had dreamed these women for years. Laughing, lascivious women. It wasn't until he was twelve years old that he found out enough about sex to know what it all meant. By then he had long since learned that any dream he had more than once was true. So when he had a dream of Father with one of the laughing women, he woke up, holding the dream in his memory. He thought through it from beginning to end, remembering all the details he could. The name of the motel. The room number. It was midnight, but Father was in California, so it was an hour earlier. Sam got out of bed and walked quietly into the kitchen and dialed directory assistance. There was such a motel. He wrote down the number. Then Mother was there, asking him what he was doing.

"This is the number of the Seaview Motor Inn," he said. "Call this number and ask for room twenty-one twelve and then ask for Dad."

Mother looked at him strangely, like she was about to

scream or cry or hit him or throw up. "Your father is at the Hilton," she said.

But he just looked right back at her and said, "No matter who answers the phone, ask for Dad."

So she did. A woman answered, and Mom asked for Dad by name, and he was there. "I wonder how we can afford to pay for two motel rooms on the same night," Mom said coldly. "Or are you splitting the cost with your friend?" Then she hung up the phone and burst into tears.

She cried all night as she packed up everything the old bastard owned. By the time Dad got home two days later, all his things were in storage. Mom moved fast when she made up her mind. Dad found himself divorced and excommunicated all in the same week, not two months later.

Mother never asked Sam how he knew where Dad was that night. Never even hinted at wanting to know. Dad never asked him how Mom knew to call that number, either. An amazing lack of curiosity, Sam thought sometimes. Perhaps they just took it as fate. For a while it was a secret, then it stopped being secret, and it didn't matter how the change happened. But one thing Sam knew for sure—the woman at the Seaview Motor Inn was not the first woman, and the Seaview was not the first motel. Dad had been an adulterer for years, and it was ridiculous for him to lie about it now.

But there was no point in arguing with him, especially when he was in the mood to slap Sam around.

"I don't like the idea of you spending so much time with an older woman," said Father.

"She's the closest thing to a doctor these people have. She needs my help and I'm going to keep helping her," said Sam.

"Don't talk to me like that, little boy."

"You don't know anything about this, so just mind your own business."

Another slap. "You're going to get tired of this before I do, Sammy."

"I love it when you slap me, Dad. It confirms my moral superiority."

Another slap, this time so hard that Sam stumbled under the blow, and he tasted blood inside his mouth. "How hard next time, Dad?" he said. "You going to knock me down? Kick me around a little? Show me who's boss?"

"You've been asking for a beating ever since we got here."

"I've been asking to be left alone."

"I know women, Sam. You have no business getting involved with an older woman like that."

"I help her wash a little girl who has bowel movements in bed, Father. I empty pails of vomit. I wash clothes and help patch leaking roofs and while I'm doing all these things we talk. Just talk. I don't imagine you have much experience with that, Dad. You probably never talk at all with the women *you* know, at least not after the price is set."

It was going to be the biggest slap of all, enough to knock him down, enough to bruise his face and black his eye. But the old bastard held it in. Didn't hit him. Just stood there, breathing hard, his face red, his eyes tight and piggish.

"You're not as pure as you think," the old bastard finally whispered. "You've got every desire you despise in me."

"I don't despise you for *desire*," said Sam.

"The guys on the crew have been talking about you and this Indian bitch, Sammy. You may not like it, but I'm your father and it's my job to warn you. These Indian women are easy, and they'll give you a disease."

"The guys on the crew," said Sam. "What do they know about Indian women? They're all fags or jerk-offs."

"I hope someday you say that where they can hear you, Sam. And I hope it happens I'm not there to stop what they do to you."

"I would never *be* around men like that, Daddy, if the court hadn't given you shared custody. A no-fault divorce. What a joke."

More than anything else, those words stung the old bastard. Hurt him enough to shut him up. He walked out of the house and didn't come back until Sam was long since asleep.

Asleep and dreaming.

* * *

Anamari knew what was on Sam's mind, and to her surprise she found it vaguely flattering. She had never known the shy affection of a boy. When she was a teenager, she was the one Indian girl in the schools of São Paulo. Indians were so rare in the Europeanized parts of Brazil that she might have seemed exotic, but in those days she was still so frightened. The city was sterile, all concrete and harsh light, not at all like the deep soft meadows and woods of Xingu Park. Her tribe, the Kuikuru, were much more Europeanized than the jungle Indians—she had seen cars all her life and spoke Portuguese before she went to school. But the city made her hungry for the land, the cobblestones hurt her feet, and these intense, competitive children made her afraid. Worst of all, true dreams stopped in the city. She hardly knew who she was, if she was not a true dreamer. So if any boy desired her then, she would not have known it. She would have rebuffed him inadvertently. And then the time for such things had passed. Until now.

"Last night I dreamed of a great bird, flying west, away from land. Only its right wing was twice as large as its left wing. It had great bleeding wounds along the edges of its wings, and the right wing was the sickest of all, rotting in the air, the feathers dropping off."

"Very pretty dream," said Sam. Then he translated, to keep in practice. "Que sonho lindo."

"Ah, but what does it mean?"

"What happened next?"

"I was riding on the bird. I was very small, and I held a small snake in my hands—"

"The feathered snake."

"Yes. And I turned it loose, and it went and ate up all the corruption, and the bird was clean. And that's all. You've got a bubble in that syringe. The idea is to inject medicine, not air. What does the dream mean?"

"What, you think I'm a Joseph? A Daniel?"

"How about a Sam?"

"Actually, your dream is easy. Piece of cake."

"What?"

"Piece of cake. Easy as pie. That's how the cookie crumbles. Man shall not live by bread alone. All I can think of are bakery sayings. I must be hungry."

"Tell me the dream or I'll poke this needle into your eye."

"That's what I like about you Indians. Always you have torture on your mind."

She planted her foot against him and knocked him off his stool onto the packed dirt floor. A beetle skittered away.

Sam held up the syringe he had been working with—it was undamaged. He got up, set it aside. "The bird," he said, "is North and South America. Like wings, flying west. Only the right wing is bigger." He sketched out a rough map with his toe on the floor.

"That's the shape, maybe," she said. "It could be."

"And the corruption—show me where it was."

With her toe, she smeared the map here, there.

"It's obvious," said Sam.

"Yes," she said. "Once you think of it as a map. The corruption is all the Europeanized land. And the only healthy places are where the Indians still live."

"Indians or half-Indians," said Sam. "All your dreams are about the same thing, Anamari. Removing the Europeans from North and South America. Let's face it. You're an Indian chauvinist. You give birth to the resurrection god of the Aztecs, and then you send it out to destroy the Europeans."

"But why do I dream this?"

"Because you hate Europeans."

"No," she said. "That isn't true."

"Sure it is."

"I don't hate *you*."

"Because you know me. I'm not a European anymore, I'm a person. Obviously you've got to keep that from happening anymore, so you can keep your bigotry alive."

"You're making fun of me, Sam."

He shook his head. "No, I'm not. These are true dreams, Anamari. They tell you your destiny."

She giggled. "If I give birth to a feathered snake, I'll know the dream was true."

"To drive the Europeans out of America."

"No," she said. "I don't care what the dream says. I won't do that. Besides, what about the dream of the flowering weed?"

"Little weed in the garden, almost dead, and then you water it and it grows larger and larger and more beautiful—"

"And something else," she said. "At the very end of the dream, all the other flowers in the garden have changed. To be just like the flowering weed." She reached out and rested her hand on his arm. "Tell me *that* dream."

His arm became still, lifeless under her hand. "Black is beautiful," he said.

"What does *that* mean?"

"In America. The U.S., I mean. For the longest time, the blacks, the former slaves, they were ashamed to be black. The whiter you were, the more status you had—the more honor. But when they had their revolution in the sixties—"

"You don't remember the sixties, little boy."

"Heck, I barely remember the seventies. But I read books. One of the big changes, and it made a huge difference, was that slogan. Black is beautiful. The blacker the better. They said it over and over. Be proud of blackness, not ashamed of it. And in just a few years, they turned the whole status system upside down."

She nodded. "The weed came into flower."

"So. All through Latin America, Indians are very low status. If you want a Bolivian to pull a knife on you, just call him an Indian. Everybody who possibly can, pretends to be of pure Spanish blood. Pure-blooded Indians are slaughtered wherever there's the slightest excuse. Only in Mexico is it a little bit different."

"What you tell me from my dreams, Sam, this is no small job to do. I'm one middle-aged Indian woman, living in the jungle. I'm supposed to tell all the Indians of America to be proud? When they're the poorest of the poor and the lowest of the low?"

"When you give them a name, you create them. Benjamin Franklin did it, when he coined the name *American* for the people of the English colonies. They weren't New Yorkers or Virginians, they were Americans. Same thing for you. It isn't Latin Americans against Norteamericanos. It's Indians and Europeans. Somos todos indios. We're all Indians. Think that would work as a slogan?"

"Me. A revolutionary."

"Nós somos os americanos. Vai fora, Europa! America p'ra americanos! All kinds of slogans."

"I'd have to translate them into Spanish."

"Indios moram na India. Americanos moram na America. America nossa! No, better still: Nossa America! Nuestra America! It translates. Our America."

"You're a very fine slogan maker."

He shivered as she traced her finger along his shoulder and down the sensitive skin of his chest. She made a circle on his nipple and it shriveled and hardened, as if he were cold.

"Why are you silent now?" She laid her hand flat on his abdomen, just above his shorts, just below his navel. "You never tell me of your own dreams," she said. "But I know what they are."

He blushed.

"See? Your skin tells me, even when your mouth says nothing. I have dreamed these dreams all my life, and they troubled me, all the time, but now you tell me what they mean, a white-skinned dream-teller, you tell me that I must go among the Indians and make them proud, make them strong, so that everyone with a drop of Indian blood will call himself an Indian, and Europeans will lie and claim native ancestors, until America is all Indian. You tell me that I will give birth to the new Quetzalcoatl, and he will unify and heal the land of its sickness. But what you never tell me is this: Who will be the father of my feathered snake?"

Abruptly he got up and walked stiffly away. To the door, keeping his back to her, so she couldn't see how alert his body was. But she knew.

"I'm fifteen," said Sam, finally.

"And I'm very old. The land is older. Twenty million years. What does it care of the quarter-century between us?"

"I should never have come to this place."

"You never had a choice," she said. "My people have always known the god of the land. Once there was a perfect balance in this place. All the people loved the land and tended it. Like the garden of Eden. And the land fed them. It gave them maize and bananas. They took only what they needed to eat, and they did not kill animals for sport or humans for hate. But then the Incas turned away from the land and worshiped gold and the bright golden sun. The Aztecs soaked the ground in the blood of their human sacrifices. The Pueblos cut down the forests of Utah and Arizona and turned them into red-rock deserts. The Iroquois tortured their enemies and filled the forests with their screams of agony. We found tobacco and coca and peyote and coffee and forgot the dreams the land gave us in our sleep. And so the land rejected us. The land called to Co-

lumbus and told him lies and seduced him and he never had
a chance, did he? Never had a choice. The land brought the
Europeans to punish us. Disease and slavery and warfare
killed most of us, and the rest of us tried to pretend we were
Europeans rather than endure any more of the punishment.
The land was our jealous lover, and it hated us for a while.''

''Some Catholic you are,'' said Sam. ''I don't believe in
your Indian gods.''

''Say *Deus* or *Cristo* instead of *the land* and the story is
the same,'' she said. ''But now the Europeans are worse
than we Indians ever were. The land is suffering from a
thousand different poisons, and you threaten to kill all of
life with your weapons of war. We Indians have been pun-
ished enough, and now it's our turn to have the land again.
The land chose Columbus exactly five centuries ago. Now
you and I dream our dreams, the way he dreamed.''

''That's a good story,'' Sam said, still looking out the
door. It sounded so close to what the old prophets in the
Book of Mormon said would happen to America; close, but
dangerously different. As if there was no hope for the Europeans anymore. As if their chance had already been lost,
as if no repentance would be allowed. They would not be
able to pass the land on to the next generation. Someone
else would inherit. It made him sick at heart, to realize what
the white man had lost, had thrown away, had torn up and
destroyed.

''But what should I do with my story?'' she asked. He
could hear her coming closer, walking up behind him. He
could almost feel her breath on his shoulder. ''How can I
fulfill it?''

By yourself. Or at least without me. ''Tell it to the Indians. You can cross all these borders in a thousand different
places, and you speak Portuguese and Spanish and Arawak
and Carib, and you'll be able to tell your story in Quechua,
too, no doubt, crossing back and forth between Brazil and
Columbia and Bolivia and Peru and Venezuela, all close
together here, until every Indian knows about you and calls
you by the name you were given in my dream.''

''Tell me my name.''

''Virgem America. See? The land or God or whatever it
is wants you to be a virgin.''

She giggled. ''Nossa senhora,'' she said. ''Don't you see?
I'm the new Virgin *Mother*. It wants me to be a *mother*; all

the old legends of the Holy Mother will transfer to me; they'll call me virgin no matter what the truth is. How the priests will hate me. How they'll try to kill my son. But he will live and become Quetzalcoatl, and he will restore America to the true Americans. That is the meaning of my dreams. My dreams and yours.''

"Not me," he said. "Not for any dream or any god." He turned to face her. His fist was pressed against his groin, as if to crush out all rebellion there. "My body doesn't rule me," he said. "Nobody controls me but myself."

"That's very sick," she said cheerfully. "All because you hate your father. Forget that hate, and love me instead."

His face became a mask of anguish, and then he turned and fled.

* * *

He even thought of castrating himself, that's the kind of madness that drove him through the jungle. He could hear the bulldozers carving out the airstrip, the screams of falling timber, the calls of birds and cries of animals displaced. It was the terror of the tortured land, and it maddened him even more as he ran between thick walls of green. The rig was sucking oil like heartblood from the forest floor. The ground was wan and trembling under his feet. And when he got home he was grateful to lift his feet off the ground and lie on his mattress, clutching his pillow, panting or perhaps sobbing from the exertion of his run.

He slept, soaking his pillow in afternoon sweat, and in his sleep the voice of the land came to him like whispered lullabies. I did not choose you, said the land. I cannot speak except to those who hear me, and because it is in your nature to hear and listen, I spoke to you and led you here to save me, save me, save me. Do you know the desert they will make of me? Encased in burning dust or layers of ice, either way I'll be dead. My whole purpose is to thrust life upward out of my soils, and feel the press of living feet, and hear the songs of birds and the low music of the animals, growling, lowing, chittering, whatever voice they choose. That's what I ask of you, the dance of life, just once to make the man whose mother will teach him to be Quetzalcoatl and save me, save me, save me.

He heard that whisper and he dreamed a dream. In his dream he got up and walked back to Agualinda, not along the path, but through the deep jungle itself. A longer way, but the leaves touched his face, the spiders climbed on him, the tree lizards tangled in his hair, the monkeys dunged him and pinched him and jabbered in his ear, the snakes entwined around his feet; he waded streams and fish caressed his naked ankles, and all the way they sang to him, song that celebrants might sing at the wedding of a king. Somehow, in the way of dreams, he lost his clothing without removing it, so that he emerged from the jungle naked, and walked through Agualinda as the sun was setting, all the Baniwas peering at him from their doorways, making clicking noises with their teeth.

He awoke in darkness. He heard his father breathing. He must have slept through the afternoon. What a dream, what a dream. He was exhausted.

He moved, thinking of getting up to use the toilet. Only then did he realize that he was not alone on the bed, and it was not his bed. She stirred and nestled against him, and he cried out in fear and anger.

It startled her awake. "What is it?" she asked.

"It was a dream," he insisted. "All a dream."

"Ah yes," she said, "it was. But last night, Sam, we dreamed the same dream." She giggled. "All night long."

In his sleep. It happened in his sleep. And it did not fade like common dreams, the memory was clear, pouring himself into her again and again, her fingers gripping him, her breath against his cheek, whispering the same thing, over and over: "Aceito, aceito-te, aceito." Not love, no, not when he came with the land controlling him, she did not love him, she merely accepted the burden he placed within her. Before tonight she had been a virgin, and so had he. Now she was even purer than before, Virgem America, but his purity was hopelessly, irredeemably gone, wasted, poured out into this old woman who had haunted his dreams. "I hate you," he said. "What you stole from me."

He got up, looking for his clothing, ashamed that she was watching him.

"No one can blame you," she said. "The land married us, gave us to each other. There's no sin in that."

"Yeah," he said.

"One time. Now I am whole. Now I can begin."

And now I'm finished.

"I didn't mean to rob you," she said. "I didn't know you were dreaming."

"I thought I was dreaming," he said, "but I loved the dream. I dreamed I was fornicating and it made me glad." He spoke the words with all the poison in his heart. "Where are my clothes?"

"You arrived without them," she said. "It was my first hint that you wanted me."

There was a moon outside. Not yet dawn. "I did what you wanted," he said. "Now can I go home?"

"Do what you want," she said. "I didn't plan this."

"I know. I wasn't talking to you." And when he spoke of home, he didn't mean the shack where his father would be snoring and the air would stink of beer.

"When you woke me, I was dreaming," she said.

"I don't want to hear it."

"I have him now," she said, "a boy inside me. A lovely boy. But you will never see him in all your life, I think."

"Will you tell him? Who I am?"

She giggled. "Tell Quetzalcoatl that his father is a European? A man who blushes? A man who burns in the sun? No, I won't tell him. Unless someday he becomes cruel, and wants to punish the Europeans even after they are defeated. Then I will tell him that the first European he must punish is himself. Here, write your name. On this paper write your name, and give me your fingerprint, and write the date."

"I don't know what day it is."

"October twelfth," she said.

"It's August."

"Write October twelfth," she said. "I'm in the legend business now."

"August twenty-fourth," he murmured, but he wrote the date she asked for.

"The helicopter comes this morning," she said.

"Good-bye," he said. He started for the door.

Her hands caught at him, held his arm, pulled him back. She embraced him, this time not in a dream, cool bodies together in the doorway of the house. The geis was off him now, or else he was worn out; her body had no power over his anymore.

"I did love you," she murmured. "It was not just the god that brought you."

Suddenly he felt very young, even younger than fifteen, and he broke away from her and walked quickly away through the sleeping village. He did not try to retrace his wandering route through the jungle; he stayed on the moonlit path and soon was at his father's hut. The old bastard woke up as Sam came in.

"I knew it'd happen," Father said.

Sam rummaged for underwear and pulled it on.

"There's no man born who can keep his zipper up when a woman wants it." Father laughed. A laugh of malice and triumph. "You're no better than I am, boy."

Sam walked to where his father sat on the bed and imagined hitting him across the face. Once, twice, three times.

"Go ahead, boy, hit me. It won't make you a virgin again."

"I'm not like you," Sam whispered.

"No?" asked Father. "For you it's a sacrament or something? As my daddy used to say, it don't matter who squeezes the toothpaste, boy, it all squirts out the same."

"Then your daddy must have been as dumb a jackass as mine."

Sam went back to the chest they shared, began packing his clothes and books into one big suitcase. "I'm going out with the chopper today. Mom will wire me the money to come home from Manaus."

"She doesn't have to. I'll give you a check."

"I don't want your money. I just want my passport."

"It's in the top drawer." Father laughed again. "At least I always wore my clothes home."

In a few minutes Sam had finished packing. He picked up the bag, started for the door.

"Son," said Father, and because his voice was quiet, not derisive, Sam stopped and listened. "Son," he said, "once is once. It doesn't mean you're evil, it doesn't even mean you're weak. It just means you're human." He was breathing deeply. Sam hadn't heard him so emotional in a long time. "You aren't a thing like me, son," he said. "That should make you glad."

Years later Sam would think of all kinds of things he should have said. Forgiveness. Apology. Affection. Something. But he said nothing, just left and went out to the clearing and waited for the helicopter. Father didn't come to try to say good-bye. The chopper pilot came, unloaded, left the chopper to talk to some people. He must have talked to Father because when he came back he handed Sam a check. Plenty to fly home, and stay in good places during the layovers, and buy some new clothes that didn't have jungle stains on them. The check was the last thing Sam had from his father. Before he came home from that rig, the Venezuelans bought a hardy and virulent strain of syphilis on the black market, one that could be passed by casual contact, and released it in Guyana. Sam's father was one of the first million to die, so fast that he didn't even write.

Page, Arizona

The State of Deseret had only sixteen helicopters, all desperately needed for surveying, spraying, and medical emergencies. So Governor Sam Monson rarely risked them on government business. This time, though, he had no choice. He was only fifty-five, and in good shape, so maybe he could have made the climb down into Glen Canyon and back up the other side. But Carpenter wouldn't have made it, not in a wheelchair, and Carpenter had a right to be here. He had a right to see what the red-rock Navaho desert had become.

Deciduous forest, as far as the eye could see.

They stood on the bluff where the old town of Page had once been, before the dam was blown up. The Navahos hadn't tried to reforest here. It was their standard practice. They left all the old European towns unplanted, like pink scars in the green of the forest. Still, the Navahos weren't stupid. They had come to the last stronghold of European science, the University of Deseret at Zarahemla, to find out how to use the heavy rainfalls to give them something better than perpetual floods and erosion. It was Carpenter who gave them the plan for these forests, just as it was Carpenter whose program had turned the old Utah deserts into the richest farmland in America. The Navahos filled their forests with bison, deer, and bears. The Mormons raised crops enough to feed five times their population. That was the

European mind-set, still in place, enough is never enough. Plant more, grow more, you'll need it tomorrow.

"They say he has two hundred thousand soldiers," said Carpenter's computer voice. Carpenter *could* speak, Sam had heard, but he never did. Preferred the synthesized voice. "They could all be right down there, and we'd never see them."

"They're much farther south and east. Strung out from Phoenix to Santa Fe, so they aren't too much of a burden on the Navahos."

"Do you think they'll buy supplies from us? Or send an army in to take them?"

"Neither," said Sam. "We'll give our surplus grain as a gift."

"He rules all of Latin America, and he needs *gifts* from a little remnant of the U.S. in the Rockies?"

"We'll give it as a gift, and be grateful if he takes it that way."

"How else might he take it?"

"As tribute. As taxes. As ransom. The land is his now, not ours."

"We made the desert live, Sam. That makes it ours."

"There they are."

They watched in silence as four horses walked slowly from the edge of the woods, out onto the open ground of an ancient gas station. They bore a litter between them, and were led by two—not Indians—Americans. Sam had schooled himself long ago to use the word *American* to refer only to what had once been known as Indians, and to call himself and his own people Europeans. But in his heart he had never forgiven them for stealing his identity, even though he remembered very clearly where and when that change began.

It took fifteen minutes for the horses to bring the litter to him, but Sam made no move to meet them, no sign that he was in a hurry. That was also the American way now, to take time, never to hurry, never to rush. Let the Europeans wear their watches. Americans told time by the sun and stars.

Finally the litter stopped, and the men opened the litter door and helped her out. She was smaller than before, and her face was tightly wrinkled, her hair steel-white.

She gave no sign that she knew him, though he said his

name. The Americans introduced her as Nuestra Señora. Our Lady. Never speaking her most sacred name: Virgem America.

The negotiations were delicate but simple. Sam had authority to speak for Deseret, and she obviously had authority to speak for her son. The grain was refused as a gift, but accepted as taxes from a federated state. Deseret would be allowed to keep its own government, and the borders negotiated between the Navahos and the Mormons eleven years before were allowed to stand.

Sam went further. He praised Quetzalcoatl for coming to pacify the chaotic lands that had been ruined by the Europeans. He gave her maps that his scouts had prepared, showing strongholds of the prairie raiders, decommissioned nuclear missiles, and the few places where stable governments had been formed. He offered, and she accepted, a hundred experienced scouts to travel with Quetzalcoatl at Deseret's expense, and promised that when he chose the site of his North American capital, Deseret would provide architects and engineers and builders to teach his American workmen how to build the place themselves.

She was generous in return. She granted all citizens of Deseret conditional status as adopted Americans, and she promised that Quetzalcoatl's armies would stick to the roads through the northwest Texas panhandle, where the grasslands of the newest New Lands project were still so fragile that an army could destroy five years of labor just by marching through. Carpenter printed out two copies of the agreement in English and Spanish, and Sam and Virgem America signed both.

Only then, when their official work was done, did the old woman look up into Sam's eyes and smile. "Are you still a heretic, Sam?"

"No," he said. "I grew up. Are you still a virgin?"

She giggled, and even though it was an old lady's broken voice, he remembered the laughter he had heard so often in the village of Agualinda, and his heart ached for the boy he was then, and the girl she was. He remembered thinking then that forty-two was old.

"Yes, I'm still a virgin," she said. "God gave me my child. God sent me an angel, to put the child in my womb. I thought you would have heard the story by now."

"I heard it," he said.

She leaned closer to him, her voice a whisper. "Do you dream, these days?"

"Many dreams. But the only ones that come true are the ones I dream in daylight."

"Ah," she sighed. "My sleep is also silent."

She seemed distant, sad, distracted. Sam also; then, as if by conscious decision, he brightened, smiled, spoke cheerfully. "I have grandchildren now."

"And a wife you love," she said, reflecting his brightening mood. "I have grandchildren, too." Then she became wistful again. "But no husband. Just memories of an angel."

"Will I see Quetzalcoatl?"

"No," she said, very quickly. A decision she had long since made and would not reconsider. "It would not be good for you to meet face-to-face, or stand side by side. Quetzalcoatl also asks that in the next election, you refuse to be a candidate."

"Have I displeased him?" asked Sam.

"He asks this at my advice," she said. "It is better, now that his face will be seen in this land, that your face stay behind closed doors."

Sam nodded. "Tell me," he said. "Does he look like the angel?"

"He is as beautiful," she said. "But not as pure."

Then they embraced each other and wept. Only for a moment. Then her men lifted her back into her litter, and Sam returned with Carpenter to the helicopter. They never met again.

* * *

In retirement, I came to visit Sam, full of questions lingering from his meeting with Virgem America. "You knew each other," I insisted. "You had met before." He told me all this story then.

That was thirty years ago. She is dead now, he is dead, and I am old, my fingers slapping these keys with all the grace of wooden blocks. But I write this sitting in the shade of a tree on the brow of a hill, looking out across woodlands and orchards, fields and rivers and roads, where once the land was rock and grit and sagebrush. This is what America wanted, what it bent our lives to accomplish. Even if we took twisted roads and got lost or injured on the way, even if we came limping to this place, it is a good place, it is worth the journey, it is the promised, the promising land.

THE WORLD MUST NEVER KNOW

by G. C. Edmondson

Born Jose Mario Gary Ordoonez Edmondson y Cotton in 1922, the Mexican-born American writer and translator known as G.C. Edmondson has never been a prolific writer by genre standards, but many of those works he has produced have been important to the development of the field . . . and for many years he was one of the few SF writers around who routinely set stories in Third World locales, and was willing to examine life from a perspective other than that of whitebread suburban North America. His 1965 novel The Ship That Sailed the Time Stream *is a minor classic of the time-travel subgenre, and his 1971 novel* Chapayeca *(also published as* Blue Face*) is one of the best and most undeservedly forgotten novels of the 70s, an intelligent and compelling Alien Contact story that draws evocatively on Edmondson's expert knowledge of the Yaqui Indian culture of Northern Mexico. Edmondson also published a long sequence of "Mad Friend" stories in* The Magazine of Fantasy and Science Fiction *throughout the early and middle 60s, which were eventually assembled in the collection* Stranger Than You Think. *Almost forgotten today, the "Mad Friend" stories were sophisticated, intelligent, witty, and full of offbeat erudition, and again were frequently set in obscure corners of Mexico and Latin America—the story that follows, "The World Must Never Know," one of the best of them, examines cultures in conflict, as much of Edmondson's work does, and demonstrates how subtle—and how deadly—such a conflict can be.*

G.C. Edmondson's *other books include* To Sail the Century Sea, The Aluminum Man, T.H.E.M, The Man Who Corrupted the Earth, *and three books written with C.M. Kotlan,* The Takeover, The Cummingham Equations, *and The*

Black Magician. *Edmondson has also written numerous Western novels, under the psuedonym of Kelly P. Gast. Edmondson lives in Chula Vista, California.*

It was very late of a dark and moonless night. My mad friend was near exhaustion and I had arrived. Crouching in a thicket of some thorny desert flora, we listened for sounds of pursuit. After a moment my friend stopped panting. "You suppose it really worked—like he said it would?"

I shrugged and a thorn raked my shoulder. "Want to go back and see?"

He climbed to his feet and helped me up. "Better get to the car before daylight," he said. We began trotting. A half hour later we collapsed in a dry arroyo and he was pecking at it again. "God would never permit such a thing," he complained.

"He permits this," I panted. "As for the rest, The World Must Never Know."

"About the icebox or about the writer?"

A horse neighed somewhere so we began running again.

The trip had been one undiluted disaster. First, the transmission had exploded. Then my agent had phoned at the last minute and stuck me with this fool's errand. About that time the only wives on friendly terms with us had decided they'd had enough Mexican desert to last the rest of their lives. In another month this town would be uninhabitable. Already, the mirages were carrying parasols.

We sat on a backless bench under the scant shade of the military society's *ramada* and surveyed the dancers who tramped and spun monotonously. My mad friend sipped asphaltum-like coffee and looked surreptitiously for a place to spit. Finding none, he swallowed. "It is my considered opinion," he pontificated, "That we pursue the wild goose."

I tasted *tizwín* and agreed. With neither ice, head, nor maturity, the *tizwín* offered little, apart from bits of fermenting maize and possibly less danger than the local water. "I only knew him by reputation," I said.

"So what makes your literary shill think he'd end up in a place like this?"

I shrugged. "Last known address."

My friend waited in silence.

"Apparently he was living in one of those Truman Crack-erbox developments, skinning mules or missiles up in California when he first started dumping his frustrations into the typewriter."

My mad friend gave me a sharp glance. "Sounds familiar."

"He had one of those weird, gingerbread styles," I continued, "Unreadable until somebody performed an adjectivotomy."

A strident chirping issued from the church as *cantoras* antiphoned their distaff portion of the mass back at the chanting maestro. A *pascola*—one of the dancing clowns—gave us each a hand-rolled cigarette and began a long, rambling story. The language was quicker than I, but the punch line, which convulsed our neighbors, seemed to involve a coyote urinating on someone.

"You suppose he spoke it?" my friend asked.

"Must've. His Spanish was as ungrammatical as Hemingway's."

"Why do you suppose he left Utopia-on-the-Freeway?"

I shrugged. "He had a job, a wife, two daughters—none of which, apparently, he cared much for."

"Gauguin syndrome," my mad friend observed. "What caused him to bolt?"

A small brown man with a large canvas musette bag appeared on the opposite side of the plaza. Standing between the cross and the whipping post, he peered uncertainly through the dancers' dust. Spotting the only foreigners, he advanced, unconsciously parodying the sacred steps as he wheeled to avoid a gyrating platoon whose skirts fooled no one, save possibly the Boy-Stealing-Devil for whom they were intended.

Having safely skirted the skirts, the small brown man stopped at our bench beneath the military society's ramada. He removed an immense hat and fanned himself before rummaging in the bag and extracting a much handled post card. "Meester EeYAHree?"

This was vaguely reminiscent of my mad friend's patrilineal handle so he took the plunge. *"Ehui."*

The small brown man brightened. "You speak the language!"

My friend lapsed into Spanish. "Not well," he admitted.

"I can never remember when the double vowels should have a glottal stop in between." He turned the post card over."

"May we buy you a drink?" I asked.

The mail carrier rearranged the one or two letters in his bag, searching for a graceful way to apprise me of my gaffe. "I am *pweplum*," he said, which meant he belonged to the club whose shade we used, and was a citizen of this city-state where we barbarians gaped. "You are *yorim*?" The word referred to races less favored by God—people of degenerate religious practice who are not quite human—and presumably excused me from knowing that Drink came from the Great Mother and was neither bought nor sold.

My mad friend said something in Arabic. It sounded like an old window shade being ripped down the middle.

"Qué hubo?" I asked.

"They twist the dagger in a still bleeding wound!"

The post card had squares for "x's" after *Was your car ready on time? Were our employees courteous? Were you satisfied with the work performed? Was the steering wheel clean?*

I sympathized, for my mad friend was acutely unhappy with the re-transmissioned and re-radiatored behemoth which languished at Road's End some 100 km below us.

"Just wait," he muttered, "Until one of those courteous, cheerful, clean-steering-wheeled pirates tools into my speed trap!" He remembered the mailman. "Will you honor us by sitting?"

The small brown man gave a furtive Indian smile and sat. A boy brought him a glass of *tizwín*.

Still shrilling, the purple crowned *cantoras* emerged from the church, surrounding Virgin & Child. Age and an unsophisticated wood-carver had given these statues a color and ethnic cast more probable than that of the Aryan travesties one encounters among Nordic Faithful.

"Murphy was lacerating his duodenum up in California," my mad friend prompted.

"Ah yes. My city slicker spent a great deal of time showing him the ropes. About the time the slicker was ready to get his money back, presto!"

My mad friend sighed.

"At first my shill thought he'd been lured away by some other razor merchant. But after several months he received a letter—"

My mad friend began dictating: " 'I take the liberty of enclosing a MS which you may find marketable. Should you decide to handle me, I must stipulate that my whereabouts remain secret.

" 'Should any unusual conjecture cross your mind, please be assured I have excellent reason for conducting my affairs in this fashion. Sincerely, Joe Blow.' "

"You got it all right but the name," I conceded. "He signed himself S. Murphy."

The mailman coughed and blew a fine spray of *tizwín* in the general direction of the dancers. "Something wrong?" I asked. He shook his head and continued gasping. My mad friend thumped him on the back and after a couple of agonized wheezes the mailman was himself again. "You are writers!" he said.

"I demand trial by jury," my mad friend hastened.

"Whatever gave you that idea?" I wondered.

"You spoke of S. Murphy. I have read his works."

"Has he been translated?"

"I read him in English," the mail carrier said.

I raised my eyebrows but did not manage to cover my bald spot. "Obviously," my friend said, "You are a man of parts."

The *cantoras* had by now escorted Virgin and Child to the Mother cross next to the whipping post. After some complicated footwork and flag waving by the village's little girls, they returned the images to the church.

"This Murphy," my mad friend prompted.

I managed another sip of *tizwín*. "You're the crime crusher. You put the clues together. He pulled the plug on his instalments and in-laws and disappeared in a transparent but satisfactory manner since the joy and fruits of his gonads didn't bother or think to trace him through his agent.

"When he incarnated as Murphy, his kookie gingerbread style was unchanged, the subject matter still autobiographical. Previous stories had dealt with an Outsider type trying rather desperately to establish some contact with his family. The new run was beach-comber-remittance man genre—about the lonely stranger who nobly bears his white man's burden through some dark and secret corner of existence."

"My old sabre wounds are throbbing," my mad friend grunted.

The mail carrier took a deep breath. "I would write," he said, "If only I could find more time."

My friend flinched from the look in my eye.

"I have many ideas," the little man continued.

My mad friend glanced upward at the *ramada* which shaded us, reminding me that as guests we were duty-bound to hear out the club bore. "You didn't know S. Murphy?" I asked.

The mailman was swallowing *tizwín*, throwing his head back chicken fashion. He waggled a finger in the Latin negative.

"And you obviously know everyone in this district," my mad friend added.

The mail carrier nodded and spat the taste of *tizwín* toward the plaza where men danced in eternal penance for having slept when the Romans came to arrest their Saviour.

"Your agent's never met Murphy?" my friend asked.

I shook my head. "In this racket those who know your most intimate secrets are people you've never seen outside of an envelope."

"Why the sudden interest in looking him up?"

I fanned myself and wished either the weather or the *tizwín* were cooler. "Our errant scribe underwent some sort of metamorphosis once he escaped the strictures of Organizationville. Maybe it was a spiritual rebirth; maybe his typewriter got gummy. (He began hitting the keys a lot harder.) But he started leaving out all those adjectives. Suddenly, he had one of those simple, effective styles which makes Genesis read rather like a comic book. Of course, he loused it up by going off on some sort of phonetic spelling kick but writers never can spell anyway."

The low slanting sun was beginning to reach us beneath the *ramada* whose shade was now transposed to the plaza where *chapayecas* in needlenosed demon masks waved wooden swords in mute menace at children who made faces at them.

"What kind of stories do you write?" the little brown mail carrier asked.

"Mostly, I write the kind everybody was buying last year."

"*Principalmente,*" my mad friend contributed, "He writes accounts of the fantasy scientific."

"—so, about this time, S. Murphy—"

The mailman had taken the bit in his teeth. Though the Spanish language was no more native to him than to me, he had a certain way with words. "It was on the island," he began, "Which lies in the sea two days N from the river mouth. There had been a burning. The people accused him of being *ñagual*. The Mexicans got wind of it and I was taken along to interpret when they arrested the headman."

"*¿Nagual?*" my mad friend asked, "You believe that?"

"Certainly not," the mail carrier said. "A man is a man and a bear is a bear. They do not trade shapes. But these island people—"

"But there are no bears on this island," I protested, "How could the belief have drifted over there?"

The mail carrier shrugged. "No one ever got to the bottom of it. I could not understand their language so finally the Mexicans shot the headman and we left.

"On the way back, after the Mexicans had gone their way and I mine I decided to pass the night at—" He whisked through the double voweled stutterings which mean Jackrabbit Drinking Place Where the American Killed Many Mexicans Before They Cut Off His Head. "You have been there?"

We nodded.

"I watered my horse and hobbled him, a large *alazán* which I had acquired from a Mexican who no longer needed him."

No longer needed was a euphemism which I understood. "But you were working for the Mexicans," I protested.

"For their money," the mail carrier corrected. "This was some years ago, before they learned to respect us.

"It was early spring and there were still a few green weeds inside the hacienda's house garden. I led my sorrel in and was getting ready to boil coffee when a light came on inside the ruined building. It startled me," the little man continued, "For I had not seen many electric lights. Since then I have been in large cities and seen the colored lights which twist into letters but I have never seen light like this. It came from everywhere, like sunlight through fog. Though there was enough to sight a rifle, it cast no shadow."

A *chapayeca* came to the *ramada* and gestured with his wooden sword. While men were bringing out the drum I studied his needlenosed mask of fresh deerhide. Around the neck, his rosary strung up and was hidden under the demon face. I glanced at my mad friend.

"Vow of silence," he explained. "They keep the crucifix in their mouth for the entire week."

The mail carrier sensed that we were not particularly interested and began speeding up his story. "He was very white. His face had the pale, corpse color—like the part of a white man which is always covered by trousers. It was hard to know where clothing ended and skin began. He had no pockets. Carried a bag like this, only smaller." The mailman smiled momentarily. "His trousers were tight but showed no bulge at the seat of courage. His hair was like dried corn silk and bristled a half centimeter over face and head. His eyes were pink, like those of a horse I stole once. He was not Mexican so even though he was alone, I did not kill him.

"I accepted his invitation. His food came in square pieces like that tasteless bread you Americans eat. I did not care for it but since I had only a handful of *piñole* and three more days to ride . . . His beer was cold. Have you ever seen a small box from which one takes soft bottles and bites off the end?"

"No, but I've seen this story."

"About once a month for the first twenty years after Stanley G. Weinbaum's *floruit*," my mad friend suggested.

"You speak of stories," the mailman protested. "This really happened."

All the more reason for its suppression, I thought, but the little man was off again. "That night he took a small thing from his knapsack. It made a noise like beans when they are first dumped into a hot skillet, then a voice in some language I didn't know and he answered questions."

"How big was this radio?" I asked.

"It was like the cigarette pack radios the *turistas* carry now."

"And this really happened?" my mad friend asked, "In what year?"

The Indian thought a moment. "1926," he said.

"I know the Indian has a flexible concept of time," my friend said, "But this is carrying things too far."

"Later that night I woke and rolled a cigarette. It was that time of year when Woman Who Plants Squash is high in the sky. While I watched, the tip of her digging stick flared for just an instant, then suddenly the star was much tinier.''

''Were any novas recorded in 1926?''

''Search me,'' my friend said, ''I thought they lasted for days or months.''

''I had seen falling stars,'' the mail carrier continued, ''But this was the first time I had seen a fixed star change. I turned to see the all white man also sitting on his blanket. 'Two minutes early,' he grunted.''

The sun had finally set and it was becoming endurable beneath the *ramada*. In ten minutes it would be dark and we had not yet decided where to spread our sleeping bags. The dancers and officials of the various societies had been on their feet and fasting since dawn. Soon they would eat and those whose vow of silence relaxed at sundown would be enjoying themselves before the tiny fires which rimmed the boundaries of sacred ground.

''I dislike to freeload on people who can ill afford it,'' my friend said. ''But we'll create a bad impression if we uncork K rations in front of them.''

''You will be welcome at my house,'' the mailman said.

''We couldn't impose on you like that.'' Mentally, I was calculating how many times this offer must be refused to strike a balance between politeness and necessity. The mailman was the only one in this village who had regarded us with other than a faintly hostile curiosity. ''You must dine and pass the night with me,'' he repeated.

A boy brought *tizwín*. My long empty stomach regarded it somewhat coldly. I wondered if its taste had something to do with the village custom of constant and indiscriminate expectation.

''So what's with S. Murphy?'' my mad friend inquired.

''Ah yes, the errant scribe. Well, along with that stark and simple style he suddenly developed a plot sense. I read the first few chapters of his magnum opus as it came in. They were (and I say it with a wrenching in the cardiac region) far superior to anything I'll ever do.''

''So what's the difficulty?''

''They were good enough,'' I continued, ''To get the granddaddy of all contracts. The prepublication campaign on this one will make the *Peyton Place* business sound like the hard sell on some starving poet's slim volume.''

My mad friend was still mystified.

"The time is overripe," I said. "If I can't find this guy and talk him into completing those last three chapters within 60 days my shill may be forced to subsist exclusively on Brand X."

"Zo vot's in it for you?"

"If the wheels fall off his pushcart my apples also scatter," By now I had fallen into the habit of automatically spitting after each sip of *tizwín*. The postman, apparently unused to stronger waters, had lost his Indian gravity and would soon by all portents approach orbital velocity.

"S. Murphy," he slurred, "A wonderful writer."

Somewhere across the plaza a harp tinkled and falsetto voices raised in plaint to the Great Mother. "I have read his books," the mailman continued in a voice from which *tizwín* had dissolved all roughness. "Have you read one—I remember not the title under which it publishes." He began sketching in plot and characters, using that verbal shorthand one writer employs with another. I decided he must know Murphy quite well to have picked it up. "Could you take me to see him?" I asked.

The mailman shook his head. "Impossible. Much distance."

My mad friend listened boredly. The plot with a bumbling Ugly American type who settled in a village remarkably like this one—a man whose roots became large and clumsy feet when he attempted to plant them. My mad friend became more apathetic as he listened to garbled authorese. "What happened to the all-white man who was using pocket radios and predicting stellar catastrophes in 1926?" he asked.

Without hesitation the mailman shifted stories in midsentence. "It frightened me that this man with the pink eyes could know a star was going to die. I had always thought only Our Lord or Earth Mother could do these things. I thought of killing him but if he were what I thought, my bullets were of the wrong metal. For a moment I wondered if he might be the same one the island people burned.

"The all-white man sensed my inquietude. 'Everywhere it is the same,' he said. 'Most people are good. They hire someone to protect them from the bad and the foolish.' "

"Always around when you don't need one," I grunted.

My mad friend whistled from Gilbert and Sullivan to the effect that a policeman's lot was not a happy one. While the postman had droned on with this utterly predictable bit of sf I had been thinking deep thoughts about the Murphy plot he'd been detailing. "¿y Murphy?" I asked.

Murphy's style seemed to have rubbed off on the mail carrier though, of course, all Spanish in literal translation has that florid, bigger-than-life quality.

"There was a man in the village who could read," the Indian continued, "so he received a salary from the Mexicans, ostensibly as mail carrier, though really they thought they were hiring a Judas. Since no one else could read, his job was a sinecure. To make ends meet on his microscopic salary he also kept store, burro-training back those bits of civilization—cartridges, matches, coffee—which cannot be grown in fields.

"The postman and the stranger became friends. Both were initiates into the sacred mysteries of Alphabet. Both knew tales of the great world below. And there was the postman's daughter, in imminent danger of becoming an old maid. She sat in inconspicuous corners while the white man told stories of a world which mountain-bred beauty would never see.

"Murphy's eyes seared the brown body which bulged beneath an all-concealing dress. The postman was optimistic. But . . .

"Perhaps she reminded the white man too much of his own daughters who by now must have been considerably older. He made no overture. Meanwhile, young men of the village stayed away, knowing they could not compete with this blond Othello who held a maid enthralled with tales of distant lands." The mailman spat again.

It was totally dark now with that velvety blackness of the tropics, unrelieved at this altitude by any flicker of love-frenzied fireflies. From the tiny fires that ringed Sacred Ground came appetizing smells of coffee and broiling meat. "I don't know about you," I said to my friend, "But I could eat the gastric contents of a *ñagual.*"

"There will be food at my house," the mailman said.

I slung saddle bags of emergency rations over one shoulder and loaded down the other with the gadget bags and cameras which I had learned earlier would be reduced to powder if I so much as popped a flashbulb toward Sacred Ground. My mad friend shouldered the sleeping bags and we trudged behind the mailman, across the plaza, up the widest of the streets which wriggled octopus-like away from it.

A couple of hundred meters uphill we entered a larger than usual compound, fenced with the usual jumble of cactus and *pitahaya* stalks. With no great surprise, I recognized the store in Murphy's novel. We passed through it into the patio between the Mother Cross and a drying rack for chiles, into a low, rambling structure whose wattle and daub walls were high enough for privacy, but lacked a full meter of reaching the oval shaped palm thatch which shaded the house, stored maize out of the hog's reach, and sustained its own ecological cycle from cockroach to scorpion via mouse to snake. We suffered a visitation of mosquitoes.

"Burn a candle for whoever invented atabrine," I muttered.

My mad friend nodded and crossed himself.

The postman's wife was a tall, mahogany colored woman who wore abundant hair in a *molote* like Mrs. Katzenjammer. She greeted her minuscule husband with a respectful affection which explained the equanimity with which he faced a large and confusing world. She extracted a palm leaf from beneath the baby in her rebozo and knelt to revive the fire in the patio. A stairstep set of daughters joined her and the eldest began slapping tortillas while others brought out the best dishes.

Soon my mad friend and I faced steaming bowls of the stewed squash blossoms which are one reason why I return regularly to this desolate land. We were poured countless cups of the asphaltum-like coffee which, after one disremembers American brews stands on its own peculiar virtue. There was chicken stewed in *mole*, a dark brown sauce made of 21 different chiles, peanut flour, ground *chocolatl*, and Ometecuhtl knows what else. When *tamales de dulce* appeared, made of fresh roasting ears macerated with stick cinnamon and loaf sugar, I began to suspect some runner had forewarned the household of our impending visit. The *tizwín* began to rest more comfortably.

After a terminal plate of beans with tortillas of the local, paper thin and yard wide variety, we stretched legs and tilted vertical backed rawhide bottomed chairs to a comfortable angle. I glanced at my mad friend who was more cognizant of local custom than I. He nodded so I extracted some emergency ration.

A daughter brought glasses. The mailman regarded the label on my rations with respect and said something which astounded us: "I'll bring some ice."

The wife had long since retired to her own part of the immense rambling structure. We were alone in the patio, save for the 15 year old daughter who bulged in all the proper places and was learning how to pose and project her protuberances. I wondered if this were instinct or sophistication. It occurred to me that this might be the same young lady who in her quiet way was giving Murphy the business.

My mad friend was oblivious to her. "Where in the name of Our Lord and Saviour did he ever get ice?" he wondered. It flabbergoosed me too; the nearest natural ice was hundreds of miles higher in the sierra and the nearest machine at least 100 km below us at Road's End.

The postman returned with a dish of ice cubes and Desdemona ceased her siren act. My mad friend sipped resignedly at his coffee while I and the postman tried to forget the taste of *tizwín*. "This Murphy plot," I pursued, "What did you say was the name of the book?"

Beguiled by the smoothness of my K ration, the postman was underestimating its effect. "Don't know," he slurred, "Not finished yet."

My mad friend raised eyebrows and I nodded, "He's been describing the one my shill sent me here to get finished," I turned back to the postman, "Now when," I insisted, "do I see S. Murphy?"

The little man's eyes flickered and he was suddenly cautious. "Not possible. Much distance."

The siren remained silent and watchful in her corner. I sneaked a glance at her and wondered why Murphy had hesitated. The postman caught me looking so I hastily poured him another drink. "What happened," my mad friend asked, "To the pink-eyed cop who shrinks stars?"

"He doesn't." I marvelled at the mailman's ability to switch subjects as rapidly as my mad friend. He skipped hurriedly through the rest of the story: "The good people paid him to watch out for the bad ones—*delincuentes juveniles*—he called them." Abruptly, the mailman lurched to his feet and staggered past the Mother cross into the darker portion of the patio. I heard sounds which suggested an incompatibility between squash blossoms and emergency ration.

My mad friend glanced meaningly to my left as a mez-quite twig flickered I saw the 15 year old still studying us unblinkingly from her dark corner. "I think," I said in English, "We observe the reason why Murphy has not finished his book."

My friend reflected a half second. "Still making up his mind how to end it?"

"Where do you suppose he's hiding and why won't he see us?"

I grinned. "Even without badge and nightstick there is in your freudian corpus a certain aura which probably shows— even through binoculars."

My mad friend sighed and again began whistling Gilbert and Sullivan. "So what do we do?" he wondered.

I shrugged. "There's at least one member of the family who'd love to have us stay."

My friend glanced worriedly at her. The siren protuber-ated visibly when she saw him looking.

Wiping away the remains of a cold sweat, the mailman returned to sit between us. "The pink-eyed man asked me," he continued, "if I had ever sat by a fire as someone in drunken glee galloped a horse through it. I remembered when Mexican soldiers amused themselves that way at the expense of the meal my mother was cooking. Thinking about it, I was almost ready again to kill the pink-eyed man when he asked, 'How would you like it if someone rode a great horse—' " The mailman stopped perplexed and looked at us. "I've seen horses drag men and cows but what kind of horse can drag a whole field with it?"

My mad friend looked blankly at me.

"The pink-eyed one spoke of galloping too close to the sun and one field interfering with another until the fire flared and went out just as when the soldiers used to ride through our village. It was annoying when people had to leave their earth and synthesize new homes. It could even be dangerous for people who do not—¿what means *teleport?*"

My mad friend sipped coffee. "Well, Dr. OneStone, there's the missing link in your Unified Field Theory."

I looked at the mailman. "Possibilities," I said. "I can't remember it's being used in sf before. Where did you get this idea?"

"That's what the pink-eyed man said. I don't understand it." He threw a stick on the fire.

"After smoking a cigarette I went back to sleep. At dawn the all-white man's radio began sizzling like frying beans. He asked questions in that other language and finally put the small radio away. He opened the cold box and took out beer. 'I must leave,' he said, handing me one and biting the top from his own. 'Do you like cold drinks?' I nodded for the sun had been up 10 minutes and the day was already hot. 'Keep the box,' he said, 'Do not open the bottom and it will never harm you. Treat it with respect and it will run forever. Anything you put in it will be cold.'

"' I am poor,' I protested, 'What can I give you?' The all-white man gave a strange, twisted smile. 'To me, nothing. But next time you're ready to kill a cop, stop and think how your world would be if there were none.'

"I tried to understand what he meant. I was asking him to explain when I noticed that he was gone. I looked all around the hacienda buildings but did not find him."

My mad friend sipped coffee and whistled Policeman's Lot in a minor key. It was quite late and I wondered where we would unroll our sleeping bags. A mezquite twig flared and illuminated the mailman's mahogany face. Some trick of the light reminded me of an idol on a vine-tangled trail halfway between Persepolis and San Francisco.

"Naguales," my friend grunted, and halfheartedly mumbled an exorcism. I decided to make a final lunge toward the main chance. "¿y Murphy?"

The brown man emerged from his white study. "Wonderful writer." He fished a melting ice cube from the dish and bathed it with K ration. I admired his fortitude. He took a long swallow which wavered briefly in his gullet before going down. "The ending is written. The pages will leave for New York whenever the post office makes up a bag."

"Didn't he send them airmail?"

"Is there need for haste?"

"Much need," I groaned, "Also much need to see Murphy."

The postman ignored this. "Two endings," he continued, "Which is most artistically satisfying? Should the bumbling stranger marry the girl and live happily or should he be consistent and put his foot in this as in everything else?"

My mad friend and I waited with unbated breath. The postman took another swallow and continued more slowly: "The stranger did not even realize that to visit the girl's father so often constituted a form of engagement. If he did not marry her, the girl would never find another husband in the village."

My mad friend yawned. "And you never saw the pink-eyed cop again?"

The mailman waggered his finger.

"Good idea," I said. "But it has the same defect as Murphy's book. You'll never get away with these up-in-the-air endings. Pin it down now—what happened to your all-white cop?—just as Murphy'll have to pin down what happened to his multiple-thumbed hero."

"Murphy had an ending," the mailman said.

My mad friend fanned himself and assassinated a brace of mosquitoes. "Might drag that wireless icebox back into the plot somehow," he maundered, "By the way, where're you getting all this ice?"

"From the icebox?"

"That one?"

"Couldn't be," I said in English. "No electricity; he's probably got a kerosene powered Servel."

The postman shook his head.

"Please," my mad friend said tiredly, "No extraterrestrials at this hour of the morning."

"I'll bring it," the mailman said. He staggered to his feet and left the circle of firelight. In a moment I heard the sound of K ration leaving by that same door wherein it went.

"I wonder what Monkey Ward Marvel he's going to palm off on us?" my friend mused.

I shrugged. "You may have noticed certain obvious parallels in this Murphy book," I began, "Also, a certain talent in our host."

My friend nodded. "Suppose he learned all his English in the last year from Murphy?"

"Probably chopped beets or picked lettuce in the States between revolutions."

"Have you considered," my friend asked, "How far we are from civilization and/or law enforcement?"

I nodded. "Suppose they've burnt any *ñaguales* around here recently?"

My mad friend tossed a gnarled mezquite branch on the fire and waited till it blazed. Somewhere in the darkness I could hear the mailman retching.

"You mentioned that Murphy's style changed. What about his typing?"

"Suddenly every letter was slammed home as if he were whacking them out with a chisel."

"Sure mark of a one finger typist."

The retching had stopped and I could hear the postman rummaging somewhere in his house. The branch flared up and I saw the fifteen year old still regarding us unwinkingly from the shadows. She commenced protuberating.

"He said Murphy *had* an end," I mused. "Also mentioned that a visit constitutes formal engagement." From the house I heard footsteps as the postman approached us. My mad friend looked at me and I looked at him. We both glanced at the hopeful sprite.

The postman stepped into the circle of firelight bearing a rectangular box, subtly different from anything I'd ever seen. "This is the refrigerator which works forever without fuel," he said.

The girl stretched and protuberated some more. I caught my friend's eye and we shared a common thought about an uncommon discovery. Suddenly we knew why Murphy's typewriter was being one-fingered, why his spelling had suddenly gone to playing by ear, and what had happened to S. Murphy. My mad friend tilted his straight backed chair forward and began rising.

But I beat him out the door.

It was very late of a dark and moonless night. Crouching in thorny desert flora, we listened. "I don't believe it," my mad friend muttered.

"So what are we running for?" I whispered back.

Somewhere in the distance a bit clinked. We shrank behind an ocotillo while a rider with rifle at ready light-footed down the trail. "They're ahead of us now," I whispered.

My mad friend pointed sky-ward. I sighted along his forearm at a line of minor but fixed stars which was slowly winking out. "Coming this way," I whispered. "You suppose that starcop was for real?"

My friend was muttering something in Latin.

"Maybe we could teleport?" I suggested.

"Please," he hissed, "I've got enough troubles already!"

We started running again.

INVADERS

by John Kessel

Here's a wry and blackly ironic story that contrasts and compares two different sorts of invaders, and draws some very uncomfortable conclusions. . . .

Born in Buffalo, New York, John Kessel now lives in Raleigh, North Carolina, where he is a professor of American literature and creative writing at North Carolina State University. Kessel made his first sale in 1975, and has since become a frequent contributor to Isaac Asimov's Science Fiction Magazine *and* The Magazine of Fantasy and Science Fiction *(for which magazine he now writes a regular column on books), as well as to many other magazines and anthologies. Kessel's first solo novel,* Good News From Outer Space, *was released in 1988 to wide critical acclaim, but before that he had made his mark on the genre primarily as a writer of highly-imaginative, finely-crafted short stories. He won a Nebula Award in 1983 for his superlative novella "Another Orphan," which was also a Hugo finalist that year, and has been released as an individual book. His story "Buffalo" won the Theodore Sturgeon Award in 1991. His other books include the novel* Freedom Beach, *written in collaboration with James Patrick Kelly. His most recent book is a collection of his short fiction,* Meeting in Infinity. *He is currently at work on a new novel,* Corrupting Dr. Nice.*

November 1532: That night no one slept. On the hills outside Cajamarca, the campfires of the Inca's army shone like so many stars in the sky. De Soto had reported that Atahualpa had perhaps forty thousand troops under arms, but looking at the myriad lights spread across those hills, de Candia realized that estimate was, if anything, low.

Against them, Pizarro could throw one hundred foot soldiers, sixty horse, eight muskets, and four harquebuses. Pizarro, his brother Hernando, de Soto, and Benalcázar laid out plans for an ambush. They would invite the Inca to a parlay. De Candia and his artillery would be hidden in the building along one side of the square, the cavalry and infantry along the others. De Candia watched Pizarro prowl through the camp that night, checking the men's armor, joking with them, reminding them of the treasure they would have, and the women. The men laughed nervously and whetted their swords.

They might sharpen them until their hands fell off; when morning dawned, they would be slaughtered. De Candia breathed deeply of the thin air and turned from the wall.

Ruiz de Arce, an infantryman with a face like a clenched fist, hailed him as he passed. "Are those guns of yours ready for some work tomorrow?"

"We need prayers more than guns."

"I'm not afraid of these brownies," de Arce said.

"Then you're a half-wit."

"Soto says they have no swords."

The man was probably just trying to reassure himself, but de Candia couldn't abide it. "Will you shut your stinking fool's trap! They don't need swords! If they only spit all at once, we'll be drowned."

Pizarro overheard him. He stormed over, grabbed de Candia's arm, and shook him. "Have they ever seen a horse, Candia? Have they ever felt steel? When you fired the harquebus on the seashore, didn't the town chief pour beer down its barrel as if it were a thirsty god? Pull up your balls and show me you're a man!"

His face was inches away. "Mark me! Tomorrow, Saint James sits on your shoulder, and we win a victory that will cover us in glory for five hundred years."

* * *

2 December 2001: "DEE-fense! DEE-fense!" the crowd screamed. During the two-minute warning, Norwood Delacroix limped over to the Redskins' special conditioning coach.

"My knee's about gone," said Delacroix, an outside linebacker with eyebrows that ran together and all the musculature that modern pharmacology could load onto his six-foot-five frame. "I need something."

"You need the power of prayer, my friend. Stoner's eating your lunch."

"Just do it."

The coach selected a popgun from his rack, pressed the muzzle against Delacroix's knee, and pulled the trigger. A flood of well-being rushed up Delacroix's leg. He flexed it tentatively. It felt better than the other one now. Delacroix jogged back onto the field. "DEE-fense!" the fans roared. The overcast sky began to spit frozen rain. The ref blew the whistle, and the Bills broke huddle.

Delacroix looked across at Stoner, the Bills' tight end. The air throbbed with electricity. The quarterback called the signals; the ball was snapped; Stoner surged forward. As Delacroix backpedaled furiously, sudden sunlight flooded the field. His ears buzzed. Stoner jerked left and went right, twisting Delacroix around like a cork in a bottle. His knee popped. Stoner had two steps on him. TD for sure. Delacroix pulled his head down and charged after him.

But instead of continuing downfield, Stoner slowed. He looked straight up into the air. Delacroix hit him at the knees, and they both went down. He'd caught him! The crowd screamed louder, a scream edged with hysteria.

Then Delacroix realized the buzzing wasn't just in his ears. Elation fading, he lifted his head and looked toward the sidelines. The coaches and players were running for the tunnels. The crowd boiled toward the exits, shedding thermoses and beer cups and radios. The sunlight was harshly bright. Delacroix looked up. A huge disk hovered no more than fifty feet above, pinning them in its spotlight. Stoner untangled himself from Delacroix, stumbled to his feet, and ran off the field.

Holy Jesus and the Virgin Mary on toast, Delacroix thought.

He scrambled toward the end zone. The stadium was emptying fast, except for the ones who were getting trampled. The throbbing in the air increased in volume, lowered in pitch, and the flying saucer settled onto the NFL logo on the forty-yard line. The sound stopped as abruptly as if it had been sucked into a sponge.

Out of the corner of his eye, Delacroix saw an NBC cameraman come up next to him, focusing on the ship. Its side divided, and a ramp extended itself to the ground. The cameraman fell back a few steps, but Delacroix held his ground. The inside glowed with the bluish light of a UV lamp.

A shape moved there. It lurched forward to the top of the ramp. A large manlike thing, it advanced with a rolling stagger, like a college freshman at a beer blast. It wore a body-tight red stretchsuit, a white circle on its chest with a lightning bolt through it, some sort of flexible mask over its face. Blond hair covered its head in a kind of brush cut, and two cup-shaped ears poked comically out of the sides of its head. The creature stepped off onto the field, nudging aside the football that lay there.

Delacroix, who had majored in public relations at Michigan State, went forward to greet it. This could be the beginning of an entirely new career. His knee felt great.

He extended his hand. "Welcome," he said. "I greet you in the name of humanity and the United States of America."

"Cocaine," the alien said. "We need cocaine."

* * *

Today: I sit at my desk writing a science-fiction story, a tall, thin man wearing jeans, a white T-shirt with the abstract face of a man printed on it, white high-top basketball shoes, and gold-plated wire-rimmed glasses.

In the morning I drink coffee to get me up for the day, and at night I have a gin and tonic to help me relax.

* * *

16 November 1532: "What are they waiting for, the shitting dogs!" the man next to de Arce said. "Are they trying to make us suffer?"

"Shut up, will you?" De Arce shifted his armor. Wedged into the stone building on the side of the square, sweating, they had been waiting since dawn, in silence for the most part except for the creak of leather, the uneasy jingle of cascabels on the horses' trappings. The men stank worse than the restless horses. Some had pissed themselves. A common foot soldier like de Arce was lucky to get a space near enough to the door to see out.

As noon came and went with still no sign of Atahualpa and his retinue, the mood of the men went from impatience to near panic. Then, late in the day, word came that the Indians again were moving toward the town.

An hour later, six thousand brilliantly costumed attendants entered the plaza. They were unarmed. Atahualpa, borne on a golden litter by eight men in cloaks of green feathers that glistened like emeralds in the sunset, rose above them. De Arce heard a slight rattling, looked down, and found that his hand, gripping the sword so tightly the knuckles stood out white, was shaking uncontrollably. He unknotted his fist from the hilt, rubbed the cramped fingers, and crossed himself.

"Quiet now, my brave ones," Pizarro said.

Father Valverde and Felipillo strode out to the center of the plaza, right through the sea of attendants. The priest had guts. He stopped before the litter of the Inca, short and steady as a fence post. "Greetings, my lord, in the name of Pope Clement VII, His Majesty the Emperor Charles V, and Our Lord and Savior Jesus Christ."

Atahualpa spoke and Felipillo translated: "Where is this new god?"

Valverde held up the crucifix. "Our God died on the cross many years ago and rose again to Heaven. He appointed the Pope as His viceroy on earth, and the Pope has commanded King Charles to subdue the peoples of the world and convert them to the true faith. The king sent us here to command your obedience and to teach you and your people in this faith."

"By what authority does this pope give away lands that aren't his?"

Valverde held up his Bible. "By the authority of the word of God."

The Inca took the Bible. When Valverde reached out to help him get the cover unclasped, Atahualpa cuffed his arm away. He opened the book and leafed through the pages. After a moment he threw it to the ground. "I hear no words," he said.

Valverde snatched up the book and stalked back toward Pizarro's hiding place. "What are you waiting for?" he shouted. "The saints and the Blessed Virgin, the bleeding wounds of Christ himself, cry vengeance! Attack, and I'll absolve you!"

Pizarro had already stridden into the plaza. He waved his kerchief. "Santiago, and at them!"

On the far side, the harquebuses exploded in an enfilade.
The lines of Indians jerked like startled cats. Bells jingling,
de Soto's and Hernando's cavalry burst from the lines of
doorways on the adjoining side. De Arce clutched his sword
and rushed out with the others from the third side. He felt
the power of God in his arm. "Santiago!" he roared at the
top of his lungs, and hacked halfway through the neck of
his first Indian. Bright blood spurted. He put his boot to the
brown man's shoulder and yanked free, lunged for the belly
of another wearing a kilt of bright red-and-white checks.
The man turned, and the sword caught between his ribs.
The hilt was almost twisted from de Arce's grasp as the
Indian went down. He pulled free, shrugged another man
off his back, and daggered him in the side.

After the first flush of glory, it turned to filthy, hard work,
an hour's wade through an ocean of butchery in the twilight,
bodies heaped waist-high, boots skidding on the bloody
stones. De Arce alone must have killed forty. Only after
they'd slaughtered them all and captured the Sapa Inca did
it end. A silence settled, broken only by the moans of dying
Indians and distant shouts of the cavalry chasing the ones
who had managed to break through the plaza wall to escape.

Saint James had indeed sat on their shoulders. Six thousand dead Indians, and not one Spaniard nicked. It was a
pure demonstration of the power of prayer.

* * *

31 January 2002: It was Colonel Zipp's third session in-
terrogating the alien. So far the thing had kept a consistent
story, but not a credible one. The only consideration that
kept Zipp from panic at the thought of how his career would
suffer if this continued was the rumor that his fellow case
officers weren't doing any better with any of the others.
That, and the fact that the Krel possessed technology that
would reestablish American superiority for another two
hundred years. He took a drag on his cigarette, the first of
his third pack of the day.

"Your name?" Zipp asked.

"You may call me Flash."

Zipp studied the red union suit, the lightning bolt. With
the flat chest, the rounded shoulders, pointed upper lip, and
pronounced underbite, the alien looked like a cross between

Wally Cleaver and the Mock Turtle. "Is this some kind of joke?"

"What is a joke?"

"Never mind." Zipp consulted his notes. "Where are you from?"

"God has ceded us an empire extending over sixteen solar systems in the Orion arm of the galaxy, including the systems around the stars you know as Tau Ceti, Epsilon Eridani, Alpha Centauri, and the red dwarf Barnard's star."

"God gave you an empire?"

"Yes. We were hoping He'd give us your world, but all He kept talking about was your cocaine."

The alien's translating device had to be malfunctioning. "You're telling me that God sent you for cocaine?"

"No. He just told us about it. We collect chemical compounds for their aesthetic interest. These alkaloids do not exist on our world. Like the music you humans value so highly, they combine familiar elements—carbon, hydrogen, nitrogen, oxygen—in pleasing new ways."

The colonel leaned back, exhaled a cloud of smoke. "You consider cocaine like—like a symphony?"

"Yes. Understand, Colonel, no material commodity alone could justify the difficulties of interstellar travel. We come here for aesthetic reasons."

"You seem to know what cocaine is already. Why don't you just synthesize it yourself?"

"If you valued a unique work of aboriginal art, would you be satisfied with a mass-produced duplicate manufactured in your hometown? Of course not. And we are prepared to pay you well, in a coin you can use."

"We don't need any coins. If you want cocaine, tell us how your ships work."

"That is one of the coins we had in mind. Our ships operate according to a principle of basic physics. Certain fundamental physical reactions are subject to the belief system of the beings promoting them. If I believe that X is true, then X is more probably true than if I did not believe so."

The colonel leaned forward again. "We know that already. We call it the 'observer effect.' Our great physicist Werner Heisenberg—"

"Yes. I'm afraid we carry this principle a little further than that."

''What do you mean?''

Flash smirked. ''I mean that our ships move through interstellar space by the power of prayer.''

* * *

13 May 1533: Atahualpa offered to fill a room twenty-two feet long and seventeen feet wide with gold up to a line as high as a man could reach, if the Spaniards would let him go. They were skeptical. How long would this take? Pizarro asked. Two months, Atahualpa said.

Pizarro allowed the word to be sent out, and over the next several months, bearers, chewing the coca leaf in order to negotiate the mountain roads under such burdens, brought in tons of gold artifacts. They brought plates and vessels, life-sized statues of women and men, gold lobsters and spiders and alpacas, intricately fashioned ears of maize, every kernel reproduced, with leaves of gold and tassels of spun silver.

Martin Bueno was one of the advance scouts sent with the Indians to Cuzco, the capital of the empire. They found it to be the legendary city of gold. The Incas, having no money, valued precious metals only as ornament. In Cuzco the very walls of the Sun Temple, Coricancha, were plated with gold. Adjoining the temple was a ritual garden where gold maize plants supported gold butterflies, gold bees pollinated gold flowers.

''Enough loot that you'll shit in a different gold pot every day for the rest of your life,'' Bueno told his friend Diego Leguizano upon his return to Cajamarca.

They ripped the plating off the temple walls and had it carried to Cajamarca. There they melted it down into ingots.

The huge influx of gold into Europe was to cause an economic catastrophe. In Peru, at the height of the conquest, a pair of shoes cost $850, and a bottle of wine $1,700. When their old horseshoes wore out, iron being unavailable, the cavalry shod their horses with silver.

* * *

21 April 2003: In the executive washroom of Bellingham, Winston, and McNeese, Jason Prescott snorted a couple of

lines and was ready for the afternoon. He returned to the
brokerage to find the place in a whispering uproar. In his
office sat one of the Krel. Prescott's secretary was about to
piss himself. "It asked specifically for you," he said.

What would Attila the Hun do in this situation? Prescott
thought. He went into the office. "Jason Prescott," he said.
"What can I do for you, Mr. . . . ?"

The alien's bloodshot eyes surveyed him. "Flash. I wish
to make an investment."

"Investments are our business." Rumors had flown
around the New York Merc for a month that the Krel were
interested in investing. They had earned vast sums selling
information to various computer, environmental, and bio-
tech firms. Several of the aliens had come to observe trading
in the currencies pit last week, and only yesterday Jason
had heard from a reliable source that they were considering
opening an account with Merrill Lynch. "What brings you
to our brokerage?"

"Not the brokerage. You. We heard that you are the most
ruthless currencies trader in this city. We worship efficiency. You are efficient."

Right. Maybe there was a hallucinogen in the toot. "I'll
call in some of our foreign-exchange experts. We can work
up an investment plan for your consideration in a week."

"We already have an investment plan. We are, as you say
in the markets, 'long' in dollars. We want you to sell dollars
and buy francs for us."

"The franc is pretty strong right now. It's likely to hold
for the next six months. We'd suggest—"

"We wish to buy $50 billion worth of francs."

Prescott stared. "That's not a very good investment."
Flash said nothing. The silence grew uncomfortable. "I
suppose if we stretch it out over a few months, and hit the
exchanges in Hong Kong and London at the same time—"

"We want these francs bought in the next week. For the
week after that, a second $50 billion. Fifty billion a week
until we tell you to stop."

Hallucinogens for sure. "That doesn't make any sense."

"We can take our business elsewhere."

Prescott thought about it. It would take every trick he
knew—and he'd have to invent some new ones—to carry this
off. The dollar was going to drop through the floor, while
the franc would punch through the sell-stops of every trader

on ten world markets. The exchanges would scream bloody murder. The repercussions would auger holes in every economy north of Antarctica. Governments would intervene. It would make the historic Hunt silver squeeze look like a game of Monopoly.

Besides, it made no sense. Not only was it criminally irresponsible, it was stupid. The Krel would squander every dime they'd earned.

Then he thought about the commission on $50 billion a week.

Prescott looked across at the alien. From the right point of view, Flash resembled a barrel-chested college undergraduate from Special Effects U. He felt an urge to giggle, a euphoric feeling of power. "When do we start?"

* * *

19 May 1533: In the fields the *purics,* singing praise to Atahualpa, son of the sun, harvested the maize. At night they celebrated by getting drunk on *chicha.* It was, they said, the most festive month of the year.

Pedro Sancho did his drinking in the dark of the treasure room, in the smoke of the smelters' fire. For months he had been troubled by nightmares of the heaped bodies lying in the plaza. He tried to ignore the abuse of the Indian women, the brutality toward the men. He worked hard. As Pizarro's squire, it was his job to record daily the tally of Atahualpa's ransom. When he ran low on ink, he taught the *purics* to make it for him from soot and the juice of berries. They learned readily.

Atahualpa heard about the ink and one day came to him. "What are you doing with those marks?" he said, pointing to the scribe's tally book.

"I'm writing the list of gold objects to be melted down."

"What is this 'writing'?"

Sancho was nonplussed. Over the months of Atahualpa's captivity, Sancho had become impressed by the sophistication of the Incas. Yet they were also queerly backward. They had no money. It was not beyond belief that they should not know how to read and write.

"By means of these marks, I can record the words that people speak. That's writing. Later other men can look at these marks and see what was said. That's reading."

"Then this is a kind of quipu?" Atahualpa's servants had demonstrated for Sancho the quipu, a system of knotted strings by which the Incas kept talleys. "Show me how it works," Atahualpa said.

Sancho wrote on the page: *God have mercy on us.* He pointed. "This, my lord, is a representation of the word 'God.' "

Atahualpa looked skeptical. "Mark it here." He held out his hand, thumbnail extended.

Sancho wrote "God" on the Inca's thumbnail.

"Say nothing now." Atahualpa advanced to one of the guards, held out his thumbnail. "What does this mean?" he asked.

"God," the man replied.

Sancho could tell the Inca was impressed, but he barely showed it. That the Sapa Inca had maintained such dignity throughout his captivity tore at Sancho's heart.

"This writing is truly a magical accomplishment," Atahualpa told him. "You must teach my *amautas* this art."

Later, when the viceroy Estete, Father Valverde, and Pizarro came to chide him for the slow pace of the gold shipments, Atahualpa tested each of them separately. Estete and Valverde each said the word "God." Atahualpa held his thumbnail out to the conquistador.

Estete chuckled. For the first time in his experience, Sancho saw Pizarro flush. He turned away. "I don't waste my time on the games of children," Pizarro said.

Atahualpa stared at him. "But your common soldiers have this art."

"Well, I don't."

"Why not?"

"I was a swineherd. Swineherds don't need to read."

"You are not a swineherd now."

Pizarro glared at the Inca. "I don't need to read to order you put to death." He marched out of the room.

After the others had left, Sancho told Atahualpa, "You ought not to humiliate the governor in front of his men."

"He humiliates himself," Atahualpa said. "There is no skill in which a leader ought to let himself stand behind his followers."

* * *

Today: The part of this story about the Incas is as histor-ically accurate as I could make it, but this Krel business is science fiction. I even stole the name "Krel" from a 1950s SF flick. I've been addicted to SF for years. In the evening my wife and I wash the bad taste of the news out of our mouths by watching old movies on videotape.

A scientist, asked why he read SF, replied, "Because in science fiction the experiments always work." Things in SF stories work out more neatly than in reality. Nothing is im-possible. Spaceships move faster than light. Atomic weap-ons are neutralized. Disease is abolished. People travel in time. Why, Isaac Asimov even wrote a story once that ended with the reversal of entropy!"

The descendants of the Incas, living in grinding poverty, find their most lucrative crop in coca, which they refine into cocaine and sell in vast quantities to North Americans.

* * *

23 August 2008: "Catalog number 208," said John Bos-tock. "Georges Seurat, *Bathers*."

FRENCH GOVERNMENT FALLS, the morning *Times* had an-nounced. JAPAN BANS U.S. IMPORTS. FOOD RIOTS IN MADRID. But Bostock had barely glanced at the newspaper over his coffee; he was buzzed on caffeine and adrenaline, and it was too late to stop the auction, the biggest day of his ca-reer. The lot list would make an art historian faint. *Guer-nica. The Potato Eaters. The Scream.* Miró, Rembrandt, Vermeer, Gauguin, Matisse, Constable, Magritte, Pollock, Mondrian. Six desperate governments had contributed to the sale. And rumor had it the Krel would be among the bidders.

The rumor proved true. In the front row, beside the so-licitor Patrick McClannahan, sat one of the unlikely aliens, wearing red tights and a lightning-bolt insignia. The famous Flash. The creature leaned back lazily while McClannahan did the bidding with a discreetly raised forefinger.

Bidding on the Seurat started at ten million and went or-bital. It soon became clear that the main bidders were Flash and the U.S. government. The American campaign against cultural imperialism was getting a lot of press, ironic since the Yanks could afford to challenge the Krel only because of the technology the Krel had lavished on them. The probability suppressor that prevented the detonation of atomic weapons. The autodidactic antivirus that cured most diseases. There was talk of an immortality drug. Of a time machine. So what if the European Community was in the sixth month of an economic crisis that threatened to dissolve the unifying efforts of the past twenty years? So what if Krel meddling destroyed humans' capacity to run the world? The Americans were making money, and the Krel were richer than Croesus.

The bidding reached $1.2 billion, at which point the American ambassador gave up. Bostock tapped his gavel. "Sold," he said in his most cultured voice, nodding toward the alien.

The crowd murmured. The American stood. "If you can't see what they're doing to us, then you don't deserve our help!"

For a minute Bostock thought the auction was going to turn into a riot. Then the new owner of the pointillist masterpiece stood, smiled. Ingenuous, clumsy. "We know that there has been considerable disquiet over our purchase of these historic works of art," Flash said. "Let me promise you, they will be displayed where all humans—not just those who can afford to visit the great museums—can see them."

The crowd's murmur turned into applause. Bostock put down his gavel and joined in. The American ambassador and his aides stalked out. Thank God, Bostock thought. The attendants brought out the next item.

"Catalog number 209," Bostock said. "Leonardo da Vinci, *Mona Lisa.*"

* * *

26 July 1533: The soldiers, seeing the heaps of gold grow, became anxious. They consumed stores of coca meant for the Inca messengers. They fought over women. They grumbled over the airs of Atahualpa. "Who does he think he is? The governor treats him like a hidalgo."

Father Valverde cursed Pizarro's inaction. That morning, after matins, he spoke with Estete. "The governor has agreed to meet and decide what to do," Estete said.

"It's about time. What about Soto?" De Soto was against harming Atahualpa. He maintained that, since the Inca had paid the ransom, he should be set free, no matter what dan-

ger this would present. Pizarro had stalled. Last week he
had sent de Soto away to check out rumors that the Tahuan-
tinsuyans were massing for an attack to free the Sapa Inca.

Estete smiled. "Soto's not back yet."

They went to the building Pizarro had claimed as his, and
found the others already gathered. The Incas had no tables
or proper chairs, so the Spaniards were forced to sit in a
circle on mats as the Indians did. Pizarro, only a few years
short of threescore, sat on a low stool of the sort that Atahualpa used when he held court. His left leg, whose old
battle wound still pained him at times, was stretched out
before him. His loose white shirt had been cleaned by some
puric's wife. Valverde sat beside him. Gathered were Estete, Benalcázar, Almagro, de Candia, Riquelme, Pizarro's
young cousin Pedro, the scribe Pedro Sancho, Valverde,
and the governor himself.

As Valverde and Estete had agreed, the viceroy went first.
"The men are jumpy, Governor," Estete said. "The longer
we stay cooped up here, the longer we give these savages
the chance to plot against us."

"We should wait until Soto returns," de Candia said,
already looking guilty as a dog. "We've got nothing but
rumors so far. I won't kill a man on a rumor."

Silence. Trust de Candia to speak aloud what they were
all thinking but were not ready to say. The man had no
political judgment—but maybe it was just as well to face it
directly. Valverde seized the opportunity. "Atahualpa plots
against us even as we speak," he told Pizarro. "As governor, you are responsible for our safety. Any court would
convict him of treason, and execute him."

"He's a king," de Candia said. Face flushed, he spat out
a cud of leaves. "We don't have authority to try him. We
should ship him back to Spain and let the emperor decide
what to do."

"This is not a king," Valverde said. "It isn't even a man.
It is a creature that worships demons, that weaves spells
about half-wits like Candia. You saw him discard the Bible.
Even after my months of teaching, after the extraordinary
mercies we've shown him, he doesn't acknowledge the pri-
macy of Christ! He cares only for his wives and his pagan
gods. Yet he's satanically clever. Don't think we can let him
go. If we do, the day will come when he'll have our hearts
for dinner."

"We can take him with us to Cuzco," Benalcázar said. "We don't know the country. His presence would guarantee our safe conduct."

"We'll be traveling over rough terrain, carrying tons of gold, with not enough horses," Almagro said. "If we take him with us, we'll be ripe for ambush at every pass."

"They won't attack if we have him."

"He would escape. We can't trust the rebel Indians to stay loyal to us. If they turned to our side, they can just as easily turn back to his."

"And remember, he escaped before, during the civil war," Valverde said. "Huascar, his brother, lived to regret that. If Atahualpa didn't hesitate to murder his own brother, do you think he'll stop for us?"

"He's given us his word," Candia said.

"What good is the word of a pagan?"

Pizarro, silent until now, spoke. "He has no reason to think the word of a Christian much better."

Valverde felt his blood rise. Pizarro knew as well as any of them what was necessary. What was he waiting for? "He keeps a hundred wives! He betrayed his brother! He worships the sun!" The priest grabbed Pizarro's hand, held it up between them so they could both see the scar there, where Pizarro had gotten cut preventing one of his own men from killing Atahualpa. "He isn't worth an ounce of the blood you spilled to save him."

"He's proved worth twenty-four tons of gold." Pizarro's eyes were hard and calm.

"There is no alternative!" Valverde insisted. "He serves the Antichrist! God demands his death."

At last Pizarro seemed to have gotten what he wanted. He smiled. "Far be it from me to ignore the command of God," he said. "Since God forces us to it, let's discuss how He wants it done."

* * *

5 October 2009: "What a lovely country Chile is from the air. You should be proud of it."

"I'm from Los Angeles," Leon Sepulveda said. "And as soon as we close this deal, I'm going back."

"The mountains are impressive."

"Nothing but earthquakes and slag. You can have Chile."

"Is it for sale?"

Sepulveda stared at the Krel. "I was just kidding."

They sat at midnight in the arbor, away from the main buildings of Iguassu Microelectronics of Santiago. The night was cold and the arbor was overgrown and the bench needed a paint job—but then, a lot of things had been getting neglected in the past couple of years. All the more reason to put yourself in a financial situation where you didn't have to worry. Though Sepulveda had to admit that, since the advent of the Krel, such positions were harder to come by, and less secure once you had them.

Flash's earnestness aroused a kind of horror in him. It had something to do with Sepulveda's suspicion that this thing next to him was as superior to him as he was to a guinea pig, plus the alien's aura of drunken adolescence, plus his own willingness, despite the feeling that the situation was out of control, to make a deal with it. He took another Valium and tried to calm down.

"What assurance do I have that this time-travel method will work?"

"It will work. If you don't like it in Chile, or back in Los Angeles, you can use it to go into the past."

Sepulveda swallowed. "Okay. You need to read and sign these papers."

"We don't read."

"You don't read Spanish? How about English?"

"We don't read at all. We used to, but we gave it up. Once you start reading, it gets out of control. You tell yourself you're just going to stick to nonfiction—but pretty soon you graduate to fiction. After that, you can't kick the habit. And then there's the oppression."

"Oppression?"

"Sure. I mean, I like a story as much as the next Krel, but any pharmacologist can show that arbitrary cultural, sexual, and economic assumptions determine every significant aspect of a story. Literature is a political tool used by ruling elites to ensure their hegemony. Anyone who denies that is a fish who can't see the water it swims in. Or the fascist who tells you, as he beats you, that those blows you feel are your own delusion."

"Right. Look, can we settle this? I've got things to do."

"This is, of course, the key to temporal translation. The

past is another arbitrary construct. Language creates reality. Reality is smoke.''

''Well, this time machine better not be smoke. We're going to find out the truth about the past. Then we'll change it.''

''By all means. Find the truth.'' Flash turned to the last page of the contact, pricked his thumb, and marked a thumbprint on the signature line.

After they sealed the agreement, Sepulveda walked the alien back to the courtyard. A Krel flying pod with Vermeer's *The Letter* varnished onto its door sat at the focus of three spotlights. The painting was scorched almost into unrecognizability by atmospheric friction. The door peeled downward from the top, became a canvas-surfaced ramp.

''I saw some interesting lines inscribed on the coastal desert on the way here,'' Flash said. ''A bird, a tree, a big spider. In the sunset, it looked beautiful. I didn't think you humans were capable of such art. Is it for sale?''

''I don't think so. That was done by some old Indians a long time ago. If you're really interested, though, I can look into it.''

''Not necessary.'' Flash waggled his ears, wiped his feet on Mark Rothko's *Earth and Green*, and staggered into the pod.

* * *

26 July 1533: Atahualpa looked out of the window of the stone room in which he was kept, across the plaza where the priest Valverde stood outside his chapel after his morning prayers. Valverde's chapel had been the house of the virgins; the women of the house had long since been raped by the Spanish soldiers, as the house had been by the Spanish god. Valverde spoke with Estete. They were getting ready to kill him, Atahualpa knew. He had known ever since the ransom had been paid.

He looked beyond the thatched roofs of the town to the crest of the mountains, where the sun was about to break in his tireless circuit of Tahuantinsuyu. The cold morning air raised dew on the metal of the chains that bound him hand and foot. The metal was queer, different from the bronze the *puric*s worked or the gold and silver Atahualpa was used to wearing. If gold was the sweat of the sun, and silver the tears of the moon, what was this metal, dull and hard like the men who held him captive, yet strong, too—stronger, he had come to realize, than the Inca. It, like the men who brought it, was beyond his experience. It gave evidence that Tahuantinsuyu, the Four Quarters of the World, was not all the world after all. Atahualpa had thought none but savages lived beyond their lands. He'd imagined no man readier to face ruthless necessity than himself. He had ordered the death of Huascar, his own brother. But he was learning that these men were capable of enormities against which the Inca civil war would seem a minor discomfort.

That evening they took him out of the building to the plaza. In the plaza's center, the soldiers had piled a great heap of wood on flagstones, some of which were still stained with the blood of the six thousand slaughtered attendants. They bound him to a stake amid the heaped fagots, and Valverde appealed one last time for the Inca to renounce Satan and be baptized. He promised that if Atahualpa would do so, he would earn God's mercy: they would strangle him rather than burn him to death.

The rough wood pressed against his spine. Atahualpa looked at the priest, and the men gathered around, and the women weeping beyond the circle of soldiers. The moon, his mother, rode high above. Firelight flickered on the breastplates of the Spaniards, and from the waiting torches drifted the smell of pitch. The men shifted nervously. Creak of leather, clink of metal. Men on horses shod with silver. Sweat shining on Valverde's forehead. Valverde stared at Atahualpa as if he desired something, but was prepared to destroy him without getting it if need be. The priest thought he was showing Atahualpa resolve, but Atahualpa saw that beneath Valverde's face he was a dead man. Pizarro stood aside, with the Spanish viceroy Estete and the scribe. Pizarro was an old man. He ought to be sitting quietly in some village, outside the violence of life, giving advice and teaching the children. What kind of world did he come from, that sent men into old age still charged with the lusts and bitterness of the young?

Pizarro, too, looked as if he wanted this to end.

Atahualpa knew that it would not end. This was only the beginning. These men would suffer for this moment as they had already suffered for it all their lives, seeking the pain blindly over oceans, jungles, deserts, probing it like a sore tooth until they'd found and grasped it in this plaza of Cajamarca, thinking they sought gold. They'd come all this way to create a moment that would reveal to them their own incurable disease. Now they had it. In a few minutes, they thought, it would at last be over, that once he was gone, they would be free—but Atahualpa knew it would be with them ever after, and with their children and grandchildren and the million others of their race in times to come, whether they knew of this hour in the plaza or not, because they were sick and would pass the sickness on with their breath and semen. They could not burn out the sickness so easily as they could burn the Son of God to ash. This was a great tragedy, but it contained a huge jest. They were caught in a wheel of the sky and could not get out. They must destroy themselves.

"Have your way, priest," Atahualpa said. "Then strangle me, and bear my body to Cuzco, to be laid with my ancestors." He knew they would not do it, and so would add an additional curse to their faithlessness.

He had one final curse. He turned to Pizarro. "You will have responsibility for my children."

Pizarro looked at the pavement. They put up the torch and took Atahualpa from the pyre. Valverde poured water on his head and spoke words in the tongue of his god. Then they sat him upon a stool, bound him to another stake, set the loop of cord around his neck, slid the rod through the cord, and turned it. His women knelt at his side and wept. Valverde spoke more words. Atahualpa felt the cord, woven by the hands of some faithful *puric* of Cajamarca, tighten. The cord was well made. It cut his access to the night air; Atahualpa's lungs fought, he felt his body spasm, and then the plaza became cloudy and he heard the voice of the moon.

* * *

12 January 2011: Israel Lamont was holding big-time when a Krel monitor zipped over the alley. A minute later one of the aliens lurched around the corner and approached him. Lamont was ready.

"I need to achieve an altered state of consciousness," the alien said. It wore a red suit, a lightning bolt on its chest.

"I'm your man," Lamont said. "You just try this. Best

stuff on the street.'' He held the vial out in the palm of his hand. ''Go ahead, try it.'' The Krel took it.

''How much?''

''One million.''

The Krel gave him a couple hundred thousand. ''Down payment,'' it said. ''How does one administer this?''

''What, you don't know? I thought you guys were hip.''

''I have been working hard, and am unacquainted.''

This was ripe. ''You burn it,'' Lamont said.

The Krel started toward the trash-barrel fire. Before he could empty the vial into it, Lamont stopped him. ''Wait up, homes! You use a pipe. Here, I'll show you.''

Lamont pulled a pipe from his pocket, torched up, and inhaled. The Krel watched him. Brown eyes like a dog's. Goofy honkie face. The rush took him, and Lamont saw in the alien's face a peculiar need. The thing was hungry. Desperate.

''I may try?'' The alien reached out. Its hand trembled.

Lamont handed over the pipe. Clumsily, the creature shook a block of crack into the bowl. Its beaklike upper lip, however, prevented it from getting its mouth tight against the stem. It fumbled with the pipe, from somewhere producing a book of matches. ''Shit, I'll light it,'' Lamont said.

The Krel waited while Lamont held his Bic over the bowl. Nothing happened. ''Inhale, man.''

The creature inhaled. The blue flame played over the crack; smoke boiled through the bowl. The creature drew in steadily for what seemed to be minutes. Serious capacity. The crack burned totally through. Finally the Krel exhaled.

It looked at Lamont. Its eyes were bright.

''Good shit?'' Lamont said.

''A remarkable stimulant effect.''

''Right.'' Lamont looked over his shoulder toward the alley's entrance. It was getting dark. Yet he hesitated to ask for the rest of the money.

''Will you talk with me?'' the Krel asked, swaying slightly.

Surprised, Lamont said, ''Okay. Come with me.''

Lamont led the Krel back to a deserted store that abutted the alley. They went inside and sat down on some crates against the wall.

''Something I been wondering about you,'' Lamont said.

"You guys are coming to own the world. You fly across the planets, Mars and that shit. What you want with crack?"

"We seek to broaden our minds."

Lamont snorted. "Right. You might as well hit yourself in the head with a hammer."

"We seek escape," the alien said.

"I don't buy that, neither. What you got to escape from?"

The Krel looked at him. "Nothing."

They smoked another pipe. The Krel leaned back against the wall, arms at its sides like a limp doll. It started a queer coughing sound, chest spasming. Lamont thought it was choking and tried to slap it on the back. "Don't do that," it said. "I'm laughing."

"Laughing? What's so funny?"

"I lied to Colonel Zipp," it said. "We want cocaine for kicks."

Lamont relaxed a little. "I hear you now."

"We do everything for kicks."

"Makes for hard living."

"Better than maintaining consciousness continuously without interruption."

"You said it."

"Human beings cannot stand too much reality," the Krel said. "We don't blame you. Human beings! Disgust, horror, shame. Nothing personal."

"You bet."

"Nonbeing penetrates that in which there is no space."

"Uh-huh."

The alien laughed again. "I lied to Sepulveda, too. Our time machines take people to the past they believe in. There is no other past. You can't change it."

"Who the fuck's Sepulveda?"

"Let's do some more," it said.

They smoked one more. "Good shit," it said. "Just what I wanted."

The Krel slid off the crate. Its head lolled. "Here is the rest of your payment," it whispered, and died.

Lamont's heart raced. He looked at the Krel's hand, lying open on the floor. In it was a full-sized ear of corn, fashioned of gold, with tassels of finely spun silver wire.

* * *

Today: It's not just physical laws that science-fiction readers want to escape. Just as commonly, they want to escape human nature. In pursuit of this, SF offers comforting alternatives to the real world. For instance, if you start reading an SF story about some abused wimp, you can be pretty sure that by chapter two he's going to discover he has secret powers unavailable to those tormenting him, and by the end of the book, he's going to save the universe. SF is full of this sort of thing, from the power fantasy of the alienated child to the alternate history where Hitler is strangled in his cradle and the Library of Alexandria is saved from the torch.

Science fiction may in this way be considered as much an evasion of reality as any mind-distorting drug. I know that sounds a little harsh, but think about it. An alkaloid like cocaine or morphine invades the central nervous system. It reduces pain, produces euphoria, enhances our perceptions. Under its influence we imagine we have supernormal abilities. Limits dissolve. Soon, hardly aware of what's happened to us, we're addicted.

Science fiction has many of the same qualities. The typical reader comes to SF at a time of suffering. He seizes on it as a way to deal with his pain. It's bigger than his life. It's astounding. Amazing. Fantastic. Some grow out of it; many don't. Anyone who's been around SF for a while can cite examples of longtime readers as hooked and deluded as crack addicts.

Like any drug addict, the SF reader finds desperate justifications for his habit. SF teaches him science. SF helps him avoid "future shock." SF changes the world for the better. Right. So does cocaine.

Having been an SF user myself, however, I have to say that, living in a world of cruelty, immersed in a culture that grinds people into fish meal like some brutal machine, with histories of destruction stretching behind us back to the Pleistocene, I find it hard to sneer at the desire to escape. Even if escape is delusion.

* * *

18 October 1527: Timu drove the foot plow into the ground, leaned back to break the crust, drew out the pointed pole, and backed up a step to let his wife, Collyur, turn the earth with her hoe. To his left was his brother, Okya; and to his right, his cousin, Tupa; before them, their wives planting the seed. Most of the *purics* of Cajamarca were there, strung out in a line across the terrace, the men wielding the foot plows, and the women or children carrying the sacks of seed potatoes.

As he looked up past Collyur's shoulders to the edge of the terrace, he saw a strange man approach from the post road. The man stumbled into the next terrace up from them, climbed down steps to their level. He was plainly excited.

Collyur was waiting for Timu to break the next row; she looked up at him questioningly.

"Who is that?" Timu said, pointing past her at the man.

She stood up straight and looked over her shoulder. The other men had noticed, too, and stopped their work.

"A *chasqui* come from the next town," said Okya.

"A *chasqui* would go to the *curaca*," said Tupa.

"He's not dressed like a *chasqui*," Timu said.

The man came up to them. Instead of a cape, loincloth, and flowing *onka,* the man wore uncouth clothing: cylinders of fabric that bound his legs tightly, a white short-sleeved shirt that bore on its front the face of a man, and flexible white sandals that covered all his foot to the ankle. He shivered in the spring cold.

He was extraordinarily tall. His face, paler than a normal man's, was long, his nose too straight, mouth too small, and lips too thin. Upon his face he wore a device of gold wire that, hooking over his ears, held disks of crystal before his eyes. The man's hands were large, his limbs long and spiderlike. He moved suddenly, awkwardly.

Gasping for air, the stranger spoke rapidly the most abominable Quechua Timu had ever heard.

"Slow down," Timu said. "I don't understand."

"What year is this?" the man asked.

"What do you mean?"

"I mean, what is the year?"

"It is the thirty-fourth year of the reign of the Sapa Inca Huayna Capac."

The man spoke some foreign word. "Goddamn," he said in a language foreign to Timu, but which you or I would recognize as English. "I made it."

Timu went to the *curaca,* and the *curaca* told Timu to take the stranger in. The stranger told them that his name was "Chuan." But Timu's three-year-old daughter, Curi, reacting to the man's sudden gestures, unearthly thinness, and piping speech, laughed and called him "the Bird." So he was ever after to be known in that town.

There he lived a long and happy life, earned trust and respect, and brought great good fortune. He repaid them well for their kindness, alerting the people of Tahuantinsuyu to the coming of the invaders. When the first Spaniards landed on their shores a few years later, they were slaughtered to the last man, and everyone lived happily ever after.

BATS

by Diane de Avalle-Arce

Born in Maplewood, New Jersey, Diane de Avalle-Arce now lives at the edge of the Los Pardres National Forest with her husband, two children, and "a cat that inhabits several parallel universes." Formerly a college professor of Spanish, she has been a full-time writer since 1984; under the pseudonym of "Pilar de Ovalle," she has published several books in Spanish, a book of translations called The Story of Mexico, *a novel called* Calabrinia Falling, *and dozens of short stories in small literary markets such as* The Antigonish Review, Pandora, Ellipsis, *and* Crosscurrents, *as well as in genre markets such as* Isaac Asimov's Science Fiction Magazine. *She is currently finishing a mystery novel, but still finds times to "sneak into the hills on horseback whenever possible."*

Here she offers us a strange, wry, and compassionate story that's about exactly what it says that it's about. . . .

It was the old and cruel custom of the shoeshine boys of Guanajuato, when they had no pressing matters on hand, to catch a bat and make it smoke. You nail the bat to a board fence, by each wing, and put a lit cigarette in the mouth as it opens in a soundless shriek. The tip of the cigarette glows and smoke curls out of the bat's nostrils, as though it were enjoying a gringo's *rubio* tobacco.

This is no longer done, by order of Manuel Aceves, chief among the shoeshine boys of the barrio of San Martin. Rose, the lady who wore white gloves, had something to do with it, and so (though he never made the connection) did Dr. Murphy, a prominent physician in the American colony. Rufina, who keeps the Bar Zotzil on top of La Valenciana, might claim some credit, but she and the grey cat have enough to do without concerning themselves about such things.

It was and is the custom for the gringos to emerge from their pink villas on the outskirts of Guanajuato just before sundown, and drive up to La Valenciana for their evening drink. They admire the view and complain about the laundress and the lack of parts for their cars. This being the hour when the hand is more willing to reach into the pocket and extend a bill, not waiting for change, Manuel Aceves with his shoeshine kit was accustomed to climb the stone steps zig-zagging up the hill to the mine, cutting the loops of the road between nopales and yucca.

The evening of his revelation, he was late; it was nearly dark, and the ground was cold in the shadow of the hill, although the sun behind the mountain gilded the twin towers of the church of La Valenciana. Manuel usually pretended he was the Emperor Moctezuma climbing the Great Temple of the Sun—though he is all four quarterings Chichimeca of Guanajuato and proud of it—but this evening he forgot the Emperor Moctezuma, watching the bats leaving the church.

They came out in a thin spiral, like smoke rising from a small fire, then in a twisted column, a pillar growing upward, larger at the top like a funnel, spinning faster and faster. The funnel danced back and forth as the wind pushed it, until the bats streamed out eastward in a cloud, passing over his head. He heard the hissing of hundreds of thousands of little wings, making a downdraft of warm ammoniac air around him. Still the bats poured out, the long cloud like the plumed serpent Quetzalcoatl, while the sky behind the mountain turned from gold to red to the clear cold green that precedes the deep indigo of night.

Already the church looked a horned bulky animal asleep, and the Cafe Zotzil crouched at its foot like a smaller animal with open glowing eyes, when Manuel Aceves humped his shoeshine box into the bar. The place was almost full, with only Rufina to run back and forth with drinks, while the grey cat minded the bar under the grinning mask of Zotzil the Bat God.

Manuel ordered a Coca Cola, and Rufina threw a dishrag at him and said she hoped that Zotzil would eat him.

"Come, Rufina," he said, "the old gods are dead. The Spaniards killed them. Then we Chichimecas killed the Spaniards, until we got tired of it, and when we wish, we will kill the gringos, too."

"Throw yourself in the well," responded Rufina, loading her tray.

The Bar Zotzil was the old well-house of La Valenciana mine, when the mine had produced silver enough to build and decorate a hundred churches a year. Those times were long gone. The mine was sealed and the church empty, but the well was still there: a hole five meters wide in the floor, with a railing. Green water rushed past the hole, over a pale sand bottom. There were no fish, but the grey cat watched the water just in case, and the gringos threw cigarette butts in it.

Manuel shrugged and made a face at Rufina's back, then composed his smooth copper mask for business. Dr. Murphy first. Grey laceless shoes with tassels on them, grey pants and jacket, grey hair, grey face with purple veins. Dr. Murphy drank whiskey in the Bar Zotzil from sundown until the bar closed, although he slept much of the time. Manuel flashed his smile and said, "Shine? Shine?" Without waiting for the answer, he went to work with his rags.

Before he'd finished, *la señora* Carol sat down at the table. A pink lady, hair like a cornfield in stubble. Manuel had once thought of charging her extra because her feet were so long. Her shoes were pink lizards, which gave him pause for thought. Rummaging through his box, he listened to the conversation; Manuel understood more English than he let on.

They talked about the restoration of the church, which *la señora* Carol said was a project close to her heart. Manuel did not think gringos had hearts, not like people had. Restoring the church was not close to Manuel's heart, but if more tourists came to the area because of it, he wanted their business. On the other hand, if the Minister of Culture came to declare the church a Historical Monument, beggars and shoeshine boys and women selling lace tablecloths from baskets would be banished. So he listened carefully. *La señora* Carol wanted Dr. Murphy to contribute to the fund for illuminating the church.

"To shine like a good deed in a naughty world?" said Dr. Murphy. "It's a robber baron's bad conscience construed in masonry. That's all it amounts to. Leave it to the bats."

"Ugh," said the lady, fanning herself with a paper napkin. "I can't *bear* bats. The illumination should get rid of them if it does nothing else. Do you think the Board of Health would bear part of the cost?''

"Why?" said Dr. Murphy. He finished his whiskey. "If they ask me, I'll tell 'em more people die in a year of church-picnic potato-salad than of bat-related disease in a century."

"You can't be serious. What about *vampire* bats, which I hope those aren't? Don't the cattle ranchers—"

"If the cow had the choice of providing *you* with a steak dinner, or a *bat* with an ounce of blood, she'd choose to accommodate the bat! Rufina! Another of these. Why, the bat's saliva is an anti-coagulant with antibiotic properties, she'd be none the worse. Whereas the *steak*—"

"Phillip, you do have the oddest take on things! I hope you're not going to set yourself up against the whole North American community *just* when we're doing something that will really make a difference!"

Manuel finished the shoes with his brightest smile and held out his dirty hand, which *la señora* Carol pretended not to see. Dr. Murphy gave him a five-hundred-peso bill and said to keep the change, which would have been better if it were not a one-hundred-peso bill with false corners pasted on it. Manuel sincerely hoped he gave money like that to *la señora* Carol for her restoration fund.

He looked around for more customers, but it was a bad evening for shoes; in dry weather, the dust of the brown hills does not cling to the mirror-surface of shoes shined by Manuel the previous evening. Helping himself to a Coke behind Rufina's back, he settled on his heels in a corner.

" 'Oh, fat white woman whom nobody loves, why do you walk through the fields in gloves?' " said Dr. Murphy through his teeth in a funny way.

Rose—the gringa round like a squash or a real person, instead of chili-shaped like the other gringos—came in like a cow with staggers and dropped into a chair. She was as red as her namesake, and pressed both her gloved hands against her breastbone; slowly, she turned white as trout-bellies.

The other gringos didn't like Rose because she lived in the town, over the shop that sells silver and turquoise birds, and gave pesos to street children and told them to go to school.

"Have a glass of water—where are your *pills,* for God's sake?"

Rose shook her head. She took a fish head out of a plastic bag and put it under her chair for the grey cat. "I can't, I told you—I can't take the pills. If I take them, I can't sleep."

"Your blood pressure is literally killing you," Dr. Murphy snapped. The grey hand trembled with the glass. "I can't understand how you've survived *this* long."

La señora Carol changed the subject, because gringos don't believe in death. They never take food to the *animas* for the Day of the Dead, *never.* Manuel knew.

"Do you know you've come just in time to see the illumination of La Valenciana? Any minute now they'll turn on the lights!"

Rose looked even sicker. "Tonight?" she said in a thread of a voice. "I thought it was next month?"

"Oh, the mayor and the American consul, and just possibly the Minister of Culture, will come next month, for the dedication of the plaque crediting the American colony. But the outside illumination is ready. It'll be wonderful, just you wait and see."

But Rose was up and blundering into the rail of the well. She grasped it and looked around. Manuel, with an eye to opportunity, was at her elbow in a moment.

She flinched, then leaned on the hard dirty little arm. "You're Manuel, aren't you? I have a job for you, if you won't be afraid."

"I, afraid? Manuel Aceves is pure Chichimeca, and the meanest shoeshine boy in barrio San Martin!"

"I thought so," said Rose.

Rufina appeared. "Does the *señora* wish to lie down?"

"No," said Rose. "Manuel and I are going to the church now."

"It will be locked, *señora.* The workmen are all gone."

"That's all right," said Rose, taking a big iron key out of her bag.

Manuel, piloting the lady out of the Bar Zotzil, was not surprised that she had a key to the church. If you pay enough, you can have the key to anything you want. But why? There was nothing of value in La Valenciana. Or *was* there? Did the gringa know of hidden treasure under the altar? Who knew what the old Spaniards might have hidden in the church, under tons of bat guano in the belfries? Manuel's step quickened.

Outside the yellow fan of light from the doorway, it was dark as Rufina's braid, although the stars blazed long trails overhead.

"The side door," said Rose. "This one."

Inside the church, it was dark as a mine. Only the high altar glinted gold from the windows, a blind naked cherub with yellow curls here, the halo of a saint there. But Rose seemed to know her way, unsteady but determined, and Manuel half-followed and half-supported her up a winding stair behind the stone baptistry. They went up and up, and Manuel realized they must be climbing the west tower.

At the top there was a door, unlocked, and Rose pushed it open. Her breathing was shallow and rapid, but Manuel held his breath, looking for the treasure. There would be gold, and silver, and emeralds, and rubies, and pearls! He would take it and buy the whole city of Guanajuato, like a plate of glazed salt-clay food for the Day of the Dead: the Market and the Fort with the Mummies; the streets full of businessmen in suits the color of flour; the taxis and buses and the cars of the gringos; the policemen and their carbines; schools and banks and bars, and houses where the women wore paint and laughed so loud you could hear them all over the barrio.

But he could see nothing in the tower but the grey rectangle of the louvers, though he knew they must be under the bell-mouths, huge and black. He smelled cold bronze, and dust, ammonia, the plastic coverings of new electrical wires. Rose tripped on something and her full weight on his shoulder made him stagger. She rummaged in her bag.

"Thank you, Manuel. You can go now. Here's a hundred *pesos*." She snapped on a little flashlight with a cloth tied over the glass. Huge flickering shadows sprang up on the walls, two figures drawn up to dizzy height, crossed by black bars of beams, blurry with cobwebs and inches of dust. There were footprints in the dust on the floor as if it were sand, workmen's boots, Rose's shoes with heels, Manuel's bare feet, rat-paws, and some marks that were none of these.

Rose sat down cross-legged, with a gasp. "Can't you find your way out, Manuel? I don't need any more help now."

"I want to stay, *señora*, truly." For Manuel was Chichimeca of Guanajuato, and any treasure there might be was his as much as anyone's.

"All right, if you won't be frightened."

Manuel, *frightened?* Never since he could remember.

Rose was speaking in a low voice, he did not know whether to herself or to him, making no move toward where treasure might be hidden. He could see no sign of it.

"The lights," she said. "They've put floodlights all over, and opened the louvers. It will be light day and night. You won't stay here, Jimmy; you can't. This will be the last time. Jimmy?"

Manuel, squatting on his heels, watching, wondered if she might be wandering in her wits, for she had drunk no whisky nor even beer at the Bar Zotzil. She took off her gloves and pushed up the yellow sleeve of her blouse. She stretched out the left arm, trembling, with the back of the hand resting on the floor. And such an arm: pale as melon, mottled with red and violet, the blue veins twisting the bone from which the flesh hung slack.

She whistled. It was a high thin sound, as to a very small dog. Manuel followed her eyes and saw a bat, not hanging but right side up, crouched in the angle of a rafter. The flashlight beam showed its pug-dog face with ears pricked, wings like an umbrella half-unfolded. The mouth opened candy-pink, but what struck Manuel most was the unblinking black eyes that didn't reflect like an animal's at night.

"Here, Jimmy," whispered Rose, and the bat dropped to the floor in a brief flutter of membrane-wings as wide as Manuel's forearm was long.

He almost thought he heard it answer, like a feather in his ear. He was so afraid he crossed himself, as he had not done since his mother died, but it was no good, a bat that lived in the bells of a church must have no fear of anything.

The bat hitched itself along the floor on its rat-feet, helping with the long wing-thumbs. Manuel did not move, and every detail printed itself on his memory, like a painting on glass. The bat looked at him, looked into his eyes as no animal could do, nor any rich person in a cafe, and saw *him*, Manuel Aceves as he was, and opened its mouth. It had tiny sharp teeth, like thorns.

"Hold still," whispered Rose. "He's nervous of you."

And Manuel held still as though a spell were on him, because here was the Bat God Zotzil in the tower of the church of La Valenciana, and he had never believed in either of them.

The bat came with its humping gait, and climbed onto Rose's fingers. The hand lay quiet but the blue veins quivered and rolled over each other. The bat nuzzled her wrist, here and there, and held to it. Rose breathed, low and steady, many times, as it sucked the vein.

At last she put out her other hand, and, with her finger, stroked the bat, like Rufina stroking her cat when she was in a good mood. The bat arched its head back, and Manuel saw a mark like ink on Rose's wrist. It didn't bleed.

"This is Jimmy," she said. "Several of them will come, but he's the only one I can pet. See if he'll let you."

And then Manuel proved he was who he was. He stretched out his own dark paw and touched the bat, like warm silk, like the finest glove leather, and felt its heart beating, and heard Rose's harsh breathing and his own in the moment before the floodlights went on, brighter than day.

No one noticed their return to the Cafe Zotzil but Rufina, because all the gringos were admiring the illuminated façade of La Valenciana—except Dr. Murphy, who was asleep in his chair with his head on the table. Manuel removed some hundreds of thousands of *pesos* from his pocket and from the handbag of *la señora* Carol, under the indifferent gaze of the grey cat, and slipped down the hill in the darkness.

There was after all no treasure, and Rose was right that the bats would never come back to La Valenciana. She died some weeks later of a heart attack in the rooms over the shop that sold silver and turquoise birds. Manuel was sorry. By then he was no longer a shoeshine boy, but a boarder in the school of the Aescolapian Brothers, because a man of power, a man who has touched the heart of the world and seen it is far, far bigger than Guanajuato, must have the education to rise above the barrio San Martin.

ACONCAGUA

by Tony Daniel

One of the fastest-rising new stars of the 90s, Tony Daniel grew up in Alabama, and now lives on Vashon Island, in Washington State. He attended the Clarion West Writers Workshop in 1989, and since then has become a frequent contributor to Asimov's Science Fiction, *as well as to markets such as* The Magazine of Fantasy and Science Fiction, Amazing, SF Age, Universe, Full Spectrum, *and elsewhere. His first novel,* Warpath, *was released simultaneously in America and England in 1993, and he is currently at work on a new science fiction novel. He won $2000 and the T. Morris Hackney Award for his as-yet unpublished novel* Ascension, *from which "Aconcagua" is adapted.*

Daniel is an enthusiastic and accomplished mountain-climber—last time I was through Seattle, for instance, he was off climbing Mt. Ranier—and his love for that dangerous sport is evident in the suspensful story that follows, in which Daniel takes us to Argentina and straight up a very tall mountain, in company with a driven man whose search for himself leads him to some unusual and potentially deadly places . . . and to some downright uncanny discoveries.

> *I approached the Antarctic peninsula on a southeastern tangent, working in and out of storms. After several weeks, whipping snow replaced rain squalls. I ran them undercanvassed, awed by the fierce, incessant blast of wind, like a steady breath from a giant skull. All I had out were storm trysail and storm jib, but* Approach *crashed along far above her official hull speed. If I were racing against anyone but myself, I would have won.*

> > —from "Still Life at the
> > Bottom of the World,"
> > by Jeremiah Fall

The drive up the Andean highway was pleasantly frigid, and Jeremiah Fall's new filling was smooth under his tongue. It felt good to get away from the chilly desert clime of Mendoza to the truly cold high places. Gil Parra, a local *Andinista,* drove, and Jeremiah sat in the passenger's seat, listening to him sing horrible Argentine folk ballads.

They were in Parra's Citroën, a car which always looked to Jeremiah like a Volkswagen that had been crunched longways between two semis. The little automobile could go practically anywhere, Parra claimed, and proved it by taking it many miles down the snow-covered mule trail which left the main road near Puente del Inca. The drive completely terrified Jeremiah. Argentinians did not share the same consensus reality with Americans when it came to driving, he had long ago decided. In the Argentine driving universe, stop signs meant "speed up and beat the other guy through the intersection," and hazardous road conditions were obstructions brought about by tidal wave or earthquake—everything else was *no problema, eh? ¡Sí. ¡Ay caramba! Sí.*

The only other human being they saw on the way was a shivering private standing outside of the army checkpoint. The Argentine military permeated the country like a bad case of rash on a dog. Police and military roadblocks and checkpoints were a daily way of life. Jeremiah found it both annoying and sinister. They always asked you your destination and your business. What possible reason could they want to know such a thing, and how could they check to see if you were telling the truth anyway? What it came down to was that they were trying to intimidate the citizens, let the people know who was *really* in charge and who could pull the rug out from under the democracy at any time they wished. Jeremiah made it a habit to answer all questions asked by police or military with a lie.

Today, however, the private was obviously a poor kid far from home. He couldn't have been much over eighteen, and as he leaned into the Citroën and asked them where they were going, he was shaking so badly that Jeremiah was terrified he'd accidentally pull the trigger on the machine gun he had strapped over his shoulder and discharge a few rounds into two innocent mountain climbers. Parra handled the situation quickly and well, however. He slipped the poor kid a little money in the bargain, and promised to carry a letter to the boy's parents on their way back out. As they drove away, Jeremiah noticed that the private was not wearing any socks.

"They make them provide their own," Parra answered when he commented on the fact. "It's part of their conscription duties. If they don't have any, they don't have any," he said, and shrugged. The shrug was the universal method used in Argentina to comment on the government's inanities. That, and the ubiquitous grafitti.

After another five miles or so—Jeremiah had tried to break the habit of always thinking in miles instead of kilometers, feet instead of meters, but never could—the trail became truly impassible. Snow had avalanched down the steep banks of the valley they were driving along and sealed off the way. Parra found a relatively level and sheltered place to park, and they got their equipment out and strapped on their snowshoes. It would be a long, long approach hike in to the mountain. Most of the people who attempted Aconcagua in the summer hired a team of mules and a guide to take their stuff on the two day trip to the base camp at Plaza de Mulas. No guides worked in winter, and besides, a mule could gain no footing in the snow they would have to walk through. Parra had climbed the mountain over ten times, however— though never before in winter—and knew the way well.

They walked diagonally up the side of the valley for a ways, hoping to reach a plateau that Parra knew to be a few hundred feet up, and so avoid the danger of an avalanche that continuing down the bottom of the valley would bring. Jeremiah couldn't see the Vacas river, which ran below, under a thick layer of snow and ice, but he could make out its meander by the shape of the valley floor. He imagined it twisting and turning in dark and secret tunnels down through the valley. Had anyone ever tried to run a snow-caved river with a kayak? But this one would be impossible, it was little more than a creek. He'd save that idea for later, when he got old and would have to let the elements do most of the work.

After a half hour of climbing, they reached the plateau, and, after that, the walking became much easier. The plateau was flat for a couple of hundred feet from its edge to where it met the rising valley walls. It was very much like a step cut into the side of the valley by some giant race of gods. Maybe the same ones who'd created the Incas? Jere-

miah thanked whatever process it was that had led to the
easier going. Still, his pack weighed nearly a hundred
pounds, and he was feeling the first effects of the altitude.
This always happened to him: a day of intense mountain
sickness, after which the thin air would not bother him at
all. At least he'd kept in decent shape, running every day
while he'd lived in Mendoza. Many times his route would
take him up to see old San Martín, and the grotesque obe-
lisk which marked his crossing of the Andes.

In winter, Mendoza clung to the *cerros* like lint, like a
fungal infection. Low ceilings, low spirits, low *everything*.
For months, Jeremiah had longed for high places, but all
he'd had was a room on the third floor of an old hotel that
had been converted into efficiency apartments. These were
rented out to rich tourists from Buenos Aires in the summer.
In the winter, he paid a cheap rate. Third floor rooms were
the cheapest, because they would be the first to collapse
when the next big quake hit.

Earthquakes were a way of life in this city. If you didn't
like some piece of architecture, stick around for a few years
and it would get shaken down to its foundations. There was
still rubble poking through the irrigated shrubbery from the
one that had hit a few years ago. Many killed, forty thousand people homeless.

Yet Mendoza was not a city that made one think of death.
Mendoza was, instead, fine wine (okay, *wine* anyway, at
least) and thin doñas in high heels. You could get good and
bloody *chorizos* here, with mustard that would reanimate a
week-old corpse and sauerkraut that could serve as an as-
tringent in a medical emergency.

He also had the highest view in town, such as it was,
because, due to the earthquakes, no building was *over* three
stories in Mendoza. Only old General San Martín on the top
of *Cerro de la Gloria* had a better view. Jeremiah had spent
hours in his apartment, gazing down the Calle 25 de Mayo
over the bare sycamores which lined the street to the Andes
beyond. Or making love to Ánalia, his *Andinista* dentist
with the perfect, white teeth.

Two days ago, he'd had no idea he would be here, with
Parra, on the way up Aconcagua. Sure, he'd intended to
climb Aconcagua *sometime*. But life in Mendoza had been

. . . not easy . . . *settled*. After the special hell of Vinson, Mendoza was, if not Heaven, then, at least, Limbo. Limbo just before the Judgment Day. Before the earthquake.

Up here, there were no trees at all. This side of the Andes was a high desert. That made the approach easier on the feet, but harder on the soul for Jeremiah. He did love trees. He loved to be *above* them, looking down at the texture they gave to the mountains. The sky was clear, but the wind was shifting and unsteady. More than once, Parra stopped short and looked around, sensing something in the air that he did not like. When Jeremiah asked him what it was, he could not say. "Maybe a storm. I don't know. Nothing." And they walked on. And on.

It was late winter, but the days were still very short. They were on the wrong side of the range for lingering sunsets. When the sun dipped below the western peaks, the air became leaden with cold. Nevertheless, Jeremiah and Parra decided to push to the base camp, and donned headlamps so that they could see as they walked. Jeremiah liked to hike at night in the winter, for the colder temperatures froze the snow fast and made avalanches less likely. But they couldn't depend on that. And they couldn't be certain that a massive avalanche wouldn't sweep them off the plateau and into the valley below, to lie buried under snow until spring, then to become fertilizer for wreaths of wildflowers.

I might not mind ending like that, Jeremiah thought, and, despite its morbidness, the idea comforted him. He felt chilly, but strong. The cold, however, was getting to Parra. Once or twice he stumbled, but insisted that they press onward. The moon came up, nearly full, and the snow shone boney blue, as if it were capillaried with blue-tinted oxygenated blood. All along, they were steadily climbing. Jeremiah's head began to pound and his bowels felt loose and weak. He knew the symptoms, and knew that there was little to be done except drink lots of water and endure. After about two hours of snow-shoeing in the darkness, they came to the Plaza de Mulas, the base camp. They had reached 13,700 feet.

Parra flung his pack to the ground and sat with his head on his knees. Jeremiah patted him on the shoulder and began to set up camp. He got out the tent; it was Parra's, but

Jeremiah had used many like it. He took the shock-corded poles and flung them out onto the snow. He always enjoyed how this seemingly random, energetic action was the exact technique for getting the separate pole sections to slide into the broadened fitting of the section next to it. The shock-cord kept the sections together and lined them up. Then Jeremiah shook the poles and all the pole sections clicked into place, forming long, pliant ribs for the tent. Next, Jeremiah leveled out a spot of snow and laid a sheet of plastic over it. The plastic would be under the tent, and would provide further protection and waterproofing for their floor. He threaded the pole-ribs through sleeves in the tent and notched them into holes on the tent's four sides. When he was done, the tent stood domed and taut. He picked it up and placed it on the plastic ground sheet. Next, he jammed their ice axes and ice tools into the snow, and anchored the four corners of the waterproof fly, which covered the tent, to the axes. He stood back and looked over his handiwork with pleasure. He loved tents, loved their smallness and coziness. A tent was all that was *necessary* for human shelter. All else, he often felt, was ostentation.

Jeremiah's apartment in Mendoza had been about the size of a tent, and a medium-sized one at that. Maybe that was part of the reason he'd felt so comfortable there, so reluctant to leave, to get on with things. That, and Ánalia. Just before he'd seen her for the last time, he'd torn himself from the small window—from gazing out in Aconcagua's general direction—and spent a half hour trying to get the apartment into some kind of presentable shape.

Papers cascaded from the brick-and-board desk like a calving glacier. He hesitated to touch them. The avalanche danger was great, and he could fall into one of those crevasses between the pages and never hit bottom.

Still, he thought that he should make it *seem* to Ánalia that he had been writing today. You should finish your book, she'd told him. If you finish your book on your Antarctic trip, I will trust you to pay me for that silver filling. That was how he'd met her. A cavity. At thirty-three years old. In Argentina. After he'd spent his last precious unconverted dollars on new, necessary climbing rope.

When he'd gotten the paper somewhat under control, he'd

sat staring at his typewriter—*her* typewriter—thinking about Antarctica. Trying to think about the bottom of the world. But nothing came. Yet surely he could get another five hundred words to show Ánalia. She couldn't read English anyway. If it were bad, he could tell her it had lost something in the translation. He had to write soon, anyway, because he needed to buy supplies. He'd spent the last of his advance money getting back from the Antarctic and getting settled in Mendoza. The climbing equipment wouldn't be a problem; he'd made sufficient friends within the local *Andinistas,* the climbing community, to beg or borrow what he would need. He already had his ax, his boots, and his crampons. He had his down sleeping bag, still salt-caked, his pack, his parka, a stove, long underwear, and windpants. He would need to buy food, though, and fuel bottles. The *Andinistas* had some sort of weird reluctance to loan out fuel bottles. He never should have given his own bottles to the guys at Palmer. I am entirely too generous, Jeremiah thought. Charlie Worth, his old climbing partner, had told him that many times, but he'd never taken it to heart. Jeremiah resolved to become more acquisitive.

He'd like to start by acquiring Ánalia for the entire afternoon. He knew she'd only committed to staying with him during siesta, but Jeremiah surveyed his current needs and found that three hours would not be enough. Yet there was little that he had left to barter with. His promises were meaning less and less to Ánalia, of that he was sure. It was funny how women trusted him so completely when they first met him, then gradually lost faith. The opposite should be the case. Why did it always come down to either keeping his promises to himself or keeping them to other people? Were love and a meaningful life mutually exclusive in the long run? For a moment, he saw the face of Mandy Asterwood in his mind's eye. His *other* climbing partner. The dead one. Her happy, windburned face smiled at him. Just before she fell three thousand feet. Stop it.

Traveling *and* women. Traveling *or* women. Which was the correct logical operand?

There was nothing to write today, and he wanted Ánalia desperately. Women. On a gloomy day like today, he would choose a woman over anything. He stared at the blank paper in his typewriter until Ánalia knocked at his door.

He opened it, and, once again, was struck by how stunning she was. Ánalia was dark for an Argentinian. This country was populated with European stock, and it constantly surprised Jeremiah to hear Spanish coming out of the mouths of the fair and blonde. But Ánalia's parents had been Uruguayan immigrants, and there was Indian in her blood. She was honey-tan, after the fashion of Polynesian women, with jet black hair and obsidian eyes. Today she was all in white, down to her white shoes. Most Argentinians dressed like sleazy Assembly of God clergy, as far as he had seen. But Ánalia was far from being a country preacher's wife.

She was smart and quick, as a woman had to be in this country of male-dominated profession. Yet she was kind. She was used to making tiny moves which hurt her patients as little as possible, and that attitude carried over into her relationship with Jeremiah. He appreciated her gentleness, even when she was probing.

Ánalia giggled as he pulled her toward him. "Do I smell like teeth?" she asked, because he'd once made an offhanded comment about that certain smell that dental offices had. Today she had on a trace of subtle perfume.

"Jaguar teeth," he said and kissed her neck. "Grizzly bear teeth, shark teeth." A kiss for each. "Giraffe teeth."

"Giraffe teeth?" She drew back playfully. "I brought you something, Jeremiah." She always pronounced the "J" as "Dj." He liked that. Djeremaya as the name of a much mellower man than Jeremiah, certainly not a man who could pronounce doom on Israel.

"What is it?" he said. He hoped it was nothing expensive, for which he would feel a debt to her.

She reached into her purse—an off-white purse to accent her outfit, he supposed—and pulled out a small package. She handed it to him, and he started to rip off the wrapping paper.

"Careful," Ánalia said. He unwrapped it more slowly.

It was exquisite. A wooden frame surrounded a mountain scene which was formed and colored by the iridescent wings of butterflies. It fitted neatly into the palm of his hand. As he turned it into the light, the overlapping scaly hills flashed and shimmered, as if the mountains were aglow with spring wildflowers.

"That big purple one in the back is Aconcagua," Ánalia said. "How do you like it?"

"I like it very much," he said. "It's amazing. How do they do this?"

"I don't know. They are very inexpensive, though, I have several myself."

He set the butterfly mosaic down on his desk and pulled Ánalia close. "Thank you," he said, and kissed her. They kissed hard and deep. Her teeth felt like curved porcelain under his tongue.

Parra climbed wearily inside the tent and dragged his non-pointy equipment along with him, but Jeremiah lingered outside. He got out his camp stove and attached the fuel line to one of Parra's fuel bottles, into which he'd put his stove's pump assembly. He gave the pump a few strokes, then lit the stove. He let it warm a moment and build the natural flow pressure out of the fuel bottle, then set some snow upon it inside a moistened stainless steel pan. The snow began to sizzle and steam. While it was melting, Jeremiah gazed up at the moon.

It was stark white this evening, a bunched, hard stone in the sky. I'd like to climb *that*, Jeremiah thought. On a small, self-contained expedition, bringing nothing but himself, leaving no trace of his passing. The moonshots were so wasteful and bottom-heavy. They were bureaucratic ladders to the sky. Like the siege tactics of expedition mountaineering—necessary perhaps, but ugly, unsymmetric. An alpine expedition to the moon. Now there was an idea! But not even Charlie Worth had the funding for *that* one.

Charlie *did* have the funding for Everest, however, the next lowest solid matter. There was money enough. Was there time? Jeremiah looked into the sky, feeling his smallness, his inconsequence. I am thirty-five. I will be thirty-six by summer. Was he too old for Everest? No. People over fifty had climbed it. But they had struggled up, and the climb had nearly done them in. Up above, the Southern Cross hung mournful in the sky, with the Magellanic Clouds smeared across its crosspieces like shining blood.

What it came down to was endurance and will.

And the ability to face the ghosts of those who had died

on the two previous attempts he'd been a part of. The chance
that it would happen again. Death at the bottom of a three
thousand foot scream. Jeremiah shuddered.

The wind whipped up and his snow sizzled faintly, and
again Jeremiah was a lone man under a big, black sky. To
the west was the blank west face of Aconcagua, glowing an
impassive white. It seemed possible that he could question
the mountain, the old Inca-god, and get some sort of response, some sort of direction. But Jeremiah knew from
long experience that the mountains did not answer. Or at
least they did not answer *directly*. Like God. After all these
years, he still believed. But he knew better than to pray.
After a while, Jeremiah made tea for himself and took a cup
in to Parra.

When he got inside the tent, Jeremiah removed his plastic
overboots, then the felt liners, wrapping them in a stuff
sack. He rolled out his thermal pad and his down sleeping
bag, and shoved the liners down to the sleeping bag's toe.
He did not want them to freeze overnight and give him
frostbite while he was climbing tomorrow. Then he climbed
into the bag. It was very cold at first, but he'd brought
warmth in with him, and the down retained most of what
his body produced. Soon he was relatively comfortable. The
bag smelled a bit moldy, a bit salty. He thought of Ánalia,
in her small house on a narrow street in Mendoza. Ánalia,
sleeping naked, brown among her white sheets. The wind
flapped the tent. All tents were like this, everywhere. It was
a separate universe he could crawl into, on any mountain
on any continent. A cocoon, the stationary point around
which all the relative world spun. Tents were a constant in
his life.

He awoke before dawn and found that his headache had
passed and his diarrhea was no longer a problem. He was
over his altitude sickness, and well on the way to becoming
acclimated. He'd had much the same experience in climbing
Vinson in Antarctica, but there the diarrhea had been a special problem, because dropping his pants to relieve himself
was a life-threatening maneuver in the cold. In the Himalayas, at much greater elevation, the mountain sickness had
laid him up for two days, not merely with discomfort, but
with exhaustion and unmoving muscles. He slept it off between fevers and vomiting, in a Sherpa's hut. Then, on the
third day, he was just *well*. There was no gradual emer-

gence; he walked out of the hut, up the trail, and joined the climbing party at base camp. By the next day, he was on the mountain.

So he was used to the altitude once more. Without disturbing Parra, Jeremiah slipped into his liners and boots—cold, but bearable—and went out to start breakfast. He would need to melt a lot of snow this morning. He needed to force himself to drink large amounts of water before he began the real climb. The eastern sky colored, and Jeremiah heard Parra stirring within the tent.

"Oatmeal's cooking," he called out, his voice a strange thing in the natural quiet.

"Nick's American Bar and Grill opens early these days," Parra said, with a laugh. It seemed that the tent was talking. "Where are my biscuits and *dulce de leche,* you stinking *norteamericano?*" After a moment, Parra stumbled out and held out his metal cup. Jeremiah filled it up with mush.

"Yvon Chouinard will not touch this stuff," Jeremiah said, wolfing down a big spoonful of his own.

"The great climber does not eat oatmeal?" Parra was incredulous.

"He got picked up for vagrancy when he was bumming out to Yosemite one time. Spent eighteen days on a work crew eating nothing but oatmeal once a day. Now he can't stand the taste of it."

Parra looked with compassion at Jeremiah. "You Yankees have it very tough when you are young, let me tell you."

"Don't call me a Yankee," Jeremiah said. "Don't ever call me *that!*"

"What are you then, amigo?"

Good question. Middle-class southern white boy who accidently ended up soloing the seven summits of the world? Well, five of them so far, anyway. And Everest would not be a solo, most likely. But he was digressing, as usual, avoiding the question.

"I don't know. But I'm *not* a Yankee."

They broke camp within an hour and started up the mountain. After snow-shoeing another mile, rocks began to poke through the snow, and then gravelly scree. Soon the snow became mixed with ice and scree entirely, and became too steep for snowshoes. They replaced them with crampons.

Their weight was more concentrated over a smaller space now, and when there was no ice or rock to support them, they plunged hip-deep into the snow and had to plow forward. The process was very physical, and, while it was tiring, Jeremiah felt fine and strong. Parra began to lag behind. The day was very cold, and the wind stole away much of the warmth they generated. Jeremiah estimated the wind speed to be about fifteen knots. This worried him somewhat, for it could be an augur of storms. When they got to camp 1, he would ask Parra what he thought.

Suddenly, from behind him, there came the familiar, chilling roar that filled many a climber's nightmares. Avalanche! It was far to their right, but angling down the slope of the mountain toward them. Where was Parra? There. He was a dot, far below Jeremiah, almost hidden by some rocks. Jeremiah watched in horror as the avalanche's edge caught the rocks and sprayed upward over them, like breaking surf. It was not a large avalanche, but *any* avalanche was big enough to kill a man if it caught him just right. Parra was lost in the powder. Jeremiah turned around and ran down the slope in long strides, turning to either side as if he were skiing.

"Gil," he called out. "Gil Parra!"

"I'm here. I'm okay."

Parra had seen the avalanche coming and made a run for the rocks which jutted out of the slope. He'd just made it to their lee side when the edge of the avalanche struck. He'd escaped with nothing worse than a dousing of snow.

"That scared the shit out of me!" he said.

"Me, too."

"I don't think it would have got me, even if I hadn't made it to the rocks," Parra said. He was gabbling in a high, nervous voice. "But it would have knocked me down. Maybe I would have broken something in the fall. Probably not."

Jeremiah agreed, but did not want to discuss the matter at the moment. Parra was badly shaken. He got out the stove and heated up some tea for Parra and himself. After drinking this, Parra seemed to calm down. They set out again. Jeremiah regulated his pace so that Parra could keep up.

The sun had already sunk behind the mountains when they reached camp 1. Chile, many miles on the other side of the rock and snow, was still bathed in light, but Mendoza would be turning on the streetlamps about now. Ánalia would be finishing up at her office. She always took a hot máte after work, the Argentine equivalent to the American South's iced tea—they drank it morning, noon, and night.

Two days ago, Ánalia had not been able to make a máte for her siesta. After kissing Jeremiah, she went to the hot plate in the apartment, but the water kettle, sitting nearby, was empty. The only source of water was the bathroom down the hall.

"I guess I will have to skip máte and get to the more important things," Ánalia said, dangling the kettle by one finger. It slipped off and clanged back onto the cold eye. She stared hard at Jeremiah with what must be deep longing—for few desires were strong enough to make an Argentinian give up her afternoon máte.

"Take a long siesta," he said. "I want you all afternoon."

"I have patients waiting already, Jeremiah."

He drew her toward him and took her purse from her, set it down, then began to undo her blouse. "I'm selfish today. Let them wait."

She laughed at this, but it was an uneasy laugh. Jeremiah finished with the blouse and it fell away. She moved to unbutton his shirt, but he stopped her. He wanted to take off her bra first. He loved the way women looked with only a skirt on. Ánalia, he corrected himself. I love the way *Ánalia* looks that way. He reached around and found the catch to her bra, and, with a rubbing motion, as if he were crushing an insect between his thumb and fingers, he undid it. Every time he did this, Ánalia would gasp. He suspected she was humoring him, but he liked even her false surprise.

"How do you *do* that so well?" she asked. "I love way you do that!"

Practice. That was the real answer, which, of course, he dare not utter. Instead, he took a nipple between his lips and licked the tip. She gently pulled away and backed up, knowing that he wanted a full view.

God, she was gorgeous. A flush under her tawny skin, crinkled nipples—brown almost to blackness. She wore no jewelry, which, when he'd first noticed, both surprised and pleased Jeremiah. Her white skirt made her skin seem even darker. She ran her long fingers over her chest, cupped a breast. Invitation enough.

What really rattled him down to his soul was this combination of European and Native American expressed in Ánalia—as if the races had re-blended to form the original Ur woman, the Earth goddess from the beginning. It was always women like this who moved him the deepest. Mandy was a sort of exception. Mandy with her perpetual mountain tan, but white as the driven snow under her long underwear. Yet still a mix of light and dark, the earth and air, in her personality. I loved her, Jeremiah thought. I love Ánalia.

After Ánalia had helped him undress, she unzipped and dropped her skirt, leaving only her curious white shoes. He knelt before her, hoping that she would take as worship what was really only a way of taking off the irritating shoes. When he stood up, he picked her up—he was pleased that his upper body strength hadn't completely deserted him since the summer—and took her toward his bed.

Or *not* the bed this time, he thought. As he walked, she wrapped her legs about his waist and, reaching down, guided him within her. He took her to the window, and leaned her back into the wall next to it. As he leaned into the wall, into Ánalia, he could see, in the corner of his eye, the distant Andes over the bare sycamores and squat buildings. He could not actually see Aconcagua from here, but he knew it was there, waiting. Frozen in place, waiting.

Let the mountain wait.

Ánalia wrapped her legs around his ass and pulled herself up and down his torso, spreading their sweat between them for a smooth slide, as if they both were covered with oil.

And then, of course, the phone rang.

He'd forgotten that he even *had* one. The ringing filled the little room with a loud insistency. Jesus Christ, where was it? Ánalia realized at the same time as Jeremiah did that there was no ignoring the sound. He eased back and she put her feet onto the floor. He pulled himself from her reluctantly, and the damn phone kept up its shrill buzz. Where the hell did the sound *come* from? He began to search the room, and Ánalia laughed at him jumping about bewildered and stark naked.

Finally, Jeremiah found the telephone under a layer of paper and extricated it with an effort. He couldn't remember anybody *ever* calling him since he'd moved in here. He wasn't in the habit of giving out his number to local people he met, and he'd told his parents only to use the number in an emergency. He wasn't sure if he'd given it to Ánalia, even. But then, she lived nearby, and physical contact was so much more enjoyable.

"Hola?"

"Don't you 'hola' me, you piece of white trash from Alabama!"

"Charlie!" he said. It wasn't a question.

"How the hell *are* you, Jeremiah Fall?" Charlie Worth sounded drunk. Or at least extremely happy.

"I'm doing okay."

"Great, great." Charlie was silent, coy even. Strange. Charlie Worth was a Texan, one of the most confident climbers Jeremiah had ever met, and a big-time financier to boot.

"What do you want, Charlie?" Jeremiah went over to the bed—the phone would barely reach—and sat down.

Again with the trace of coyness in his voice, Charlie said, "Why? Am I disturbing you?"

"Would I let you disturb me?" Jeremiah looked over at Ánalia. She was smiling, a bit nonplussed, since she could not understand the English he was speaking. "It's an old friend," he said in Spanish.

"Somebody there with you?" Charlie asked. "I should have known. But if I can't even call you in the middle of the *day* and not interrupt your fun, I don't know *when* it would be possible!"

"It's okay, Charlie. What do you want?"

"You getting over climbing Vinson yet?" Charlie asked. After Jeremiah had gotten back from Antarctica, Charlie had been the first person he'd called to brag to.

"I'm getting there."

"Feel like doing some more climbing soon?"

"Could be. What's up?" What *was* up? Surely Charlie wasn't about to offer him a place on a climb. Hadn't Charlie quit for good after that horrible storm cost him most of a foot on Nanga Parbat?

"I was thinking about climbing Mount Everest, myself," Charlie said, deadpan. "I was wondering if you'd like to come along."

So, it was a joke he wasn't getting. Maybe he'd been away from the States for so long that American humor didn't make sense to him anymore.

"I'm serious as a heart attack," Charlie said, correctly interpreting Jeremiah's silence. "I want to climb Everest. I'm willing to pay large sums of money to be able to do so, and I'm asking you if you want to do it *with* me, Jeremiah Fall."

Right. Charlie Worth climb Everest. At forty, with one and half feet.

"Charlie, you may be biting off more than you can chew," Jeremiah said, trying to let his friend down easily.

"Don't patronize me, you son-of-bitch!" Charlie shot back. "You're as bad as that damn guide!"

"What damn guide?"

"I climbed the Eiger, Jeremiah. I said I'd never climb again, but I did it."

"*You* climbed the Eiger?"

"Hell *yes* I did! And I want *more*. Higher!"

"Don't you think you should try something intermediate? Like maybe K2 or something?"

"I mean it, Jeremiah," Charlie said. Jeremiah could tell he was getting agitated, getting into that excited-nervous funk which only Charlie could achieve with wince-producing perfection. "*Everest,* Jeremiah!"

Everest. Just the thought of her made Jeremiah shudder. He always thought of her that way, as female, as if she were a boat, with her high mast puncturing the stratosphere and trailing a great permanent plume like a masthead pendant. For the last ten years, she'd filled his dreams. And there was one dream, the bad one, which he would awaken from shuddering and sweaty. He and the other climbers he had known were clinging to the mountain like sailors clinging to the rigging, caught in a hurricane. Then the screams as one by one they lost their grips and fell into the miasma below. Finally, Jeremiah was the only one left. His hands were black with frostbite and he watched in horror as his fingers separated from his palms, oozing away like bananas squeezed in two. There was no way to hold on any longer, with only broadened stumps for hands. And Jeremiah fell. And fell. And *fell*.

Ánalia saw Jeremiah shake at the memory and came over to the bed and put her arms about him.

"What's got into you, Charlie?" he heard himself saying.

"I decided that it was *necessary* for me to climb it."

"*Why,* for Godsake?"

Charlie was quiet for a long time, and the line almost sounded dead. It was amazing how little static there was on it, considering the distance.

"I've asked *you* that same question a bunch of times, and you've never given *me* a satisfactory answer," Charlie finally said.

Well, he's got me there, Jeremiah thought. Everest. A third attempt. Up until now, he'd put the mountain out of his conscious mind. *Since Mandy fell and I couldn't catch her.* But Everest was always there, looming massively in his dreams, his nightmares, his desires.

"Just how are you planning to go *about* this little adventure?" Jeremiah asked. "You know we're talking three-quarters of a million to a million?"

"I'm prepared to invest whatever it takes. I have ten million which is relatively liquid, and I can get more if it's necessary. A lot more."

Ten million. Charlie's expert system interpreter was apparently selling very well. That solved *that* problem.

"There's permits," Jeremiah said weakly. "You know Nepal is hell on giving out permits, and there's no way you're talking about trying the Chinese side."

"No, I think Nepal is the way to go," said Charlie, sounding like a hardheaded businessman closing in on a deal. "There are several expeditions which have permits for next summer, I understand. I'll bet you know one of those expedition leaders, and that you could suggest to them that, ah, we could give them a good price for a chance to participate."

"Bribe our way onto a team?" It had been done. Climbers took funding where they could get it, and sometimes it came with extra human baggage.

Everest.

Jesus Christ, when Charlie dreamed big, he didn't have very many scruples about making his dreams come true. Jeremiah tried to remember who had permits for next year. The Japanese had a team. Akima was the leader. There was a Canadian-American effort out of Seattle, too.

I can't believe I'm even considering this, thought Jeremiah. I am a barbarian. No ethics. No *way.* No fucking way.

But *Everest.*

"You think about it, Jeremiah," said Charlie. "I'm ready to do this. I need your help or there's no way, though."

"I'm sure you could find some way to arrange it without me," Jeremiah replied.

"Maybe. But we climb well together. Have you ever thought that the reason you didn't make it up Everest those other times is because you didn't have *me* along?"

"*You* had retired. At least that's what you told me."

"Yeah, well, now I'm *un*retired."

Suddenly, the entire conversation was enormously funny to Jeremiah. He couldn't control himself, he was shaking with mirth. Ánalia held him tighter and caressed him. She probably thinks I'm in pain. Maybe she thinks someone has called to tell me that my parents died or something.

"Don't worry," he told her. "It's nothing. It's okay."

"Okay?" she whispered.

"Well, more or less."

"Hey, tell her howdy for me, whoever she is, won't you, Jeremiah," said Charlie.

"Uh huh."

"And you *think* about this. This is my dream, Jeremiah. I need this, more than I've ever needed anything before. It's a matter of life and death for me."

"I see," said Jeremiah.

"I *mean* it."

"I know." And he *did.* He could tell Charlie Worth was not shitting him.

"Call me in a week," said Charlie. Then he hung up. Jeremiah stayed on the phone as the connections broke—U.S. to satellite to Buenos Aires to Mendoza—one by one. Click. Click. Click. Click.

He slowly hung up the phone. He found that he had lost his breath for a second and was breathing in quick gasps. The room smelled very much like sex.

"That was Charlie," he said. "My best friend and partner since I was twenty years old and climbed my first mountain." And then he told her the rest. After he finished, Ánalia was silent for a long time.

She pulled back a little bit. There was the tiniest crack between them, Jeremiah thought. Just big enough to jam in a finger for a good hold in rock climbing. But flesh was not rock. "Do you think you are going to do this?" she asked.

"I don't know."

"Then let me ask you another question. Do you think there is a place for *me* in this thing?"

The question he dreaded. The question he had been asked so many times, and had never known how to answer.

"I don't know that either."

"When are you going to know?"

"I have to decide what to do soon. There are many arrangements to be made."

"You have to climb Aconcagua very soon then."

"Yes."

"It can't wait for summer?"

"This summer, I will be in Nepal making preparations. It'll be winter there, of course. *If* I go."

"Who will go with you to Aconcagua?"

He looked at her long, hard, objectively. She was too soft. Not because she was a woman. Nothing of the sort. Because she wasn't *him*.

"Some *Andinista* I know. Gil Parra, probably. But I was thinking of soloing the summit."

"I couldn't make it?"

"No."

"You will go this week?"

"It would be best. Gil could go, as support."

"That would probably be for the best," she said. The crack was widening. In space, in time.

"Then there is something I would like to tell you," Ánalia said.

"What? What is it?"

"You have another cavity developing. I saw it when I filled the other. I knew you didn't have any money, and silver is expensive."

"Ah."

"I will cancel my appointments this afternoon and fill it for you."

He looked at Ánalia closely then. She was crying softly, dabbing her eyes with the cover from his bed.

I cannot say why I decided to sail to Antarctica alone. I do know where and when I came up with the notion of climbing the Vinson Masif. I was working my way through the infamous Rock Band of Mt. Everest. This was my second trip to the mountain, and I had every hope of being on the summit team. Everest is not only the highest point on Planet Earth, it is—perhaps beside the point—the highest peak in Asia. I had already climbed McKinley—Denali it is also called—in Alaska, so I had North America's highest point under my belt. I thought that, after I finished the big one—Everest—I could go and do the rest in short order. This was not to be.

As we neared the summit of Everest, the team which was to establish the last camp before the top made a mistake. Nobody knows what the mistake was. Or maybe it was not a mistake. Maybe it was a pure accident. Accidents and mistakes have the same outcome in the Himalayas. One of the members of that team was a friend. A woman I had loved, and asked to marry me. In all, three people fell to their deaths, roped together physically, by fate, by the mistake of one team member. By the accidental callousness of the universe. Like ants on the sticky tongue of the anteater.

I found her body the next day, but it was too dangerous to carry her out. I knew she wouldn't have wanted me to risk it. After that, I went sailing for a long time. Some months later, I found myself in New Zealand.

—From "Still Life at the Bottom of the World"

For the first time, that night, Jeremiah took from his pack the little mountain scene made from butterfly wings which Ánalia had given him. In the light of the waxing moon, the colors were gone, but the texture was accented, so that the mountains looked furry, as if they were covered with great hordes of moths.

He and Parra set up the tent in the flattest place they could find, and partially buried it in the snow, for the insulation. Jeremiah was not entirely happy about the location, though it did not look prone to avalanches. There was a gully off to the side a few hundred yards that the falling snow would most likely channel down if it *did* come in the night. Winter mountaineering was in every way a careful man's game.

After they'd burrowed into their sleeping bags, Jeremiah discussed the weather with Parra.

"I think there is a storm coming," Parra told him. "But I'm not sure when. We may have several days . . . I do not have so much experience in the winter here."

"Tomorrow we will climb to the Berlin hut."

"That is something I wanted to talk with you about, amigo," said Parra. "I'm beginning to think your solo idea is the best one."

They'd discussed it before. Jeremiah had done the other five highest continental peaks alone. Of course Kilimanjaro and Elbrus were merely long walks. And climbing Australia's Kosciusko was comparable to hiking up Cheaha, back in Alabama. Denali had been a bitch, though. He'd done that one in winter, also. But Jeremiah had never experienced hardship like he had on Vinson. After the sheer unmanning cold, the worst part was knowing that, even though there was a small contingent of well-wishers below in base camp, if he hurt himself, the nearest hospital was hundreds and hundreds of miles away—and the airplane came on schedule, period. Even if you were dying. That was the way it had to be in the Antarctic.

But Parra had been undecided about whether he wanted to make the winter ascent, and it *was* mostly Parra's equipment, after all. Jeremiah had decided to let the mountain take care of the decision. Apparently, it had done so, just as Jeremiah had expected.

"Do you want to stay here, or go down to Plaza de Mulas?" Jeremiah asked. "And are you sure?"

"Yes, I am sure," Parra said. "I am feeling bad luck for myself on this one. But it will be okay for me to stay here and keep some hot tea on for you."

Parra was making a brave gesture, and Jeremiah respected it. He could not have found a better person to come into the Andes with. Parra would be a perfect team member on Everest.

"Thank you, amigo," Jeremiah said. "When I come back down, I may have something to discuss with you."

"What?"

"A climb."

"Well, when you come back down, we will discuss it."

Jeremiah had difficulty sleeping that night. It was very cold, and he was going over his route again and again. He'd memorized a photograph of the winter west face of Aconcagua, but here on the mountain, there was no way to stand back and gain perspective on where he was. He'd need to be thoughtful as well as strong if he were to make it. They were at 16,200 feet. Nearly a half-mile above the tallest of

the Rockies, Jeremiah reflected. Tomorrow would be real
mountain climbing.

Parra woke Jeremiah up before dawn with a cup of tea
and some oatmeal. They ate in silence. Jeremiah got out his
pack, and, by the light of his headlamp, began to examine
and discard anything he wouldn't need. A daypack to carry
things in. The tent would stay. He'd have to carve out a
snow cave, for the climb would require one or possibly two
overnight bivouacs. But not having to carry the tent's weight
was an acceptable tradeoff. He would not need rope. Rope
was what you used when you went with a partner. It was
why you went with a partner. Safety. No rope. An ice ax,
and a shorter tool. Stove, fuel, and food. Camera. Sunglasses. He had on long underwear, synthetic fleece pants
and jacket, a toboggan on his head. Heavy woolen socks.
Wind pants over the fleece pants. A down parka. A parka
shell. Gaiters over his boots. Crampons. Silk undergloves.
Wool gloves. Nylon overmitts to keep away the frostbiting
wind.

I am an astronaut, Jeremiah thought. All I need is a jet
backpack. That *would* make the whole thing simpler,
wouldn't it? He slung his daypack into position. It was
very much lighter. Maybe forty pounds. He could barely
feel it.

"Go with God," said Parra. Jeremiah shook Parra's hand,
then began climbing the mountain. The going was easy at
first. The snow surface was hard-frozen overnight, and his
crampons gripped it with precision. He felt fine, very
strong. As the sun came up, Jeremiah began to sing. It was
an old Eagles tune from his college days, "Peaceful, Easy
Feeling." Charlie had liked that one, too. They'd nearly
worn it out on the Walkman they'd carried on their bumming
trip in the Chamonix valley, when they'd done three peaks
a day for a week. As the day went on, he continued to make
good time. Yet the summit looked no nearer. Jeremiah began to fall into a sort of trance, but an alert trance. He
carefully cramponed up the moderate slope, using classic
single-ax technique expertly and unconsciously. His short
ax was lashed to his daypack.

As the sun moved higher overhead, the snow's surface
began to weaken. Jeremiah found himself slogging through
deep drifts, sometimes up to his shoulders. The climbing

was grueling, and he only made a few hundred feet an hour. The altitude also began to take its toll. No matter how good the condition he was in, there were built-in limits to what the human body could do, without proper oxygen. He used his tiredness to gauge how high he was. Quite tired at 17,000. Screaming for air was 18,000 to 18,500. Nearing exhaustion at 19,000. At 19,700 he'd had all he could take in one day. But he'd arrived at Camp Berlin. In the summer, there was an iron hut here, roofless, more of a landmark than any kind of shelter. He could barely see the tip of its frame poking through the snow. It was located in an excellent spot for avoiding avalanches, however, and Jeremiah wearily began to dig a snow cave into the snow bank that had drifted near to the hut. After an hour of work, he struck the hut's side, and, amazingly, half of its front door. He dug back into the hut a ways more, then paused, his lungs and arms aching. He was very satisfied with his work, and spread his thermal pad and sleeping bag out into the cave. Then, wrapped in his bag, he lit the stove and boiled water for tea and dinner soup. Jeremiah felt very safe and comfortable, despite the cold and the altitude.

Outside, he could see, just over the lip of his cave, that the snow was blood red with the dying embers of the sun. *Practice what you preach, Jeremiah,* he heard a voice say. What the hell? He unzipped his bag and crawled to the entrance. Nobody there, but the mountainside was on fire with the sun. He was dazed by the beauty, and sat for a long time, lost, mesmerized by the play of sun on snow. There were shades to the red, as the contours of the mountain caught the light in different ways. Not what you'd expect. In places, some deep crevasses and gullies were alight, as if a beacon burned within them. On the flat snow, the crystalline ice sparkled, and the spindrift cascade that was always flowing down the mountain blushed nearly pink, looking like scars on the mountain's face. But traveling scars.

And there was someone here, nearby. He could *feel* her presence. *Her.* That voice. Was it Mandy's? It had been so long now. With a deep sadness, he found that he could not remember what she'd sounded like. *Be careful tomorrow,* the voice said. He spun around. Did he catch a glimpse of something, someone? A flash of parka as she turned to leave? Or was it just the shimmering snow? It's the *altitude,* is what it is, he told himself. He slid back into his shelter and pulled his sleeping bag tight around him. He slept fitfully, hearing the voice again and again in his dreams. Sometimes it was Mandy's. But awake, he could not be sure.

When he awoke for the last time, the sky was lightening. Jeremiah had the feeling in his bones that it was going to be a dangerous morning.

Nevertheless, the climbing was not extremely difficult at first. Jeremiah came to steeper sections which had shed their snow and were covered with ice, or bare. The ice was good, for he was a strong ice climber and had a fine technique. He front-pointed up several steep slopes, driving in his ice axes, steadying himself, and then kicking in the tips of his crampons. It looked very dangerous, as if he were stuck to the mountain by the thinnest of margins, and indeed, the blades of the axes and the points of his crampons were less than an inch into the ice. But Jeremiah had climbed giant frozen waterfalls using this procedure, and was completely at home with it.

As he neared the summit pyramid, he began to face some exposure, with drops of a half-mile and more to one side or the other. Jeremiah had always been afraid of heights, and that was part of the reason he'd been so attracted to climbing. He found this fear exhilarating, for—after he'd faced it the first time—he knew that it was a fear he could overcome and use.

After Jeremiah was up the ice slope, the going got rougher. The snow and ice slopes, which had been horribly tiring, but straightforward, gave way to seracs—ice and snow blocks as big as Citroëns and shaped not unlike them—and Jeremiah had to pick his way through them carefully. All the time, he was aware that the snow underfoot could shift slightly and one of these blocks could tumble over onto him. He would die. It had happened in the great Icefall near the base of Everest, though never on a team he'd been on. *His* friends seemed to die more spectacularly.

Finally, he was through the worst of this band of seracs and came out upon a slightly flattened area. Another man-made structure, half-destroyed, barely protruding from the snow. It was a shattered A-frame which had once been a hut. Camp Independencia, Parra had called it. Jeremiah decided that this was as good a place as any to take a break. He got out his stove once more and began to brew tea water. He'd had an extraordinary morning so far, climbing a little over 1,200 feet in three hours. "Who took all the fucking *air?*" he said. It was an old joke, a ritual really, which he performed whenever he was over 20,000 feet. He made his tea and sat quietly. His voice had disturbed the silence of the morning, and, with it, some of his repose. He wanted to get that back. Only the gentle hiss of the stove disturbed the quiet. Then came another hiss from far below, the wrenching squeak of ice on ice. A thunderous roar, growing in intensity, as the sound of a car on a gravel road will as it gets closer and closer. What in God's name? Jeremiah walked to the edge of his level resting place and looked down.

Aconcagua was on the move. Ice torrents poured down either side of the mountain, while down its middle a giant section of snow had broken away and was tumbling down, taking everything in its path with it, growing, *growing*. It completely obliterated his path back down, turning it into an unstable mush of snow, ice, and rock. He'd never *seen* an avalanche so huge! He watched and watched, as it rolled on and seemed to never end. He thought of Parra down below, waiting. Even such an avalanche as *this* would probably not make it to the flattened-out area where they'd pitched camp 1. But who could say? This was beyond measurement, beyond belief. What could have caused it?

And how the hell was he going to get back *down?*

After what seemed hours, the icefall subsided. If he had not been climbing as well as he had this morning, if he'd not heeded the strange voice from yesterday, he'd have been a part of that, a corpse, rapidly freezing, lost from sight until the spring thaws. Of course, there was *still* that possibility.

He looked at the summit. Lenticular clouds were forming, space-saucer prophets of storm. Great. More snow's coming. No way down except maybe over the summit and down the other side. To *what?* There were no shepherds in the high valleys at this time of year. He'd perish with no

food and no way to melt snow for water. His only hope was
that Parra had survived and was waiting for him. He had to
find a way down to him. But first, he had to survive the
coming storm.

Having thought the situation through, he felt better. He
had all afternoon. He could dig a cozy snow cave here in
that time on this relatively flat ledge. Its position should
protect it from avalanches. But, Christ, how could he tell?
There was no precedent that he knew of for the way this
mountain had behaved.

He began to dig, and was just finishing up the cave when
the first snow began to fall. He crawled inside, made a cup
of tea, then settled into his sleeping bag. It might be a long
wait. Hours, if he were lucky. Days, if he weren't. With the
way things had gone so far today, he'd better count on the
latter. He would have to conserve food and fuel, but even
with miserly rations, he had only enough to last two more
days. It was far more important to keep drinking than to
eat, so he sorted out all the food which required rehydration
and threw it away. He hated to leave trash on the mountain,
but . . . ah hell, he picked the packets back up. He might
die, but he wouldn't be a litterbug. His mother had taught
him that much.

Jeremiah began to feel a deep longing to see his parents
once again. It had been years now. And his sister in California, even longer. Good middle-class folks.

How did somebody like *me* get strained out of these
genes? he wondered. He'd gone to a fine copy of a fine
Eastern private school. Seen what there was to be had by
the rich and influential, and was none too impressed. And
so he'd applied his ambitions elsewhere.

What a neat analysis. It had more open crevasses than
a glacier in August. Living in the South seemed so long
ago, so far away. It had no hold on him anymore. He was
free. That was the thing, to let go of the past and be free.
Except there was Charlie, his Texas connection. Charlie
wouldn't let go. And Mandy. He could never let go of
Mandy, no matter how far he fell into the future and she,
like an immovable stone, remained fixed in the past, set
there forever. And Ánalia? What subtle ropes attached
him to Ánalia?

Outside, the wind was howling like a bear caught in a foot trap. *Like the scream of a woman falling through space.* Soon, however, snow covered the entrance hole, and the sound abated. Jeremiah slept in fits and starts. He had many dreams of falling.

In the morning, he broke out into the sunlight and found that the storm had passed. Aconcagua was blanketed with a snow coating almost as thick as the one it had had before yesterday's avalanche. Still, the path down looked impassible, ready to come loose and avalanche again. The mountainside could remain like this for some time, for weeks even. He tried to think of other ways out of his predicament, and grew anxious with himself. For the first time, he was afraid. Before, there had been just too much amazement. But anxiety was useless. What the hell could he *do?*

He could climb *up.* There was that. He scanned the summit pyramid. Its exposed rock was whitish-gray, as if the rock itself were suffering from frostbite. This was icing, but should be relatively crumbly. It was too cold for a coating of verglas—the enemy of the climber trying to negotiate rock—to develop. There were many cliffs on the pyramid which were dangerously corniced with snow—snow that could give at any time and sweep him down the mountainside along with it. He could just make out the route which Parra had suggested, up a small gully which cut up into the summit pyramid like a ready-made ramp. It was called the Canaleta.

Without really deciding to do so, Jeremiah found himself climbing upward. After so many mountains, it was an old habit, an instinct which took over when one was not thinking or could not think. He climbed. That was what he did.

Within a couple of hours, he was at the Canaleta. This was not going to be as easy as he'd supposed it would be. The slope was moderate, but rock and ice cannonballs shot down it at random intervals. For once in his climbing career, he wished he'd brought a helmet. But a helmet would do him little good against one of *those* suckers anyway. The trick was to be lucky and not get hit. Not a very sound technique. Jeremiah studied the falling stone and ice more carefully. There was a pattern to it, albeit a con-

voluted one. Stationary boulders were placed in strategic
locations all the way up the ramp. If he could shuffle from
boulder to boulder, only exposing himself to the falling
shit on the traverses *between* rocks . . . it wasn't a perfect
plan, but it would increase his chances greatly. And the
floor of the gully was mostly ice, too steep for snow to
collect. He could use his ice-climbing skills to full advantage. So. Start.

The first few traverses were easy and eventless, but as he
got higher, the boulders got smaller and provided less protection. Once, a cannonball rock slammed directly into the
boulder Jeremiah was sheltering behind. He ducked, but
part of his back was exposed, and he was stung with the
broken shrapnel of the exploded cannonball. He shook off
the pain and skirted to a better shelter. And finally, he was
up and *out,* over to one side of the gully. He was on the
final ridge.

And the rest was easy. He climbed steadily through deep
snow, which got harder and shallower as he got near the
summit. When he crested the mountain, he was walking
almost normally—except for the inch-long spikes on his feet.

There was an aluminum cross which marked the highest
point on the summit; it was half-buried in snow. Jeremiah
rammed in one of his ice axes and afixed his camera to a
screw atop the ax. He flipped the self-timer button, jogged
over to stand by the cross. The jogging left him winded and
panting hard. The camera clicked. He went and set it again
and got another. Proof. Okay. He finally took a good look
around.

To the north and south, there was a sea of mountains
which disappeared into the distance. To the east was a falling line which led ultimately to Mendoza. To Ánalia. To the
west was Chile. All of the mountain peaks were below him,
as far as he could see. Jeremiah Fall was standing on the
highest point of land in the Western Hemisphere. 22,835
feet. Western Man, on top of the West.

From his daypack, Jeremiah took out the butterfly mosaic. It glimmered in the sun. Here's to us, Ánalia. Here's
to a taste of the warm South, even in winter time. Jeremiah
set the mosaic down next to the aluminum cross. He backed
away, started to take a picture of it.

No. He felt the female presence again, heard a voice and

saw a flickering, just on the edge of his vision. It could have been the altitude, the lack of oxygen. *You'll need that,* said the voice.

"What do you mean?" he found himself saying. The wind carried his words away, over to the west, out toward Chile. "Tell me what you mean."

You'll need it on Everest.

"I'm not going there. I'm never going back there. People *die* when I go there."

But the presence was gone. *She* was gone.

Jeremiah was utterly alone.

With a bewildered heart, Jeremiah retrieved the picture and began his descent. Now was the time when the most concentration, the most care, was needed. He tried to free his mind of all thoughts but climbing down. To where? At least to Camp Independencia. He could hole up there. For how long? Three days. Maybe longer. And then? The way down might be easier. But no. That was no ordinary avalanche. It would take a long time for the mountain to restabilize after *that* one.

A cannonball rock caromed past. It barely missed taking Jeremiah's head off. Shit. Pay attention. Once, coming down the Canaleta's final run, he slipped and fell. This was bad, for he would accelerate rapidly on the ice and shoot out of the run so fast it would send him tumbling down the mountain. With expert movement, he got himself turned right and used his ice ax to self-arrest. On ice, the procedure was delicate and required experience, else one could start spinning completely out of control. He dug in the blade and bottom spike of the ax and barely grazed the forepoints of his crampons against the ice, applying just enough pressure to keep him from sliding on past the ice ax, but not enough to stop him short and spin him around upside down. It worked, and he was lucky— for the fall had carried him nearly out of the Canaleta. He rose shakily and got all the way out as quickly as he could. *Shoom* went a block of ice, shooting past right after he'd gotten out of the way. The Canaleta was a bad place, and he was glad to be rid of it.

From this point, climbing down was easier. Still, he had to be careful, for there was no one but himself to arrest him if he started falling, and the self-arrest on the Canaleta had taken much of the strength from his arms. He doubted he could stop himself again. Noon was nearing when he got back to Camp Independencia with its wrecked A-frame. He had decided what to do. Looking over the edge, the avalanche remains appeared as dangerous as ever. Yet there was a line of descent he could imagine which would skirt the worst of the debris—provided he could find his route once he was down there.

Everest. The voice had said he was going to Everest. That had to mean he would make it down off this hill, didn't it? Christ, I'm listening to voices in my *head* for advice now, he thought. It wasn't funny, and he didn't laugh. *Was* he going to Everest, then? Had the inarticulate right side of his brain decided that he was going and provided him with a prophetic voice to inform him of that decision? A rational explanation. He doubted it immediately.

What I *really* hate is standing here undecided, Jeremiah thought, freezing my ass off. I feel strong. I'm climbing well. I want to *do* something. He imagined what staying here for several days would do to him. First he would dehydrate after his fuel ran out and he could no longer melt snow. Or he'd try to eat snow, and die from hypothermia. If he didn't die, he'd be forced to descend in weakened condition, and he truly did not believe that the climbing conditions below were going to get any better.

"I'm going," Jeremiah said, as if, by speaking aloud, his decision would somehow be recorded, known—whatever the outcome. First, Jeremiah made himself a cup of hot tea. Then he sorted his equipment. He left behind his stove, food, and fuel, taking only his camera, ice axes, and sleeping bag. If he did not make it all the way down, he might need to bivouac one more night. He'd die without his sleeping bag, of that he was sure. *"Okay,"* he said, and started down.

The going was incredibly complex, with a mixture of snow, ice, and rock which changed composition with each step, and none of which was stable. He found himself slipping and sliding down stretches that were nearly vertical. Only by taking long loping steps for yards on end, partially out of control, was he able to retain his balance and not fall on down the hill to his death. Jeremiah tried to follow a diagonal which avoided the main line of the avalanche, but found seracs and plain old boulders constantly blocking his way. As a consequence, he had to zig-zag downward, trying desperately to work his way to the left side of the avalanche's primary path.

But, midway down, he came upon a line of rising stone and ice that could not be surmounted. Jeremiah tried to work his way in or around the barrier, but there was just no way. He was boxed into the most dangerous place he could be, and could do nothing about it. In fear and despair, Jeremiah turned back to his right, and descended the surface of the avalanche.

The day progressed, and he ground his way onward, downward. He hoped that the setting of the sun and the general cooling off which followed would harden the snow a bit, decrease the chances for a major breakaway. But there was no guarantee. He climbed downward.

As the sun set behind the western peaks, Jeremiah realized that he had left his headlamp back at Independencia, in his daypack. There was nothing he could do about that, either. As blackness filled the sky, he continued his descent. The darkness seemed to be sapping him of his will, as if it were creeping into his soul as it was creeping across the West. He'd just been to the top of the West, and had felt a kind of semi-mystic identification with it. Would the night descend on him before he could descend the mountain? Slipping and sliding, afraid that each new step would be his last, Jeremiah kept climbing down.

And the moon rose. This was immensely cheering to Jeremiah, for now the moon was practically full. He began to see better, and picked up his pace a little. Then he was off of the rock-and-ice mixture, and onto pure snow. The going got tougher. He was slogging through. Jeremiah could no longer feel his feet, and was certain that his toes were frost-bitten. This was a shame, for he'd always thought his feet were one of the better parts of his body, and he'd had a special fondness for his toes. Probably they would have to come off. If he lived long enough to have that to worry about. He pushed on.

And thought he saw, far below—a light. But then it was gone, and he was sure that he was mistaken. Then, there it was *again*, far, far below. Was it Parra, in the tent with a candle lantern? As if in answer, the light flickered, then came back on. Oh God, oh God sweet Jesus, let it be.

That was when he heard the roar coming from above him.

He couldn't see a thing. Running downward was impossible in the deep snow. All he could do was stand and wait for the avalanche to bear him away. He was going to die with a blank, bewildered mind.

Jeremiah didn't have long to wait. Within seconds, the snow was upon him. He was swept up like a stick in an ocean wave and spit out onto the avalanche surface. But soon he was rolling, being turned under again. There was something you could do. Something you did in an avalanche. No guarantee. A last hope. But he couldn't think, couldn't remember.

Suddenly, the presence was there again, rolling along with him, speaking a wordless calm. Then a word. *Swim,* she said. Yes. That was it! You kick your legs, you flail your arms; you pretend you're swimming. You *are* swimming, swimming through snow. Jeremiah swam. Swam the American crawl, like the *norteamericano* that he was.

> *I sailed to Antarctica in order to climb Mt. Vinson, the highest peak on that continent. I climbed it alone out of necessity, but I would have done so anyway. For I was in mourning for a lost love, and I had thoughts of throwing myself off into that desolate wasteland. But with every step up the mountain, every plunge of my ax into the snow, I was healing. I was healing. And that is the reason I went to Antarctica, and the reason I sailed there alone, and the reason I climbed. The reason I climb. For there is a wound in me which seeing the mountains opened long ago, that seeing death on the mountains reopens often enough. And the only cure is climbing. I can only find healing for this wound in the highest of places.*
>   —from "Still Life at the Bottom of the World"

And he was swimming, and turning his head for air, and breathing, breathing, and churning, kicking, *swimming.* Then slowly, slowly, the avalanche subsided, struck a deal with gravity to hold for this one time, to hold. And Jeremiah came to rest. He lay there for a long time, facedown in the snow. Then he heard something, a humming sound, a human sound.

He picked himself up. Not five hundred yards away was camp 1, and the glowing aura of the tent. Jeremiah stood up and walked down to camp. As he grew nearer, he could hear the whistling hiss of a stove. He quickened his pace. After his eyes got used to the brighter light, he could see Parra, sitting half in the tent, but with the stove outside, heating water. Parra looked up at him and nearly turned the stove over and spilled everything, but regained himself. He smiled in the huge way that only Argentinians had.

"I'm back," said Jeremiah.

"Yes," said Parra. "And I'll have your tea in a moment. Did you know there was a big earthquake?"

The huge avalanche, thought Jeremiah. *That* was the cause. That, or an aftershock. There were two avalanches.

"If I could feel it all the way up here," Parra said, "It must have hit Mendoza *hard*."

And all at once, Jeremiah knew where the voice had come from, to whom it belonged. Not to Mandy. Or at least, not to Mandy alone. The longer he lived, the deeper the hurt—and the higher the mountains must be. Suddenly not only his feet were numb, his whole body was numb, his soul was numb. He whispered a name. It came out choked and dry, as if his throat were full of autumn leaves.

"Ánalia."

THE SKY PEOPLE

by Poul Anderson

Here's a big, vivid, and powerful novella, full of color and action, that examines a subtle point with a good deal of profundity: just what is civilization, anyway? And are you sure you'll recognize it when you see it. . . ?

One of the best-known and most prolific writers in science fiction, Poul Anderson made his first sale in 1947, and in the course of his subsequent 46-year career has published almost a hundred books (in several different fields, as Anderson has written historical novels, fantasies, and mysteries, in addition to SF), sold hundreds of short pieces to every conceivable market, and won seven Hugo Awards, three Nebula Awards, and the Tolkien Memorial Award for life achievement. His books include, among many others) The High Crusade, The Enemy Stars, Three Hearts and Three Lions, The Broken Sword, Tau Zero, The Night Face, Orion Shall Rise, *and* The People of the Wind, *as well as the two multi-volume series of novels about his two most popular characters, Dominic Flandry and Nicholas van Rijn. His short work has been collected in* The Queen of Air and Darkness and Other Stories, Guardians of Time, The Earth Book of Stormgate, Fantasy, The Unicorn Trade *(with Karen Anderson),* Past Times, *and* Time Patrolman. *His most recent books are the novels* The Boat of a Million Years, The Shield of Time, *and* The Time Patrol, *and the collection* Explorations. *Coming up is a new novel,* Harvest of Stars. *Anderson lives in Orinda, California, with his wife (and fellow writer) Karen.*

The rover fleet got there just before sunrise. From its height, five thousand feet, the land was bluish gray, smoked with mists. Irrigation canals caught the first light as if they were full of mercury. Westward the ocean gleamed, its far edge dissolved into purple and a few stars.

Loklann sunna Holber leaned over the gallery rail of his flagship and pointed a telescope at the city. It sprang to view as a huddle of walls, flat roofs, and square watchtowers. The cathedral spires were tinted rose by a hidden sun. No barrage balloons were aloft. It must be true what rumor said, that the Perio had abandoned its outlying provinces to their fate. So the portable wealth of Meyco would have flowed into S' Antón, for safekeeping—which meant that the place was well worth a raid. Loklann grinned.

Robra sunna Stam, the *Buffalo*'s mate, spoke. "Best we come down to about two thousand," he suggested. "To make sure the men aren't blown sideways, to the wrong side of the town walls."

"Aye." The skipper nodded his helmeted head. "Two thousand, so be it."

Their voices seemed oddly loud up here, where only the wind and a creak of rigging had broken silence. The sky around the rovers was dusky immensity, tinged red gold in the east. Dew lay on the gallery deck. But when the long wooden horns blew signals, it was somehow not an interruption, nor was the distant shouting of orders from other vessels, thud of crew feet, clatter of windlasses and hand-operated compressor pumps. To a Sky Man, those sounds belonged in the upper air.

Five great craft spiraled smoothly downward. The first sunrays flashed off gilt figureheads, bold on sharp gondola prows, and rioted along the extravagant designs painted on gas bags. Sails and rudders were unbelievably white across the last western darkness.

"Hullo, there," said Loklann. He had been studying the harbor through his telescope. "Something new. What could it be?"

He offered the tube to Robra, who held it to his remaining eye. Within the glass circle lay a stone dock and warehouses, centuries old, from the days of the Perio's greatness. Less than a fourth of their capacity was used now. The normal clutter of wretched little fishing craft, a single coasting schooner . . . and yes, by Oktai the Stormbringer, a monster thing, bigger than a whale, seven masts that were impossibly tall!

"I don't know." The mate lowered the telescope. "A foreigner? But where from? Nowhere in this continent—"

"I never saw any arrangement like that," said Loklann.

"Square sails on the topmasts, fore-and-aft below." He
stroked his short beard. It burned like spun copper in the
morning light; he was one of the fair-haired blue-eyed men,
rare even among the Sky People and unheard of elsewhere.
"Of course," he said, "we're no experts on water craft. We
only see them in passing." A not unamiable contempt rode
his words: sailors made good slaves, at least, but naturally
the only fit vehicle for a fighting man was a rover abroad
and a horse at home.

"Probably a trader," he decided. "We'll capture it if
possible."

He turned his attention to more urgent problems. He had
no map of S' Antón, had never even seen it before. This
was the farthest south any Sky People had yet gone plundering, and almost as far as any had ever visited; in bygone
days aircraft were still too primitive and the Perio too strong.
Thus Loklann must scan the city from far above, through
drifting white vapors, and make his plan on the spot. Nor
could it be very complicated, for he had only signal flags
and a barrel-chested hollerer with a megaphone to pass orders to the other vessels.

"That big plaza in front of the temple," he murmured.
"Our contingent will land there. Let the *Stormcloud* men
tackle that big building east of it . . . see . . . it looks like
a chief's dwelling. Over there, along the north wall, typical
barracks and parade ground—*Coyote* can deal with the soldiers. Let the *Witch of Heaven* men land on the docks, seize
the seaward gun emplacements and that strange vessel, then
join the attack on the garrison. *Fire Elk*'s crew should land
inside the east city gate and send a detachment to the south
gate, to bottle in the civilian population. Having occupied
the plaza, I'll send reinforcements wherever they're needed.
All clear?"

He snapped down his goggles. Some of the big men
crowding about him wore chain armor, but he preferred a
cuirass of hardened leather, Mong style; it was nearly as
strong and a lot lighter. He was armed with a pistol, but
had more faith in his battle ax. An archer could shoot almost as fast as a gun, as accurately—and firearms were getting fabulously expensive to operate as sulfur sources
dwindled.

He felt a tightness which was like being a little boy again,
opening presents on Midwinter Morning. Oktai knew what

treasures he would find, of gold, cloth, tools, slaves, of battle and high deeds and eternal fame. Possibly death. Someday he was sure to die in combat; he had sacrificed so much to his josses, they wouldn't grudge him war-death and a chance to be reborn as a Sky Man.

"Let's go!" he said.

He sprang up on a gallery rail and over. For a moment the world pinwheeled; now the city was on top and now again his *Buffalo* streaked past. Then he pulled the ripcord and his harness slammed him to steadiness. Around him, air bloomed with scarlet parachutes. He gauged the wind and tugged a line, guiding himself down.

II

Don Miwel Carabán, calde of S' Antón d' Inio, arranged a lavish feast for his Maurai guests. It was not only that this was a historic occasion, which might even mark a turning point in the long decline. (Don Miwel, being that rare combination, a practical man who could read, knew that the withdrawal of Perio troops to Brasil twenty years ago was not a "temporary adjustment." They would never come back. The outer provinces were on their own.) But the strangers must be convinced that they had found a nation rich, strong, and basically civilized, that it was worthwhile visiting the Meycan coasts to trade, ultimately to make alliance against the northern savages.

The banquet lasted till nearly midnight. Though some of the old irrigation canals had choked up and never been repaired, so that cactus and rattlesnake housed in abandoned pueblos, Meyco Province was still fertile. The slant-eyed Mong horsemen from Tekkas had killed off innumerable peons when they raided five years back; wooden pitchforks and obsidian hoes were small use against saber and arrow. It would be another decade before population had returned to normal and the periodic famines resumed. Thus Don Miwel offered many courses, beef, spiced ham, olives, fruits, wines, nuts, coffee, which last the Sea People were unfamiliar with and didn't much care for, et cetera. Entertainment followed—music, jugglers, a fencing exhibition by some of the young nobles.

At this point the surgeon of the *Dolphin*, who was rather drunk, offered to show an Island dance. Muscular beneath tattoos, his brown form went through a series of contortions which pursed the lips of the dignified Dons. Miwel himself remarked, "It reminds me somewhat of our peons' fertility rites," with a strained courtesy that suggested to Captain Ruori Rangi Lohannaso that peons had an altogether different and not very nice culture.

The surgeon threw back his queue and grinned. "Now let's bring the ship's wahines ashore to give them a real hula," he said in Maurai-Ingliss.

"No," answered Ruori. "I fear we may have shocked them already. The proverb goes, 'When in the Solmon Islands, darken your skin.' "

"I don't think they know how to have any fun," complained the doctor.

"We don't yet know what the taboos are," warned Ruori. "Let us be as grave, then, as these spike-bearded men, and not laugh or make love until we are back on shipboard among our wahines."

"But it's stupid! Shark-toothed Nan eat me if I'm going to—"

"Your ancestors are ashamed," said Ruori. It was about as sharp a rebuke as you could give a man whom you didn't intend to fight. He softened his tone to take out the worst sting, but the doctor had to shut up. Which he did, mumbling an apology and retiring with his blushes to a dark corner beneath faded murals.

Ruori turned back to his host. "I beg your pardon, S'ñor," he said, using the local tongue. "My men's command of Spañol is even less than my own."

"Of course." Don Miwel's lean black-clad form made a stiff little bow. It brought his sword up, ludicrously, like a tail. Ruori heard a smothered snort of laughter from among his officers. And yet, thought the captain, were long trousers and ruffled shirt any worse than sarong, sandals, and clan tattoos? Different customs, no more. You had to sail the Maurai Federation, from Awaii to his own N'Zealann and west to Mlaya, before you appreciated how big this planet was and how much of it a mystery.

"You speak our language most excellently, S'ñor," said Doñita Tresa Carabán. She smiled. "Perhaps better than we, since you studied texts centuries old before embarking, and the Spañol has changed greatly since."

Ruori smiled back. Don Miwel's daughter was worth it.

The rich black dress caressed a figure as good as any in the world; and, while the Sea People paid less attention to a woman's face, he saw that hers was proud and well formed, her father's eagle beak softened to a curve, luminous eyes and hair the color of midnight oceans. It was too bad these Meycans—the nobles, at least—thought a girl should be reserved solely for the husband they eventually picked for her. He would have liked her to swap her pearls and silver for a lei and go out in a ship's canoe, just the two of them, to watch the sunrise and make love.

However—

"In such company," he murmured, "I am stimulated to learn the modern language as fast as possible."

She refrained from coquetting with her fan, a local habit the Sea People found alternately hilarious and irritating. But her lashes fluttered. They were very long, and her eyes, he saw, were gold-flecked green. "You are learning cab'llero manners just as fast, S'ñor," she said.

"Do not call our language 'modern,' I pray you," interrupted a scholarly-looking man in a long robe. Ruori recognized Bispo Don Carlos Ermosillo, a high priest of that Esu Carito who seemed cognate with the Maurai Lesu Haristi. "Not modern, but corrupt. I too have studied ancient books, printed before the War of Judgment. Our ancestors spoke the true Spañol. Our version of it is as distorted as our present-day society." He sighed. "But what can one expect, when even among the well born, not one in ten can write his own name?"

"There was more literacy in the high days of the Perio," said Don Miwel. "You should have visited us a hundred years ago, S'ñor Captain, and seen what our race was capable of."

"Yet what was the Perio itself but a successor state?" asked the Bispo bitterly. "It unified a large area, gave law and order for a while, but what did it create that was new? Its course was the same sorry tale as a thousand kingdoms before, and therefore the same judgment has fallen on it."

Doñita Tresa crossed herself. Even Ruori, who held a degree in engineering as well as navigation, was shocked. "Not atomics?" he exclaimed.

"What? Oh. The old weapons, which destroyed the old world. No, of course not." Don Carlos shook his head. "But in our more limited way, we have been as stupid and sinful as the legendary forefathers, and the results have been parallel. You may call it human greed or el Dío's punishment as you will; I think the two mean much the same thing."

Ruori looked closely at the priest. "I should like to speak with you further, S'ñor," he said, hoping it was the right title. "Men who know history, rather than myth, are rare these days."

"By all means," said Don Carlos. "I should be honored."

Doñita Tresa shifted on light, impatient feet. "It is customary to dance," she said.

Her father laughed. "Ah, yes. The young ladies have been getting quite impatient, I am sure. Time enough to resume formal discussions tomorrow, S'ñor Captain. Now let the music begin."

He signalled. The orchestra struck up. Some instruments were quite like those of the Maurai, others wholly unfamiliar. The scale itself was different. . . . They had something like it in Stralia, but—a hand fell on Ruori's arm. He looked down at Tresa. "Since you do not ask me to dance," she said, "may I be so immodest as to ask you?"

"What does 'immodest' mean?" he inquired.

She blushed and tried to explain, without success. Ruori decided it was another local concept which the Sea People lacked. By that time the Meycan girls and their cavaliers were out on the ballroom floor. He studied them for a moment. "The motions are unknown to me," he said, "but I think I could soon learn."

She slipped into his arms. It was a pleasant contact, even though nothing would come of it. "You do very well," she said after a minute. "Are all your folk so graceful?"

Only later did he realize that was a compliment for which he should have thanked her; being an Islander, he took it at face value as a question and replied, "Most of us spend a great deal of time on the water. A sense of balance and rhythm must be developed or one is likely to fall into the sea."

She wrinkled her nose. "Oh, stop," she laughed. "You're as solemn as S' Osé in the cathedral."

Ruori grinned back. He was a tall young man, brown as all his race but with the gray eyes which many bore in memory of Ingliss ancestors. Being a N'Zealanner, he was not tattooed as lavishly as some Federation men. On the other hand, he had woven a whalebone filigree into his queue, his sarong was the finest batik, and he had added thereto a fringed shirt. His knife, without which a Maurai felt obscenely helpless, was in contrast: old, shabby until you saw the blade, a tool.

"I must see this god, S' Osé," he said. "Will you show me? Or no. I would not have eyes for a mere statue."

"How long will you stay?" she asked.

"As long as we can. We are supposed to explore the whole Meycan coast. Hitherto the only Maurai contact with the Merikan continent has been one voyage from Awaii to Calforni. They found desert and a few savages. We have heard from Okkaidan traders that there are forests still farther north, where yellow and white men strive against each other. But what lies south of Calforni was unknown to us until this expedition was sent out. Perhaps you can tell us what to expect in Su-Merika."

"Little enough by now," she sighed, "even in Brasil."

"Ah, but lovely roses bloom in Meyco."

Her humor returned. "And flattering words in N'Zealann," she chuckled.

"Far from it. We are notoriously straightforward. Except, of course, when yarning about voyages we have made."

"What yarns will you tell about this one?"

"Not many, lest all the young men of the Federation come crowding here. But I will take you aboard my ship, Doñita, and show you to the compass. Thereafter it will always point toward S' Antón d' Inio. You will be, so to speak, my compass rose."

Somewhat to his surprise, she understood, and laughed. She led him across the floor, supple between his hands.

Thereafter, as the night wore on, they danced together as much as decency allowed, or a bit more, and various foolishness which concerned no one else passed between them. Toward sunrise the orchestra was dismissed and the guests, hiding yawns behind well-bred hands, began to take their departure.

"How dreary to stand and receive farewells," whispered Tresa. "Let them think I went to bed already." She took Ruori's hand and slipped behind a column and thence out onto a balcony. An aged serving woman, stationed to act as duenna for couples that wandered thither, had wrapped up in her mantle against the cold and fallen asleep. Otherwise the two were alone among jasmines. Mists floated around the palace and blurred the city; far off rang the "*Todos buen*" of pikemen tramping the outer walls. Westward the balcony faced darkness, where the last stars glittered. The seven tall topmasts of the Maurai *Dolphin* caught the earliest sun and glowed.

Tresa shivered and stood close to Ruori. They did not speak for a while.

"Remember us," she said at last, very low. "When you are back with your own happier people, do not forget us here."

"How could I?" he answered, no longer in jest.

"You have so much more than we," she said wistfully. "You have told me how your ships can sail unbelievably fast, almost into the wind. How your fishers always fill their nets, how your whale ranchers keep herds that darken the water, how you even farm the ocean for food and fiber and . . ." She fingered the shimmering material of his shirt. "You told me this was made by craft out of fishbones. You told me that every family has its own spacious house and every member of it, almost, his own boat . . . that even small children on the loneliest island can read, and have printed books . . . that you have none of the sicknesses which destroy us . . . that no one hungers and all are free— oh, do not forget us, you on whom el Dío has smiled!"

She stopped, then, embarrassed. He could see how her head lifted and nostrils dilated, as if resenting him. After all, he thought, she came from a breed which for centuries had given, not received, charity.

Therefore he chose his words with care. "It has been less our virtue than our good fortune, Doñita. We suffered less than most in the War of Judgment, and our being chiefly Islanders prevented our population from outrunning the sea's rich ability to feed us. So we—no, we did not retain any lost ancestral arts. There are none. But we did re-create an ancient attitude, a way of thinking, which has made the difference—science."

She crossed herself. "The atom!" she breathed, drawing from him.

"No, no, Doñita," he protested. "So many nations we have discovered lately believe science was the cause of the old world's ruin. Or else they think it was a collection of cut-and-dried formulas for making tall buildings or talking at a distance. But neither is true. The scientific method is only a means of learning. It is a . . . a perpetual starting afresh. And that is why you people here in Meyco can help us as much as we can help you, why we have sought you out and will come knocking hopefully at your doors again in the future.''

She frowned, though something began to glow within her. "I do not understand," she said.

He cast about for an example. At last he pointed to a series of small holes in the balcony rail. "What used to be here?'' he asked.

"Why . . . I do not know. It has always been like that.''

"I think I can tell you. I have seen similar things elsewhere. It was a wrought-iron grille. But it was pulled out a long time ago and made into weapons or tools. No?''

"Quite likely,'' she admitted. "Iron and copper have grown very scarce. We have to send caravans across the whole land, to Támico ruins, in great peril from bandits and barbarians, to fetch our metal. Time was when there were iron rails within a kilometer of this place. Don Carlos has told me.''

He nodded. "Just so. The ancients exhausted the world. They mined the ores, burned the oil and coal, eroded the land, until nothing was left. I exaggerate, of course. There are still deposits. But not enough. The old civilization used up the capital, so to speak. Now sufficient forest and soil have come back that the world could try to reconstruct machine culture—except that there aren't enough minerals and fuels. For centuries men had been forced to tear up the antique artifacts, if they were to have any metal at all. By and large, the knowledge of the ancients hasn't been lost; it has simply become unusable, because we are so much poorer than they.''

He leaned forward, earnestly. "But knowledge and discovery do not depend on wealth," he said. "Perhaps because we did not have much metal to cannibalize in the Islands, we turned elsewhere. The scientific method is just as applicable to wind and sun and living matter as it was to oil, iron, or uranium. By studying genetics we learned how to create seaweeds, plankton, fish that would serve our purposes. Scientific forest management gives us adequate timber, organic-synthesis bases, some fuel. The sun pours down energy which we know how to concentrate and use. Wood, ceramics, even stone can replace metal for most purposes. The wind, through such principles as the airfoil or the Venturi law or the Hilsch tube, supplies force, heat, refrigeration; the tides can be harnessed. Even in its present early stage, paramathematical psychology helps control population, as well as—no, I am talking like an engineer now, falling into my own language. I apologize.

"What I wanted to say was that if we can only have the help of other people, such as yourselves, on a worldwide scale, we can match our ancestors, or surpass them . . . not in their ways, which were often shortsighted and wasteful, but in achievements uniquely ours. . . ."

His voice trailed off. She wasn't listening. She stared over his head, into the air, and horror stood on her face.

Then trumpets howled on battlements, and the cathedral bells crashed to life.

"What the nine devils!" Ruori turned on his heel and looked up. The zenith had become quite blue. Lazily over S' Antón floated five orca shapes. The new sun glared off a jagged heraldry painted along their flanks. He estimated dizzily that each of them must be three hundred feet long.

Blood-colored things petaled out below them and drifted down upon the city.

"The Sky People!" said a small broken croak behind him. "Sant'sima Marí, pray for us now!"

III

Loklann hit flagstones, rolled over, and bounced to his feet. Beside him a carved horseman presided over fountain waters. For an instant he admired the stone, almost alive; they had nothing like that in Canyon, Zona, Corado, any of the mountain kingdoms. And the temple facing this plaza was white skywardness.

The square had been busy, farmers and handicrafters setting up their booths for a market day. Most of them scattered in noisy panic. But one big man roared, snatched a stone hammer, and dashed in his rags to meet Loklann. He was covering the flight of a young woman, probably his wife, who held a baby in her arms. Through the shapeless sack dress Loklann saw that her figure wasn't bad. She would fetch a price when the Mong slave dealer next visited Canyon. So could her husband, but there wasn't time now, still encumbered with a chute. Loklann whipped out his pistol and fired. The man fell to his knees, gaped at the blood seeping between fingers clutched to his belly, and collapsed. Loklann flung off his harness. His boots thudded after the woman. She shrieked when fingers closed on her arm and tried to wriggle free, but the brat hampered her. Loklann shoved her toward the temple. Robra was already on its steps.

"Post a guard!" yelled the skipper. "We may as well keep prisoners in here, till we're ready to plunder it."

An old man in priest's robes tottered to the door. He held up one of the cross-shaped Meycan josses, as if to bar the way. Robra brained him with an ax blow, kicked the body off the stairs, and urged the woman inside.

It sleeted armed men. Loklann winded his oxhorn bugle, rallying them. A counterattack could be expected any minute. . . . Yes, now.

A troop of Meycan cavalry clanged into view. They were young, proud-looking men in baggy pants, leather breastplate and plumed helmet, blowing cloak, fire-hardened wooden lances but steel sabres—very much like the yellow nomads of Tekkas, whom they had fought for centuries. But so had the Sky People. Loklann pounded to the head of his line, where his standard bearer had raised the Lightning Flag. Half the *Buffalo*'s crew fitted together sections of pike tipped with edged ceramic, grounded the butts, and waited. The charge crested upon them. Their pikes slanted down. Some horses spitted themselves, others reared back screaming. The pikemen jabbed at their riders. The second paratroop line stepped in, ax and sword and hamstringing knife. For a few minutes murder boiled. The Meycans broke. They did not flee, but they retreated in confusion. And then the Canyon bows began to snap.

Presently only dead and hurt cluttered the square. Loklann moved briskly among the latter. Those who weren't too badly wounded were hustled into the temple. Might as well collect all possible slaves and cull them later.

From afar he heard a dull boom. "Cannon," said Robra, joining him. "At the army barracks."

"Well, let the artillery have its fun, till our boys get in among 'em," said Loklann sardonically.

"Sure, sure." Robra looked nervous. "I wish they'd let us hear from them, though. Just standing around here isn't good."

"It won't be long," predicted Loklann.

Nor was it. A runner with a broken arm staggered to him. *"Stormcloud,"* he gasped. "The big building you sent us against . . . full of swordsmen. . . . They repulsed us at the door—"

"Huh! I thought it was only the king's house," said Loklann. He laughed. "Well, maybe the king was giving a party. Come on, then, I'll go see for myself. Robra, take over here." His finger swept out thirty men to accompany him. They jogged down streets empty and silent except for their bootfalls and weapon-jingle. The housefolk must be huddled terrified behind those blank walls. So much the easier to corral them later, when the fighting was done and the looting began.

A roar broke loose. Loklann led a dash around a last corner. Opposite him he saw the palace, an old building, red-tiled roof and mellow walls and many glass windows. The *Stormcloud* men were fighting at the main door. Their dead and wounded from the last attack lay thick.

Loklann took in the situation at a glance. "It wouldn't occur to those lardheads to send a detachment through some side entrance, would it?" he groaned. "Jonak, take fifteen of our boys and batter in a lesser door and hit the rear of that line. The rest of you help me keep it busy meanwhile."

He raised his red-spattered ax. "A Canyon!" he yelled. "A Canyon!" His followers bellowed behind him and they ran to battle.

The last charge had reeled away bloody and breathless. Half a dozen Meycans stood in the wide doorway. They were nobles: grim men with goatees and waxed mustaches, in formal black, red cloaks wrapped as shields on their left arms and long slim swords in their right hands. Behind them stood others, ready to take the place of the fallen.

"A Canyon!" shouted Loklann as he rushed.

"Quel Dío wela!" cried a tall grizzled Don. A gold chain of office hung around his neck. His blade snaked forth.

Loklann flung up his ax and parried. The Don was fast, riposting with a lunge that ended on the raider's breast. But hardened six-ply leather turned the point. Loklann's men crowded on either side, reckless of thrusts, and hewed. He

struck the enemy sword; it spun from the owner's grasp.
"Ah, no, Don Miwel!" cried a young person beside the
calde. The older man snarled, threw out his hands, and
somehow clamped them on Loklann's ax. He yanked it away
with a troll's strength. Loklann stared into eyes that said
death. Don Miwel raised the ax. Loklann drew his pistol
and fired point blank.

As Don Miwel toppled, Loklann caught him, pulled off
the gold chain, and threw it around his own neck. Straight-
ening, he met a savage thrust. It glanced off his helmet. He
got his ax back, planted his feet firmly, and smote.

The defending line buckled.

Clamor lifted behind Loklann. He turned and saw weapons gleam beyond his own men's shoulders. With a curse
he realized—there had been more people in the palace than
these holding the main door. The rest had sallied out the
rear and were now on his back!

A point pierced his thigh. He felt no more than a sting,
but rage flapped black before his eyes. "Be reborn as the
swine you are!" he roared. Half unaware, he thundered
loose, cleared a space for himself, lurched aside and over-
saw the battle.

The newcomers were mostly palace guards, judging from
their gaily striped uniforms, pikes, and machetes. But they
had allies, a dozen men such as Loklann had never seen or
heard of. Those had the brown skin and black hair of Injuns,
but their faces were more like a white man's; intricate blue
designs covered their bodies, which were clad only in
wraparounds and flower wreaths. They wielded knives and
clubs with wicked skill.

Loklann tore his trouser leg open to look at his wound.
It wasn't much. More serious was the beating his men were
taking. He saw Mork sunna Brenn rush, sword uplifted, at
one of the dark strangers, a big man who had added a rich-
looking blouse to his skirt. Mork had killed four men at
home for certain, in lawful fights, and nobody knew how
many abroad. The dark man waited, a knife between his
teeth, hands hanging loose. As the blade came down, the
dark man simply wasn't there. Grinning around his knife,
he chopped at the sword wrist with the edge of a hand.
Loklann distinctly heard bones crack. Mork yelled. The foreigner hit him in the Adam's apple. Mork went to his knees,
spat blood, caved in, and was still. Another Sky Man

charged, ax aloft. The stranger again evaded the weapon, caught the moving body on his hip, and helped it along. The Sky Man hit the pavement with his head and moved no more.

Now Loklann saw that the newcomers were a ring around others who did not fight. Women. By Oktai and man-eating Ulagu, these bastards were leading out all the women in the palace! And the fighting against them had broken up; surly raiders stood back nursing their wounds.

Loklann ran forward. "A Canyon! A Canyon!" he shouted.

"Ruori Rangi Lohannaso," said the big stranger politely. He rapped a string of orders. His party began to move away.

"Hit them, you scum!" bawled Loklann. His men rallied and straggled after. Rearguard pikes prodded them back. Loklann led a rush to the front of the hollow square.

The big man saw him coming. Gray eyes focused on the calde's chain and became full winter. "So you killed Don Miwel," said Ruori in Spañol. Loklann understood him, having learned the tongue from prisoners and concubines during many raids further north. "You lousy son of a skua."

Loklann's pistol rose. Ruori's hand blurred. Suddenly the knife stood in the Sky Man's right biceps. He dropped his gun. "I'll want that back!" shouted Ruori. Then, to his followers: "Come, to the ship."

Loklann stared at blood rivering down his arm. He heard a clatter as the refugees broke through the weary Canyon line. Jonak's party appeared in the main door—which was now empty, its surviving defenders having left with Ruori.

A man approached Loklann, who still regarded his arm. "Shall we go after 'em, Skipper?" he said, almost timidly. "Jonak can lead us after 'em."

"No," said Loklann.

"But they must be escorting a hundred women. A lot of young women too."

Loklann shook himself, like a dog coming out of a deep cold stream. "No. I want to find the medic and get this wound stitched. Then we'll have a lot else to do. We can settle with those outlanders later, if the chance comes. Man, we've a city to sack!"

IV

There were dead men scattered on the wharves, some burned. They looked oddly small beneath the warehouses, like rag dolls tossed away by a weeping child. Cannon fumes lingered to bite nostrils.

Atel Hamid Seraio, the mate, who had been left aboard the *Dolphin* with the enlisted crew, led a band to meet Ruori. His salute was in the Island manner, so casual that even at this moment several of the Meycans looked shocked. "We were about to come for you, Captain," he said.

Ruori looked toward that forest which was the *Dolphin*'s rig. "What happened here?" he asked.

"A band of those devils landed near the battery. They took the emplacements while we were still wondering what it was all about. Part of them went off toward that racket in the north quarter, I believe where the army lives. But the rest of the gang attacked us. Well, with our gunwale ten feet above the dock, and us trained to repel pirates, they didn't have much luck. I gave them a dose of flame."

Ruori winced from the blackened corpses. Doubtless they had deserved it, but he didn't like the idea of pumping flaming blubber oil across live men.

"Too bad they didn't try from the seaward side," added Atel with a sigh. "We've got such a lovely harpoon catapult. I used one like it years ago off Hinja, when a Sinese buccaneer came too close. His junk sounded like a whale."

"Men aren't whales!" snapped Ruori.

"All right, Captain, all right, all right." Atel backed away from his violence, a little frightened. "No ill-speaking meant."

Ruori recollected himself and folded his hands. "I spoke in needless anger," he said formally. "I laugh at myself."

"It's nothing, Captain. As I was saying, we beat them off and they finally withdrew. I imagine they'll bring back reinforcements. What shall we do?"

"That's what I don't know," said Ruori in a bleak tone. He turned to the Meycans, who stood with stricken, uncomprehending faces. "Your pardon is prayed, Dons and Doñitas," he said in Spañol. "He was only relating to me what had happened."

"Don't apologize!" Tresa Carabán spoke, stepping out ahead of the men. Some of them looked a bit offended, but they were too tired and stunned to reprove her forwardness, and to Ruori it was only natural that a woman act as freely as a man. "You saved our lives, Captain. More than our lives."

He wondered what was worse than death, then nodded. Slavery, of course—ropes and whips and a lifetime's unfree toil in a strange land. His eyes dwelt upon her, the long hair disheveled past smooth shoulders, gown ripped, weariness and a streak of tears across her face. He wondered if she knew her father was dead. She held herself straight and regarded him with an odd defiance.

"We are uncertain what to do," he said awkwardly. "We are only fifty men. Can we help your city?"

A young nobleman, swaying on his feet, replied: "No. The city is done. You can take these ladies to safety, that is all."

Tresa protested: "You are not surrendering already, S'ñor Dónoju!"

"No, Doñita," the young man breathed. "But I hope I can be shriven before returning to fight, for I am a dead man."

"Come aboard," said Ruori curtly.

He led the way up the gangplank. Liliu, one of the ship's five wahines, ran to meet him. She threw arms about his neck and cried, "I feared you were slain!"

"Not yet." Ruori disengaged her as gently as possible. He noticed Tresa standing stiff, glaring at them both. Puzzlement came—did these curious Meycans expect a crew to embark on a voyage of months without taking a few girls along? Then he decided that the wahines' clothing, being much like his men's, was against local mores. To Nan with their silly prejudices. But it hurt that Tresa drew away from him.

The other Meycans stared about them. Not all had toured the ship when she first arrived. They looked in bewilderment at lines and spars, down fathoms of deck to the harpoon catapult, capstans, bowsprit, and back at the sailors. The Maurai grinned encouragingly. Thus far most of them looked on this as a lark. Men who skindove after sharks, for fun, or who sailed outrigger canoes alone across a thousand ocean miles to pay a visit, were not put out by a fight.

But they had not talked with grave Don Miwel and merry

Don Wan and gentle Bispo Ermosillo, and then seen those people dead on a dance floor, thought Ruori in bitterness.

The Meycan women huddled together, ladies and servants, to weep among each other. The palace guards formed a solid rank around them. The nobles, and Tresa, followed Ruori up on the poop deck.

"Now," he said, "let us talk. Who are these bandits?"

"The Sky People," whispered Tresa.

"I can see that." Ruori cocked an eye on the aircraft patrolling overhead. They had the sinister beauty of as many barracuda. Here and there columns of smoke reached toward them. "But who are they? Where from?"

"They are Nor-Merikans," she answered in a dry little voice, as if afraid to give it color. "From the wild highlands around the Corado River, the Grand Canyon it has cut for itself—mountaineers. There is a story that they were driven from the eastern plains by Mong invaders, a long time ago; but as they grew strong in the hills and deserts, they defeated some Mong tribes and became friendly with others. For a hundred years they have harried our northern borders. This is the first time they have ventured so far south. We never expected them—I suppose their spies learned most of our soldiers are along the Río Gran, chasing a rebel force. They sailed southwesterly, above our land—" She shivered.

The young Dónoju spat. "They are heathen dogs! They know nothing but to rob and burn and kill!" He sagged. "What have we done that they are loosed on us?"

Ruori rubbed his chin thoughtfully. "They can't be quite such savages," he murmured. "Those blimps are better than anything my own Federation has tried to make. The fabric . . . some tricky synthetic? It must be, or it wouldn't contain hydrogen any length of time. Surely they don't use helium! But for hydrogen production on that scale, you need industry. A good empirical chemistry, at least. They might even electrolyze it . . . good Lesu!"

He realized he had been talking to himself in his home language. "I beg your pardon," he said. "I was wondering what we might do. This ship carried no flying vessels."

Again he looked upward. Atel handed him his binoculars. He focused on the nearest blimp. The huge gas bag and the gondola beneath—itself as big as many a Maurai ship—formed an aerodynamically clean unit. The gondola seemed to be light, woven cane about a wooden frame, but strong.

Three-fourths of the way up from its keel a sort of gallery
ran clear around, on which the crew might walk and work.
At intervals along the rail stood muscle-powered machines.
Some must be for hauling, but others suggested catapults. Evidently the blimps of various chiefs fought each other occasionally, in the northern kingdoms. That might be worth knowing.
The Federation's political psychologists were skilled at the
divide-and-rule game. But for now . . .

The motive power was extraordinarily interesting. Near
the gondola bows two lateral spars reached out for some
fifty feet, one above the other. They supported two pivoted
frames on either side, to which square sails were bent. A
similar pair of spars pierced the after hull: eight sails in all.
Shark-fin control surfaces were braced to the gas bag. A
couple of small retractable windwheels, vaned and pivoted,
jutted beneath the gondola, evidently serving the purpose
of a false keel. Sails and rudders were trimmed by lines
running through block and tackle to windlasses on the gallery. By altering their set, it should be possible to steer at
least several points to windward. And, yes, the air moved
in different directions at different levels. A blimp could descend by pumping out cells in its gas bag, compressing the
hydrogen into storage tanks; it could rise by reinflating or
by dropping ballast (though the latter trick would be reserved for home stretches, when leakage had depleted the
gas supply). Between sails, rudders, and its ability to find
a reasonably favoring wind, such a blimp could go roving
across several thousand miles, with a payload of several
tons. Oh, a lovely craft!

Ruori lowered his glasses. "Hasn't the Perio built any air
vessels, to fight back?" he asked.

"No," mumbled one of the Meycans. "All we ever had
was balloons. We don't know how to make a fabric which
will hold the lifting-gas long enough, or how to control the
flight. . . ." His voice trailed off.

"And being a nonscientific culture, you never thought of
doing systematic research to learn those tricks," said Ruori.

Tresa, who had been staring at her city, whirled about
upon him. "It's easy for you!" she screamed. "You haven't
stood off Mong in the north and Raucanians in the south for
century after century. You haven't had to spend twenty years
and ten thousand lives making canals and aqueducts, so a
few less people would starve. You aren't burdened with a

peon majority who can only work, who cannot look after themselves because they have never been taught how because their existence is too much of a burden for our land to afford it. It's easy for you to float about with your shirtless doxies and poke fun at us! What would you have done, S'ñor Almighty Captain?''

"Be still," reproved young Dónoju. "He saved our lives.''

"So far!'' she said, through teeth and tears. One small dancing shoe stamped the deck.

For a bemused moment, irrelevantly, Ruori wondered what a doxie was. It sounded uncomplimentary. Could she mean the wahines? But was there a more honorable way for a woman to earn a good dowry than by hazarding her life, side by side with the men of her people, on a mission of discovery and civilization? What did Tresa expect to tell her grandchildren about on rainy nights?

Then he wondered further why she should disturb him. He had noticed it before, in some of the Meycans, an almost terrifying intensity between man and wife, as if a spouse were somehow more than a respected friend and partner. But what other relationship was possible? A psychological specialist might know; Ruori was lost.

He shook an angry head, to clear it, and said aloud: "This is no time for inurbanity." He had to use a Spañol word with not quite the same connotation. "We must decide. Are you certain we have no hope of repelling the pirates?''

"No unless S' Antón himself passes a miracle," said Doñoju in a dead voice.

Then, snapping erect: "There is only a single thing you can do for us, S'ñor. If you will leave now, with the women—there are high-born ladies among them, who must not be sold into captivity and disgrace. Bear them south to Port Wanawato, where the calde will look after their welfare.''

"I do not like to run off," said Ruori, looking at the men fallen on the wharf.

"S'ñor, these are *ladies!* In el Dío's name, have mercy on them!''

Ruori studied the taut, bearded faces. He did owe them a great deal of hospitality, and he could see no other way he might ever repay it. "If you wish," he said slowly. "What of yourselves?''

The young noble bowed as if to a king. "Our thanks and prayers will go with you, my lord Captain. We men, of course, will now return to battle." He stood up and barked in a parade-ground voice: "Atten-tion! Form ranks!"

A few swift kisses passed on the main deck, and then the men of Meyco had crossed the gangplank and tramped into their city.

Ruori beat a fist on the taffrail. "If we had some way," he mumbled. "If I could do something." Almost hopefully: "Do you think the bandits might attack us?"

"Only if you remain here," said Tresa. Her eyes were chips of green ice. "Would to Marí you had not pledged yourself to sail!"

"If they come after us at sea—"

"I do not think they will. You carry a hundred women and a few trade goods. The Sky People will have their pick of ten thousand women, as many men, and our city's treasures. Why should they take the trouble to pursue you?"

"Aye . . . aye. . . ."

"Go," she said. "You dare not linger."

Her coldness was like a blow. "What do you mean?" he asked. "Do you think the Maurai are cowards?"

She hesitated. Then, in reluctant honesty: "No."

"Well, why do you scoff at me?"

"Oh, go away!" She knelt by the rail, bowed head in arms, and surrendered to herself.

Ruori left her and gave his orders. Men scrambled into the rigging. Furled canvas broke loose and cracked in a young wind. Beyond the jetty, the ocean glittered blue, with small whitecaps; gulls skimmed across heaven. Ruori saw only the glimpses he had had before, as he led the retreat from the palace.

A weaponless man, his head split open. A girl, hardly twelve years old, who screamed as two raiders carried her into an alley. An aged man fleeing in terror, zigzagging, while four archers took potshots at him and howled laughter when he fell transfixed and dragged himself along on his hands. A woman sitting dumb in the street, her dress torn, next to a baby whose brains had been dashed out. A little statue in a niche, a holy image, a faded bunch of violets at its feet, beheaded by a casual war-hammer. A house that burned, and shrieks from within.

Suddenly the aircraft overhead were not beautiful.

To reach up and pull them out of the sky!

Ruori stopped dead. The crew surged around him. He heard a short-haul chantey, deep voices vigorous from always having been free and well fed, but it echoed in a far corner of his brain.

"Casting off," sang the mate.

"Not yet! Not yet! Wait!"

Ruori ran toward the poop, up the ladder and past the steersman to Doñita Tresa. She had risen again, to stand with bent head past which the hair swept to hide her countenance.

"Tresa," panted Ruori. "Tresa, I've an idea. I think—there may be a chance—perhaps we can fight back after all."

She raised her eyes. Her fingers closed on his arm till he felt the nails draw blood.

Words tumbled from him. "It will depend . . . on luring them . . . to us. At least a couple of their vessels . . . must follow us . . . to sea. I think then—I'm not sure of the details, but it may be . . . we can fight . . . even drive them off—"

Still she stared at him. He felt a hesitation. "Of course," he said, "we may lose the fight. And we do have the women aboard."

"If you lose," she asked, so low he could scarcely hear it, "will we die or be captured?"

"I think we will die."

"That is well." She nodded. "Yes. Fight, then."

"There is one thing I am unsure of. How to make them pursue us." He paused. "If someone were to let himself . . . be captured by them—and told them we were carrying off a great treasure—would they believe that?"

"They might well." Life had come back to her tones, even eagerness. "Let us say, the calde's hoard. None ever existed, but the robbers would believe my father's cellars were stuffed with gold."

"Then someone must go to them." Ruori turned his back to her, twisted his fingers together and slogged toward a conclusion he did not want to reach. "But it could not be just anyone. They would club a man in among the other slaves, would they not? I mean, would they listen to him at all?"

"Probably not. Very few of them know Spañol. By the

time a man who babbled of treasure was understood, they might be halfway home.'' Tresa scowled. ''What shall we do?''

Ruori saw the answer, but could not get it past his throat.

''I am sorry,'' he mumbled. ''My idea was not so good after all. Let us be gone.''

The girl forced her way between him and the rail to stand in front of him, touching as if they danced again. Her voice was altogether steady. ''You know a way.''

''I do not.''

''I have come to know you well, in one night. You are a poor liar. Tell me.''

He looked away. Somehow, he got out: ''A woman—not any woman, but a very beautiful one—would she not soon be taken to their chief?''

Tresa stood aside. The color drained from her cheeks.

''Yes,'' she said at last. ''I think so.''

''But then again,'' said Ruori wretchedly, ''she might be killed. They do much wanton killing, those men. I cannot let anyone who was given into my protection risk death.''

''You heathen fool,'' she said through tight lips. ''Do you think the chance of being killed matters to me?''

''What else could happen?'' he asked, surprised. And then: ''Oh, yes, of course, the woman would be a slave if we lost the battle afterward. Though I should imagine, if she is beautiful, she would not be badly treated.''

''And is that all you—'' Tresa stopped. He had never known it was possible for a smile to show pure hurt. ''Of course. I should have realized. Your people have your own ways of thinking.''

''What do you mean?'' he fumbled.

A moment more she stood with clenched fists. Then, half to herself: ''They killed my father; yes, I saw him dead in the doorway. They would leave my city a ruin peopled by corpses.''

Her head lifted. ''I will go,'' she said.

''You?'' He grabbed her shoulders. ''No, surely not you! One of the others—''

''Should I send anybody else? I am the calde's daughter.''

She pulled herself free of him and hurried across the deck, down the ladder toward the gangway. Her gaze was turned from the ship. A few words drifted back. ''Afterward, if there is an afterward, there is always the convent.''

He did not understand. He stood on the poop, staring after her and abominating himself until she was lost to sight. Then he said, "Cast off," and the ship stood out to sea.

V

The Meycans fought doggedly, street by street and house by house, but in a couple of hours their surviving soldiers had been driven into the northeast corner of S' Antón. They themselves hardly knew that, but a Sky chief had a view from above; a rover was now tethered to the cathedral, with a rope ladder for men to go up and down, and the companion vessel, skeleton crewed, brought their news to it.

"Good enough," said Loklann. "We'll keep them boxed in with a quarter of our force. I don't think they'll sally. Meanwhile the rest of us can get things organized. Let's not give these creatures too much time to hide themselves and their silver. In the afternoon, when we're rested, we can land parachuters behind the city troops, drive them out into our lines and destroy them."

He ordered the *Buffalo* grounded, that he might load the most precious loot at once. The men, by and large, were too rough—good lads, but apt to damage a robe or a cup or a jeweled cross in their haste; and sometimes those Meycan things were too beautiful even to give away, let alone sell.

The flagship descended as far as possible. It still hung at a thousand feet, for hand pumps and aluminum-alloy tanks did not allow much hydrogen compression. In colder, denser air it would have been suspended even higher. But ropes snaked from it to a quickly assembled ground crew. At home there were ratcheted capstans outside every lodge, enabling as few as four women to bring down a rover. One hated the emergency procedure of bleeding gas, for the Keepers could barely meet demand, in spite of a new sunpower unit added to their hydroelectric station, and charged accordingly. (Or so the Keepers said, but perhaps they were merely taking advantage of being inviolable, beyond any kings, to jack up prices. Some chiefs, including Loklann, had begun to experiment with hydrogen production for themselves, but it was a slow thing to puzzle out an art that even the Keepers only half understood.)

Here, strong men replaced machinery. The *Buffalo* was soon pegged down in the cathedral plaza, which it almost filled. Loklann inspected each rope himself. His wounded leg ached, but not too badly to walk on. More annoying was his right arm, which hurt worse from stitches than from the original cut. The medic had warned him to go easy with it. That meant fighting left-handed, for the story should never be told that Loklann sunna Holber stayed out of combat. However, he would only be half himself.

He touched the knife which had spiked him. At least he'd gotten a fine steel blade for his pains. And . . . hadn't the owner said they would meet again, to settle who kept it? There were omens in such words. It could be a pleasure to reincarnate that Ruori.

"Skipper. Skipper, sir."

Loklann glanced about. Yuw Red-Ax and Aalan sunna Rickar, men of his lodge, had hailed him. They grasped the arms of a young woman in black velvet and silver. The be-weaponed crowd, moiling about, was focusing on her; raw whoops lifted over the babble.

"What is it?" said Loklann brusquely. He had much to do.

"This wench, sir. A looker, isn't she? We found her down near the waterfront."

"Well, shove her into the temple with the rest till—oh." Loklann rocked back on his heels, narrowing his eyes to meet a steady green glare. She was certainly a looker.

"She kept hollering the same words over and over: *'Shef, rey, ombro gran.'* I finally wondered if it didn't mean 'chief,' " said Yuw, "and then when she yelled 'khan' I was pretty sure she wanted to see you. So we didn't use her ourselves," he finished virtuously.

"Aba tu Spañol?" said the girl.

Loklann grinned. "Yes," he replied in the same language, his words heavily accented but sufficient. "Well enough to know you are calling me 'thou.' " Her pleasantly formed mouth drew into a thin line. "Which means you think I am your inferior—or your god, or your beloved."

She flushed, threw back her head (sunlight ran along crow's-wing hair) and answered: "You might tell these oafs to release me."

Loklann said the order in Angliz. Yuw and Aalan let go. The marks of their fingers were bruised into her arms. Loklann stroked his beard. "Did you want to see me?" he asked.

"If you are the leader, yes," she said. "I am the calde's daughter, Doñita Tresa Carabán." Briefly, her voice wavered. "That is my father's chain of office you are wearing. I came back on behalf of his people, to ask for terms."

"What?" Loklann blinked. Someone in the warrior crowd laughed.

It must not be in her to beg mercy, he thought; her tone remained brittle. "Considering your sure losses if you fight to a finish, and the chance of provoking a counterattack on your homeland, will you not accept a money ransom and a safe-conduct, releasing your captives and ceasing your destruction?"

"By Oktai," murmured Loklann. "Only a woman could imagine we—" He stopped. "Did you say you came back?"

She nodded. "On the people's behalf. I know I have no legal authority to make terms, but in practice—"

"Forget that!" he rapped. "Where did you come back from?"

She faltered. "That has nothing to do with—"

There were too many eyes around. Loklann bawled orders to start systematic plundering. He turned to the girl. "Come aboard the airship," he said. "I want to discuss this further."

Her eyes closed, for just a moment, and her lips moved. Then she looked at him—he though of a cougar he had once trapped—and she said in a flat voice: "Yes. I do have more arguments."

"Any woman does," he laughed, "but you better than most."

"Not that!" she flared. "I meant—no. Marí, pray for me." As he pushed a way through his men, she followed him.

They went past furled sails, to a ladder let down from the gallery. A hatch stood open to the lower hull, showing storage space and leather fetters for slaves. A few guards were posted on the gallery deck. They leaned on their weapons, sweating from beneath helmets, swapping jokes; when Loklann led the girl by, they yelled good-humored envy.

He opened a door. "Have you ever seen one of our vessels?" he asked. The upper gondola contained a long room, bare except for bunk frames on which sleeping bags were laid. Beyond, a series of partitions defined cabinets, a sort of galley, and at last, in the very bow, a room for maps, tables, navigation instruments, speaking tubes. Its walls slanted so far outward that the glazed windows would give a spacious view when the ship was aloft. On a shelf, beneath racked weapons, sat a small idol, tusked and four-armed. A pallet was rolled on the floor.

"The bridge," said Loklann. "Also the captain's cabin."

He gestured at one of four wicker chairs, lashed into place. "Be seated, Doñita. Would you like something to drink?"

She sat down but did not reply. Her fists were clenched on her lap. Loklann poured himself a slug of whiskey and tossed off half at a gulp. "Ahhh! Later we will get some of your own wine for you. It is a shame you have no art of distilling here."

Desperate eyes lifted to him, where he stood over her. "S'ñor," she said, "I beg of you, in Carito's name—well, in your mother's, then—spare my people."

"My mother would laugh herself ill to hear that," he said. Leaning forward: "See here, let us not spill words. You were escaping, but you came back. Where were you escaping to?"

"I—does that matter?"

Good, he thought, she was starting to crack. He hammered: "It does. I know you were at the palace this dawn. I know you fled with the dark foreigners. I know their ship departed an hour ago. You must have been on it, but left again. True?"

"Yes." She began to tremble.

He sipped molten fire and asked reasonably: "Now, tell me, Doñita, what you have to bargain with. You cannot have expected we would give up the best part of our booty and a great many valuable slaves for a mere safe-conduct. All the Sky kingdoms would disown us. Come now, you must have more to offer, if you hope to buy us off."

"No . . . not really—"

His hand exploded against her cheek. Her head jerked from the blow. She huddled back, touching the red mark, as he growled: "I have no time for games. Tell me! Tell me this instant what thought drove you back here from safety, or down in the hold you go. You'd fetch a good price when the traders next visit Canyon. Many homes are waiting for you: a woods runner's cabin in Orgon, a Mong khan's yurt in Tekkas, a brothel as far east as Chai Ka-Go. Tell me now, truly, what you know, and you will be spared that much.''

She looked downward and said raggedly: ''The foreign ship is loaded with the calde's gold. My father had long wanted to remove his personal treasure to a safer place than this, but dared not risk a wagon train across country. There are still many outlaws between here and Fortlez d' S' Er-nán; that much loot would tempt the military escort itself to turn bandit. Captain Lohannaso agreed to carry the gold by sea to Port Wanawato, which is near Fortlez. He could be trusted because his government is anxious for trade with us; he came here officially. The treasure had already been loaded. Of course, when your raid came, the ship also took those women who had been at the palace. But can you not spare them? You'll find more loot in the foreign ship than your whole fleet can lift.''

''By Oktai!'' whispered Loklann.

He turned from her, paced, finally stopped and stared out the window. He could almost hear the gears turn in his head. It made sense. The palace had been disappointing. Oh, yes, a lot of damask and silverware and whatnot, but nothing like the cathedral. Either the calde was less rich than powerful, or he concealed his hoard. Loklann had planned to torture a few servants and find out which. Now he realized there was a third possibility.

Better interrogate some prisoners anyway, to make sure—no, no time. Given a favoring wind, that ship could outrun any rover without working up a sweat. It might already be too late to overhaul. But if not—h'm. Assault would be no cinch. That lean, pitching hull was a small target for para-troopers, and with rigging in the way . . . Wait. Bold men could always find a road. How about grappling to the upper works? If the strain tore the rigging loose, so much the better: a weighted rope would then give a clear slideway to the deck. If the hooks held, though, a storming party could nevertheless go along the lines, into the topmasts. Doubt-less the sailors were agile too, but had they ever reefed a rover sail in a Merikan thunderstorm, a mile above the earth?

He could improvise as the battle developed. At the very least, it would be fun to try. And at most, he might be reborn a world conqueror, for such an exploit in this life.

He laughed aloud, joyously. ''We'll do it!''

Tresa rose. "You will spare the city?" she whispered hoarsely.

"I never promised any such thing," said Loklann. "Of course, the ship's cargo will crowd out most of the stuff and people we might take otherwise. Unless, hm, unless we decide to sail the ship to Calforni, loaded, and meet it there with more rovers. Yes, why not?"

"You oathbreaker," she said, with a hellful of scorn.

"I only promised not to sell you," said Loklann. His gaze went up and down her. "And I won't."

He took a stride forward and gathered her to him. She fought, cursing; once she managed to draw Ruori's knife from his belt; but his cuirass stopped the blade.

Finally he rose. She wept at his feet, her breast marked red by her father's chain. He said more quietly, "No, I will not sell you, Tresa. I will keep you."

VI

"Blimp ho-o-o!"

The lookout's cry hung lonesome for a minute between wind and broad waters. Down under the mainmast, it seethed with crewmen running to their posts.

Ruori squinted eastward. The land was a streak under cumulus clouds, mountainous and blue-shadowed. It took him a while to find the enemy, in all that sky. At last the sun struck them. He lifted his binoculars. Two painted killer whales lazed his way, slanting down from a mile altitude.

He sighed. "Only two," he said.

"That may be more than plenty for us," said Atel Hamid. Sweat studded his forehead.

Ruori gave his mate a sharp look. "You're not afraid of them, are you? I daresay that's been one of their biggest assets, superstition."

"Oh, no, Captain. I know the principle of buoyancy as well as you do. But those people are tough. And they're not trying to storm us from a dock this time; they're in their element."

"So are we." Ruori clapped the other man's back. "Take over. Tanaroa knows what's going to happen, but use your own judgment if I'm spitted."

"I wish you'd let me go," protested Atel. "I don't like being safe here. It's what can happen aloft that worries me."

"You won't be too safe for your liking." Ruori forced a grin. "And somebody has to steer this tub home to hand in those lovely reports to the Geoethnic Research Endeavor."

He swung down the ladder to the main deck and hurried to the mainmast shrouds. His crew yelled around him, weapons gleamed. The two big box kites quivered taut canvas, lashed to a bollard and waiting. Ruori wished there had been time to make more.

Even as it was, though, he had delayed longer than seemed wise, first heading far out to sea and then tacking slowly back, to make the enemy search for him while he prepared. (Or planned, for that matter. When he dismissed Tresa, his ideas had been little more than a conviction that he could fight.) Assuming they were lured after him at all, he had risked their losing patience and going back to the land. For an hour, now, he had dawdled under mainsail, genoa, and a couple of flying jibs, hoping the Sky People were lubbers enough not to find that suspiciously little canvas for this good weather.

But here they were, and here was an end to worry and remorse on a certain girl's behalf. Such emotions were rare in an Islander; and to find himself focusing them thus on a single person, out of earth's millions, had been horrible. Ruori swarmed up the ratlines, as if he fled something.

The blimps were still high, passing overhead on an upper-level breeze. Down here was almost a straight south wind. The aircraft, unable to steer really close-hauled, would descend when they were sea-level upwind of him. Regardless, estimated a cold part of Ruori, the *Dolphin* could avoid their clumsy rush.

But the *Dolphin* wasn't going to.

The rigging was now knotted with armed sailors. Ruori pulled himself onto the mainmast crosstrees and sat down, casually swinging his legs. The ship heeled over in a flaw and he hung above greenish-blue, white-streaked immensity. He balanced, scarcely noticing, and asked Hiti: "Are you set?"

"Aye." The big harpooner, his body a writhe of tattoos and muscles, nodded a shaven head. Lashed to the fid where he squatted was the ship's catapult, cocked and loaded with one of the huge irons that could kill a sperm whale at a blow. A couple more lay alongside in their rack. Hiti's two mates and four deckhands poised behind him, holding the

smaller harpoons—mere six-foot shafts—that were launched
from a boat by hand. The lines of all trailed down the mast
to the bows.

"Aye, let 'em come now." Hiti grinned over his whole
round face. "Nan eat the world, but this'll be something to
make a dance about when we come home!"

"If we do," said Ruori. He touched the boat ax thrust
into his loincloth. Like a curtain, the blinding day seemed
to veil a picture from home, where combers broke white
under the moon, longfires flared on a beach and dancers
were merry, and palm trees cast shadows for couples who
stole away. He wondered how a Meycan calde's daughter
might like it . . . if her throat had not been cut.

"There's a sadness on you, Captain," said Hiti.

"Men are going to die," said Ruori.

"What of it?" Small kindly eyes studied him. "They'll
die willing, if they must, for the sake of the song that'll be
made. You've another trouble than death."

"Let me be!"

The harpooner looked hurt, but withdrew into silence.
Wind streamed and the ocean glittered.

The aircraft steered close. They would approach one on
each side. Ruori unslung the megaphone at his shoulder.
Atel Hamid held the *Dolphin* steady on a broad reach.

Now Ruori could see a grinning god at the prow of the
starboard airship. It would pass just above the topmasts, a
little to windward. . . . Arrows went impulsively toward it
from the yardarms, without effect, but no one was excited
enough to waste a rifle cartridge. Hiti swiveled his catapult.
"Wait," said Ruori. "We'd better see what they do."

Helmeted heads appeared over the blimp's gallery rail. A
man stepped up—another, another, at intervals; they whirled
triple-clawed iron grapnels and let go. Rutor saw one strike
the foremast, rebound, hit a jib. . . . The line to the blimp
tautened and sang but did not break; it was of leather. . . .
The jib ripped, canvas thundered, struck a sailor in the belly
and knocked him from his yard. . . . The man recovered to
straighten out and hit the water in a clean dive. Lesu grant
he lived. . . . The grapnel bumped along, caught the gaff
of the fore-and-aft mainsail, wood groaned. . . . The ship
trembled as line after line snapped taut.

She leaned far over, dragged by leverage. Her sails
banged. No danger of capsizing—yet—but a mast could be

pulled loose. And now, over the gallery rail and seizing a rope between hands and knees, the pirates came. Whooping like boys, they slid down to the grapnels and clutched after any rigging that came to hand.

One of them sprang monkeylike onto the mainmast gaff, below the crosstrees. A harpooner's mate cursed, hurled his weapon, and skewered the invader. "Belay that!" roared Hiti. "We need those irons!"

Ruori scanned the situation. The leeward blimp was still maneuvering in around its mate, which was being blown to port. He put the megaphone to his mouth and a solar-battery amplifier cried for him: "Hear this! Hear this! Burn that second enemy now, before he grapples! Cut the lines to the first one and repel all boarders!"

"Shall I fire?" called Hiti. "I'll never have a better target."

"Aye."

The harpooner triggered his catapult. It unwound with a thunder noise. Barbed steel smote the engaged gondola low in a side, tore through, and ended on the far side of interior planking.

"Wind 'er up!" bawled Hiti. His own gorilla hands were already on a crank lever. Somehow two men found space to help him.

Ruori slipped down the futtock shrouds and jumped to the gaff. Another pirate had landed there and a third was just arriving, two more aslide behind him. The man on the spar balanced barefooted, as good as any sailor, and drew a sword. Ruori dropped as the blade whistled, caught a mainsail grommet one-handed, and hung there, striking with his boat ax at the grapnel line. The pirate crouched and stabbed at him. Ruori thought of Tresa, smashed his hatchet into the man's face, and flipped him off, down to the deck. He cut again. The leather was tough, but his blade was keen. The line parted and whipped away. The gaff swung free, almost yanking Ruori's fingers loose. The second Sky Man toppled, hit a cabin below and spattered. The men on the line slid to its end. One of them could not stop; the sea took him. The other was smashed against the masthead as he pendulumed.

Ruori pulled himself back astride the gaff and sat there awhile, heaving air into lungs that burned. The fight ramped around him, on shrouds and spars and down on the decks. The second blimp edged closer.

Astern, raised by the speed of a ship moving into the wind, a box kite lifted. Atel sang a command and the helmsman put the rudder over. Even with the drag on her, the *Dolphin* responded well; a profound science of fluid mechanics had gone into her design. Being soaked in whale oil, the kite clung to the gas bag for a time—long enough for "messengers" of burning paper to whirl up its string. It burst into flame.

The blimp sheered off, the kite fell away, its small gunpowder load exploded harmlessly. Atel swore and gave further orders. The *Dolphin* tacked. The second kite, already aloft and afire, hit target. It detonated.

Hydrogen gushed out. Sudden flames wreathed the blimp. They seemed pale in the sun-dazzle. Smoke began to rise, as the plastic between gas cells disintegrated. The aircraft descended like a slow meteorite to the water.

Its companion vessel had no reasonable choice but to cast loose unsevered grapnels, abandoning the still outnumbered boarding party. The captain could not know that the *Dolphin* had only possessed two kites. A few vengeful catapult bolts spat from it. Then it was free, rapidly falling astern. The Maurai ship rocked toward an even keel.

The enemy might retreat or he might plan some fresh attack. Ruori did not intend that it should be either. He megaphoned: "Put about! Face that scum-gut!" and led a rush down the shrouds to a deck where combat still went on.

For Hiti's gang had put three primary harpoons and half a dozen lesser ones into the gondola.

Their lines trailed in tightening catenaries from the blimp to the capstan in the bows. No fear now of undue strain. The *Dolphin*, like any Maurai craft, was meant to live off the sea as she traveled. She had dragged right whales alongside; a blimp was nothing in comparison. What counted was speed, before the pirates realized what was happening and found ways to cut loose.

"*Tohiha, hioha, itoki, itoki!*" The old canoe chant rang forth as men tramped about the capstan. Ruori hit the deck, saw a Canyon man fighting a sailor, sword against club, and brained the fellow from behind as he would any other vermin. (Then he wondered, dimly shocked, what made him think thus about a human being.) The battle was rapidly concluded; the Sky Men faced hopeless odds. But half a dozen Federation people were badly hurt. Ruori had the few surviving pirates tossed into a lazaret, his own casualties taken below to anesthetics and antibiotics and cooing Doñitas. Then, quickly, he prepared his crew for the next phase.

The blimp had been drawn almost to the bowsprit. It was canted over so far that its catapults were useless. Pirates lined the gallery deck, howled and shook their weapons. They outnumbered the *Dolphin* crew by a factor of three or four. Ruori recognized one among them—the tall yellow-haired man who had fought him outside the palace; it was a somehow eerie feeling.

"Shall we burn them?" asked Atel.

Ruori grimaced. "I suppose we have to," he said. "Try not to ignite the vessel itself. You know we want it."

A walking beam moved up and down, driven by husky Islanders. Flame spurted from a ceramic nozzle. The smoke and stench and screams that followed, and the things to be seen when Ruori ordered cease fire, made the hardest veteran of corsair patrol look a bit ill. The Maurai were an unsentimental folk, but they did not like to inflict pain.

"Hose," rasped Ruori. The streams of water that followed were like some kind of blessing. Wicker that had begun to burn hissed into charred quiescence.

The ship's grapnels were flung. A couple of cabin boys darted past grown men to be first along the lines. They met no resistance on the gallery. The uninjured majority of pirates stood in a numb fashion, their armament at their feet, the fight kicked out of them. Jacob's ladders followed the boys; the *Dolphin* crew swarmed aboard the blimp and started collecting prisoners.

A few Sky Men lurched from behind a door, weapons aloft. Ruori saw the tall fair man among them. The man drew Ruori's dagger, left-handed, and ran toward him. His right arm seemed nearly useless. "A Canyon, a Canyon!" he called, the ghost of a war cry.

Ruori sidestepped the charge and put out a foot. The blond man tripped. As he fell, the hammer of Ruori's ax clopped down, catching him on the neck. He crashed, tried to rise, shuddered, and lay twitching.

"I want my knife back." Ruori squatted, undid the robber's tooled leather belt, and began to hogtie him.

Dazed blue eyes looked up with a sort of pleading. "Are you not going to kill me?" mumbled the other in Spañol.

"Haristi, no," said Ruori, surprised. "Why should I?"

He sprang erect. The last resistance had ended; the blimp was his. He opened the forward door, thinking the equivalent of a ship's bridge must lie beyond it.

Then for a while he did not move at all, nor did he hear anything but the wind and his own blood.

It was Tresa who finally came to him. Her hands were held out before her, like a blind person's, and her eyes looked through him. "You are here," she said, flat and empty voiced.

"Doñita," stammered Ruori. He caught her hands. "Doñita, had I known you were aboard, I would never have . . . have risked—"

"Why did you not burn and sink us, like that other vessel?" she asked. "Why must this return to the city?"

She wrenched free of him and stumbled out onto the deck. It was steeply tilted, and bucked beneath her. She fell, picked herself up, walked with barefoot care to the rail and stared out across the ocean. Her hair and torn dress fluttered in the wind.

VII

There was a great deal of technique to handling an airship. Ruori could feel that the thirty men he had put aboard this craft were sailing it as awkwardly as possible. An experienced Sky Man would know what sort of thermals and downdrafts to expect, just from a glance at land or water below; he could estimate the level at which a desired breeze was blowing, and rise or fall smoothly; he could even beat to windward, though that would be a slow process much plagued by drift.

Nevertheless, an hour's study showed the basic principles. Ruori went back to the bridge and gave orders in the speaking tube. Presently the land came nearer. A glance below showed the *Dolphin,* with a cargo of war captives, following on shortened sail. He and his fellow aeronauts would have to take a lot of banter about their celestial snail's pace. Ruori did not smile at the thought or plan his replies, as he would have done yesterday. Tresa sat so still behind him.

"Do you know the name of this craft, Doñita?" he asked, to break the silence.

"He called it *Buffalo*," she said, remote and uninterested.

"What's that?"

"A sort of wild cattle."

"I gather, then, he talked to you while cruising in search of me. Did he say anything else of interest?"

"He spoke of his people. He boasted of the things they have which we don't . . . engines, powers, alloys . . . as if that made them any less a pack of filthy savages."

At least she was showing some spirit. He had been afraid she had started willing her heart to stop; but he remembered he had seen no evidence of that common Maurai practice here in Meyco.

"Did he abuse you badly?" he asked, not looking at her.

"You would not consider it abuse," she said violently. "Now leave me alone, for mercy's sake!" He heard her go from him, through the door to the after sections.

Well, he thought, after all, her father was killed. That would grieve anyone, anywhere in the world, but her perhaps more than him. For a Meycan child was raised solely by its parents; it did not spend half its time eating or sleeping or playing with any casual relative, like most Island young. So the immediate kin would have more psychological significance here. At least, this was the only explanation Ruori could think of for the sudden darkness within Tresa.

The city hove into view. He saw the remaining enemy vessels gleam above. Three against one . . . yes, today would become a legend among the Sea People, if he succeeded. Ruori knew he should have felt the same reckless pleasure as a man did surfbathing, or shark fighting, or sailing in a typhoon, any breakneck sport where success meant glory and girls. He could hear his men chant, beat wardrum rhythms out with hands and stamping feet. But his own heart was Antarctic.

The nearest hostile craft approached. Ruori tried to meet it in a professional way. He had attired his prize crew in captured Sky outfits. A superficial glance would take them for legitimate Canyonites, depleted after a hard fight for the captured Maurai ship at their heels.

As the northerners steered close in the leisurely airship

fashion, Ruori picked up his speaking tube. "Steady as she goes. Fire when we pass abeam."

"Aye, aye," said Hiti.

A minute later the captain heard the harpoon catapult rumble. Through a port he saw the missile strike the enemy gondola amidships. "Pay out line," he said. "We want to hold her for the kite, but not get burned ourselves."

"Aye, I've played swordfish before now." Laughter bubbled in Hiti's tones.

The foe sheered, frantic. A few bolts leaped from its catapults; one struck home, but a single punctured gas cell made slight difference. "Put about!" cried Ruori. No sense in presenting his beam to a broadside. Both craft began to drift downwind, sails flapping. "Hard alee!" The *Buffalo* became a drogue, holding its victim to a crawl. And here came the kite prepared on the way back. This time it included fish hooks. It caught and held fairly on the Canyonite bag. "Cast off!" yelled Ruori. Fire whirled along the kite string. In minutes it had enveloped the enemy. A few parachutes were blown out to sea.

"Two to go," said Ruori, without any of his men's shouted triumph.

The invaders were no fools. Their remaining blimps turned back over the city, not wishing to expose themselves to more flame from the water. One descended, dropped hawsers, and was rapidly hauled to the plaza. Through his binoculars, Ruori saw armed men swarm aboard it. The other, doubtless with a mere patrol crew, maneuvered toward the approaching *Buffalo*.

"I think that fellow wants to engage us," warned Hiti. "Meanwhile number two down yonder will take on a couple of hundred soldiers, then lay alongside us and board."

"I know," said Ruori. "Let's oblige them."

He steered as if to close with the sparsely manned patroller. It did not avoid him, as he had feared it might; but then, there was a compulsive bravery in the Sky culture. Instead, it maneuvered to grapple as quickly as possible. That would give its companion a chance to load warriors and rise. It came very near.

Now to throw a scare in them, Ruori decided. "Fire arrows," he said. Out on deck, hardwood pistons were shoved into little cylinders, igniting tinder at the bottom; thus oil-soaked shafts were kindled. As the enemy came in range, red comets began to streak from the *Buffalo* archers.

Had his scheme not worked, Ruori would have turned off. He didn't want to sacrifice more men in hand-to-hand fighting; instead, he would have tried seriously to burn the hostile airship from afar, though his strategy needed it. But the morale effect of the previous disaster was very much present. As blazing arrows thunked into their gondola, a battle tactic so two-edged that no northern crew was even equipped for it, the Canyonites panicked and went over the side. Perhaps, as they parachuted down, a few noticed that no shafts had been aimed at their gas bag.

"Grab fast!" sang Ruori. "Douse any fires!"

Grapnels thumbed home. The blimps rocked to a relative halt. Men leaped to the adjacent gallery; bucketsful of water splashed.

"Stand by," said Ruori. "Half our boys on the prize. Break out the lifelines and make them fast."

He put down the tube. A door squeaked behind him. He turned, as Tresa reentered the bridge. She was still pale, but she had combed her hair, and her head was high.

"Another!" she said with a note near joy. "Only one of them left!"

"But it will be full of their men." Ruori scowled. "I wish now I had not accepted your refusal to go aboard the *Dolphin*. I wasn't thinking clearly. This is too hazardous."

"Do you think I care for that?" she said. "I am a Carabán."

"But I care," he said.

The haughtiness dropped from her; she touched his hand, fleetingly, and color rose in her cheeks. "Forgive me. You have done so much for us. There is no way we can ever thank you."

"Yes, there is," said Ruori.

"Name it."

"Do not stop your heart just because it has been wounded."

She looked at him with a kind of sunrise in her eyes.

His boatswain appeared at the outer door. "All set, Captain. We're holding steady at a thousand feet, a man standing by every valve these two crates have got."

"Each has been assigned a particular escape line?"

"Aye." The boatswain departed.

"You'll need one too. Come." Ruori took Tresa by the hand and led her onto the gallery. They saw sky around them, a breeze touched their faces and the deck underfoot moved like a live thing. He indicated many light cords from the *Dolphin*'s store, bowlined to the rail. "We aren't going to risk parachuting with untrained men," he said. "But you've no experience in skinning down one of these. I'll make you a harness which will hold you safely. Ease yourself down hand over hand. When you reach the ground, cut loose." His knife slashed some pieces of rope and he knotted them together with a seaman's skill. When he fitted the harness on her, she grew tense under his fingers.

"But I am your friend," he murmured.

She eased. She even smiled, shakenly. He gave her his knife and went back inboard.

And now the last pirate vessel stood up from the earth. It moved near; Ruori's two craft made no attempt to flee. He saw sunlight flash on edged metal. He knew they had witnessed the end of their companion craft and would not be daunted by the same technique. Rather, they would close in, even while their ship burned about them. If nothing else, they could kindle him in turn and then parachute to safety. He did not send arrows.

When only a few fathoms separated him from the enemy, he cried: "Let go the valves!"

Gas whoofed from both bags. The linked blimps dropped.

"Fire!" shouted Ruori. Hiti aimed his catapult and sent a harpoon with anchor cable through the bottom of the attacker. "Burn and abandon!"

Men on deck touched off oil which other men splashed from jars. Flames sprang high.

With the weight of two nearly deflated vessels dragging it from below, the Canyon ship began to fall. At five hundred feet the tossed lifelines draped across flat rooftops and trailed in the streets. Ruori went over the side. He scorched his palms going down.

He was not much too quick. The harpooned blimp released compressed hydrogen and rose to a thousand feet with its burden, seeking sky room. Presumably no one had yet seen that the burden was on fire. In no case would they find it easy to shake or cut loose from one of Hiti's irons.

Ruori stared upward. Fanned by the wind, the blaze was smokeless, a small fierce sun. He had not counted on his fire taking the enemy by total surprise. He had assumed they would parachute to earth, where the Meycans could attack. Almost, he wanted to warn them.

Then flame reached the remaining hydrogen in the collapsed gas bags. He heard a sort of giant gasp. The topmost vessel became a flying pyre. The wind bore it out over the city walls. A few antlike figures managed to spring free. The parachute of one was burning.

"Sant'sima Marí," whispered a voice, and Tresa crept into Ruori's arms and hid her face.

VIII

After dark, candles were lit throughout the palace. They could not blank the ugliness of stripped walls and smoke-blackened ceilings. The guardsmen who lined the throne room were tattered and weary. Nor did S' Antón itself rejoice, yet. There were too many dead.

Ruori sat throned on the calde's dais, Tresa at his right and Páwolo Dónoju on his left. Until a new set of officials could be chosen, these must take authority. The Don sat rigid, not allowing his bandaged head to droop; but now and then his lids grew too heavy to hold up. Tresa watched enormous-eyed from beneath the hood of a cloak wrapping her. Ruori sprawled at ease, a little more happy now that the fighting was over.

It had been a grim business, even after the heartened city troops had sallied and driven the surviving enemy before them. Too many Sky Men fought till they were killed. The hundreds of prisoners, mostly from the first Maurai success, would prove a dangerous booty; no one was sure what to do with them.

"But at least their host is done for," said Dónoju.

Ruori shook his head. "No, S'ñor. I am sorry, but you have no end in sight. Up north are thousands of such aircraft, and a strong hungry people. They will come again."

"We will meet them, Captain. The next time we shall be prepared. A larger garrison, barrage balloons, fire kites, cannons that shoot upward, perhaps a flying navy of our own . . . we can learn what to do."

Tresa stirred. Her tone bore life again, though a life which hated. "In the end, we will carry the war to them. Not one will remain in all the Corado highlands."

"No," said Ruori. "That must not be."

Her head jerked about; she stared at him from the shadow of her hood. Finally she said, "True, we are bidden to love our enemies, but you cannot mean the Sky People. They are not human!"

Ruori spoke to a page. "Send for the chief prisoner."

"To hear our judgment on him?" asked Dónoju. "That should be done formally, in public."

"Only to talk with us," said Ruori.

"I do not understand you," said Tresa. Her words faltered, unable to carry the intended scorn. "After everything you have done, suddenly there is no manhood in you."

He wondered why it should hurt for her to say that. He would not have cared if she had been anyone else.

Loklann entered between two guards. His hands were tied behind him and dried blood was on his face, but he walked like a conqueror under the pikes. When he reached the dais, he stood, legs braced apart, and grinned at Tresa.

"Well," he said, "so you find these others less satisfactory and want me back."

She jumped to her feet and screamed: "Kill him!"

"No!" cried Ruori.

The guardsmen hesitated, machetes half drawn. Ruori stood up and caught the girl's wrists. She struggled, spitting like a cat. "Don't kill him, then," she agreed at last, so thickly it was hard to understand. "Not now. Make it slow. Strangle him, burn him alive, toss him on your spears—"

Ruori held fast till she stood quietly.

When he let go, she sat down and wept.

Páwolo Dónoju said in a voice like steel: "I believe I understand. A fit punishment must certainly be devised."

Loklann spat on the floor. "Of course," he said. "When you have a man bound, you can play any number of dirty little games with him."

"Be still," said Ruori. "You are not helping your own cause. Or mine."

He sat down, crossed his legs, laced fingers around a knee, and gazed before him, into the darkness at the hall's end. "I know you have suffered from this man's work," he said carefully. "You can expect to suffer more from his kinfolk in the future. They are a young race, heedless as children, even as your ancestors and mine were once young. Do you think the Perio was established without hurt and harm? Or, if I remember your history rightly, that the Spañol people were welcomed here by the Inios? That the Ingliss did not come to N'Zealann with slaughter, and that the Maurai were not formerly cannibals? In an age of heroes, the hero must have an opponent.

"Your real weapon against the Sky People is not an army, sent to lose itself in unmapped mountains. . . . Your priests, merchants, artists, craftsmen, manners, fashions, learning—there is the means to bring them to you on their knees, if you will use it."

Loklann started. "You devil," he whispered. "Do you actually think to convert us to . . . a woman's faith and a city's cage?" He shook back his tawny mane and roared till the walls rung. "No!"

"It will take a century or two," said Ruori.

Don Páwolo smiled in his young scanty beard. "A refined revenge, S'ñor Captain," he admitted.

"Too refined!" Tresa lifted her face from her hands, gulped after air, held up claw-crooked fingers and brought them down as if into Loklann's eyes. "Even if it could be done," she snarled, "even if they did have souls, what do we want with them, or their children or grandchildren . . . they who murdered our babies today? Before almighty Dío— I am the last Carabán and I will have my following to speak for me in Meyco—there will never be anything for them but extermination. We can do it, I swear. Many Tekkans would help, for plunder. I shall yet live to see your home burning, you swine, and your sons hunted with dogs."

She turned frantically toward Ruori. "How else can our land be safe? We are ringed in by enemies. We have no choice but to destroy them, or they will destroy us. And we are the last Merikan civilization."

She sat back and shuddered. Ruori reached over to take her hand. It felt cold. For an instant, unconsciously, she returned the pressure, then jerked away.

He sighed in his weariness.

"I must disagree," he said. "I am sorry. I realize how you feel."

"You do not," she said through clamped jaws. "You cannot."

"But after all," he said, forcing dryness, "I am not just a man with human desires. I represent my government. I must return to tell them what is here, and I can predict their response.

"They will help you stand off attack. That is not an aid you can refuse, is it? The men who will be responsible for Meyco are not going to decline our offer of alliance merely to preserve a precarious independence of action, whatever a few extremists may argue for. And our terms will be most reasonable. We will want little more from you than a policy working toward conciliation and close relations with the Sky People, as soon as they have tired of battering themselves against our united defense."

"What?" said Loklann. Otherwise the chamber was very still. Eyes gleamed white from the shadows of helmets, toward Ruori.

"We will begin with you," said the Maurai. "At the proper time, you and your fellows will be escorted home. Your ransom will be that your nation allow a diplomatic and trade mission to enter."

"No," said Tresa, as if speech hurt her throat. "Not him. Send back the others if you must, but not him—to boast of what he did today."

Loklann grinned again, looking straight at her. "I will," he said.

Anger flicked in Ruori, but he held his mouth shut.

"I do not understand," hesitated Don Páwolo. "Why do you favor these animals?"

"Because they are more civilized than you," said Ruori.

"What?" The noble sprang to his feet, snatching for his sword. Stiffly, he sat down again. His tone froze over. "Explain yourself, S'ñor."

Ruori could not see Tresa's face, in the private night of her hood, but he felt her drawing farther from him than a star. "They have developed aircraft," he said, slumping back in his chair, worn out and with no sense of victory; *O great creating Tanaroa, grant me sleep this night!*

"But—"

"That was done from the ground up," explained Ruori, "not as a mere copy of ancient techniques. Beginning as refugees, the Sky People created an agriculture which can send warriors by the thousands from what was desert, yet plainly does not require peon hordes. On interrogation I have learned that they have sunpower and hydroelectric power, a synthetic chemistry of sorts, a well-developed navigation with the mathematics which that implies, gunpowder, metallurgics, aerodynamics. . . . Yes, I daresay it's a lopsided culture, a thin layer of learning above a largely illiterate mass. But even the mass must respect technology, or it would never have been supported to get as far as it has.

"In short," he sighed, wondering if he could make her comprehend, "the Sky People are a scientific race—the only one besides ourselves which we Maurai have yet discovered. And that makes them too precious to lose.

"You have better manners here, more humane laws, higher art, broader vision, every traditional virtue. But you are not scientific. You use rote knowledge handed down from the ancients. Because there is no more fossil fuel, you depend on muscle power; inevitably, then, you have a peon class, and always will. Because the iron and copper mines are exhausted, you tear down old ruins. In your land I have seen no research on wind power, sun power, the energy reserves of the living cell—not to mention the theoretical possibility of hydrogen fusion without a uranium primer. You irrigate the desert at a thousand times the effort it would take to farm the sea, yet have never even tried to improve your fishing techniques. You have not exploited the aluminum which is still abundant in ordinary clays, not sought to make it into strong alloys; no, your farmers use tools of wood and volcanic glass.

"Oh, you are neither ignorant nor superstitious. What you lack is merely the means of gaining new knowledge. You are a fine people; the world is the sweeter for you; I love you as much as I loathe this devil before us. But ultimately, my friends, if left to yourselves, you will slide gracefully back to the Stone Age."

A measure of strength returned. He raised his voice till it filled the hall. "The way of the Sky People is the rough way outward, to the stars. In that respect—and it overrides all others—they are more akin to us Maurai than you are. We cannot let our kin die."

He sat then, in silence, under Loklann's smirk and Dónoju's stare. A guardsman shifted on his feet, with a faint squeak of leather harness.

Tresa said at last, very low in the shadows: "That is your final word, S'ñor?"

"Yes," said Ruori. He turned to her. As she leaned for-

ward, the hood fell back a little, so that candlelight touched
her. And the sight of green eyes and parted lips gave him
back his victory.

He smiled. "I do not expect you will understand at once.
May I discuss it with you again, often? When you have seen
the Islands, as I hope you will—"

"You *foreigner!*" she screamed.

Her hand cracked on his cheek. She rose and ran down
the dais steps and out of the hall.

FURTHER READING
ABOUT SOUTH AMERICA

Novels
James Blish, THE NIGHT SHAPES, Ballantine.
Avram Davidson, CLASH OF STAR KINGS, Ace.
G.C. Edmondson, BLUE FACE, DAW.
Arthur Conan Doyle, THE LOST WORLD, Doran.
Pat Murphy, THE FALLING WOMAN, Tor.
Lucius Shepard, LIFE DURING WARTIME, Bantam.
Lewis Shiner, DESERTED CITIES OF THE HEART, Bantam.

Anthologies and Collections
Jorge Luis Borges, Ed., THE BOOK OF FANTASY, Carroll & Graf.
L. Sprague de Camp, THE CONTINENT MAKERS, Signet.
G.C. Edmondson, STRANGER THAN YOU THINK, Ace.
Frederik Pohl & Elizabeth Ann Hull, Eds., TALES OF PLANET EARTH, St. Martin's Press.

STORIES WITH
SOUTH AMERICAN THEMES

John Brunner, "The First Since Ancient Persia," *Amazing*, July 1990.
Avram Davidson, "El Vilvoy de las Islas," *IA sfm*, Aug. 1988.
Avram Davidson, "The Power of Every Root," *Strange Seas and Shores*.
Avram Davidson, "Sleep Well of Nights," F&SF, Aug. 1978.
L. Sprague de Camp, "Yellow Man," *The Purple Pterodactyls*.

Samuel R. Delany, "Driftglass," *Driftglass.*

Karen Joy Fowler, "Duplicity," *IA sfm,* Dec. 1989.

Robert Frazier, "Cruising Through Blueland," *IA sfm,* Mid-Dec 1991.

Howard H. Hendrix, "Singing the Mountain to the Stars," ABO SF, Jan.-Feb. 1991.

Frank Herbert, "Greenslaves," *On the Way to the Future.*

Bruce McAllister, "Songs From a Far Country," *IA sfm,* Feb. 1988.

Barry N. Malzberg, "Panama," *Full Spectrum 3,* Bantam, 1991.

Richard Mueller, "Meditations on the Death of Cortez," *IA sfm,* Sept. 1988.

Pat Murphy, "Clay Devils," *Points of Departure.*

Pat Murphy, "In the Islands," *Points of Departure.*

Richard Paul Russo, "For a Place in the Sky," *IA sfm,* May 1986.

Lucius Shepard, "A Traveller's Tale," *The Jaguar Hunter.*

Lucius Shepard, "Aymara," *The Ends of the Earth.*

Lucius Shepard (with Robert Frazier), "The All-Consuming," *Playboy,* July 1990.

Lucius Shepard, "Black Coral," *The Jaguar Hunter.*

Lucius Shepard, "The End of Life As We Know It," *The Jaguar Hunter.*

Lucius Shepard, "Fire-Zone Emerald," *The Ends of the Earth.*

Lucius Shepard, "On the Border," *The Ends of the Earth.*

Lucius Shepard, "Surrender," *The Ends of the Earth.*

Lewis Shiner, "Cabrican," *IA sfm,* Oct. 1986.

Robert Silverberg, "The Clone Zone," *Playboy,* March 1991.

Robert Silverberg, "Enter A Soldier. Later: Enter Another," *IA sfm,* June 1989.

Bruce Sterling, "Spook," *Crystal Express.*

S.P. Somtow, "Kingdoms in the Sky," *IA sfm,* Feb. 1992.

James Tiptree, Jr., "Beam Us Home," *Ten Thousand Light Years From Home.*

James Tiptree, Jr., "Yaqui Doodle," *IA sfm,* July 1987.

Steven Utley, "The Glowing Cloud," *IA sfm,* Jan. 1992.

Steven Utley, "Haiti," *IA sfm,* May 1992.

Science Fiction Anthologies

☐ **FUTURE EARTHS: UNDER AFRICAN SKIES**   UE2544—$4.99
Mike Resnick & Gardner Dozois, editors
From a utopian space colony modeled on the society of ancient Kenya, to a shocking future discovery of a "long-lost" civilization, to an ingenious cure for one of humankind's oldest woes—a cure that might cost too much—here are 15 provocative tales about Africa in the future and African culture transplanted to different worlds.

☐ **FUTURE EARTHS: UNDER SOUTH AMERICAN SKIES**
Mike Resnick & Gardner Dozois, editors   UE2581—$4.99
From a plane crash that lands its passengers in a survival situation completely alien to anything they've ever experienced, to a close encounter of the insect kind, to a woman who has journeyed unimaginably far from home—here are stories from the rich culture of South America, with its mysteriously vanished ancient civilizations and magnificent artifacts, its modern-day contrasts between sophisticated city dwellers and impoverished villagers.

☐ **MICROCOSMIC TALES**   UE2532—$4.99
Isaac Asimov, Martin H. Greenberg, & Joseph D. Olander, eds.
Here are 100 wondrous science fiction short-short stories, including contributions by such acclaimed writers as Arthur C. Clarke, Robert Silverberg, Isaac Asimov, and Larry Niven. Discover a superman who lives in a *real* world of nuclear threat . . . an android who dreams of electric love . . . and a host of other tales that will take you instantly out of this world.

☐ **WHATDUNITS**   UE2533—$4.99
☐ **MORE WHATDUNITS**   UE2557—$5.50
Mike Resnick, editor
In these unique volumes of all-original stories, Mike Resnick has created a series of science fiction mystery scenarios and set such inventive sleuths as Pat Cadigan, Judith Tarr, Katharine Kerr, Jack Haldeman, and Esther Friesner to solving them. Can you match wits with the masters to make the perpetrators fit the crimes?

Buy them at your local bookstore or use this convenient coupon for ordering.

PENGUIN USA P.O. Box 999, Dept. #17109, Bergenfield, New Jersey 07621

Please send me the DAW BOOKS I have checked above, for which I am enclosing $_____ (please add $2.00 per order to cover postage and handling. Send check or money order (no cash or C.O.D.'s) or charge by Mastercard or Visa (with a $15.00 minimum.) Prices and numbers are subject to change without notice.

Card #_____ Exp. Date _____

Signature_____

Name_____

Address_____

City _____ State _____ Zip _____

For faster service when ordering by credit card call **1-800-253-6476**

Please allow a minimum of 4 to 6 weeks for delivery.

DAW

Introducing 3 New DAW Superstars . . .

GAYLE GREENO

☐ **THE GHATTI'S TALE:**
  Book 1—Finders, Seekers   UE2550—$5.50

Someone is attacking the Seekers Veritas, an organization of
Truth-finders composed of Bondmate pairs, one human, one a
telepathic, catlike ghatti. And the key to defeating this deadly
foe is locked in one human's mind behind barriers even her
ghatta has never been able to break.

S. ANDREW SWANN

☐ **FORESTS OF THE NIGHT**   UE2565—$3.99

When Nohar Rajasthan, a private eye descended from geneti-
cally manipulated tiger stock, a moreau—a second-class hu-
manoid citizen in a human world—is hired to look into a human's
murder, he find himself caught up in a conspiracy that includes
federal agents, drug runners, moreau gangs, and a deadly
canine assassin. And he hasn't even met the real enemy yet!

DEBORAH WHEELER

☐ **JAYDIUM**   UE2556—$4.99

Unexpectedly cast adrift in time and space, four humans from
different times and universes unite in a search to find their way
back—even if it means confronting an alien race whose doom
may prove their only means of salvation.
